PATRIOT

By Ted Bell

Fiction

PATRIOT
WARRIORS
PHANTOM
WARLORD
TSAR
SPY
PIRATE
ASSASSIN
HAWKE

Novellas

WHITE DEATH
WHAT COMES AROUND
CRASH DIVE

Young Adult Novels

THE TIME PIRATE
NICK OF TIME

TED BELL

PATRIOT

AN ALEX HAWKE NOVEL

WILLIAM MORROW

An Imprint of HarperCollinsPublishers

Several chapters of this novel have previously appeared in the novella *What Comes Around*, also by Ted Bell.

WILLIAM MORROW
An Imprint of HarperCollins*Publishers*
195 Broadway
New York, New York 10007

Copyright © 2015 by Theodore A. Bell
ISBN 978-0-06-227943-9

First William Morrow premium printing: July 2016
First William Morrow hardcover printing: September 2015

For Lucinda Watson and Byrdie Bell,
with abiding love

The wolves must eat too.

—ANCIENT RUSSIAN MOTTO

PROLOGUE

THE SIXTH-RICHEST MAN IN ENGLAND DUCKED his head.

Pure instinct, it was. A tight formation of four Russian MiG-35s suddenly came screaming out of the blinding sun, thundering directly over Lord Alexander Hawke's Royal Navy watch cap. Silver wings flashing, thrusters howling, the fighter jets quickly shed altitude and skimmed over his position, their squat air brakes down for landing.

"*What the hell?*" Alex Hawke muttered to himself. The British intelligence officer was looking straight up as four fighter jets thundered not a hundred feet over his head! MiG-35s in bloody *Cuba*? He'd have to alert his superiors at MI6 London straightaway.

These MiG fighters were the most radical thing aloft these days; their mere presence here on the island of Cuba confirmed one of Hawke's worst suspicions about his mission: the Russians were no longer fooling around playing, the unconvincing role of "advisors" to the aging Castro brothers. Despite Cuba's impending and highly problematic "detente" with America, the Muscovites had clearly returned to this island paradise to stay. And they meant business.

The plain and simple fact was that his imminent mission, if successful, would soon bring about a head-on political collision between Britain, America, and Russia. The true facts about Cuba's double-dealing would soon flare into stark relief, both in the espionage community and on front pages of newspapers around the world. Welcome to sunny Cuba! Welcome to Planet Tinderbox.

And welcome to realpolitik 2012, Hawke thought to himself.

His four-man stick, or assassination team, and their Cuban guide were crouched in the heavy tangle of verdant jungle encroaching on the airfield. His current position was a scant hundred yards or so from the wide white airstrip. In the recent past, he'd noted on his mental pad, all the cracks in the cheap concrete had been patched, crisscrossed with slapdash splashes of black tar, and the uneven surface mostly cleared of choking weeds and overgrowth.

This very long tactical runway had been chopped into the top of the mountain by the Soviets more than a half century earlier, and it certainly looked its age. One famous legacy the Russians had left behind on the island, seriously crappy concrete.

One after another, the fighter planes scorched the far end of the runway. Puffs of bluish-white smoke spurted from the blistered tyres as, with jets howling, the four aircraft landed in sequence. They then taxied in single file to the far boundary of the field. Maneuvering adroitly, the Russian fighter pilots nested wing to wing in the shadows of a few rusty Quonset hangars overarched with climbing vines. An antiquated control tower, also built by the bloody Sovs during a brief warm spell in the Cold War, provided little in the way of shade.

Commander Hawke motioned to his squad as he rose to his feet, squinting against the high hard dazzle of the sky. "Move out," the Englishman said softly, and he and his men melted back into the protective cover of the dense jungle canopy encroaching on the field. He wanted to get closer to that tower. The MiGs were interesting, but they were not what he'd come all the way from Britain to see.

Ten minutes and a few hundred yards later the commandos had relocated; they were now nearly in spitting distance of yet another Russian airplane, albeit one vastly less sophisticated than the four gleaming MiGs. The first new arrival, having landed a scant few minutes ahead of its fighter escort, was now parked on the tarmac, broiling under the intense Caribbean sun.

The nearby control tower, almost completely enwreathed in cascading flowering vines, loomed above the airplane but provided no shade at all. The fact that all the tower windows were either shattered or completely missing and that there were no controllers present up there seemed to be of little concern to the five Russian pilots recently arrived.

Hawke raised the Zeiss binoculars to his eyes and studied this aviation relic from another century. Unlike the four silver MiG 35s, this was a very old number indeed. It was a dilapidated twin-engine Ilyushin 12 transport, at once a venerable and veritable blast from the past. Hawke caught a sudden glimpse of garish color out of the corner of his eye and quickly shifted his focus left.

A vintage Cadillac limo, painted a ripe old shade of lavender, now rolled to a stop a few feet from the starboard wingtip of the IL 12. A small aluminum ladder was hung down from the opened cabin door aft of the wing. One of the uniformed crew, looking very much like a yachtsman in white trousers and a blue blazer, appeared at the aircraft hatchway.

This chap, clearly DGI, the Cuban secret service unit under the control of the KGB, was shielding his eyes from the fierce sunshine and carrying a serious submachine gun. He climbed down the ladder, circled the faded and rusting limo, and bent to examine the driver's paperwork. Apparently finding everything in order, the armed steward called up to another man still aboard the airplane. A big chap in full jungle camo was now standing in the opening in the fuselage. Hawke smiled. He knew the Russian army officer by the nickname given him by his German father. But he had made his real reputation fighting rebels in Chechnya: a savage butcher.

Der Wolf.

The man climbed down the steps to the tarmac with a good deal of athleticism, Hawke noticed. He held a heavy leather suitcase in his hand, but he handled it as if it were a spy novel he'd been reading on the flight. He was a big, bald man, with masses of bunched muscle around his neck and shoulders. His shirtsleeves were rolled up to the elbows, revealing powerful forearms. The whole gristly package came with a right bullet of a head, too, gleaming with sweat.

Hawke zoomed in on the face, on the hooded dark and bushy-browed eyes of the arriving passenger.

He took a good long look at the fellow and then handed the glasses to his old friend, an ex–Navy SEAL and former New York Jet, a human mountain from West 129th Street in Harlem known by the name of Stokely Jones Jr. A much-decorated counterterrorist for hire, he was oft described by Alex Hawke as "about the size of your average armoire."

"It's him, Stoke," Hawke said. "Ivanov."

Stokely Jones took a quick peek and confirmed Hawke's opinion. There was no doubt. The man they'd come to Cuba to kill had arrived right on schedule.

THAT NIGHT IT TURNED COLD IN THE MOUNTAINS. From his vantage point in the jungle peaks of the Sierra Maestra, Commander Hawke could see the misty lights of Cabo Cruz, a small fishing village on the northeastern coast of Cuba, on the coastline far below. To the east, a few more such villages were visible from his vantage point. Dim clusters of light scattered along the black coastline, as if tiny gold coins had been flung out by some giant hand.

These were the only signs of civilization visible in the darkness from the mountainside campsite.

Hawke pulled his collar up as he looked seaward. The wind was up, heralding a cold front moving north. He knew from CIA ops briefings in Miami that a tropical storm was brewing up to the south of Cuba. It was headed this way, a cold wind out of Jamaica, drawn northward by warmer Caribbean waters. Hawke swore softly under his breath. Sometimes inclement weather worked in your favor; and sometimes it decidedly did not.

Among the five men living at the makeshift campsite, the mood around the deliberately low-burning campfire was one of quiet, confident expectation. The tiny village of Cabo Cruz, just below them, was their target tonight. In that village was the man the commando squad been tracking for the last forty-eight hours, ever since the Ilyushin 12 had touched down at the secret airstrip.

His name was General Sergey Ivanovich Ivanov.

He was a high-ranking Russian officer on a mission from Moscow, a much-feared veteran of the Spetsnaz brigade who'd written their names in blood on the killing fields of Chechnya. Special forces, the crème de la crème of Putin's much vaunted advance combat brigades.

Earlier that afternoon, the general, along with two civilian aides cum bodyguards and his plain-clothes entourage of advisors, had checked into a seaside hotel called Illuminata de los Reyes, Light of the Kings. They'd taken the entire top floor of the pale-pink-washed building. The general's quarters were on the third floor, a capacious suite with a balcony overlooking the sea. That night before, Sergey had left the French doors open to the wind and waves; at around midnight, he'd ventured out onto the balcony for a last Montecristo cigar and vintage brandy.

Hawke's four-man stick was a British MI6-initiated counterterrorist team, operating in tandem with the CIA. The Englishman's mission, under the direction of Sir David Trulove, chief of MI6, was straightforward enough: travel to Miami, then Cuba, and gather intelligence about Russian operations on the island. And then take out *der Wolf.*

A forward espionage base in North America was long rumored to be under consideration by Vladimir Putin's top generals as a KGB spy outpost. Human intel reports out of CIA Miami indicated scouting had already begun for a prime location on a small island off the southwestern coast of Cuba.

Hawke's joint force of CIA and MI6 commandos had a clear-cut objective: kill the man sent by Moscow to supervise the design and construction of a major Russian military facility on the Isla de Pinos. In 1953, Fidel had been imprisoned at a notorious facility there, a house of horrors built by Batista. And his brother Raúl had recommended the small island to the Kremlin as the ideal location for a major spy base.

Now, the Castro brothers, despite increasingly friendly diplomatic overtures from Washington, had revealed their true colors: despite any rhyme or reason, the Cuban sympathies still lay with Moscow. Sir David Trulove, Hawke's superior at MI6, had once joked to Hawke that *los hermanos* must have missed the memo: "Communism is dead."

Los hermanos, Spanish for "the brothers," was Sir David's pet sobriquet for that notorious pair of tenacious banana republic dictators.

It had been estimated by British-run undercover operatives in Havana that the general's imminent demise would set back top secret Russian espionage initiatives by at least eighteen months to two years. Time sorely needed by the Western powers to get their act together on the new realities shaping the Latin America geopolitical arena.

The CIA/MI6 hit team consisted of four warriors: Commander Hawke himself, ex–Royal Navy; the former Navy SEAL Stokely Jones Jr.; a young ex-Marine sniper named Captain Alton Irby; and a freelance Aussie SAS demolition expert, Major Sean Fitzgerald.

They had picked up a fifth member, a local guide, shortly after they'd arrived. He was a good-looking young kid named Rico Alonso. He was moody and hot-tempered, but Hawke put up with him. Rico exuded complete confidence, something he'd gained through prior dealings with British and American commandos traveling in harm's way. He'd done it all before, apparently with much success. And he had an encyclopedic knowledge of the jungle regions of the central Cuba's mountains that Hawke was in desperate need of.

The stick had been put ashore on the northeastern coast by an American submarine, *Hammerhead*, out of Guantanamo Bay; the insertion location was a small port city called Mayacamas. That had been two days earlier, the night before they'd scouted the airstrip. Since then they'd been tracking the movements of the target, using Rico to gather intel from the village locals about the Russian general's movements, weapons, and sleep habits.

Tonight, *Hammerhead* had returned to the Mayacamas LZ on the coast. The attack submarine was loitering offshore even now, scheduled for a rendezvous with Hawke at 0400 hours this morning. It was a full moon, and the brightness presented its own set of dangers.

Six hours gave the four-man stick and Rico plenty of time to make their way down to the village, suppress resistance, if any, in and around the hotel, and gain access to the top-floor room where the Russian target was now presumably sleeping. The team would assassinate him and then make their way back along the coast to the exfiltration point as quickly as possible.

It all sounded straightforward enough, and in reality, it was. But war, as Alex Hawke had learned long ago, had its own reality. If things could go wrong, they would. Even if things could not possibly go wrong, things could always find a way. And, sometimes, incredibly, things would go *right* at the very moment when you'd lost all hope. That was just the way it was in the fog of war.

BEHIND THE KEENING NOTE OF THE FRESHENING wind, the sea boomed softly at the bottom of the cliffs. Alex Hawke got to his feet, kicked dirt onto the smoldering embers, and began a final check of his automatic weapon and ammunition. He carried a machine pistol and an FN SCAR assault rifle with a grenade launcher mounted on the lower rail. Grenades hung like grape clusters from his utility belt.

"Let's move out," Hawke said softly, putting a match to the Marlboro jammed in the corner of his mouth.

"Time," Stoke said to the other men. "You heard the man."

Stoke, like the others, was surreptitiously watching their leader, his old friend Alex Hawke. Hawke, especially in his muddy jungle camo, was hardly the picture of a typical British lord in his midthirties. To be sure, there was nothing typical about the man. He was, as one of his former Etonian classmates once put it, "a masterpiece of contradictions." He was a British intelligence officer and former Royal Navy combat pilot about whom it had oft been said: the naturally elegant Lord Hawke is also quite naturally good at war.

Now, on the eve of battle, the man grew ever more calm and at peace with himself. He was unmoving, quietly smoking in the flickering firelight, the smoke a visible curl, rising into the cool night air. Stoke alone knew that behind Hawke's wry smile and placid exterior was, after all, a creature of radiant violence.

This man, whom Stokely had befriended twenty years earlier, was a natural leader; equal parts self-containment, fierce determination, and cocksure animal magnetism. Women and men alike seemed drawn to him like water to the moon.

Even in repose Hawke was noticeable, for he possessed the palpable gravity of a man who had been there and back. A pure and elemental warrior, necessarily violent, riveting, nature itself. Well north of six feet, incredibly fit for someone his age, this was a man who swam six miles in open ocean every day of his life.

He possessed a full head of unruly black hair, had a chiseled profile, and sported a deepwater tan from weeks at sea. And then there were those "arctic blue" eyes. A prominent London gossip columnist once declared in *Tatler* that his eyes looked like "pools of frozen rain." She had thus further embellished his reputation as one of London's most sought-after bachelors. Hawke's two vices, Bermudian rum and American cigarettes, were the only two left to him since he'd given up on women.

"Awright, let's hit the road," Captain Irby, said, kicking enough damp earth onto the fire to extinguish it. And the five heavily armed men began to make their way down the seaward face, hacking their way through rugged terrain covered by dense vegetation. Rico first, then Irby, Fitzgerald, Stoke, and, finally, Hawke, covering the rear.

It was slow going.

The trail was switchbacked, snaking down the mountain, hairpin turns giving on sheer drops. Almost immediately, Hawke began to second-guess the wisdom of taking Rico's advice. For one thing, the trail was very steep and soon began to grow narrow in places. The commandos were forced to use their machetes simply to keep hacking their way forward. Rico offered constant assurances, saying more than once that it would widen out soon. It didn't. Now, it was barely wide enough for passage.

And then it got worse.

Walls of green now pressed in on them from either side, slowing them down even more. Thick, loopy vines and exposed ficus roots underfoot grabbed at their boots. Hawke, having seen Irby suddenly trip and pitch forward, didn't like it one bit. Not that it mattered much now. Retracing their steps and coming down the open face was not an option at this late stage in the mission.

So there was nothing for it. Hawke grimly kept his mouth shut and told the chattering Rico to do the same . . .

Thirty minutes into the descent, the jungle closed in, then narrowed to a complete standstill. They stumbled into an apparent dead end. A tiny space inside a cathedral of hundred-foot-high palms, the fronds chattering loudly high overhead in the stiff winds, the air in the green hollows cool and damp. Rico was slashing at the solid green walls that remained before them, cursing loudly as he flailed away with his ivory-handled machete.

"Look, Commandante!" the young Cuban kid cried out over his shoulder. "All clear ahead now!"

Hawke looked. Rico had disappeared through the now invisible opening he had slashed between two trees in the wall of palms. The squad pressed forward in an attempt to follow his lead.

"Shut that damn kid up, Stoke," Hawke said, using his assault knife to whack at the dangling morass of thick green vines as he, too, tried to follow Rico's path forward. Captain Irby was now in the lead, and he was pulling back elephant leaves and palm fronds, seeking a way forward.

"I don't like this, boss," Stoke said, watching Irby struggle. "Something is not—"

"*Down!* Everybody get fucking *down!*" Captain Irby croaked, turning to face them, his face stricken. Stoke took one look at the man's clouding eyes and knew they were in deep trouble.

"Hey, Captain, you okay, man?" Stoke said to him, reaching out to help. There was so much blood. The man had something stuck in his . . . oh, Jesus, it looked like Rico's ivory-handled machete. It was buried up to the hilt, near the top of Irby's chest, just above his Nomex body armor. Irby's fixed and glazed eyes stared out at nothing, and he fell facedown at Major Fitzgerald's feet.

"Oh, God, I didn't think he would—" the Aussie said, dropping to his knees to see what he could do for his dead or dying comrade.

And that's when the thick jungle surrounding the natural cathedral erupted in a storm of sizzling lead. Heavy machine-gun fire came from all directions, muzzle flashes visible everywhere they looked, rounds shredding the foliage over their heads and all around the trapped commandos. Masses of shrieking green parrots, macaws, and other tropical birds loudly rose up into the moonlit skies in terror as the incoming fire increased in ferocity.

"Get down now! Take cover!" Hawke shouted.

He dove left, but not before he heard the young Aussie scream, "I'm hit! I'm hit!" And then he was silent.

"Damn it to hell!" Hawke cried, getting back on his feet to go to the wounded man's aid.

"Forget him, boss! He's gone," Stoke cried out.

Hawke felt a visceral torque in his gut. In a rage, he opened up with both his assault rifle and his machine pistol, firing both weapons on full auto until he'd exhausted his ammo and reached for more. Stoke had his back, the two of them stood there back-to-back, leaning against each other as they spun in unison, unleashing a 360-degree hail of lead with overlapping fields of fire. The thumping roar of Stoke's heavy M-60 machine gun seemed to be having an impact on the enemy hidden in the jungle.

"Gotta be getting the hell out of here, boss!" Stoke said, grabbing Hawke's shoulder and spinning him around. "Back up the mountain! It's the only way . . ."

"Go, go!" Hawke said. He heaved two frag grenades over his shoulder while turning to follow his friend's upward retreat. He'd taken two steps forward when a high-caliber round slammed him in the lower back, spun him around, and dropped him to his knees.

"Boss!" Stoke cried, seeing Hawke trying vainly to get to his feet and firing his weapon blindly.

"Keep bloody moving, damn it!" Hawke shouted. "I'll take care of these bastards. Leave me be."

"Not today," Stoke said.

Stoke whirled around and bent down, firing his

weapon with his left hand and scooping Hawke up with his right. He flung Hawke over his broad shoulders and started running flat out straight up the mountain. The giant with his wounded friend tore through the dense foliage as if it didn't exist.

They got maybe a few hundred yards before all hope of salvation vanished. A broad rope net, weighted with stones, was released by three Cuban soldiers perched on branches high in the canopy. The net fell, entrapping the two enemy combatants, driving them to the ground, and ending for good any hope they still harbored of escape.

WHEN HAWKE CAME TO, HE WAS GAZING INTO THE sweat-streaked face of the Russian general he'd come to Cuba to kill.

Ivanov was bent over from the waist, smiling into his prisoner's glazed eyes. His thick lips were moving, his Adam's apple was bobbing up and down, but he wasn't making any sounds Hawke could understand as he drifted in and out of consciousness. Alex blinked rapidly, trying to focus. He saw Stoke out of the corner of his eye.

His friend was bound by his ankles with rough cordage and suspended upside down from a heavy wooden rafter. He appeared to be naked. And there was a lot of blood pooled on the floor beneath his head for some reason. Had he been shot, too, and hung to bleed out? Hawke's own wound was radiating fire throughout his body. He fought to stay awake . . . heard a familiar laugh and looked across the room.

The kid, Rico, was there, too, sitting at a bat-

tered wooden table, smoking a cigarette and swig-
ging from a bottle of rum with some other Cuban
guards. He seemed to be talking to Stokely out of
the side of his mouth. Every now and then he'd get
up, walk over to the suspended black man, scream
epithets into his bleeding ears, and then backhand
him viciously across the mouth with his pistol. A
few white teeth shone in the puddle of blood under
Stoke's head.

Stoke, perhaps the toughest man Hawke had ever
met, was a stoic of the first order. Hawke had never
once heard his friend cry out in pain.

Hawke felt a white-hot flare of anger. Bloody
hell. He had to do something! He tried to rise from
the chair but felt himself slipping away again. He
could not seem to keep his eyes open. How long
had he been awake? They never let him sleep. No
food. Some poisonous water out of a rusty coffee
can now and then. It was cold sleeping on the dirt
floor of the dank cement building after the sun
dropped . . .

They'd both been stripped naked the first night.
Allowed to keep nothing but their heavy combat
boots with no laces. The bullet was still in Alex's
back, and the wound had turned into one hot
mess, all right, but he fought to ignore the searing
pain and keep his wits about him. He shook his
head and tried to remember where he was despite
the spiking fever that made straight thinking so
difficult.

It was a compound built in a clearing in the
middle of the jungle. Palm tree fronds brushed the
ground. High wire fences. Dogs. Every evening the

Russians came, including General Ivanov. They drank vodka and played rummy with the Cubans. The general and Rico interrogated the two prisoners until they got bored with torture and retreated deeper and deeper into drink.

The worst brutality the two prisoners had endured was called the "Wishing Well." Every morning at dawn, two burly guards would march them naked through the jungle to a spot away from the compound. There, two fifty-gallon drums had been stacked one on top of the other and buried in the soil. Hawke and Jones were made to lie down in the dirt beside the well. One guy would bind each of their ankles to a stout bamboo pole while the other one kept his MAC-10 machine pistol trained on both of them.

Then they'd lift them up off the ground by turns and dunk them headfirst down into the foul, slop-filled hole. Sometimes for a few seconds, other times for a couple of minutes. Or longer. Neither man knew how long his head would be submerged. Each would come up sputtering. The hole was brimming with a fetid stew of urine and feces.

What the Wishing Well actually was, Hawke and Stokely soon realized, was the Cuban soldiers' latrine.

"I can't take much more of this, Stoke," Hawke said at dawn one morning, before the guards came for them. "I'm deadly serious, man. This will break me. I thought Iraq was bad. But, this? Hell, I'll just start talking, man."

"We are just not ever going to do that, boss."

"I know."

So that morning was different. The two guards arrived and marched the naked and manacled prisoners outside the fenced perimeter and single file into the jungle. The Cubanos laughing and shouting to each other out of habit. Another hot day, another hilarious game of dunk the prisoners headfirst into the latrine.

One guard was in front, Hawke right behind him. Then Stoke, then the other guard at the rear with his gun aimed at the back of Stoke's head. No talking allowed for the two captives. Hawke obeyed that rule until they got within sight of the Wishing Well. That's when he said the one word Stoke was waiting to hear:

"NOW!"

In that instant, Hawke got his manacled wrists over the guard's head and cinched tight around the stocky Cuban's throat. Hawke yanked him backward off his feet, got him on the ground, and began pummeling his face with his two bound fists, using the steel manacles as a weapon. Stoke, meanwhile, planted one foot and whirled, whipping his bound hands in a great sweeping arc, slamming his enjoined fists against the side of the other guard's head and knocking him off his feet.

Hawke had little memory of the ensuing skirmish. Both Cubans acquitted themselves rather nicely, knowing full well they were fighting for their lives. Hawke was fairly sure he'd bit both ears off his guy and done terrible things to his eyes and teeth. And, ultimately, to the vertebrae in his cervical spine. C3, C4, and C5, damaged beyond repair.

Meanwhile, Stoke used his enormous size and

weight to his advantage. He sat atop the guy long enough to break the index finger of the thrashing right hand by removing his gun while his finger was still inside the trigger guard. Then he bounced up and down on his chest a couple of times until all his ribs fractured pretty much at once. Until something sharp and splintery pierced his heart and lungs.

FOR THREE DAYS THEY FOUGHT TO SURVIVE IN THE wild. Naked, hungry, no food, no water, no map. They followed the sun during the day. Kept well clear of the occasional dirt roads. Survived on snakes, bugs, and bark. Made a little shelter with palm fronds every night to keep the cold rain off their hides. And so it went.

On the fourth night, they heard booming surf in the distance. That's when they came upon a high wire fence. They had little strength left to go around it. Hawke was in far worse shape than Stokely; he'd lost a lot of blood and still battled a raging fever. Somehow, they both found enough strength to scale the fence and drop to the ground on the other side.

HAWKE WOKE UP IN SICK BAY THE NEXT MORNING with no memory of how he'd come to be there.

"Good morning, handsome," a pretty red-haired American nurse said to him, holding the straw in his orange juice next to his parched lips. "There's someone here to see you."

Hawke smiled.

"Who is it?"

"I'll go get him, honey," the nurse said.

Now a strange man appeared at his bedside.

American military. Brass, obviously. A U.S. naval officer, who was also smiling down at him in a friendly way. Where the bloody hell was he? On a U.S. destroyer?

"Good morning, Admiral," Hawke managed, very happy to see a familiar uniform and a friendly face.

"Good morning," the old man said, pulling a chair up to his bedside. "Son, I don't know who the hell you are or where the hell you came from, but I will tell you one goddamn thing. You ruined my golf game, sailor."

"Sorry, sir?"

"You heard me. I came up the seventh fairway this morning half expecting to find my ball in a sand trap. Instead, I found you. Bare assed, except for your goddamn shoes. Damnedest thing I ever saw. And no tracks in the sand anywhere around you. Like you'd dropped out of the blue."

"From the top of the fence, Admiral."

"But how the hell did you—Never mind."

"I'm sorry, sir."

"Oh, hell, don't apologize. I hit my sand wedge out of there and sank it for a birdie! Almost had to take your foot off to get my club face on the ball. Never had a human hazard before! Welcome to the Guantanamo Bay Naval Base Golf and Country Club, son! We're glad to have you and your Navy SEAL friend Mr. Jones here as our guests."

Then the admiral laughed and handed him a fat Montecristo cigar. He helped Hawke get it lit and then said, "Tell me, what can I do for you, son? You look to me like a man who could use a helping hand right about now."

Hawke smiled and said, "There is one thing you could do for me, sir."

"Name it."

"Got any drones?" Hawke said, taking another puff and feeling instantly much improved. The fog seemed to be lifting. He saw a small green bird alight on his sunny windowsill, and it seemed to him a harbinger of happy days to come.

"Hell, yeah, I got drones, son. Shitload of them. What exactly do you have in mind?"

"Well, Admiral, you see, there's this little pink hotel over on the northeast coast of Cuba. Place called the Illuminata de los Reyes. One of the guests there, a Russian chap of my acquaintance, was exceptionally rude to my friend Stokely Jones and me recently. Killed a couple of my chaps in an ambush. And I thought, well, perhaps you could teach him a lesson in old-fashioned Anglo-American manners."

"Done and done!" The admiral laughed. "I'll have my guys get a couple of birds in the air before lunchtime. That little hotel you mentioned, that's the pretty pink one over in Cabo Cruz, am I right?"

"That's the one all right, Admiral."

"I'm on it."

And damn if it wasn't done that very day.

Done, and done, as they say.

ONE

Y OU SEE, THE WHOLE DAMN BUSINESS STARTED
with the USS *Cole*.

The *Cole* is a serious U.S. Navy warship, mind
you. Think billion-dollar baby. She's a 505-foot-long
Arleigh Burke–class guided-missile destroyer. She
carries a vast array of advanced radar equipment,
not to mention her torpedoes, machine guns, Toma-
hawk missiles, and, well—you get the picture. Bad
mammajamma.

Big, badass damn boat. Kept afloat by a crew of
young navy seamen. And you won't find as nice a
gang of fine young men and women as you will in
the U.S. Navy. "Yes, sir," "No, ma'am," kids, all of
them. Manners, remember those? Good haircuts?
Pants actually held up with belts? Yeah, I didn't
think so.

Along about August 2000—remember, this was

about a year before the attack on the Twin Towers—USS *Cole* sailed from NAS Norfolk to join the U.S. Fifth Fleet in the Arabian Gulf. A few months later she called at the seaport of Aden, situated by the eastern approach to the Red Sea. A city, weird as it might seem, built in the crater of a dormant volcano. What were they thinking? Anyway, the day it all went down, the Big Wake-Up Call, I like to call it, the *Cole* was under a security posture known as Threatcon Bravo. We're talking the third of five alert levels used by the U.S. Navy to label impending terrorist threats.

Sunny day. Hot as Hades. Most of the crew was busy with daily shipboard routine, but a bunch of guys had their shirts off, sunning on the foredeck, playing cards, shooting the breeze, or, more accurately, the shit, as they say in the navy.

One of the guys, out of the corner of his eye, notices a small fiberglass fishing boat making its way through the busy harbor. Kinda boat local fishermen used to ply their trade around the harbor. Nothing fancy and certainly nothing scary.

The boat seemed to be headed right for the ship's port side, or, so thought Seaman Foster Riggs anyway. Now, on a normal day, you understand, most of the harbor's waterborne inhabitants sensibly gave the *Cole* a wide berth. Which is why Seaman Riggs got up and went to the port rail to have a closer look at the approaching vessel. Something odd about it, he was thinking.

It was going pretty fast for conditions, number one. Two locals stood side by side at the helm station. Young guys, bearded, T-shirts and faded shorts.

Had the throttle cranked, the boat up on plane. Out for a cruise, a couple of amigos just having a good time, was what it looked like.

Nothing looked all that out of the ordinary to Riggs, even as the fishing boat drew ever nearer to the *Cole.* Big smiles on the local yokels' faces as they pulled along the destroyer's port side.

As the boat settled, they were raising their hands up in the air, waving hello at the friendly young sailor staring down at them. Friendlies themselves, Riggs was thinking. But then they did something funny, something that should have sounded crazy loud alarm bells banging big-time inside that young seaman's head.

The two men looked up at the skinny sailor on the foredeck, snapped to attention, and then saluted smartly. Riggs noticed something really strange then: the smiles were gone from their faces.

A second later, those two boys were vaporized. They had just exploded a whole boatload of C-4 plastic explosive. At the moment of the explosion, the little skiff was about five feet from the warship's hull. And that much C-4 at close range? Hell, that is the equivalent of seven hundred pounds of TNT blowing up in your face.

The blast shattered windows and shook the buildings along the waterfront. It also opened a forty-foot-by-forty-foot gash in the destroyer's reinforced steel hull. And turned the inside of that ship into an abattoir. Seventeen of our young warriors were killed instantly or mortally wounded. Thirty-nine more were seriously injured. It was bad. It was real bad, brother.

The *Cole* incident, that was the single worst attack on an American target since the 1998 bombings of U.S. embassies in Kenya, Nairobi, and Dar es Salaam, Tanzania.

That attack was bad enough.

And then it got worse.

The blast in the Gulf of Aden sent shock-wave repercussions rolling down the corridors of the Pentagon.

The navy brass had finally gotten the wake-up call heard round the world. Decades of the USN's woefully outdated policies and training procedures had finally come back to bite the navy's ass, bigtime. The much disputed Rules of Engagement, well, that's exactly what had put the *Cole* in the crosshairs of two young terrorists hell-bent on killing American sailors.

And the *Cole*? Hell, she had been a sitting duck. Never had a chance.

Crew members started reporting that the sentries' Rules of Engagement, set up by the ship's captain according to navy guidelines, "would have prevented them from defending the ship even if they'd detected a threat." The crew would not have been permitted to fire *without being fired upon first*! You're beginning to see the problem. But, wait, there's more.

A petty officer manning a .50 cal. at the stern of the *Cole* moments after the explosion that fateful day saw a second boat approaching and was ordered to turn his weapon away unless and until he was actively shot at. "We're trained to hesitate," the young sailor told the board of inquiry. "If somebody had seen something that looked or even smelled wrong and fired his weapon, sir? That man would have been court-martialed."

The commander of the U.S. Navy's Fifth Fleet concluded: "Even had the *Cole* implemented Threatcon Bravo measures flawlessly, there is total unity among the flag officers that the ship would not and could not have prevented or even deterred this attack."

Hello?

Now you got yourself a Class A shitstorm brewing in the Pentagon. Now you got the commander of the Fifth Fleet—which patrols five million square miles, mind you, including the Red Sea, the Arabian Gulf, the Arabian Sea, and parts of the Indian Ocean—saying, hold on, a U.S. Navy destroyer versus a crappy little fishing boat? And the fishing boat *wins*?

That's when the call for help went out. And that's where I come in.

My outfit, a little ole Texas company at that time, called Vulcan Inc., was just one of many providers contacted by the U.S. Navy and the Department of Defense. They wanted to see just how quickly people like me could respond to their "urgent and compelling" need for the immediate training of twenty thousand sailors in force protection over the next six months. The navy was basically saying to all of us, *Look, we have to train X number of sailors at X types of ranges and we need to do it now. Can you handle that?*

My name is Colonel Brett "Beau" Beauregard. I'm the founder and CEO of Vulcan Inc. And I knew this was my shot. Mine was the only company that checked every box on the navy's list. At the time, I had only twenty full-time employees. At Vulcan's original training facility on the Gulf of Mexico south of Port Arthur, Texas, hell, we hadn't even trained a measly three thousand people.

That was the total ever since opening our doors three years earlier. But Beau? Nothing if not aggressive. First in my class at West Point, decorated U.S. Army Ranger, strong as a team of oxen, captain of the Army gridiron team that beat Navy to win the Thanksgiving Army-Navy game my senior year.

Go, Army! And as I always say, "It ain't braggin' if it's true."

That navy contract? It was worth over seven million dollars. I was worth about seven cents. And I had only thirty days to get my guys ready. I got myself started bright and early next morning, you better believe I did.

I began construction on a little idea I'd cooked up called a "ship-in-a-box." It was a floating superstructure made of forty-foot steel tractor-trailer containers. It was painted battleship grey and fitted with watertight doors and railings. Imagine an elaborate ship's bridge on a movie set, but one designed to withstand live ammunition in real-life firefights. Stone cool.

For one month, no one around here slept much. But the old colonel's magical training boat-in-a-box was ready for the navy when day 30 rolled around. To my great surprise, and delight, Vulcan won that damn navy contract. Over the next six months down at Port Arthur, Vulcan personnel trained nearly a thousand new sailors a week! We taught them to identify threats, engage enemies, and defeat terrorist attacks while aboard ships either in port or at sea.

Almost immediately, I identified one of the navy's biggest problems. This was the original gang that couldn't shoot straight! It had been maybe years since a whole lot of these guys had even held guns in their hands. U.S. Navy sailors who had never even used a firearm since boot camp!

Hundreds of sailors started flowing through the facility every week. The ATFP approach developed by my team, Anti-Terrorism Force Protection, was the very finest available on the planet at that time. We ramped up the manning, training, and equipping of naval forces to better realize a war fighter's physical security at sea. ATFP became the U.S. Navy's primary focus of every mission, activity, and event. This mind-set was instilled in every one of the sailors who went through the program.

Vulcan was so successful that in 2003, Vulcan would train roughly seventy thousand sailors at our rapidly growing Port Arthur, Texas, facility.

One night I told my brand-new wife, Margaret Anne, I felt like that scrappy little dog who finally caught that school bus he'd been chasing. We expanded the Port Arthur operation again and again—up to over seven thousand acres, more than twelve square miles, including considerable conservation areas to preserve wetlands and restore wildlife habitat. I made sure we reseeded hundreds of acres with native oak and swamp cypress.

And I made one other important addition to the facility.

I'd shot me a massive black bear over in Red River County east of Dallas. Took that bad boy with a black powder rifle. Old Blackie now stood on his hind legs in the lobby of the main Lodge, a 598-pound symbol of Vulcan's trademark tenacity—jaws frozen open, right paw raised high, ready to strike. It became the corporate logo, on every piece of paper my company generated in the years that followed. I've still got the T-shirt.

In a few short years, Vulcan achieved worldwide fame. We were providing private military assistance to any country that could afford our services. And here's the thing: we did not play favorites, and politics never entered into the equation. I was a soldier of fortune, after all, and this soldier was looking to make his fortune. I was soon working with the military and military intelligence agencies of countries around the world. And not once did I show a trace of favoritism toward any client or any government; that's what kept me in the game.

I got pretty good at building impenetrable firewalls between our clients. The degree of security afforded each major account was so highly regarded that the Americans, the Russians, and even the Chinese were all equally comfortable that their most closely held secrets were safe with us. Hell, at one point early on, Vulcan could claim both Israel and the Iranians as clients at one and the same time!

My own journey to the pinnacle of power had begun; and neither America nor, later, the world, had a clue what they were in for. I made it to the very top, and I clung to my position tenaciously. But the center would not hold. Events, politics, politicians, and most devastating of all, the media, overtook me in the end. The whole world would turn on me, viciously, and bring me down.

Because in the end, me and my guys, the former heroes of Vulcan, we who had taken bullets for the Americans and everyone else, would become objects of scorn and ridicule in the press and everywhere else. And many believed it was all through no fault of our own. Hell, I believe it to this day! Did some innocent people get shot? Yeah, it's called war. Did we shoot first? My opinion? No, we did not. I've seen the evidence. I stand by my troops to this day.

First America, and then the rest of the world, like dominoes, threw Colonel Beauregard under the bus. My men were labeled wanton murderers in the world press. Cowboys with neither scruples nor morality. Hired killers who would turn on anyone if the price was high enough. Eventually, the old colonel disappeared from the front pages of the media . . . some said I was only biding my time. Some said I wanted nothing to do with the world anymore and had gone into seclusion in some remote location down in the Caribbean. And that's just what I damn well did.

Now, here comes the funny part.

That I would return to the front lines one day in the not too distant future, exponentially more powerful than ever before, was unthinkable at that dark time. Or that I would seek my ultimate revenge on a duplicitous world that had shamed me, nearly destroying me.

As it all turned out in the end, Vulcan's rapid fall

from grace and glory was not the end of me. Not by a long shot. As one of my hardasses said when he saw me back in a Jeep, "The colonel has definitely not left the building."

In fact, all this ancient history I been telling you? It was only the beginning of my story.

Respectfully Submitted, November 2015
Colonel Brett T. Beauregard, U.S. Army, Ret.
Aboard *Celestial*
Royal Bermuda Yacht Club
Hamilton, Bermuda

TWO

———

———

MOST EVENINGS, LIKE TONIGHT, HARDING TORrance walked home from the office. His cardiac guy had told him walking was the best thing for his ticker. Harding liked walking. He even wore one of those FitBit thingamajigs on his wrist to keep track of his steps. Doctor's orders after a couple of issues popped up in his last stress test. But the truth was, Harding liked walking in Paris, especially in the rain.

Ah, April in Paris.

And the women on the streets, too, you know? God in heaven. Paris has the world's most beautiful women, full stop, hands down. The clothes, the jewelry, the hair, the way they walked, the posture, the way . . . the way they dangled their dainty little *parapluies*, the way they goddamn *smelled*. And, it wasn't perfume, it was natural.

Plus, his eight-room Beaux-Arts apartment was an easy stroll home from his office. His ultradeluxe building was located on the rue du Faubourg Saint-Honoré, right next to Sotheby's. Saint-Honoré was the shopping street in one of the fancier arrondissements on the Right Bank. Where there are beautiful shops, there are beautiful women, *n'est-ce pas?* Especially in this extremely ritzy neighborhood. Or arrondissement, as the froggies like to say.

Tell the truth, he'd lived here in Paris for ten years or more and he still didn't have any idea which arrondissement was which. Somebody would ask him, *Which is which?* He'd shrug his shoulders with a smile. He had learned a handy little expression in French early on which had always served him well in his expatriate life: "*Je ne sais pas.*"

I don't know!

At any rate, his homeward route from the office took him past the newly renovated Ritz Hotel, Hermès (or "Hermeez" as the bumpkins called his ties whenever he wore one when he visited Langley), plus, YSL, Cartier, et cetera, et cetera. You get the picture. Ritzy real estate, like he said. And, just so you know, Hermès is pronounced "Air-mez."

Very ritzy.

Oddly enough, the ritziest hotel on the whole rue was not the one *called* the Ritz. It was the less obvious one called Hôtel Le Bristol. Now, what he liked about the Bristol, mainly, was the bar. At the end of the day, good or bad, he liked a quiet cocktail or three in a quiet bar before he went home to his wife. That's all there was to it, been doing it all his life. His personal happy hour.

The Bristol's lobby bar was dimly lit, church quiet, and hidden away off the beaten path. It was basically a dark paneled room lit by a roaring fire situated off the lobby where only the cognoscenti, as they say, held sway. Harding held sway there because he was a big, good-looking guy, always impeccably dressed in Savile Row threads and Charvet shirts of pale pink or blue. He was a big tipper, a friendly guy, great smile. Knew the bar staff's names by heart and discreetly handed out envelopes every Christmas.

Sartorial appearances to the contrary, Harding Torrance was one hundred percent red-blooded American. He even worked for the government, had done, mostly all his life. And he'd done very, very well, thank you. He'd come up the hard way, but he'd come up, all right. His job, though he'd damn well have to kill you if he told you, was station chief, CIA, Paris. In other words, Harding was a very big damn deal in anybody's language.

El Queso Grande, as they used to say at Langley.

He'd been in Paris since right after 9/11. His buddy from Houston, the new president, had posted him here because the huge Muslim population in Paris presented a lot of high-value intel opportunities. His mandate was to identify the al-Qaeda leadership in France, then whisk them away to somewhere nice and quiet for a little enhanced interrogation.

He was good at it, he stuck with it, got results, and got promoted, boom, boom, boom. The president had even singled him out for recognition in an Oval Office reception, had specifically said that he and his team had been responsible for saving countless lives on the European continent and in the United Kingdom. What goes around, right? Let's just say he was well compensated.

Harding had gone into the family oil business after West Point and a stint with the Rangers out of Fort Bragg. Spec-ops duty, two combat tours in Iraq. Next, working for Torrance Oil, he was all over Saudi and Yemen and Oman, running his daddy's fields in the Middle East. He was no silver spooner, though; no, he had started on the rigs right at the bottom, working as a ginzel (lower than the lowest worm), working his way up to a floorhand on the kelly driver, and then a bona fide rig driller in one year.

That period of his life was his introduction to the real world of Islam.

Long story short?

Harding knew the Muslims' mind-set, their language, their body language, their brains, even, knew the whole culture, the mullahs, the warlords, where all the bodies were buried, the whole enchilada. And so, when his pal W needed someone uniquely qualified to transform the CIA's Paris station into a first-rate intelligence clearinghouse for all Europe? Well. Who was he to say? Let history tell the tale.

His competition? Most guys inside the Agency, working in Europe at that time, right after the Twin Towers? Didn't know a burqa from a kumquat and that's no lie—

"Monsieur Torrance? Monsieur Torrance?"

"*Oui?*"

"*Votre whiskey, monsieur.*"

"Oh, hey, Maurice. Sorry, what'd you say? Scotch rocks?" he said to the head bartender, distracted, not even remembering ordering this fresh one. "Sure. One more. Why not?"

"*Mais oui, m'sieur.* There it is. *C'est ça!*"

Apparently his drink had arrived and he hadn't even noticed. That was *not* a first, by the way.

"Oh, yeah. Merci."

"*Mais certainement, Monsieur Torrance. Et voilà.*"

His drink had come like magic. Had he already ordered that? He knocked it back, ordered another, and relaxed, making small talk, *le bavardage*, with Maurice about the rain, the train bombing in Marseilles. Which horse might win four million euros in the Prix de l'Arc de Triomphe at Longchamp tomorrow. The favorite was an American thoroughbred named Buckpasser. He was a big pony, heralded in the tabloids as the next Secretariat, Maurice told him.

"Really? Listen. There will never, *ever*, be another 'Big Red,' Maurice. Trust me on that one."

"But of course, sir. Who could argue?"

Harding swiveled on his barstool, sipping his third or fourth scotch, depending, checking the scenery, admiring his fellow man . . .

And woman . . .

And this one rolled in like thunder.

THREE

HE'D ALWAYS SAID HE'D BEEN BORN LUCKY. AND just look at him. Sitting in a cozy bar on a cold and rainy Friday night. He'd told his wife, Julia, not to expect him for dinner. Just in case, you know, that *something came up*. He'd explained to her that, well, honey, something troubling *had* come up. That whole thing with the state visit of the new Chinese president to the Élysée Palace on Sunday? About to go *au toilette*!

"Sorry, is this seat taken?" the scented woman said.

What the hell? He'd seen her take an empty stool at the far end of the bar. Must have changed her mind after catching a glimpse of the chick magnet at the other end . . .

"Not at all, not at all," he told her. "Here, let me

remove my raincoat from the barstool. How rude of me."

"Thank you."

Tres chic, he registered. *Very elegant*. Blond. Big American girl. Swimmer, maybe, judging by the shoulders. California. Stanford. Maybe UCLA. One of the two. Pink Chanel, head to toe. Big green Hermès Kelly bag, all scruffed up, so loaded. Big rock on her finger, so married. A small wet puffball of a dog and a dripping umbrella, so ducked in out of the rain. Ordered a martini, so a veteran. Beautiful eyes and fabulous cleavage, so a possibility . . .

He bought her another drink. Champagne, this time. Domaines Ott Rosé. So she had taste.

"What brings you to Paris, Mrs. . . ."

"I'm Crystal. Crystal Methune. And you are?"

"Harding," he said, in his deepest voice.

"Harding. Now that's a good strong name, isn't it? So. Why *are* we here in Paris? Let me see. Oh, yes. Horses. My husband has horses. We're here for the races at Longchamp."

"And that four million euros' purse at Longchamp, I'll bet. Maurice here and I were just talking about that. Some payday, huh? Your horse have a shot? Which horse is it?"

"Buckpasser."

"Buckpasser? That's your horse? That's some horse, honey."

"I suppose. I don't like horses. I like to shop."

"Attagirl. Sound like my ex. So where are you from, Crystal?"

"We're from Kentucky. Louisville. You know it?"

"Not really. So where are you staying?"

"Right upstairs, honey. My hubby took the penthouse for the duration."

"Ah, got it. He's meeting you here, is he?"

"Hardly. Having dinner with Felix, his horse trainer, somewhere in the Bois de Boulogne, out near the track is more like it. The two of them are all juned up about Buckpasser running on a muddy track tomorrow. You ask a lot of questions, don't you, Harding?"

"It's my business."

"Really? What do you do?"

"I'm a writer for a quiz show."

She smiled. "That's funny."

"Old joke."

"You're smart, aren't you, Harding? I like smart men. Are you married?"

"No. Well, yes."

"See? You are funny. May I have another pink champagne?"

Harding twirled his right index finger, signaling the barman for another round. He briefly tried to remember how many scotches he'd had and gave up.

"Cute dog," he said, bending down to pet the pooch, hating how utterly pathetic he sounded. But, hell, he was hooked. Hooked, gaffed, and in the boat. He'd already crawl through a mile of broken glass just to drink her bathwater.

"Thanks," she said, lighting a gold-tipped cigarette with a gold Dupont lighter. She took a deep drag and let it out, coughing a bit.

"So you enjoy smoking?" Harding said.

"No, I just like coughing."

"Good one. What's the little guy's name?"

"It's a her. Rikki Nelson."

"Oh. You mean like . . ."

"Right. In the Ozzie and Harriet reruns. Only this little bitch on wheels likes her name spelled with two 'k's. Like Rikki Martinez. You know? Don't you, precious? Yes, you do!"

"Who?"

"The singer?"

"Oh, sure. Who?"

"Never mind, honey. Ain't no thing."

"Right. So, shopping. What else do you like, Crystal?"

"Golf. I'm a scratch golfer. Oh, and jewelry. I really like jewelry."

"Golfer, huh? You heard the joke about Arnold Palmer's ex-wife?"

"No, but I'm going to, I guess."

"So this guy marries Arnold Palmer's ex. After they make love for the *third* time on their wedding night, the new groom picks up the phone. 'Who are you calling?' Arnie's ex asks. Room service, he says, I'm starved. That's not what Arnold would've done, she says. So the guy says, okay, what would Arnold have done? Arnold would have done it again, that's what. So they did it again. Then the guy picks up the phone again and she says, 'You calling room service again?' And he says, 'No, baby, I'm calling Arnold. Find out what par is on this damn hole.'"

He waited.

"I don't get it."

"Well, see, he's calling Arnold because he—"

"Shhh," she said, putting her index finger to her lips.

She covered his large hand with her small one and stroked the inside of his palm with her index finger.

She put her face close to his and whispered, "Frankly? Let's just cut the shit. I like sex, Harding."

"That's funny, I do, too," he said.

"I bet you do, baby. I warn you, though. I'm a big girl, Harding. I am a big girl with big appetites. I wonder. Did you read *Fifty Shades of Grey*?"

"Must have missed that one, sorry. You ever read Mark Twain?"

"No. Who wrote it?"

"What?"

"I said, who wrote it? The Mark Twain thing."

"Doesn't matter, tell me about *Fifty Shades of Grey*."

"Doesn't matter. I found it terribly vanilla," she said.

"Hmm."

"Yeah, right. That's what men always say when they don't know what the hell a girl is talking about."

"Vanilla. Not kinky enough."

"Not bad, Harding. Know what they used to say about me at my sorority house at UCLA? The Kappa Delts?"

"I do not."

"That Crystal. She's got big hair and big knockers and she likes big sex."

He turned to face her and took both her perfect hands in his.

"I'm sorry. Would you ever in your wildest dreams consider leaving your rich husband and marrying a poor, homeless boy like me?"

"No."

"Had to ask."

"I do like to screw. You do get that part, right?"

"Duly noted."

"Long as we're square on this, Harding."

"We're square."

"I'm gonna tie you to the bed and make you squeal like Porky Pig, son. Or, vice versa. You with me on this?"

He just looked at her and smiled.

Jackpot.

THE ELEVATOR TO THE PENTHOUSE SUITE OPENED inside the apartment foyer. It was exquisite, just as Harding would have imagined the best rooms in the best hotel in Paris might be, full of soft evening light, with huge arrangements of fresh flowers everywhere, and through the opened doors, a large terrace overlooking the lights of Paris and the misty gardens directly below.

Crystal smiled demurely and led him into the darkened living room. She showed him the bar and told him to help himself. She'd be right back. Slipping into something a little more comfortable, he imagined, smiling to himself as he poured two fingers of Johnnie Walker Blue and strolled over to a large and very inviting sofa by the fireplace.

He kicked his shoes off, stretched out, and took a sip of whisky. He was just getting relaxed when he heard an odd streaming sound. Looking down at the floor, he saw that the little fuckhead Rikki Nelson had just peed all over his Guccis.

"Shit!" he said, under his breath.

"Hey!" he heard Crystal yell.

"What?"

"Turn on some music, Harding; Momma wants to dance, baby!" she called out from somewhere down a long dark hall.

He got to his feet and staggered a few feet in the gloom, cracking his shin on an invisible coffee table.

"What? Music? Where is it?"

"Right below the bar glasses. Just push 'on.' It's all loaded up and ready to rip."

He limped over to the bar and hit the button.

Dean Martin's "That's Amore" filled the room.

"Is that it?" he shouted over Dino.

"Hell, yeah, son. Crank it!"

He somehow found the volume control, cranked it, and went out to the terrace, away from the bar's booming overhead speakers. The rain was pattering on the drooping awning overhead and the night smelled like . . . like what . . . jasmine? No, that wasn't it. Something, anyway. It definitely smelled like something out here. But—

"Hey, you!" she shouted from the living room's open doorway. "There he is! There's my big stud. Come on in here, son. Let's dance! Waltz your ass on in here, baby boy, right now!"

He downed his drink and went inside. Crystal stood in the center of the room wearing a skintight S&M outfit. A black leather bodysuit that would have put Catwoman to shame. She had little Rikki Nelson cuddled atop her bulging tits, nuzzling her with kisses.

"Where's the whip, kitten?" he said.

"Oh, I'll dig one up somewhere, don't worry."

Harding collapsed into the nearest armchair and stared.

"Why are you staring like that at me and Rikki?" she pouted.

"Just trying to figure out whether or not that diamond-studded leash of yours is on the wrong bitch."

Give her credit, she laughed.

"I sure hope to hell you know how to dance, mister," she said. "Now get up and get with it, I mean it."

He hauled himself manfully up out of the leather chair.

You do what you have to do, he reminded himself.

And he danced.

And danced some more.

FOUR

H E WAS DRENCHED IN SWEAT AND PANTING LIKE an old bird dog. Even the sheets were wet. Somehow he'd managed to give her three Big Os, two traditional and, last, one utterly exhausting one. He'd never worked so hard in his life. "Outside the box," she called it, that last one.

He managed a weak smile. "Wow, you are something else, aren't you, girl? I need a cigarette."

"No time. Back in the saddle, cowboy. You got me hot, now. This cowgirl's itching to ride!"

"Crystal, seriously. I need a little breather here."

"Don't be a pussy, Harding. Momma's waiting. Turn over."

"Oh, Christ."

He rolled over onto his back and stared at the ceiling. She took his wrists and tied them to the bedposts with two Hermès scarves she'd plucked from the bedside table.

He didn't even bother trying to fight her.

"Are you trying to kill me, or what?"

"Don't you worry yourself, baby. The Cialis will kick in any minute now."

"I don't take Cialis, Crystal."

"You do now, stud. I put two in your drink down at the lobby bar. When you bent down to pat Rikki Nelson. Remember that?"

"What? Are you kidding me? F'crissakes, Crystal . . ."

"Don't say I didn't warn you, hon. Big sex, re-member? Okay, I'll get on top this time. Oh, yes . . . *somebody's* ready for Momma down there. That Cialis is a bitch, isn't it? Just think, two pills, you might have an erection lasting *eight* hours . . ."

"Listen, Crystal, you've really got to stop this . . . untie me . . . I've got a pain in my chest . . . I mean it!"

"Pussy is always the best cure for whatever ails you, son. Hang on, Momma's gonna ride this buck-ing bronco . . ."

"Damn it, get off! I've got a cardiac condition! Doc says I'm supposed to take it easy . . . Goddam-mit, I'm serious! Now my arm really hurts . . . call the doctor, Crystal. Now. They must have a house doctor on call and. . . . oh, Christ almighty, it hurts . . . do something!"

"Like what?"

"My pills! My nitro pills! They're over there in my trouser pocket. . . ."

"Hold on a sec . . ."

She reached over and picked up the bedside phone, never breaking her rhythmic stride, and asked for the hotel operator.

He must have passed out from the pain. Everything was foggy, out of focus. The room was dark, the rain beating hard against the windowpanes. Just a single lamp light from a table over in the corner.

Crystal, still naked, was sitting at the foot of the bed, smoking a cigarette and talking to the doctor in hushed tones. Her head was resting on the doctor's shoulder. He couldn't make out what they were saying. He was bathed in a cold, clammy sweat and the pain had spread from behind his breastbone into and out along his left arm. Fucking hell. His wrists were still tied to the bedposts? Was she insane?

Then he noticed something that totally weirded him out. The fucking doctor? His savior?

He was naked.

He heard a sob escape his own lips, and then a cry of pain from the phantom elephant sitting atop his chest.

"Shhh," the doctor said, getting to his feet and coming to the head of the bed to stand beside him. He put his finger to his lips and said, "Shhh," again.

"You've gotta do CPR or something, Doc," Harding croaked. "My pills! They're in the right pocket of my trousers. Please. I feel like I'm going to die . . ."

"That's because you are going to die, Harding," the man said.

"What?"

"You heard me."

"Wait. Who are you?" He squinted his eyes, but he couldn't make out the physician's features.

"Vengeance, sayeth the Lord, Harding. That's who I am. Vengeance."

"You're not a doctor. . . . You're . . ."

"Dr. Death will do for now."

"Who . . . no, you're not . . . you're somebody else. You're . . ."

"Don't you recognize me anymore, Harding? I've had a little surgery recently. A bit of Botox. But, still, the eyes are always a dead giveaway. Look close."

"Spider?"

"Bingo."

"No, can't be . . . You're *Spider*, f'crissakes," the dying man croaked.

"Right. Spider Payne. Your old buddy. Come rain or come shine. Tonight, it's rain. Look out the window, Harding. It's goddamn pouring out there. Ever see it rain so hard?"

"Gimme a break here, Spider. What are you doing . . ."

"It's called poetic justice. A little twist of fate shall we say?"

Pain scorched Torrance's body and he arched upward, straining against his bonds, coming almost completely off the bed. He didn't think anything could hurt this much.

His old nemesis knelt on the floor by the bed and started gently stroking his hair. When he spoke, it was barely above a whisper.

"You fucked me royally, Harding. Remember that? When I needed you most? When the French government, whom you always claimed to have in your pocket, nailed my balls to the wall? Kidnapping and suspicion of murder. Thirty years to life? Ring a bell?"

"That wasn't my fault, f'crissakes! Please! You gotta help me!"

"That's my line. Help *me*. You don't get to use it. Way too late for that, I'm afraid, old soldier. You're catching the next train, partner."

"I can't . . . I can't breathe . . . I can't catch my . . ."

"This is how it works, Harding. You fucked with the wrong honchos in Moscow, buddy. *Really* wrong. Ever heard of a dude goes by the name of Uncle Joe? A dead ringer for Joe Stalin. You pissed off Putin's number one henchman in the Kremlin, compadre. He's the reason I'm here. Your ass is *mine*, pal."

"Who—"

"Doesn't matter now. It's so simple, isn't it? Judgment Day. How it all works out in the end? In that dark hour when no treason, no treachery, no bad deed goes unpunished."

"I can't . . . can't . . ."

Harding Torrance opened his eyes wide in fear and pain. And as the blackness creeped in around him, and his life ran away from him like a man fleeing a burning building, he heard Spider Payne utter the last words his brain would ever register.

"You fucked me, right? But, in the end, Crystal Meth and the old Spider, well, I guess they fucked you."

"Who's Uncle Joe?" Harding Torrance whispered with the last breath left in his body.

FIVE

NORTH HAVEN, MAINE

T HE BRIGHT BLUE WATERS OF PENOBSCOT BAY
beckoned. Cam Hooker, buttoning up a light
blue and freshly laundered Brooks Brothers shirt,
paused to throw open his dressing room window.
Glorious morning, all right. Sunlight sparkled on
the bay, white seabirds flashed and dove above.
He leaned out the window, took a deep breath of
pine-scented Maine air, and assessed the morning's
weather.

Fresh breeze out of the east, and a moderate
chop, fifteen knots sustained, maybe gusting to
thirty. Barometer falling, increased cloudiness,
possible thunderheads moving in from the west by

midmorning. Chance of rain showers later on, oh, sixty to seventy percent, give or take.

Perfect.

Certainly nothing an old salt like Cameron Hooker couldn't handle.

It was Sunday, praise the Lord, his favorite day of the week. The day he got to take himself, his *New York Times*, and whatever tattered paperback spy novel he was currently headlong into reading for the third time (an old Alastair MacLean) out on his boat for a few tranquil hours of peace and quiet and bliss.

Hooker had sailed her, his black ketch *Maracaya*, every single Sunday morning of his life, for nigh on forty years now, rain or shine, sleet, hail or snow.

Man alone. A singleton. Solitary.

It was high summer again, and summer meant grandchildren by the dozen. Toddlers, rug rats, and various ragamuffins running roughshod throughout his rambling old seaside cottage on North Haven Island. *Haven?* Hah! Up and down the back stairs they rumbled, tearing roughshod through the rose gardens, dashing inside and out, darting through his vegetable patches and into his library, all the while shouting at peak decibels some mysterious new battle cry, "Huzzah! Huzzah!" picked up God knows where.

It was the victory cheer accorded to General George Washington, he knew that, but this intellectually impoverished gizmo generation had not a clue who George Washington was! Of that much, at least, he was certain.

You knew you were down in the deep severe when

not a single young soul in your entire family had the remotest clue who the hell the Father of Our Country was!

In his day, portraits of the great man beamed benevolence down on students from every wall of every classroom. He was our Father, the Father of our country. *Your* country! Why, if someone had told young Cam back then that in just one or two generations, the general himself would have been scrubbed clean from our—why, he would have—

"What are you thinking about, dear?" his wife, Gillian, said, interrupting Cam's dark reverie at the breakfast table later that morning. She was perusing what he'd always referred to as the "Women's Sports Section." Also sometimes known as the bridal pages in the Sunday edition of the *New York Times*. Apparently, the definitive weekly "Who's Who" of who'd married whom last week. For all those out there who, like his wife of sixty years, were still keeping score, he supposed.

"You're frowning, dear," she said.

"Hmm."

He scratched his grizzled chin and sighed, gazing out at the tall forests of green trees marching down to the bright harbor. Even now, a mud-caked munchkin wielding a blue Frisbee bat advanced stealthily up the hill, stalking Cam's old chocolate Lab, Captain, sleeping in the foreground.

"Will you look at that?" he mused.

Gillian put the paper down and peered at him over the toaster.

"What is it, dear?"

"Oh, nothing. It's July, you know," he said, rapping sharply on the window to alert his dog and scare the munchkin away.

"July? What about it?"

"It *is* the cruelest month," he said. "Not April. July. That's all."

"Oh, good heavens," she said, and snatched away her section of the paper.

Dismissed, he stood and leaned across the table to kiss his wife's proffered cheek.

"It's your own damn fault, Cam Hooker," she said, stroking his rosy cheek. "If you'd relent for once in your life, if you'd only let them have a television to watch, just one! That black-and-white set gathering dust up in the attic would do, the one you watched the Watergate thing on. Or even one of those hand-held computer thingies, whatever they're called; silence would reign supreme in this house once more. But no. Not you."

"A *television*? In this house?" he said. "Oh, no. Not in this house. Never! I'll buy more books if I have to!"

"There's no *room* for more books, Cam!"

Grabbing his newspapers, book, and canvas sail bag and swinging out into the backyard, slamming the screen door behind him, he headed down the sloping green lawn to his dock. The old Hooker property, some fifteen acres of it, was right at the tip of Crabtree Point, with magnificent views of the Fox Islands Thorofare inlet and the Camden Hills to the west. Cameron was the fifth-generation Hooker to summer on this island, not that anyone cared a whit about such things anymore. Traditions, history, common sense, and common courtesy, things like that, all gone to hell or by the wayside. Hell, they were trying to get rid of *Christmas*! Some goddamn school district in Ohio had banned the singing of "Silent Night." "Silent Night"?

Next thing you knew they'd be banning Old Glory in the goddamn schools.

He could see the old girl out there at the far end of the dock when he crested the hill. Just the sight of her never failed to move him. His heart skipped a beat, literally, every time she hove into view.

Maracaya.

She was an old Alden-design ketch, and he'd owned her for longer than time. Forty feet on the waterline, wooden hull, gleaming black Awlgrip, with a gold cove stripe running along her flank beneath the gunwales. Her decks were teak, her spars were Sitka spruce, and she was about as yar as any damn boat currently plying the waters of coastal Maine, in his not-so-humble, humble opinion.

Making his way down the hill to the sun-dappled water, Cam couldn't take his eyes off her.

She'd never looked better.

He had a young kid this summer, sophomore at Yale, living down here in the boathouse. The boy helped him keep *Maracaya* in proper Bristol fashion. She was a looker, all right, but she was a goer, too. He'd won the Block Island Race on her back in '87, and then the Nantucket Opera Cup the year after that. Now, barely memories, just dusty trophies on the mantel in some peoples' goddamn not-so-humble opinion.

"Morning, Skipper," the crew-cut blond kid said,

popping his head up from the companionway. "Coffee's on below, sir. You're good to go."

"Thanks, Ben, good on ya, mate."

"Good day for it, sir," the boy said, looking up at the big blue sky with his big white smile. He was a good kid, this Ben Sparhawk. Sixth-generation North Haven—his dad and granddad were both hardworking lobstermen. Came from solid Maine stock too. Men from another time, men who could toil at being a fisherman, a farmer, a sailor, a lumberman, a shipwright, and a quarryman, all rolled into one. And master of all.

Ben was a history major at New Haven, on a full scholarship. He had a head on his shoulders, he did, and he used it. He came up from the galley below and quickly moved to the port-side bow, freeing the forward, spring, and aft mooring lines before leaping easily from the deck down onto the dock.

"Prettiest boat in the harbor, sir," Ben said, looking at her gleaming mahogany topsides with some pride.

"Absofuckinlutely, son," Cam said, laughing out loud at his good fortune, another golden day awaiting him out there on the water. He was one of the lucky ones and he knew it. A man in good health, of sound mind, and looking forward to the precious balance of his time here on earth, specifically in the great state of Maine.

SIX

CAM HOOKER WAS SEMIRETIRED FROM THE Agency now. He'd been the director under George H. W. Bush and had had a good run. Under his watch, the CIA was a tightly run ship. No scandals, no snafus, no bullshit, just a solid record of intelligence successes around the world. He was proud of his service to his country, and it pained him to see the condition it was in now. *Diminished*, that was the word, goddammit. How could the bastards, all of them, let this happen to his magnificent country?

He shook off such thoughts, leaving them well ashore as he stepped aboard his boat. He went aft and climbed down into the cockpit and kicked his topsiders off so he could feel the warm teak decks on the soles of his feet. He felt better already. Smell that air!

Ben Sparhawk had thoughtfully removed and

stowed the sail cover from the mainsail. Cam grabbed the main halyard, took a couple of turns around the starboard winch, and started grinding, the big mainsail blooming with fresh Maine air as it rose majestically up the stick.

Some days, when there was no wind, he'd crank up the old Universal diesel, a 42-horsepower lump of steel that had served him well over the decades. Now, with a fresh breeze, he winched the main up, loosing the sheets and letting her sails flop in the wind. The jib was roller-furling, one of his few concessions to modernity, and at his advancing age, a godsend for its ease of use. He also had a storm trysail rigged that he'd deploy when he got out beyond the harbor proper.

"Shove her bow off for me, Ben, willya?" he said, putting the helm over and sheeting in the main.

"Aye, Skipper," the boy said, and moments later Cam was pointed in the right direction and moving away from the dock toward the Thorofare running between North Haven and Vinalhaven Islands.

He turned to wave good-bye to the boy, saw him smiling and waving back with both hands, and found his old blue eyes suddenly gone all blurry with tears.

By God, he wished he'd had a son like that.

HE THREADED HIS WAY, TACKING SMARTLY THROUGH the teeming Thorofare. It was crowded as hell, always was this time of year, especially this Fourth of July weekend. Boats and yachts of every description hove into view: the Vinalhaven ferry steaming stolidly across, knockabouts and dinghies, a lovely old Nat Herreshoff gaff-headed Bar Harbor 30; and here came one of the original Internationals built in Norway, sparring with a Luders; and even a big Palmer Johnson stinkpot anchored just off Foy Brown's Yard, over a hundred feet long he'd guess, with New York Yacht Club burgees emblazoned on her smokestack. Pretty damn fancy for these parts, if you asked him.

As was his custom, once he was in open water, Cam had put her hard over, one mile from shore and headed for the pretty little harbor over on the mainland at Rockport. Blowing like stink out here now. Clouding up. Front moving in for damn sure. He stood to windward at the helm, both hands on the big wheel, his feet planted wide, and sang a few bars of his favorite sailor's ditty, sung to the tune of the old English ballad "Robin on the Moor":

It was a young captain on Cranberry Isles did dwell;
He took the schooner Arnold, one you all know well.
> *She was a tops'l schooner and*
> *hailed from Calais, Maine;*
> *They took a load from Boston*
> *to cross the raging main—*

THE WORDS CAUGHT IN HIS THROAT.

He'd seen movement down in the galley below. Not believing his eyes, he looked again. Nothing. Perhaps just a light shadow from a porthole sliding across the floor as he fell off the wind a bit? Nothing at all; and yet it had spooked him there for a second but he—

"Hello, Cam," a strange-looking man said, suddenly making himself visible at the foot of the steps down in the galley. And then he was climbing up into the cockpit.

"What the hell?" Cam said, startled.

"Relax. I don't bite."

"Who the hell are you? And what the hell are you doing aboard my boat?"

Cam eased the main a bit to reduce the amount of heel and moved higher to the windward side of the helm station. He planted himself and bent his knees, ready for any false move from years of habit in the military and later as a special agent out in the field. The stranger made no move other than to plop himself down on a faded red cushion on the leeward side of the boat and cross his long legs.

"You don't recognize me? I'm hurt. Maybe it's the long hair and the beard. Here, I know. Look at the eyes, Cam, you can always remember the eyes."

Cam looked.

Was that *Spider*, for God's sake?

IT COULDN'T BE. BUT IT WAS. SPIDER PAYNE, FOR crissakes. A guy who'd worked for him at CIA briefly the year before Cam had retired. Good agent, a guy on the way up. He'd lost track of him long ago . . . and now?

"Spider, sure, sure, I recognize you," Cam said, keeping his voice as even as he could manage. His right hand had started twitching involuntarily and he stuck it in the pocket of his jeans. His mind was ramped up, searching wildly for some kind of explanation as to how the hell this man came to be here. It just didn't make any damn sense at all.

"What in God's name is going on?"

"See? I knew this might freak you out. You know, if I just showed up on the boat like this. Sorry. I drove all night from Boston, then came over to the island on the ferry from Rockland last night. Parked my truck at Foy Brown's boatyard and went up to that little inn, the Nebo Lodge. Fully booked, not a bed to be had, wouldn't you know. Forgot it was the Fourth weekend. Stupid, I guess."

"Spider, you know this is highly goddamn unprofessional. Showing up like this. Uninvited. Are you all right? What's this all about?"

"How I found you, you mean?"

"*Why* you found me, Spider."

SEVEN

Now that's an interesting question, Cam. Well, I remembered you always had a picture of a sailboat in your office at Langley. An oil painting. A black boat at a dock below your summer house in Maine. I even remembered the boat's name. *Maracaya*. So when I couldn't get a room, I went downstairs to the bar there and had a few beers. Asked around about a boat called *Maracaya*. One old guy said, 'Ayuh. Alden ketch. She's moored out to the Hooker place, out to the end of Crabtree Point.' And here I am."

"No. Not *here you fucking are*, you idiot. How'd you get aboard? I've got a kid, looks after the boat. He'd never let you aboard."

"Cam, c'mon. It was four in the morning. Everyone was asleep. I climbed aboard and slept in the sail locker up forward. Say, it's blowing pretty good out here! Twenty knots? Think you should put in a reef?"

"Spider, you better tell me quick why you're here or you're swimming back. I am dead serious."

"I sent you a letter. A while back. You remember that? I asked for your help. I was in a little trouble with the French government. Arrested by the French for kidnapping and suspicion of murder. No body, no proof. But. Sentenced to thirty years for kidnapping a known Arab terrorist off the streets of Paris. The guy believed responsible for the Metro bombing in 2011. I was the number two guy in our Paris station, Cam! Operating within the law. Rendition was what we did then."

"Come to the point. I don't need all this history."

"I'd had a brilliant career. Not a blemish. And when I got in trouble, the Agency threw me under the bus."

"The Agency, Spider, had nothing to do with it. That decision came down out of the White House. It may surprise you to learn that the president was more concerned about our relationship with one of our most powerful European allies than you. It was a delicate time. You're a victim of bad timing."

"My whole fucking life is destroyed because of *bad timing*?"

"I'm sorry about that. But it's got nothing to do with me. I retired prior to 9/11, remember? Frankly? I never approved of rendition in the first place. Enhanced interrogation. Abu Ghraib. All those 'black funds' you had at your disposal. Not the way we played the game, son. Not in my day."

"Look. I asked you to help me. I've yet to get

a response, Cam. So now I'm here. In person. To ask you again. Right now. Will you help me? They ruined my life, man! I lost everything. My job, my shitty little farm in Aix-en-Provence. My wife took the children and disappeared. Now there's an international warrant for my arrest and my own country won't step in, Cam. All my savings gone to lawyers on appeal. I'm broke, Cam. I'm finished. Look at me. I'm falling out the window."

"Jesus Christ, Spider. What do you want? Money?"

"I want help."

"Fuck you."

"Really?"

"You screwed up, mister. Big-time. You jumped the shark, pal. You're not my problem."

"Really? You don't think I'm your problem, Cam? Are you sure about that?"

Spider stood up and took a step closer to the helm. Cam turned his old blue eyes on him, eyes that had cowed far tougher men than this one by a factor of ten.

"Are you threatening me, son? I see it in your eyes. You think I may be getting a little long in the tooth, don't you, pal, but I'll rip your beating heart out, believe me."

"That's your response then. You want me to beg? I come to you on bended knee, humbly, to beseech you for help. And you say you'll rip my heart out?"

The man was weeping.

"Listen, Spider. You're obviously upset. You need help, yes. But not from me. You need to see someone. I can help you do that. I'll even pay for it. I'm going to flip her around now and head back to the dock. I'll see that you get proper care. Uncleat that mainsheet, will you, and prepare to come about. It's really blowing out here now, so pay attention to what you're doing."

They locked eyes for what seemed an eternity.

"Do what I said," Cam told him.

Cam realized too late what Spider was going to do.

In one fluid motion, the rogue agent freed the mainsail sheet to swing the boom free, grabbed the helm, put her hard over to leeward and jibed. The jibe is the single most violent action you can take on board a big sailboat in a blow. You put yourself in mortal danger when you turn your bow away from the wind instead of up into it. You stick your tail up into the face of the wind and she kicks your ass. Hard and fast.

The standing rigging and sails shrieked like wounded banshees as the mainsail and the heavy wooden boom caught the wind from behind and came whipping across the cockpit at blinding speed.

Spider knew the boom was coming, of course, and ducked in the nick of time. Cam was not so lucky.

The boom slammed into the side of the old man's head, pulverizing the skull, spilling his brains into the sea, and carrying him out of the cockpit and up onto the deck. Only the lifelines saved him from rolling overboard.

Spider stared down at his old mentor with mixed emotions. At one point, he'd worshipped this man. But rage is a powerful thing. He'd been ruined by Cam and others like him at the highest levels of the

Agency. He knew he himself was going down soon, but he was determined not to go down alone. Revenge is another powerful thing.

He knelt down beside the dead man, trying to sort out his feelings. A lock of white hair had fallen across Cam's eyes and he lifted it away. He tried for remorse but couldn't find it inside himself anymore.

It looked like someone had dropped a cantaloupe on the deck from up at the masthead. A dark red stain flowed outward from Hooker's crushed and splintered head, soaking into the teak. What more was there to say? An unfortunate accident but it happens all the time? *Tough luck, Cam*, he thought to himself with a thin smile.

Another victim of bad timing.

Spider grabbed the helm, sheeted in the main, and headed up dead into the wind. When the boat's forward motion stalled, he grabbed the binoculars hanging from the mizzen and raised them to his eyes. He did a three-hundred-sixty-degree sweep of the horizon. Nothing, no other vessels in sight, nobody on the shore. He was about a mile and a half from the rocky shoreline. The trees encroaching down to the rocky shorebreak would provide good cover.

He looked at his watch and went below to don his wet suit for the short swim to shore. The old ketch would drift with the currents. He could disappear into the woods, bury the wet suit, and walk to town in his bathing suit, flip-flops, and T-shirt. Just another hippy tourist day-tripper, come to celebrate America's independence.

The next ferry to the mainland was at noon.

He'd checked off yet another name on his list.

Maybe it was true what they said about him, the old hands at the Agency when they got to drinking and speculating. That the old Spider was indeed a man without a future.

But he still had plenty of time to kill.

EIGHT

BERMUDA

Teakettle Cottage, in Bermuda, is no ordinary house. For starters, it is the home of the sixth-richest man in England, though you'd never guess that from the looks of the place. A rather small affair compared to its grander neighbors, it has survived, barely, at least half a dozen hurricanes in the last century. And it is, after all, the sanctum sanctorum of a very private man. Few people have ever seen it. And even to do that, first they've got to find it.

Anyone driving the coast road along the southern shore of Bermuda would find the modest limestone house hidden from view. The seaward property consists of a grove of ancient *lignum vitae*, kapok, and fragrant cedar trees. Only a narrow sandy lane gives a clue as to Teakettle's existence. A lane resembling a green tunnel finally arrives at the house, but only after winding through an incredibly dense banana grove.

Here, on a headland, Lord Alexander Hawke had resurrected an old ruin he'd promptly named Teakettle Cottage. Trees surround it on all sides except the sea, which it practically overhangs. Great windows capture every breeze, to cool, even on the hottest day, the large white rooms. The windows that look toward the sea are glassless but equipped with heavy outside shutters against the rain, enormous quadrilaterals surrounded by dark wooden frames that enclose a prospect of sea and cloud and sky, and tame the elements, as it were, into an overhanging fresco of which one could never tire.

Upon first glimpse of the house, visitors realize the cottage actually does look like a teakettle. The main portion is a rounded dome, formerly a limestone mill works. A crooked white-bricked watchtower on the far, seaward side of the house forms the teakettle's "spout." The whole affair stands out on a rocky promontory above the waves crashing against the rocks some fifty feet below.

Inside is the oval whitewashed living room. The floors are polished, well-worn Spanish red tile floors. The owner has furnished the main room with old planter's chairs and an assortment of castoffs and gifts donated by various residents seeking their own dream of solitude over the years.

Douglas Fairbanks Jr. had donated the massive

carved monkey-wood bar after a long stay during the Second World War. The battered mahogany canasta table where most of the indoor meals were taken was a gift of Errol Flynn. Flynn took refuge here during his stormy divorce from Lili Damita. Hemingway had left his Underwood typewriter on the desk where he'd written *Islands in the Stream*. The shortwave radio on the bar had been used by Admiral Sir Morgan Wheelock during World War II to monitor the comings and goings of Nazi U-boats just offshore from the cottage.

A lot of less celebrated visitors had left behind the detritus of decades, much of which had been severely edited by the new owner. He wasn't a fussy man, but he'd pulled down all the pictures of snakes some prior inhabitant had hung in his small bedroom.

The owner of this rather eccentric dwelling, Lord Hawke, won't tolerate the use of his title and has never used it himself. The only one who is allowed usage is his ancient friend and household retainer, Pelham Grenville, a man whom he has known since birth. Pelham refers to his employer simply as "m'lord."

Hawke was not a man one could simply glance at and ignore. It was not just his size, his armory of biceps, musculature, rock hardness, and the vast reserves of strength these suggested.

There was a certain nobility of bearing in him; a warrior's bearing, inherited from the knights at King Arthur's table, as well as the proud pirate captains of the Caribbean. All by way of saying that it would have been readily apparent to even the most casual of strangers that here was a man apart. A gentle, introspective man, unless aroused sufficiently to unleash the furies of hell upon you. And yet, he was usually contrite afterward, in the event that he'd been forced to use his strength.

His blue eyes were startling and had a range from merriment and charm to profound earnestness. Cross him, and he could fire a searing flash of blue across an entire room. Hawke had a high, clear brow, and a straight, imperious nose above a well-sculpted mouth with just a hint of cruelty at the corners of a smile.

When crossed, it was a much changed Alex Hawke one encountered: at that moment, those friendly blue eyes were as cold and steady as gun barrels.

Hawke's job (senior counterintelligence officer at Britain's MI6) demanded that he stay fit. Though he had a weakness for Mr. Gosling's local Bermuda rum and Morland's English cigarettes, he watched his diet and followed his old Royal Navy fitness regime religiously. He also spent endless hours at the firing range, and regularly climbed into the boxing ring with men half his age.

Attractive, yes, but it was his *What the hell?* grin, a look so freighted with charm that no woman, and even few men, could resist, that made him the man he was.

As the talk in certain circles in London had it, he was a hale fellow well met, one whom men wanted to stand a drink; and whom women much preferred horizontal.

ALEX HAWKE HAD BEEN DOZING OUT ON THE CO-quina shell terrace that fanned out from doors and windows flung open to the sea on a blue day like this. He had nothing on for today, just supper with his dear friends, the former chief inspector of Scotland Yard, Ambrose Congreve, and his wife, Lady Diana née Mars, at their Bermuda home, Shadowlands, at seven this evening.

"Sorry to disturb you, m'lord," Pelham Grenville said, having shimmered across the sunlit terrace unseen.

"Then don't," Hawke said, deliberately keeping his eyes closed against the sun.

Pelham was the octogenarian valet who'd been in service to the Hawke family in England for decades. When Hawke was but seven years old, he had witnessed his parents' tragic murder aboard their yacht in the Caribbean. Pelham and Chief Inspector Ambrose Congreve had immediately stepped in to raise the child. No one who'd survived that lengthy process would claim that it was easy, but the three men had all remained the closest of friends ever after.

"I think you might wish to take this call, sir."

"Really? Why?"

"It's your friend, the director, m'lord."

"I have many friends who are directors, Pelham. Which one?"

"CIA, sir; he says it's rather important."

"You're joking. Brick Kelly?"

"On the line as we speak, sir."

Hawke gazed out at the rolling blue Atlantic,

pausing a second to gather his wits about him before taking Brick's call. There were few things in life he felt any certainty about anymore. But he knew damn well that CIA director Brick Kelly *never* called him with good news.

NINE

HAWKE HAD MET CIA DIRECTOR KELLY A DECADE earlier, in prison. Patrick Brickhouse Kelly was a U.S. Army spec-ops colonel back then, a man who'd been caught red-handed trying to assassinate a Sunni warlord in his mountain village. And Hawke's Royal Navy fighter plane had been shot down over the desert only a few miles from the Iraqi prison. Their treatment was something less than five-star; it was no mints-on-the-pillow operation.

The guards were inhuman and merciless. These were animals, savages who laughed at the CIA and its ridiculous waterboarding, which to them was only mildly worse than having no hot water in the shower.

One night, after months of inhumanity, Kelly had been dragged away from their cell for yet another brutal beating coupled with electroshock to his genitals. Brick had looked so broken and weak that Hawke decided he'd not survive another day of malnutrition and the cruelest of tortures. The sound of his friend's screams reverberating off the stone walls of the cell down the hall galvanized him into action.

That night, Hawke planned and managed to effect an escape, killing most of the guards and destroying half the prison in the doing of it. He carried Brick Kelly on his shoulders out into the burning desert. It was four long days before they were rescued by friendlies, both men delirious with hunger, sunstroke, and dehydration. It's the kind of defining experience that brings men of a certain caliber together for the balance of their lives.

He and Brick Kelly had been thick as thieves ever since. Hawke was godfather to Brick's eldest child. Brick had been standing beside him as best man at Hawke's tragic wedding. They had learned to survive the worst with each other's help and it had stood them in good stead.

Some of Hawke's happiest memories had been springtime visits to Brick and his wife Jane's glorious Virginia estate, Burning Tree Farm in McLean, Virginia. A horse farm just outside of Washington, D.C., it was a few hundred acres of rolling green hills, perfect white fences, and some of America's most highly prized thoroughbred horses.

Hawke went inside to take the call. He moved quickly across the room to the antique black Bakelite phone sitting atop the monkey-wood bar and picked up the receiver.

"Hullo?" he said. By force of habit, he was always

noncommittal when answering any phone call. Even this one.

"Hullo?" he repeated.

"Hawke? Is that you?"

"Brick?"

"Yeah. It's a secure transmission, Alex, no worries. I know you're lying low for a while. Well-deserved R&R and all that stuff. Listen. Sorry to even bother you but something's happened I felt you should know about."

"Trouble?"

"No, not exactly. Sadness is more like it. Alex, your old friend Cameron Hooker died this past weekend."

"Hook died? Was he sick? He never said a word."

"No. It was an accident."

"Ah, hell, Brick. Damn it. What happened?"

"He went for a sail on Sunday morning. Up at his house on North Haven Island in Maine. Did it every Sunday of his life apparently. When he wasn't back home by noon, and his wife couldn't reach his cell, Gillian called the sheriff. They found the boat run aground on a small island near Stonington. Hook was in the stern, dead."

"Heart attack? Stroke?"

"His head was bashed in."

"Foul play?"

"No. He was alone, apparently. At least he was when he left the dock, according to a young fellow hired on for the summer."

"What happened?"

"I don't know much about sailing, Alex. As you

well know. Apparently, he attempted some kind of accidental tack in heavy wind and the big wooden boom swung round and hit him in the head."

"A jibe," Hawke said. "The most dangerous move you can attempt on a sailboat in a blow."

"Right, jibe, that's the word the boy used. It was blowing pretty good, I suppose. Certainly enough force for something that heavy to kill him. But . . ."

"But what?"

"I hate to even bring this up, Alex. But in the last six weeks, a number of other high-level Agency guys of his era have died. Lou Gagosian, Taylor Greene, Max Cohen, and Nicola Peruggia. And last April in Paris, Harding Torrance."

"Suspicious deaths? Any of them?"

"No. Not on the surface, anyway. No evidence of foul play at all. It's just the sheer number and timing that's troublesome. And the high number may just be coincidence."

"Or maybe not."

"Something like that, yeah."

"Want me to look into it?"

"No. Not yet, anyway. All these poor widows and families are in mourning still. And I don't really have any degree of certainty about my suspicions, just my usual extrasensory paranoia."

"But."

"Yeah. But. So, the question is this. Who is killing the great spies of Europe?"

"Look here. Hook was a good friend of mine, Brick. If someone killed him, I damn well want to find out who."

"I'm sure you do. I'll tell you what. Let's give it

a month or so. See what happens. Anything suspicious, we go full bore. Okay with you?"

"Sure. You know best. When's the funeral? Where?"

"Up at Hook's place, Cranberry Farm, in Maine. Family cemetery on the property. The service is next Friday afternoon at two. North Haven Island. Out in Penobscot Bay east of Camden. If you're going to fly up from Bermuda, there's a private airstrip at the old Watson place."

"I've used it a few times, but thanks."

"That's right, I forgot, you've been out there before. Okay. I'll see you there, then. Sorry, Alex. I know you two guys were close."

"I'm sorry, too, Brick. Last of the old breed. He was a very, very good guy. See you there."

TEN

North Haven, Maine

A PERFECT DAY FOR A FUNERAL.

It was raining steadily, but softly. Dripping from the leaves, dripping from the eaves of the old Maine cottage on the hill. Tendrils of misty grey fog curled up from the sea only to disappear into the steaming pine forests. Thin, ragged clouds scudded by low overhead.

Hook's burial service was in the overgrown family plot. A hallowed patch of small worn gravestones dotting a hilltop clearing overlooked the busy harbor. There were rows and rows of folding white chairs arranged on the grass surrounding the gravesite, filled with mourners hidden beneath rows and rows of gleaming black umbrellas.

There was even a piper in full regalia standing by the freshly opened wound in the rich earth. A white-bearded fellow wearing tartans, an old friend of Hook's who'd rowed over from Vinalhaven for the three o'clock service.

At the center of it all, a yawning grave.

Alex Hawke was seated in the very last row beside Brick Kelly. Hawke let his eyes wander where they would, taking it all in, the simple beauty of the rainy Maine day and the still and perfect sadness all around him.

Down at the dock, Hook's black ketch was flying signal flags of muted color from stem to masthead to stern, thanks to young Ben, the good-looking college kid Cam Hooker had hired that summer. Ben was sitting with the Hooker clan's grandchildren now, trying to keep them still. Earlier, he'd been trying to catch Hawke's attention. Curious enough.

Now that they'd moved down to the house after the service, Hawke wanted to find out why the young man seemed so interested in talking to him.

Finally, Hawke said, "Can I help you with something?"

"You're Lord Hawke, is that correct, sir?" They stood together, both holding plates, everyone inching forward in the buffet line circling through the living and dining rooms. Both rooms were full of musty old furniture, scrimshaw, cracked marine paintings, and frayed oriental rugs made all the more beautiful by the fade of age and deliberate lack of care.

"I am, indeed," Hawke said, puzzled. Why should anyone here know who he was? He stood out, he supposed, in his uniform. Royal Navy Blue, No. 1

Dress, no sword. Bit of a spectacle, but nothing for it, it was regulation for service funerals.

"Ben Sparhawk, sir. I worked for Director Hooker this past summer. Helping out with *Maracaya* and around the dock. I wonder if we might have a word outside, sir?"

Curiosity piqued, Hawke said, "Of course. What about?"

The boy looked around and lowered his voice.

"I'd really rather not discuss it here if you don't mind, sir."

Hawke looked at the long line of people slowly snaking toward the buffet tables set up in the dining room. "Let's go out onto the porch and get some air," the Englishman said. "I'm not really hungry anyway."

"Thank you," the boy replied, somewhat shakily. He followed the older man outside into the damp air, misty rain blowing about under the eaves. "I really appreciate your taking the time."

"Something's bothering you, Ben," Hawke said, his hands on the railing, admiring Camden Harbor across the bay and the beautiful Maine coastline visible from the hilltop. "Just relax and tell me what it is."

"I don't really know quite where to start and . . ."

It occurred to Hawke that he'd always loved this part of the world. That someday he would very much like to own an old house up here. The fresh summer air full of white clouds and diving white seabirds, the endlessly waving tops of green forests, the deep rolling swells of the blue sea. Bermuda was lovely, but it wasn't this. For the first time he understood viscerally what his old friend Hook had known and cherished all his life. Down East Maine was closer to heaven than most places you could name. And you probably couldn't even name one.

"I'm sorry, sir. I don't know the proper form of address I should use. Is it 'Your lordship'?"

"It's Alex, Ben. Just plain old Alex."

The handsome young man smiled. "First of all, I haven't said a word to anyone. About what I'm going to tell you, I mean. But I know who you are and I figured you'd be someone who'd listen. Mr. Hooker talked about you a lot, all the sailing you two had done up here over the years. Northeast Harbor, Nova Scotia, Trans-Atlantic."

"We had some good times," Hawke said, wistful for those fleeting moments, sadly missing his old friend.

"So he often said. Hook always said you were the finest blue water sailor he'd ever known, sir, and one of his closest friends. But he was a good sailor, too, wouldn't you say? I was only aboard with him a couple of times out in the bay. But you can tell, right?"

"Absolutely. Hook was a lifelong salt if ever there was one. Still competitive in the Bermuda Race until a few years ago. Why? What is troubling you?"

"Okay. Here goes. There is just no way on earth I can see what happened out there on the water as accidental. None."

"Why?"

"Here's the thing, sir. On the day it happened? Well, it was blowing pretty good out there, all right. Steady at fifteen, gusting to twenty-five, thirty knots. But nothing Cam Hooker couldn't handle. Had I thought otherwise, I'd have volunteered to go with him. Not that he would have let me, but still."

"Go on."

"I know accidents happen at sea all the time, sir. Hell, I've had my share. But what I cannot understand, what I do *not* understand is why on earth Cam Hooker would jibe that big boat, out there all alone, blowing like stink. I'm sure you'd agree that it's the *last* thing he would do! It's the dead last thing *anyone* would do in a blow. Especially someone sailing alone."

"I agree. Why in the hell would he do that? . . . But what makes you think that's what happened?"

"Okay, here's what I know. I had a few beers down at Nebo's the other night with Jimmy Brown. He's the chief of police here on the island. And he told me that when they found *Maracaya*, she'd drifted awhile and finally run aground on the rocks, out there on Horse Neck Island. The main sheet, which Cam would have obviously kept cleated, was free. Why? Also, from where Cam was found, the position of the body near the gunwale, it was clear the boom must have knocked him completely out of the cockpit. And he was not a small man, sir."

Hawke nodded his head, seeing it happen.

"That much force could only have resulted from an accidental jibe."

"Yes, sir. And it was no glancing blow, either. His skull, sir, it was . . . almost completely disintegrated."

Ben Sparhawk looked away, his eyes filling up.

"Damn it, sir. I'm sorry. I just . . . I just don't buy it. Accident, human error, Cam's old age, dementia, all that police bullcrap. What they're saying in town . . ."

"What do you think really happened, Ben?"

"Maybe I'm crazy, I dunno. But—"

"But what, Ben. Tell me."

"Murder. To tell you the God's honest truth, sir, it was murder. I think someone murdered him."

ELEVEN

MURDER'S A STRONG WORD, BEN."

"I know, I know. No idea how it happened. No idea why. But you asked me what I think and now you know."

"Take me through it, Ben. Step by step. I'll ask a few questions. Any information you think I need to have, give it to me. Can you do that?"

"Absolutely, sir."

"First. He was alone on board when he left the dock? Is that right?"

"Yes, sir."

"And he sailed out of your sight alone?"

"He did."

"But, once around the point down there, he could have seen a friend on the town docks, or someone on another boat in the harbor could have hailed him over. He could have stopped to let them aboard. A friend along for the ride or something."

"He could have. But—"

"But what?"

"But he just never would have done it. Sunday was his day. He treasured every second he got to spend alone aboard that old boat. He didn't go to church, you know. That boat was his church. His place of refuge. You know what he said to me early on in the summer?"

"I don't."

"He said, 'I discovered something about sailing at a very early age, Ben. Something about the doing of it makes people want to keep their eyes and ears open and their goddamn mouths shut. I like that.'"

Hawke smiled. "He hated idle chitchat, all right. Always said they called it small talk for a very good reason."

"Yes, sir. He said sailing all alone had been his salvation as he grew older. That's what I think he believed anyway. I know he had a wonderful family, too. Hell, everyone on this island loved him. Look at them all."

"But you think he would never have stopped to take someone else aboard before he headed for open water."

"Not unless they were drowning."

"Which means the killer, if there was one, had to be hiding aboard when he left the dock."

"Had to be. Only way."

"But you would have seen someone, hiding aboard, I mean."

"Not really, sir. All I did below that morning was clean up the galley, plug in the espresso machine, check the fuel and water, and turn the batteries on. Didn't check the bilges, didn't check the sail locker forward. No reason to, really. But, still. I wish to God I had."

"Don't even think of laying this off on yourself, Ben."

"Well. I'm just sayin', is all."

"When did you last check those two places?"

"The afternoon before. One of the bilge pumps needed rewiring and I climbed down there and did that. And I'd bought some new running rigging from Foy Brown's. I stowed it forward in the sail locker until I could get around to it. Nothing, no sign of anyone on board."

"But it had to be a stowaway, Ben. If you're right about all this."

"Yes, sir. It did. But where was he?"

Hawke looked away to the horizon for a moment, thinking it through.

"Assume this is premeditated. He's been watching his victim for some time now. Knows all his habits, his routines."

"Like his weekly Sunday morning sail."

"Exactly. So. Saturday night, early Sunday morning. Our stowaway comes aboard in the wee hours, when everyone's asleep. Finds the boat unlocked, so he goes below. Finds room enough to hide in the sail locker up at the bow. Sleeps up forward on top of the sails and prays no one needs a reason to open that hatch before she next left the dock."

"That would work."

"Comes up on deck after she clears the harbor. Confronts his victim. Has a gun or a knife. Words are exchanged. Sees how hard it's blowing. Sees the opportunity for an 'accidental' jibe. No one is around to see. He realizes on the spot that he can make the murder look like an accident."

Ben nodded in the affirmative. "Maybe Cam knows him. Maybe not afraid of him. The killer stands there talking in the cockpit, making Cam relax, let his guard down. Then he suddenly frees the mainsheet and puts the helm hard over. Wham! She jibes! Cam never saw that boom coming at him."

"Was there brain tissue found on the boom, Ben?"

"Yes, sir, there was. Consistent with where it would have struck a man Cam's height standing at the helm."

"Then what happens?"

"Looks around. Makes sure he hasn't been seen, I guess. Leaves Cam lying there like that. Maybe dead, maybe still alive. He uncleats the main sheet, the jib sheet, lets her drift."

"How does he get off the boat? Water's freezing and it's a long swim."

"Has a wet suit stowed up in the sail locker and swims ashore?" Ben said.

"Exactly." Hawke paused, then asked, "Are you thinking a native of North Haven? Cam have any enemies at all on this island, Ben? By that I mean serious enemies."

"No, sir. He did not. Had a few run-ins with plumbers and caretakers, the usual disagreements over money or the quality of work over the years.

But, as I say, most everybody who knew him loved him. And nobody hated him. I would have known. Everybody knows everything around here, believe me."

"So some guy comes over from the mainland by boat the day before. Late Saturday night, let's say. His own boat, maybe, or a rental, or stolen in Camden Harbor. Something to check out with your friends at the local constabulary. Sails over to North Haven from Rockport or Camden. Hides his skiff somewhere along the shore for the night. Hikes out here to Cranberry Point sometime after midnight and climbs aboard the ketch. Tucks in for the night. Main hatch leading below was not locked I'd assume."

"Never. There's one other option. He takes the ferry from Rockport the afternoon before. Brings his car aboard. Or leaves it at the mainland ferry station. Either way."

"You're right. We've established opportunity. So all we need is a motive."

"I suspect you'd know a lot more than me about that kind of thing, sir."

"I suspect I would, too, Ben. If I don't, CIA director Brick Kelly sure does. Thank you for coming to me. It was the right thing to do. Does Cam's wife know anything about your suspicions?"

"No, sir, she does not. I would never have disturbed her grief with what might still be a whole lot of nothing. You are the one and only person I have discussed any of this with."

"I may need your help here on the island, Ben. I'll talk to the director."

"Anything at all. I loved the old guy, sir."

"Look, Ben, I'm flying back to Bermuda first thing tomorrow morning. But if Director Kelly and I both conclude that you're onto something here, I'd like you stick around North Haven as long as you can. Just in case we have any follow-up questions for the sheriff or other things we'd like you to look into. When do you have to be back at New Haven?"

"I guess I'm pretty much free now, until fall term starts I mean, sir. Since Cam had no sons who'd cared for sailing, he left me his boat. I think I'll sail her up to the coast of Nova Scotia. He always took her up there in August and—sorry. Still pretty shook up, sir."

"Understandable. I'll talk to Director Kelly tonight. If he concurs, you're working for the CIA now, Mr. Sparhawk. Just temporarily, of course."

"Yes, sir!" Ben Sparhawk said with a smile. For a second, Hawke was afraid he was going to salute.

"Don't get too excited, Ben; you don't get the secret decoder ring just yet."

TWELVE

AFTER THE SERVICE, HAWKE TOLD BRICK KELLY they needed to talk. Something that couldn't wait until next morning, when Hawke was giving the director a lift down to Washington in his plane. He'd drop him off at Andrews Air Force Base before heading back to Bermuda.

The two old friends walked in light rain down into town from the Hooker place. They were quiet, admiring the lights just coming on in the little village of North Haven, the old boatyards, and the casino before climbing the hill to the Nebo Lodge. The inn overlooked the sailboats swinging on their moorings in the tranquil sunset harbor. Hawke saw the familiar white picket fence with the hand-carved sign on the gate, NEBO LODGE. Inside was the only restaurant on the island and it was a damn good one.

They ate in the bar. Every face Hawke saw there that night he'd seen earlier at Hook's funeral. None of the lobstermen or their families paid the slightest mind to the two off-islanders talking quietly at a corner table. Hawke had discreetly given the hostess a substantial gratuity to ensure no one was seated near them.

Their drinks came and Brick solemnly raised his glass of amber whiskey, no ice.

"To Hook," the Virginian said. "None finer, and many a damn sight worse."

"We loved you, Hooker," Hawke said simply and downed his rum.

"We sure as hell did," Brick said and signaled the waitress for another round.

He looked at Hawke, glad of his company. It had been far too long since they'd been able to spend a quiet evening together in a place like this. Something they used to do all the time. Just bullshit each other and drink. Small talk would come later tonight, though; they had real business to discuss first.

"Well? You said you had something to tell me," Brick said. "Now's as good a time as any."

The tall and lanky Virginian settled back with his chair tilted toward the window, his curly red hair aflame in the sunset's last rays, his sea-blue eyes alight. Brick had always had an old-fashioned, almost Jeffersonian air about him that Hawke found both admirable and fine in a man of his stature and accomplishment. He even looked a good deal like old Tom Jefferson, to some people, with his reddish-blond hair.

Hawke said, "And you said you had something you wanted to tell me. You first."

Brick Kelly laughed.

"All right, if that's how you want to be. There was a message waiting for me upstairs in my room after the funeral. The deputy director at Langley. Ready?"

"Ready."

"Remember I told you one of my guys who died recently was a guy named Harding Torrance? He was the chief of station in Paris. A lifer. Old friend of the Houston oil crowd, Bush 41 appointee."

"I remember him, yeah. Cowboyish, as I recall."

"Yeah, well, let me explain what more we've learned."

"Okay."

"Died with his boots on, apparently. In a suite at the Hotel Bristol in Paris. He was with a woman, married, whom he'd just met in the hotel bar. Her room; she was a registered guest. You should know that this was not unusual behavior on his part. Torrance considered himself quite the swordsman. Neither here nor there, he never let it interfere with his work. He saved a lot of innocent lives in the aftermath of 9/11."

"Cause of death?"

"Coronary. Big-time. Massive. Happened in the sack. According to his inamorata, they were having some kind of kinky sex when the event occurred. She immediately called for the house doctor and administered CPR, but it was too late. Apparently her husband walked in while she was still nude and attempting mouth-to-mouth on the victim, but that's only hearsay. One of my guys on the scene, you know how they are."

"Foul play?"

"The gendarmes have already called it. Natural causes."

"No sign of succinylcholine in his bloodstream? Or that new disappearing heart attack dart?"

"I ordered an autopsy. Nada on the drugs, so far. No denatured poisons, and no sign of a dart entry."

"Dart leaves a mark? I didn't know that."

"Yeah, a tiny red dot on the skin. Easy to miss. Goes away quickly though."

"So? Clean?"

"Yeah, maybe. I still don't like the timing, but yeah, I guess he just had a heart attack brought on by excessive sexual exertion. Happens all the time. I guess."

"You guess? You never guess. What's wrong, Brick?"

"Hell, I don't know. Maybe nothing. My guys found heart meds in his pocket. This coronary was no surprise attack. Nitro pills and beta-blockers in his pocket? We checked. He's under the care of the top cardiac specialist in Paris. He feels a heart attack coming on, he immediately tells the woman to call his doctor and to go get his damn pills, right? Like, right *now*?"

"Anybody ask the woman that question about that?"

"They will tomorrow morning. I'm having her brought in. So that's my latest tale of woe. Let's order some dinner and you tell me yours."

Hawke told Kelly everything Ben Sparhawk had said about Cam's death.

Hawke waited a beat and said, "Can you connect any dots, Brick? Between these two guys and the other ones?"

Brick took a bite of his steak and said, "Not yet. But I'm on it, don't worry. I'll call your Bermuda number end of the day tomorrow if I get any hits."

THE RAIN HAD STOPPED.

After dinner, Hawke and Brick walked back up to the Hooker place, taking the main road along the harbor. It was a full moon, bright and white and big in the sky. Each man knew what the other was thinking. There was no need of talking about it.

Finally, as they turned into the long Hooker drive, Brick stopped and looked at his friend.

"What's your gut telling you, Alex?" Brick said. "Right this minute."

"Torrance and Cam dying within a couple of months of each other is no coincidence. That you've got a rogue agent running around the planet systematically killing your own guys."

"Yeah. That's where I come out, too."

"Let me find him for you, Brick."

"Are you kidding? It's my problem, not yours. My agency. My people getting killed. God knows, MI6 has got enough of its own problems these days. That intel meltdown in Syria, for starters."

"This guy, whoever he is, killed my friend Cam, Brick. That makes him my problem, too."

"You're serious. You want to take this on?"

"I do."

"You even have time to do this?"

"I've got another two weeks before C wants me to mysteriously appear in a Damascus souk, looking to purchase some bargain-rate sarin gas."

Brick looked at him and they started climbing the hill.

"Two weeks isn't a long time to find a seasoned operative who's gone to ground without a trace. But, listen, Alex. Hell, I won't stop you from looking. Nobody is better at this than you. Just tell me what you need."

"Don't worry, I will. This is obviously not an MI6 operation. And C at MI6 will pitch a fit if he finds out I've gone freelance. So I need somebody attached to this op at Langley. Files on every possible disaffected agent who had ties to multiple victims for starters. Active and inactive. Send everything to Bermuda. I'll get Ambrose Congreve on this with me. He's there in Bermuda now, as luck would have it."

"Your very own 'weapon of mass deduction.' If he can't solve this, no one can."

"Exactly."

"I'll tell you one thing," Brick said, never breaking his stride but taking a deep breath and staring up at the blazing moon. "I'm really going to miss Hook, that old bastard, won't you, Alex?"

"I sure as hell will. But I'll feel a whole lot better when I catch the sonofabitch who bloody killed him, I can tell you that bloody much."

"Easy," Brick said. "Easy there, old compadre."

"Who the hell, I ask you, would ever want to murder a fine old gentleman like Hook?"

"Go find out, Alex. Whoever he is, he needs killing."

"Yeah."

"Ambrose will have every shred of evidence we can pull together within forty-eight hours. Give him three or four days to analyze his findings and come up with something."

"Sooner the better. Tell him he's got two days."

THIRTEEN

———

Teakettle Cottage, Bermuda

It didn't take Congreve all that long to get his evidential ducks in a row.

"Sorry to disturb you, sir," Pelham said, a day and a half later.

"Not at all, Pelham."

"It's Chief Inspector Ambrose Congreve here to see you, sir," Pelham said, edging farther out into the sunshine. "A matter of some urgency, apparently."

It was a brilliant blue Bermuda day, but towering embankments of purple cloud were stacking up out over the Atlantic. Storm front moving due east. Hawke put down the book he was reading, a wonderful novel called *The Sea*, by John Banville. It made him want to read every single word the man had ever written.

"Thank you, Pelham. Won't you show him out?"

"Indeed, I shall, m'lord."

"Offer him a bit of refreshment, will you, please?"

"But of course, my lord."

Pelham withdrew soundlessly back into the shadows of the house. Pelham never "moved" anywhere. The old soul seemed always to *shimmer* from here to somewhere.

Hawke smiled as he watched the old fellow disappear.

These stilted conversational formalities had not been necessary for years. But it was something Hawke and Pelham Grenville found so amusing they continued the charade, much in the spirit of that show on the telly, *Downton Abbey*. Both men found an odd comfort in their hoary Victorian manners and exchanges. It was a secret code they shared; and the fact that an outside observer would find them old-fashioned and ridiculous made their small secret all the more enjoyable.

Moments later, Ambrose Congreve walked out onto the terrace at Teakettle Cottage with a wide smile on his face. He was wearing a three-piece white linen suit with a navy blue bow tie knotted at his neck and a floppy straw planter's hat on his head, a vision only Tennessee Williams might have conjured up. He was even dabbing at his forehead with a white linen handkerchief as Big Daddy might have done in *Cat on a Hot Tin Roof*.

Congreve had been busy. He had spent the last

two days in his home office at Shadowlands, sifting through mobile intercepts, e-mails, old dossiers, photographs, all the reams of material Brick Kelly had forwarded from Langley. And, judging by appearances this morning, the famous criminalist had come up with the goods.

"Oh, hullo, Ambrose," Hawke said, raising his sunglasses onto his forehead. "Pray, why are you in such a diabolically good humor this morning?"

"Does it show?"

"Not much. Just the feathers on your chin. You look like you've been sitting off somewhere in a dark corner eating canaries all morning."

Congreve waved the ridiculous comment away and sat down on the nearest rattan chair. He carried a lot of weight around the waterline and was always glad of a sit.

"Alex, pay attention. This is serious. You don't by any chance remember someone, a former CIA officer by the name of Artemis Payne, do you?"

Hawke looked up.

"Who did you say?"

"Payne. Artemis Payne."

"You're joking."

"I assure you that I am not, Alex, joking."

Hawke scratched his chin, realizing he'd forgotten to shave. Bermuda did that to you. Turned a man brown and hairy and hungover.

"We called him Spider Man," Hawke said. "Or, to his face, Spider. No idea where it came from. But it fit."

"Tell me about him."

"Spider Payne. I knew him all right. I worked with him a couple of times in the past. Africa, mostly. A deeply troubled man. Why?"

"He might be your chap, Alex. You can draw straight lines through the late Steven Daedalus, CIA head in Dublin, to Harding Torrance in Paris, to Cam Hooker at Langley, and they all intersect in the same place. The doorstep of one Artemis Payne. He's your man, all right. I'd bet the farm on it if I had one."

"Apart from the CIA intersections, is there any other evidence that makes you think he's our guy?"

Ambrose got to his feet, laced his fingers behind his back, and began pacing back and forth. A little affectation he'd picked up from his idol Sherlock Holmes, Hawke had always assumed. "Are you quite ready?" Ambrose said.

"Quite."

"Artemis Payne, known in the press at the time of his trial as the 'Spider Man.' Currently wanted for kidnapping and murder by the French government. Interpol has a standing warrant for his arrest for murder. He received a thirty-year sentence in French courts and skipped. A CIA rendition op gone bad, apparently. Shortly after 9/11, a French citizen, believed to be an al-Qaeda commander, was kidnapped off a Paris street and never seen again by his wife and family. The French police went after Payne for it. Arrested and convicted. The White House disavowed his existence. So did CIA. Payne was politically inconvenient. Hung out to dry. There's your motive, obviously. Lost everything, house, family, money, and went underground. Nobody's seen him since."

"Hmm."

"Is that *really* all you have to say? Hmm? After the mountains of bloody intel I've been sifting through the past two days?"

"Oh, do sit down and relax. I know you're wound up about all this but it's bad for your nerves to be so excitable. And a bit donnish and sniffy, to be honest."

"Alex, if I somehow have conveyed the illusion that I drove all the way out here to be subjected to your sarcasm and—"

Hawke looked up, his blue eyes suddenly gone dead serious as Ambrose's grave news began to sink in. He said, "Spider is extraordinarily dangerous. In a bad way, I mean."

"There's a good way?"

"Yeah. People like me. Stokely. And even you. Good dangerous."

Ambrose sat back on the planter's chair and accepted a frosty iced tea delivered by Pelham on a silver tray.

"Will that be all, m'lord?" Pelham asked Hawke.

"Thank you, Pelham, yes. Most kind."

"I endeavor to be of service, your lordship," he said, and shimmered into the ether.

"Splendid chap, is he not?"

Congreve watched this formal, Downtonesque exchange with a wry smile of bemused indulgence and said, "We've now got about one week. We're going to need a lot of help to find this shadowy character, Alex. No trail at all. He went from Europe to

Miami to Anguilla. Then it goes cold. We're going to need formidable manpower and sufficient time to organize logistics and then—"

"Not necessarily."

"No? Why not? What are you thinking?"

"Did you check NSA?"

"I did not, no. Should I have?"

"No. You wouldn't know. NSA tracks all these guys who go rogue. To the four corners of the earth. E-mails, mobile calls, obviously. Constantly updating. All I need is a number for him. Everyone has a number, no matter where they're hiding."

"Then what?"

"I call him up. Out of the blue. Long time, no see, Spider. What are you up to these days, little buddy? Doing well? That old demon gout still acting up now and then?"

"Alex, please. Don't be ridiculous. You don't think that will arouse suspicion? Payne knows you have close ties to CIA at the highest levels. He'll be lying in wait for you."

"I want the bastard to be suspicious. Listen. He compromised my position once. Morocco. Long time ago. I was working out of a small suite at *La Mamounia*, running a former al-Qaeda warlord for months, had him buying Stinger missiles at the underground arms bazaar for me. Spider, who always owed the wrong people a lot of money, got offered a tidy sum for my name and hotel address and he bloody well gave me up. Almost got me killed, that bastard. I went looking. Found him hiding in some hellish rathole or other in Tangiers. Locked myself inside with him for two days. Came close to turning out his lights. Told him if I ever saw his face again, I bloody well would kill him."

"He's afraid of you."

Hawke laughed.

"Oh, I'd say so. Yes. I would say Spider is most definitely afraid of me."

"Then follow the logic, Alex. As soon as he knows you've got his scent and now you're looking for him, he'll run. As long and fast as he can. He'll dive deep. Or, worse, he'll lay a trap for you out in the future."

"I don't think so. You don't know him like I do. I think as soon as he believes I'm looking for him, he'll come looking for me. That's what any smart guy like Spider would do. You don't sit around and wait, you don't spend the rest of your life looking over your shoulder. No. You go on offense. Eliminate the threat. It's the smart play. That's what I'd do, too."

"You want him to come here? To Bermuda?"

"I do. And, believe me, he will."

"Then what?"

"I have no earthly idea."

"What?"

"I have to make these things up as I go, Ambrose. I'm not a genius like you."

"There is that, I suppose."

"Right. And you have to help me because this guy is very, very good. And he's not only smart, he's a vicious killer, and he's utterly ruthless. And, to make matters worse, at this point, what's he got left to lose? Seriously, Ambrose, think it through."

"Have you been experiencing any suicidal thoughts lately, Alex?"

"Please, Constable, don't be ridiculous. Many people have tried to kill me over the course of my career and, more often than not, I've managed to show them the folly of that ambition."

Congreve expelled one of his trademark heaving sighs of exasperation.

"All right, then. What do you need, Alex? I mean, right now?"

"You have a picture of this character?"

"Of course I do."

"Good. Your brain's kicking in. I'll need people watching the airport round the clock, people who know what Spider looks like. Also, same setup over at the steamship docks in Hamilton and out at the Royal Naval Dockyard where the cruise ships land. I want to know the second the Spider Man sets foot on this enchanted isle."

"Done. What else?"

"Your massive brain, if you're not using all of it at the moment. We need to figure out where and how this little reunion should occur."

Congreve said, "Do it here."

"What?"

"Right here at Teakettle Cottage. Gives you the advantage."

"Why?"

"Your own turf, that's why. You cannot arrange something like this, Alex. You've got to sit tight and let the spider come to the fly, as it were."

Hawke laughed at that.

"Stop being childish and pay attention. Your bloody life is at stake here. This cottage is where he will come looking for you. And this is where the damn fly should await the spider."

"I agree, I suppose. But I don't want dear Pelham in the house or anywhere near me until this blows over. Can he come stay with you and Diana for a few days?"

"Of course. I've a lovely guest room for him at Shadowlands, right on the sea. The Blue Room."

"Perfect. Spoil him rotten, will you? The old soul deserves it, God knows."

"We'd like nothing better. Now, what else?"

"I'd like the airport and cruise ship spotters to report to you, not me. As soon as he lands somewhere, they alert you. Then you keep track of his movements until he is about to arrive at my doorstep. Just call my house phone, let it ring three times and hang up. Spider's not the type to lob a bomb down the chimney and hope it explodes. He'll want a confrontation. He'll want to talk. He'll want all the drama. Show me how fearless and brilliant he is before he pulls a knife or a gun. That's his style. One of those fellows who always thinks he's the smartest, most dangerous man in the room. Dangerous, yes. Smartest, no."

"You do realize, Alex, that if you've even slightly miscalculated, and this man does manage to kill you, that it is my rather prominent posterior that will be in a wringer with Sir David and not yours?"

"Mine will be taking a well-deserved dirt nap. Sir David will be bereft over me and extraordinarily pissed off with you. It won't be pleasant. Please accept my abject apologies in advance for the firestorm you will incur."

"You'll need a gun, I daresay."

Hawke smiled.

"You know what Stokely Jones always says whenever someone tells him he'll need a gun?"

"What does he say?"

"*I am a gun.*"

FOURTEEN

THE PHONE RANG.

Once. Twice. Three times.

Hawke waited.

It did not ring again.

Game on.

He closed his eyes, sat forward, and concentrated on sensory input. He listened intently to the stillness, heard nothing amiss. He eased back and rested his chin in one hand, periodically sipping his cold coffee and staring into the pitch-black night beyond his windows. The crackling fire he'd lit provided barely enough heat to reach his bones.

The minutes crawled by. Interminable . . . he fantasized briefly about a short rum and a cigarette but forced himself to concentrate. See, hear, smell, feel . . .

The wind was up. Shrieking under the eaves

and down the chimney. On the seaward side of the house, he could hear the rolling sea booming on the rocks far below and the rain lashing at the windows.

That cold front he'd seen had moved in over the island in the late afternoon; now it seemed like it had been raining all evening. The temperature had plummeted and palm fronds and banana leaves rustled and scratched against the windows. All the doors and shutters had been made fast against the approaching storm. And any random intruder.

There was only one way inside and that was through the front door.

Hawke sat forward once more. He had heard another kind of noise this time, muffled and distant. An automobile, its tyres hissing on the rain-wet tarmac ribbon of the coast road. He got up from his chair facing the front door. Inside the trees a fissure of pure white split the air, illuminating the clouds and all that lay below. He moved quickly from one to another of the northern exposure windows, all facing the solid wall of banana trees and the coast road beyond the groves.

Turn left out of his drive and visitors would eventually wind their way along the coast and reach the Royal Naval Dockyard. Turn right and they had a half hour's drive until they reached the Bermuda airport. The car seemed to be approaching from the right.

Peering out through the shutters into the darkness of the groves, he could see distant flashes, hazy arrows of light in the rain-drenched night. The flashes soon resolved into steady twin beams of yellowish light. Periodically, they would flare up and spike the blackness deep within the impenetrable groves. He could see the dense trees out there, their broad green leaves waving wet and storm tossed like the top of the sea.

He was on full alert now.

The wavering headlamp beams would disappear for a few seconds, and then reappear a few seconds closer still, meandering through his groves, stabbing through the trees as if reaching out for him.

Each time a little closer to his cottage . . .

. . . *came the spider to the fly.*

But the fly had no fear.

Moments like these were what Alex Hawke had lived and breathed for all his life. He was good at war. His father had once said that he was a boy born with a heart for any fate. And the fate he'd been born for was war. He felt the reassuring weight of his weapon on his right side. A big six-shot revolver, the most reliable weapon in his arsenal. A single box of ammo in the loose pocket of his pants should he have need of it.

He was wearing loose-fitting black Kunjo pants from Korea. Strapped to his right thigh was a .357 Colt Python revolver in a nylon swivel holster. It was his "Dirty Harry Special": it had a six-inch barrel, with six magnum parabellum rounds loaded in the cylinder. He wore a black Royal Navy woolen jumper, four sizes too big. It came almost to his knees, giving him freedom of movement and concealing his weapon. He'd cut a hole in the right side pocket so he could keep his hand on his gun without it being seen.

He was barefoot despite the cold marble beneath his feet . . .

He padded silently across the dark room, returning to the wooden armchair facing the door. He sat down and waited. He looked at the clock again. Only eight minutes had passed since Ambrose had called him with the agreed-upon signal. Time was elongated, stretching every minute into two or three . . .

A sudden flash of the headlamps across the ceiling.

Outside, he heard the automobile roll to a stop some twenty or thirty feet from the entrance.

Automobile tyres made a loud crunching sound on the crushed-shell drive leading up to Teakettle Cottage. A primitive alarm system, perhaps, but it worked. He jumped up and went to the window again, pulling back the curtain just as the headlamps were extinguished.

A black sedan, undistinguished, a cheap rental from the airport.

Hello, Spider.

Because of the car's misty, rain-spattered windows Hawke couldn't see inside the vehicle. Only the dark silhouette of a large man behind the wheel. He waited for the car's interior lights to illuminate. It remained dark. There was no movement at all from the driver, and the four doors remained closed.

He went back to his chair, sat, and waited in the dark for a knock on the heavy cedar door.

It didn't come.

The storm had suddenly died down. The cottage was stone silent save the ticking of the clock above the bar. No noise or movement inside, nor any noise or movement outside. He tried to imagine what Spider might be doing out there. Just sitting in his car, trying to spook his prey? Trying, somewhat successfully, he had to admit, to psyche his opponent out?

Enough of this, Hawke thought, reaching for his weapon. He'd go outside and confront the man there.

He was about to get out of his chair when his thick wooden door suddenly blew inward and off its hinges. A thunderous explosion, a blast of sound and light sufficiently powerful to blind him momentarily and disorient him. His chair was knocked arse over teakettle and he hit the floor hard after upending a very solid oak table.

He was just vaguely aware that his heavy front door was hurtling through space directly toward him when it crashed against the wall behind him, a few feet above his head, and splintered into vicious flying daggers of wood.

Alex got to his feet, shaking his head to clear the circuits. He was shaken, perhaps, but seemingly unscathed. The room was full of smoke and whirling debris, and javelin-sharp splinters of wood littered the floor.

"Hello, Lord Hawke," a rumbling voice said.

The voice of Spider Payne.

THE MAN WAS SUDDENLY STANDING IN THE DOORway. Hawke would know that voice anywhere. Gravelly, edgy, and deep, meant to intimidate. Hawke looked down at his clothes, casually dusting himself off with the back of his hand.

"Next time, try knocking, Spider," Hawke said with a thin smile.

"Right. I'll try to remember that."

All in black Nomex, Artemis Payne was wearing full night-combat fatigues, even a helmet with night-vision goggles. He had an M4A1 assault rifle slung from his shoulder and what looked like a SIG Sauer 9mm sidearm hung from each hip. Clearly he had connections on this island and they had access to the good stuff. They'd provided the assassin with full-bore weapons and gear.

"But then again," Spider added, "there won't be any next time for you and me, old buddy." He took a few steps forward into the room.

"No, I don't suppose that there will be," Hawke said, righting his chair. "I'd invite you in, but you're already in."

"Fuck off, Hawke."

"Spider, I don't mean to be rude, but have you put on a little weight?"

Hawke realized his voice showed a lot more confidence than he was feeling. He was seriously disadvantaged here, clearly having made the old mistake of bringing a knife to a gunfight. Definitely outgunned here, the big Python suddenly feeling more like a peashooter. His mind went into overdrive. He needed a new plan. Somehow, he had to remove himself from this confrontation and hit the reset button. Had to keep Payne talking. Right now Hawke was in mortal danger and both men knew it.

"Sorry about your old buddy Hook," Payne said. "I figured I might hear from you when you heard about the old bastard's accident."

"The accident."

"Yeah, well. Shit happens, y'know."

"So you came here to kill me, too. You think I threw you under the bus for that joint op fiasco in Paris? Nothing to do with it, Spider. Some people think you got a raw deal. Maybe you did."

"Save it, Alex. I was on North Haven. I went back for the funeral just to see what I could see. What I saw is you and your bosom buddy Brick Kelly huddled up at a back table at the Nebo Lodge. Didn't take much to figure out what you were talking about. Then I get a phone call from you out of the blue. That's why I'm here, Lord Hawke. Preemptive strike. You know the drill."

"Really? Going to be tough to make this one look like natural causes, Spider, my bloody door blown off the hinges and just imagine all the blood . . ." Hawke had both hands in his pockets under his sweater. He moved his right hand to the Colt Python's grips and swiveled the holster upward . . . easing the hammer back to the cocked position . . . finger applying light pressure to the trigger . . .

"I don't give a shit anymore, Alex. Kelly will have the whole fuckin' CIA on my ass now. My plan was to stay alive as long as I can. And take as many of those Agency assholes with me as I can. You understand that kind of thinking, right? Hell, I can see you doing the same damn thing if you got screwed by MI6 the way I did by CIA. Tell me you wouldn't because I know—"

Hawke fired twice.

The heavy mag rounds caught Payne high on his right side. Spider spun around in a mad pirouette and staggered backward through the doorway and into the rain. At the same time he brought up the muzzle of his automatic weapon and squeezed off a long burst, the staccato rattle deafening inside the small cottage, bullets spraying everywhere.

Hawke dove behind the upended wooden table. The high-powered rounds splintered bits and chunks of wood all around him. Couldn't remain here a second longer . . . his cover was disintegrating before his eyes.

Hawke popped up and fired again.

He missed high and left, but caused Spider to duck down, move sideways on the front steps, and take cover outside behind the exterior wall. Now Spider had his head down and was bullrushing him up the walk.

Hawke turned and bolted down the hallway leading to the seaward part of the house. That's where his bedroom was and that's where he'd just decided to make his final stand.

HAWKE DASHED INSIDE HIS ROOM.

Spider was right on his heels, pounding down the long hallway, his murderous threats echoing throughout the house.

Inside the small bedroom, Hawke whirled around and slammed the heavy wooden door behind him. He double bolted it and then slid his large mahogany dresser in front of it, thinking of how this could play out, trying to see it in his mind. Spider had come prepared for all-out war. He was wearing ceramic body armor plates inside his combat jumpsuit. In order to survive, Hawke had to put a round between one of the seams between the armor plates . . . and hope to hit a vital organ. . . .

And how the hell did you do that staring down the barrel of an assault rifle throwing lead at you? He looked around the room, trying to subdue the fear that was creeping around the edges on his conscious mind . . . a weapon? Some way out of this . . . had to be! He spotted one of Pelham's round needlepoint rugs in the center of the bedroom floor.

Hold on.

There might actually be a way . . . an escape hatch!

FIFTEEN

HAWKE'S BEDROOM WAS DIRECTLY ABOVE THE sea. A long time ago he'd had the crazy notion of installing a fireman's pole beneath a trapdoor in his bedroom floor. He would use the brass pillar to slide down the twenty or thirty feet and into the clear blue lagoon that lay just beneath his room. He'd envisioned it as a great way to wake up each morning. Slide naked and half-asleep from his bed, grab the pole, and wake up in the fresh cold seawater . . . the novelty had soon worn off . . . but the pole was still there whenever he felt like a quick dunk!

He stepped quickly to the center of his small room. Lifted up the circular hooked rug with a sailboat depicted on it. Beneath it was the round hatch he'd disguised to look like the wooden flooring, never thinking he'd need an escape hatch, but just wanting to have it as a secret, like some bookcase that swung open to reveal a hidden passage.

He hooked his finger under an edge of the trap-door and lifted.

Spider was now hammering on the heavy bed-room door with his fist, kicking it hard with his heavy boots. Telling Hawke it was over, useless, time to die. It would be the work of a few moments before the powerful brute gained entry.

Yes! Twenty feet directly below Hawke's room he could just see the gleaming pole disappearing into the dark waves below, frothing up against the rocky walls.

Delirious with frustration, Spider was firing his weapon at the heavy wooden door, splintering the timbers. Hawke knew he didn't have long—

He jumped, embraced the pole, and slid down-ward, lowering himself just a couple of feet. Then he reached up and pulled the hatch cover with its attached rug firmly back into place . . . if Spider got inside now, well, Alex had just bought himself a little time . . . a minute, maybe two . . . now . . .

Go!

He let go and slid swiftly and silently down.

The cold dark water shocked him, pumping even more adrenaline into his system. He got his bear-ings, kicking his feet as hard as he could, and swam submerged out the inlet and into open sea.

His head popped up above the surface, expect-ing to see his little white cottage up on the rocky promontory. Everything was black! Spider had shut the lights off inside. He whirled around in the surf, disoriented, looking for the shoreline. There! The pale pink garden lights up on his terrace. He started clawing water, swimming as hard as he could for land.

A minute later he reached the set of wide stone steps that ascended all the way up the rock face to his broad terrace.

He pulled his weapon from its holster and raced to the top, taking the steps three at a time.

Spider!

Through an exterior window, he'd caught a glimpse of him. He was still out in the hall, slamming his big shoulder against the splintering bedroom door and firing his weapon, screaming loudly in frustration. Hawke sprinted across the terrace, kicked open one of the flimsy exterior doors, and stepped inside.

The hallway leading to his room was to his immediate left. Spider was inside, a raging beast, firing his weapon blindly.

Moving as quietly and quickly as he could, Hawke entered the darkened hall and paused.

He knew he'd only get one shot at this.

He felt along the wall with his left hand, searching for the light switch. Spider was standing in the doorway and firing into the bedroom in a hailstorm of frustration.

Hawke raised the big revolver, sighting on Spider's broad back as he paused to take a breath.

Then he flipped the light switch.

The hall was instantly flooded with bright incandescent light.

"Spider!" he cried out, the gun now extended with two hands in front of him, braced in a shooter's stance.

The big man whirled to face him, his own face a mask of shock and bloodlust. Hawke saw the muzzle of the man's assault rifle come up, Spider firing crazy rounds, zinging off the marble floor as he raised the weapon toward his enemy.

Hawke fired the Python.

Once into the right side of Spider's chest, hoping to catch the seam and his heart.

And once more into his right eye.

The man's skull was slammed back against the door. He was still somehow struggling to lift his weapon as he fired blindly . . . rounds still ricocheting off the marble floors as all his lights winked out.

And then and there Artemis Payne breathed his last, sliding slowly to the floor, leaving a bloody smear on Alex Hawke's wall, collapsing into a shapeless black heap of flesh and bone, now rendered useless.

Hawke went to him, knelt down, and pressed two fingers to his carotid artery, just to make sure.

No pulse.

The rogue was finally dead.

"HULLO, AMBROSE," HAWKE SAID, ANSWERING HIS mobile a few moments later. "Are you there? Speak up."

"Well, since it appears to be you on the phone, one can only deduce that you survived the encounter."

"Excellent deduction, Constable. One of your best."

"Do you require any medical help, by chance?"

"That would be nice. Thank you for asking. Where are you? Enjoying a pipe by a cozy fireside somewhere?"

"Hardly. Standing about twenty feet outside what used to be your front door, soaked to the bone and waiting in the pouring rain for all the shooting to die down in there."

"Ah, you're here. Well. Do come in, won't you? Door's open, as you can see," Hawke said. "Meet me at the bar, will you? We would seem to owe ourselves a libation, some sort of restorative, I suppose. What's your pleasure, old warrior?"

Mobile to his ear, Ambrose spoke while he picked his way gingerly through the destruction. "A gin and bitters should do nicely. Boodles, if you have it."

"I certainly do. A tumbler of best rum would do me nicely."

"What about your guest? Will he be joining us?"

"Oh, I don't think he'll be having anything this evening, thank you. He's moved on, you see."

"His departure shall go unlamented, I fear. I'll see you at the bar. Two minutes."

"Cheerio, then."

"Cheerio."

Hawke looked down at the corpse at his feet. Brass cartridges glittered everywhere on the marble floor. He used one bare foot to roll the man over onto his back, saw one dead black eye staring blindly back at him.

"I should have killed you that night in Tangiers, Payne. I could have done without that funeral in Maine, you miserable prick," he said.

ALEX FOUND AMBROSE STANDING BEHIND THE BAR, his cold meerschaum pipe jammed into one corner of his mouth, pouring a healthy dollop of Gosling's rum into Hawke's favorite tumbler. Congreve smiled as he poured, "Ah, yes, m'lord. The ambrosial nectar of the gods awaits," he said.

"Indeed."

Hawke took the proffered glass, downed the contents in a single draught, and held it out for another splash.

"What shall we drink to, then?" Congreve asked, now raising his own glass.

Hawke plucked a gold-ringed cigarette from the silver stirrup cup on the bar, lit up, and thought about his response for a brief moment before speaking.

"Absent friends and dead enemies," Hawke said, raising his tumbler.

And that was the end of it.

Or so they thought.

SIXTEEN

GRADUALLY, LIFE AT TEAKETTLE COTTAGE RE-turned to something resembling normalcy. Vivid reminders of Spider's explosive and bloody midnight visit were still readily apparent through-out the property, both inside and outside the small house. Hawke was determined to soldier on in his bombed-out house. And why not? he reasoned. Sto-icism and the stiff upper were, after all, twin arteries that ran like broad motorways through the Hawke family bloodlines.

During the last war, in the midst of the London Blitz, his beloved grandfather had gone on with life despite the utter destruction of his large Belgrave Square mansion. It had all come tumbling down around his ears when a barrage of Nazi bombs during the wee small hours had reduced it to smok-ing rubble.

Grandfather Hawke had cheerfully pitched a striped canvas atop the great mountain of smoking debris, installed a surviving lounge chair, bed, and table, and remained happily ensconced atop his ruined residence for the duration. Or, something like that, so the story goes.

In this present situation, Hawke had so far replaced his splintered front door with one of solid Bermuda cedar, varnished to gleaming perfection. The antique Georgian door knocker, a snarling bulldog, had survived and was remounted. Same with the Georgian dresser in his bedroom.

He and Pelham then set about the thankless task of patching up all the countless bullet holes in the plaster walls and applied paint touch-ups where necessary throughout the bloodstained house.

They had, Hawke reckoned, been able to bleach almost all the blood spatter out of the rear hallway, scene of the final confrontation, as well as the dark brownish-orange splotches from the rugs in the living room. A few years and you'd never notice it, he assured Pelham.

The sprays of bullet holes in the ceilings proved somewhat more problematic for want of a ladder of sufficient height. "Mere pockmarks," Hawke said to Pelham, staring up at them. "Like the souvenirs the Nazis left along the Mall during the Blitz. Lends the place a certain plucky authenticity, wouldn't you agree, Pelham? Battle-scarred. I mean to say, it all adds a certain rough-hewn character in my view. Rather charming. Yes?"

"No."

"No?"

"Not really, m'lord."

"Not really?"

"No."

Still, Hawke thought the old place had cleaned up pretty well, he told a weary Pelham later that afternoon in the gardens. They were even now hard at work on the shrubbery and flower beds around the entrance to the house. Digging up the blackened trellis and remains of the climbing roses and burned boxwood hedges that had surrounded the entrance and replacing them with morning glories, high among the pantheon of Hawke's favorite flowers.

Much of the masonry surrounding the front door was still blackened and gunpowder blasted, but Hawke was not willing to replaster the whole house and repaint it. Damned if he would agree to such a waste of blood, sweat, and treasure. No, he would not. Ivy, more climbing roses, and trailing wisteria would cover a lot of sins, he assured his old friend.

"Looks almost as if nothing sinister had ever happened, wouldn't you say so, Pelham?" Hawke asked, swiping a soaked handkerchief across his glistening brow and standing back to admire his handiwork. It was a brutally hot day for Bermuda, and he couldn't wait for his daily ocean swim up to Bloody Bay and back. Six miles, but worth every inch of it.

Pelham, regarding their joint efforts with something akin to dismay, considered a measured response. These conversations were always dicey. His lordship was decidedly upbeat about their progress thus far. And Lord Hawke never, ever, appreciated rain on any of his many and various parades.

"Not quite, sir."

"Really? What do you mean, 'not quite'?"

"I mean, m'lord, that the cottage still very much looks like some battered ruin in a war zone. Like someone blew a hole in the house with high-powered explosives and a platoon of heavily armed and jackbooted infantry marched through the place firing at will. With all due respect, m'lord, all that smoke damage up under the eaves, the charred remains of the two lovely old carriage lamps to either side of what was once the front door, the—"

Pelham saw the anger at being challenged in such a way welling up in Lord Hawke. It was most unusual, though sadly more common lately. He'd come to notice the odd tic recurring, a slight trembling of the right hand at moments of stress.

Privately, he had felt for some time that his lordship had suffered a far graver wound over the loss of his cherished Anastasia than even he could admit to himself. He thought the man suffered from a malaise the French called a *folie circulaire*, a madness that rose up only to recede and manifest itself again and again later.

These horrible disorders afflict, haphazardly, the smart and the simple, and men as well as women. Even great warriors, like Hawke himself, can suffer the affliction, even with the best luck and the most supportive families and the warmest encouragement and the wisest of friends. It's the inability of all those other things to keep them sane that makes them tragic heroes.

At that moment they heard the distinctly Italian two-tone toot of an automobile horn and turned to see a long, low, red 1927 Lagonda roadster swerving into view, crunching over the shell drive. The former Lady Mars, now Diana Congreve since her joyous wedding last Christmas to Ambrose, was behind the wheel, a colorful scarf streaming from beneath her proud chin.

She appeared to be frowning as she applied the emergency brake.

"Good afternoon, my darling Diana!" Hawke cried, striding toward her automobile, an oversized grin on his face. "Wait until you see all the progress we've made today! By God, we are nothing if not two workaholic beavers, am I right, Pelham?"

"Progress?" Lady Mars said, looking askance at the charred devastation around her. "It's appalling! You two men simply cannot go on living in this horrific state of disrepair," Diana Congreve said, climbing out of the car, the skirt rising on her long tanned thighs. She turned and lifted a large casserole dish from the rear seat.

"This is for you two bachelors. A *cassoulet des legumes*. Still warm. I made it myself. Ambrose says the gas and power lines into your house were cut or blown up in the melee and that you two have no ability to cook. Or see. Is that correct?"

She handed off the casserole dish to Pelham and strode with quiet determination into the rubble, stepping over some very sizable chunks of bomb-blasted limestone scattered about what used to be the lawn.

"My God, just look at this place!" she exclaimed.

"Fabulous, is it not?" Hawke beamed, seeing her obvious excitement. "Take note, Pelham. Lady

Mars is known throughout the civilized world for her great style and extraordinarily beautiful homes."

"Indeed she is, m'lord."

"Fabulous it is certainly not, dear boy," she said, cocking one eyebrow.

"Well, I think we—" Hawke said, looking hastily to Pelham for some support, "we haven't quite gotten around to repairing *everything* that was damaged. But, still and all, this . . . uh . . . aromatic cassoulet is awfully kind of you, Diana, and—well, we've got to be getting back to work. Finishing touches, you know, the icing on the cake."

She waved him off and pulled a long handwritten list from inside her green Kelly bag.

"Alex, dear, please take this list and use it. I insist."

"What is it?"

"The names of everyone you'll need. My architect. My interior decorator. My painters and roofers. My plumbers. My gardeners. Everybody. I will be happy to provide on-site decorative oversight of the project. In fact, judging by the mess you've already made, I must insist upon it. Think of it as spring cleaning!"

Pelham raised a fist to his mouth and coughed his thoroughly discreet cough. He said: "With all due respect, Lady Mars, it will come as no surprise to you to learn that his lordship is a gentleman who likes his spring without the cleaning."

Diana threw her head back and laughed as Pelham endeavored mightily to maintain a straight face.

"No surprise at all, dear Pelham."

Hawke looked from one to the other, afraid that he might have missed a joke somewhere along the way.

He said: "Oh, I don't think any lists and such will be at all necessary, Diana. You see, Pelham and I are quite capable of this kind of thing and—both handy, you know, and—"

Pelham snatched the list out of Hawke's hand.

"Thank you, madam. I shall make sure this list is put to good use immediately. Last night the rain off the ocean poured in through his lordship's roof and smashed windows all night long, thereby soaking his bedclothes and leaving him soaked to the skin in the doing of it. Small wonder he hasn't caught pneumonia. But of course, as you well know, listening to reason is not his strong suit in matters of this nature."

Hawke snatched the list back from him, crumpled it, and jammed it down into the side pocket of his paint-spattered khaki trousers.

"Pelham, listen very clearly. I cannot, and will not, live in a house full of carpenters and painters and whatnot. I won't do it! Enough to drive any man insane. I can't do it!"

"Of course you can't, m'lord," Pelham said.

"Of course, you can't, Alex, dear. No one would expect you to," Diana chirped. "Would we, Pelham?"

"Certainly not, your ladyship."

"I wonder . . ." Hawke said, eyeing his octogenarian valet through narrowed lids. "You didn't by any chance summon Lady Mars to the premises this morning, did you, Pelham? Nothing in the way of a conspiracy here?"

"Certainly not, sir!"

"Oh, my, Alex, I just happened to be passing by en route to Trimingham's," Diana trilled. "To do a little shopping for Ambrose's big birthday next week. Thought I'd bring you a cassoulet."

"Hmm."

"No good deed goes unpunished, as they say."

Hawke looked from one to the other, dubious to say the least. Finally, beaten by this conspiracy of angels, he said, "And, for heaven's sake, Diana, please don't ask Pelham and me to come stay with you and Ambrose at Shadowlands. Oh, no. I hate being a guest. Not my cup of tea by a long shot. Sleeping upon some downy bed swathed in fancy French linen. Coming down to breakfast every day, trying to be polite in the bloody morning before I've even had a cup of my morning joe and, besides—"

Pelham, sensing her ladyship's bristling offense at this tirade against guesting skills, coughed, again ever so discreetly, into his closed fist.

"With respect, sir, I would remind your lordship that the small sailing yacht you recently purchased in Jamaica, *Santana*, arrived early yesterday from her refit in the Turks and Caicos. She's moored at the Royal Bermuda Yacht Club docks as we speak."

Diana brightened.

"Well, there you are, Alex! Perfect solution! Your new sailboat! There's your answer, right there, isn't it? After all, it's only for a fortnight or so and then— there are far worse places on earth for two young bachelors than the bustling RBYC docks, if I'm not mistaken."

Hawke considered this new notion for a long moment and grinned. His club was notorious for the numbers of beautiful women prowling the docks in search of suntanned old salts like himself, the young and the old, the strong and the infirm, the rich and the poor . . . Hawke had once said that the best thing about winning the annual Newport to Bermuda Race was that the prettiest girls had not yet been plucked away at the finish line.

He considered the notion of such a move to his club. As Pelham might say, such a move was "not without its particular merits and feasibilities." That was certainly true in this case, wasn't it? Diana, after all, for all her smothering motherly instincts, was in fact a good egg who had only his best interests at heart.

Why fight it?

Opportunity, as Shakespeare or someone of that ilk once said, taken at the flood, leads on to fortune. Omitted, all the voyage of life is bound in shallows and miseries.

Quite right, as usual, Shakespeare.

SEVENTEEN

A ND SO IT WAS THAT ALEX HAWKE AND HIS VALET
temporarily abandoned Teakettle Cottage and
installed themselves aboard the gracious seventy-
foot ketch *Santana*. After that first week of living
aboard, he felt tanned and rested. He spent lazy days
wearing nothing but his bathing trunks and catching fish off the stern. One evening, sipping a Dark
'n Stormy up on deck as the sun sank, Hawke had a
revelation of sorts. He decided it would be hard to
imagine a more pleasant place to spend one's days
and nights than on a beautiful boat moored at the
Royal Bermuda Yacht Club.

The salmon-colored clubhouse, surrounded by
swaying royal palms, was situated on the famously
beautiful Hamilton Harbour, right in the heart of
the charming old town. And the club's cedar-paneled
bar was among the coziest spots on the planet, he

thought, smiling at the barman as he strolled in for his evening restorative.

Horace Spain, known since memory as "Cap," was a twelfth-generation Bermudian and had been behind that lovely old mahogany bar since Hawke could remember and—someone was smiling and waving madly at him from across the room—who she was, he hadn't the foggiest.

"Hey! If it ain't my old buddy himself, Lord Hawke," said an amply curved blonde in a tight silk blouse. She was hailing him from a small corner table. "Come sit down and let me buy you a drink, honey. Dark 'n Stormy, if I remember right?"

"Crystal?"

"Hell, yes, son!"

Crystal Methune, from Louisville, Kentucky, Hawke's memory registered. He'd met her two nights earlier at the club's Annual Regatta Committee cocktail reception. An altogether alluring package, she was a newly minted divorcée. She had arrived in Bermuda on Sunday aboard *Celestial*. The spectacular 250-foot motor yacht had been awarded to her, she claimed, by a benevolent judge in her hell-to-pay-honey divorce in Palm Beach.

Hawke had liked her instantly. And it wasn't the champagne courtesy of the Regatta Committee. There was something about her saucy sense of humor that reminded him slightly of his mother; she was also a southern belle, but born on the Louisiana banks of the muddy Mississippi rather than Crystal's red clay topsoil of Kentucky horse country. She'd let it drop that she was the owner of the Horse of the Year, a spectacular racehorse named Buckpasser.

The Englishman had always found women from the American southland to be both funny, wise, and, beneath a brave facade . . . somewhat sad and vulnerable, a combination that equaled charm . . . in his mind anyway.

Hawke looked at the woman and her attendant cleavage and then smiled at Cap, the old black barman, shrugging his shoulders in the *what the hell are you going to do?* manner that all men instinctively understood, and pulled out a chair.

"Crystal," he said, "I thought you were sailing on the morning tide for Nantucket."

"Decided to stick around, darlin'. Fishing's pretty good here right about now. Especially around the docks. Know what I mean?"

"Ah, I fish, too," Hawke said, brightening.

"Not the way I do, honey."

"Sorry?"

"I mean I never stop. Until I got 'em hooked, gaffed, and thrashing around in the bottom of the boat. Trick is not to marry 'em."

Hawke, amused by the image of a woman marrying a cold fish, laughed, took a sip of his drink, and turned the high beams on her. A little female companionship might do him good. It had been a long, long time. Besides, why the hell not?

"You have plans for dinner tonight, Crystal?"

"Listen, honey, I hope to hell I do."

"I make a mean spaghetti bolognese. It's simmering away down in the galley aboard my little boat as we speak. Hope you like garlic."

She looked him up, down, and back again. Then she reared up at the table and mimed hauling back and reeling on a deep sea fishing rod. She said: "And so the gleaming sunlit trophy fish, twisting and writhing on my silvery hook, rises majestically to the bait . . ."

"And yet you seem like such a nice girl, Crystal." Hawke smiled.

"Pure as the driven slush, honey," she replied.

Hawke laughed, a portion of his beloved Dark 'n Stormy going down the wrong way.

ABOARD CELESTIAL, THE CREW WAS GOING ABOUT its duties. Colonel Beau Beauregard, the soldier of fortune who was the 250-foot yacht's owner, was in his quarters. He had asked not to be disturbed. He'd informed the steward in the galley that he'd be dining alone tonight in the owner's stateroom.

He was stretched out on the oversized round bed, naked beneath his black silk-paisley dressing gown from Charvet. He was a big man, heavily muscled but sleek and quick, with a steely intelligence belied by his overpowering aspect and athletic appearance.

His eyes were so dark that many people thought they were black. Black with startling glints of red when he was angry, they said, fierce fits of rage that occurred with ever increasing frequency since his public humiliation and fall from grace. The colonel tried to mask his anger with the courtly manners of a southern gent, but it was far too intense for him to cover up. He literally *seethed* anger.

And woe unto those who crossed him. Here was a man who had won worldwide fame and amassed a vast fortune by killing for money. Look in the dictionary under "mercenary"? You see his picture.

Now only one thing motivated Colonel Beauregard and it wasn't money: it was a bottomless pit boiling in his soul, filled to overflowing fiery hatred and the overwhelming need to exact revenge.

The stateroom was nearly black, only a few hidden lights in the overhead giving a soft pearly glow.

He was staring at a dark blue ceiling pinpointed with lights depicting in real time the shifting positions of constellations, a pair of high-tech headphones covering his ears. He pressed a hidden button and a wall-sized mirror behind his bed slid silently back into the bulkhead.

Revealed were the winking red eyes of power indicators on computers and routers and surge protectors. It was a mainframe IBM computer linked to a massive telecommunications system with global satellite capabilities similar to the one that afforded U.S. presidents worldwide links aboard *Air Force One*.

He knew what was back there. His company, Vulcan, which, before his epic fall from grace, had been the worldwide leader in mercenary troops and weaponry for hire, had helped design both systems for the United States Air Force.

His headphones crackled and his ears perked up. He was now privy to anything being said or done aboard Lord Hawke's yacht, *Santana*. What he hoped, what he really wanted, was for his favorite gun-for-hire, Crystal Meth, he called her, to fuck the guy before she delivered the lethals. Yeah, that would be good. Like that drunken CIA dickhead she did in Paris at the Bristol in the spring. And it was icing on the cake she'd been able to team up with Spider Payne, who had his own agenda in that escapade. What a hoot.

His headphones went live again, so clear and static free: "Miss Crystal Methune is arrived back on deck, m'lord," he heard an elderly Englishman, obviously a butler, say. "I offered her champagne but she asked for our best bourbon, sir."

"Ah, good. What do we have on board?" he heard Lord Hawke reply.

"I suggest the Knob Creek, sir. She says she is formerly from Kentucky. Louisville, I believe."

"Make it so, dear soul. And inform our lovely guest that I shall be with her momentarily."

"Indeed, sir."

BEAUREGARD CLASPED HIS HANDS BEHIND HIS HEAD, leaned back against the pillows, and smiled as his favorite constellation, Orion, arced overhead across the twinkling ceiling. His "Furies" as he called Crystal Meth and his stable of female assassins, were the best in the world. Relentlessly seductive, they found ever more inventive ways to kill without a trace; ways that could never, ever, be traced back to him.

"This is going to be good," Beauregard whispered to himself, a wide grin spreading across his bronzed face. Besides money and women, nothing held more appeal for the Texan than ice cold revenge.

"I've got you, you rich, MI6 fuck," the colonel said aloud, savoring the sounds of his words.

And he was just getting warmed up. Sooner or later, the whole damn world would feel his wrath, his terrible vengeance. Like his old daddy once said during the Texas High School Football Championship when he knocked a big tackle from Lubbock unconscious, "People got to learn sooner or later, Beau, you fuck with a truck, you get run over. You're a truck, boy, and don't you ever forget it."

EIGHTEEN

AFTER DINNER, HAWKE STRETCHED BACK against the faded red cockpit cushions. He lit a Cohiba Torpedo with his old steel Zippo, puffing to get it fully lit. There was a slight chill in the air, that cold front moving in from the west. Unfortunately for his dinner plans, it had begun to rain during the first course, misty and light, but steady, and he was grateful to Pelham for rigging the overhead canopy from the boom. The sound of soft rain drumming on taut canvas above had always soothed him.

And, since this was Bermuda, the shower stopped suddenly and the late sun was shining once more. He watched Crystal pat her lips with her napkin, ever so demurely.

"Damn that spaghetti was good, darlin'," Crystal said, sipping her bourbon neat. "You were right,

Lordy, that wasn't a mean bolognese, that was serial killer bolognese."

During dinner her short skirt had ridden up on her tanned brown thighs, revealing a glimpse of bright lacy pink at the nexus of her long bare legs. She caught him looking and smiled. Then, turning her head this way and that to catch the late rays of the sun, she asked, "This side? Or this one? What do you think, Lordy? Which side do you think is my best side?"

"I think you're sitting on it."

Crystal exploded with laughter, spewing bourbon everywhere, including Lord Hawke's pristine white linen blazer.

"You certainly give as good as you get, don't you, buddy boy?" she said.

"Mmmm," Hawke murmured, looking quickly away, his thoughts already elsewhere. He couldn't help wondering if this woman aimed to get him deep in the feathers tonight. Or, if she did, if he even should. His heart was in another place, after all.

The woman looked at her diamond wristwatch and said, "Oh Lordy! It's way past my bedtime!"

His lonely heart was back in England. It was with Nell, the woman who cared for and protected his son, Alexei. It was with her that his heart had once more found some small measure of peace and solace.

"Hello? Are you in there, Lord? I asked you a question," Crystal said.

"Sorry. I was listening to the distant cry of the seabirds. And please don't call me 'Lord' or 'Lordy,' Crystal. My name is Alex, as I told you when we met. You sound like the Apostle John, addressing Jesus, if you must know."

Crystal leaned forward to give him the benefit of her very unapostolic cleavage and smiled.

"The birds. Isn't that sweet? You're listening to the birds."

"Yes. Lovely, isn't it? Those are petrels, you know."

"Petrels."

"The Storm Petrel, to be exact. So named by ornithologists because it is always the first bird to appear as a harbinger of bad weather. The sight of petrels heralds an approaching storm, you see, to seaman everywhere."

A brief silence fell. In that moment, she placed her hand on his thigh, stroking him with a repetitive motion that was not unwelcome. Like it or no, it had been a very long time indeed.

"So, Mr. Hawke, Alex, do I get a personal tour of this floating gin palace or not? I got more curiosity in me than a roomful of female cats in heat."

"Ah. Lovely image. Would you like to go up forward? Brilliant view of the harbor at twilight from up there on the bow deck."

"No. Not up forward. I'd like to go down belowward."

"Not much to see down below, I'm afraid. Standard-issue yacht configuration. Galley and saloon amidships, two staterooms forward, owner's stateroom aft."

"Really?"

"Really."

"Hmm. It's got beds somewhere, I'll bet."

Hawke laughed. "Well, I suppose there are a few of those down there, yes."

"Well, hell, Lordy, let's go get a look at them. Test out them springs."

"Well, interesting notion, Crystal. But there is Pelham, you see, and—"

"Pelham. That old coot. Can't you give him the rest of the night off?"

"Ah. Coot, did you say? Not really. You see, my dear woman, Pelham, that old coot, as you call him, happens to be a lifelong friend of mine, actually, and—"

Her eyes were gleaming in the candlelit gloom, soft one moment, and then hard; Crystal had turned what is sometimes referred to as a gimlet eye upon him. Not a woman who cherished criticism, apparently.

Hawke returned the stone-cold glance in kind. The woman had crossed a line. People insulted Pelham at their peril on this boat.

And, at that awkward moment, as if on cue, Pelham crystallized on deck.

"Dreadfully sorry to disturb, m'lord, but there's a call on the encrypted ship-to-shore, sir. Caller wouldn't give his name, I'm afraid."

"He didn't have to. I know who it is. Thank you, Pelham. I'm sorry, Crystal. I need to take this call. Business, you see. I shan't be long I don't think. Please ask Pelham for anything you need."

She still looked awfully put out, to put it mildly.

"Swell," she said, unable to keep the sarcastic peevishness out of her voice.

"Yes, I'm sure," Hawke murmured under his breath, disappearing below. *Women*, he thought. Hell hath no fury and all that. No place for them on a small boat. You needed space, to parry and thrust . . . and, sometimes, to escape.

HAWKE DESCENDED THE WIDE MAHOGANY STEPS and settled into the small leather chair at the nav station. It was just forward of the galley. He took a deep breath and removed the transceiver from its cradle on the radio.

"Brick," Hawke said to the CIA director. "What's up?"

"Bad news, m'lord," the Virginian said, in his soft southern drawl.

"Blurt it out."

"I will, I will, as soon as you're sitting down, old man."

"Sounds bad. Tell me."

"Your late, unlamented colleague, Artemis Payne."

"Spider? He's dead. What about him?"

"Artemis, apparently, was not, as we both imagined, the end of the current nightmare, Alex."

"No?"

"No. He was maybe just the beginning. Maybe Spider was working for someone besides himself. Someone who had lots of other little spiders running around."

"You're not serious."

"Deadly serious, I'm afraid. You've heard of a Kremlin biggie named General Nastase Borkov? 'Nasty,' as he's known far and wide."

"Yeah. A very bad actor. At the very top of the

pyramid, or close enough. Volodya's right-hand man and BFF inside the Kremlin."

"BFF?"

"Best friend forever, a rather dated expression, now."

"What?"

"Never mind, Brick. What happened to Borkov?"

"He was spending a long weekend aboard Putin's new yacht, *Tsar*, in Monte Carlo harbor. He went to the casino, got pissed on vodka cosmos, took a woman back out to the yacht. Now he's dead. Your pal Volodya, or President Vladimir Putin, as those of us not in his inner circle call him, rang me up at 0600 this morning and—by the way—you been talking to him lately?"

"No. Not for months."

"Well. That's odd. He seemed to know all the details of the deaths of our two CIA officials in both Maine and Paris. And he seemed to have a working knowledge of your role in bringing the Spider matter to . . . closure. You and Congreve. How you two lured the killer to Bermuda and took him out at your cottage. And since we three are the only living souls who know exactly what happened that night, well, that's why I'm naturally curious about your speaking to—"

Hawke kept his rising anger in check.

"I have not spoken to Putin, Brick. All right? I would never do that without telling you immediately. Are we clear on that?"

"Yeah, yeah. Well, be careful of what you say from now on. There might be someone close to you who shouldn't be."

"Thanks for the heads-up, Brick."

"You're welcome. Anyway, Putin was not aboard the yacht on the weekend. The chief steward found Borkov in his stateroom sometime early next morning, dead of a massive coronary. He immediately called the Kremlin. Putin, upon hearing the very familiar M.O., put two and two together and called me. Said Borkov's death sounded suspiciously like the work of Artemis Payne. A seductress who packs a heart attack. Was his information on the recent death of Payne accurate? I told him it was. And was he correct about your role in the matter? When I told him yes, he asked me to see if you would look into the present matter, the Borkov thing. As a personal favor to him."

"Hold on. I'm supposed to investigate the murder of a top KGB guy?"

"I can always say no. But—"

"But what? Doesn't KGB usually clean up its own messes?"

"Listen, Alex, I'll be honest with you. I called the president immediately after Putin hung up. Told him the facts. POTUS was adamant. He definitely wants you to do it. Rosow says he'll call C personally and ask for MI6 assistance in getting to the bottom of this. Assistance, in this case, meaning you."

"Why?"

"Why?"

"That's what I said."

"Think about it a moment. Rosow and Putin are toe to toe over Russia's new desire to acquire more and more real estate that used to belong to them but doesn't anymore. Crimea and the Ukraine have made the West look like a hobbled giant. The rest of Ukraine will soon fall to the Russians and we won't even squeal. CIA intel is that Estonia is the next item on Putin's shopping list. He considers it already his, anyway, and he will have it. Washington is toxic these days, Alex, and our military is running on fumes. Our friends don't trust us, and our enemies don't fear us. I've never seen it this bad. And, since Rosow's hands are tied, meaning he can hardly start World War III to prevent Vlad from doing whatever earthly hell-raising he wants to do, you appear to be the White House's best option at the moment."

"In what sense?"

"A fox in their henhouse, that's you, Alex. Gather intelligence inside the Kremlin. Pick Putin clean. Feed him misinformation about NATO's planned retaliatory war games; I don't know specifics yet. Those I'll need to hear from the White House. You'll tell him he's pissed off the wrong generals at NATO HQ. The American people have him down for a nut job. Tell him anything you want. Say that the Chinese are secretly planning to make a massive incursion across his Siberian border to lay claim to his vast lumber forests. Make it all up. You're good at this stuff, remember?"

"What about UN sanctions? They always work."

"Sanctions? Work? Seriously?"

"That was a joke, Brick. The synonym for joke in my book is UN sanctions. But, hold on, you went along with Rosow on this loony idea?"

"Yeah. Because the president's right for a change. By inviting you, Putin's handing us an opening ripe with possibilities. All good. You two have the weirdest of all historical political alliances, but you do seem to get along, correct? For God's sake, Alex, he wants you to come over to his side! He's open about it! This guy has no shame, no fear. You cannot make this stuff up. Even le Carre couldn't make it up. It's as if George Patton and Hitler were somehow secretly best buds all during the Battle of the Bulge . . . I mean—it's just too offing weird to—"

"Calm down, Brick. I'll do it. I'll do it."

"What? You will?"

"Putin saved my son's life, Brick, remember? When Anastasia gave birth to Alexei, Volodya personally stepped in and stopped some KGB tsarist goons from bashing my newborn baby's skull against the walls of the Lubyanka Prison maternity ward."

"You do owe him a favor, I suppose."

"You think? I put him back on the throne. My son still has a price on his head, Brick. Because I took out the old-guard KGB's beloved Count Korsakova, and freed Putin from his prison. Which indeed put him back on the throne. But, duty always calls, doesn't it. Tell the president I'm in, I'll go see Volodya. See what I can dig up."

"Good call. The president will be delighted. He wants you at the White House so he can brief you before you go to Monte Carlo. Tomorrow evening. I'll be there, too, to hold your hand. Oh, and by the way, President Rosow has asked that you bring your friend Chief Inspector Congreve along for the ride."

"As in, Ambrose, the real brains of the outfit?"

"Something like that, yes. Rosow's got a major Sherlock Holmes fetish and he knows Congreve's a serious Sherlockian as well. So. Will Ambrose do it? Go to Monte Carlo?"

"Try and stop him. An exotic murder mystery in a famous watering hole? He lives for this stuff. Brick, you know that."

"I'm going to send a government Gulfstream G650 over there to Bermuda to pick you two up. I've booked a two-bedroom suite for you two lover boys at the Hay Adams right across the street from 1600. Our meeting with POTUS is scheduled for 1800 hours tomorrow evening."

"And transport to Monte Carlo?"

"Same G-stream smoking out of Andrews at 0700 next morning. You'll fly to Nice. An air force chopper will meet you at a remote part of the field and ferry you over to Monte Carlo harbor. *Tsar*, Putin's personal floating pussy palace, has a pad on the stern."

"You make it sound like you think this is all going to be one big laugh riot, a fun-filled holiday."

"You don't?"

"Fun? I have to be honest, Brick. I'm going into this with my eyes wide open. To be serious for a moment, I have to say, something about the whole thing smells funny."

"Everything I touch smells funny these days, Alex. It's the way the world is right now. A big hot mess. It's starting to stink from the core. There's no there there, anymore. Know what I mean?"

"I worry about Alexei. Despite your attempt to portray this new adventure in the most lighthearted fashion, I am about to put myself and my family in an unusually vulnerable situation by doing this."

"I realize that. But, just remember. Your family at least has round-the-clock security at the highest level from Scotland Yard's Royalty Protection squad. Buckingham Palace has nothing on you. Wills and Kate should be so lucky."

"I know. Like I said, Brick, I'm worried."

"I don't want you to be. You're going to be walking a very fine line over there. I need your full attention. So, tell me. What can I do for you? What will help you?"

"I'm doing you guys a rather large favor, am I not?"

"You certainly are."

"Thought so. I want Alexei and Nell living in the White House until this is over. Under full Secret Service protection. Round the clock. Same level as that enjoyed by the president and his family."

"What?"

"You heard me."

"You're serious."

"Deadly."

"Well, what the hell. The White House. Uh, yeah, why not. I think I can arrange that."

"It's a deal breaker, Brick. I'm serious."

"I trust your instincts at least as much as my own, Alex, perhaps more. Don't worry. I'll make it happen."

"Good. I'll ring Nell in London and tell her to pack up. My pilot will ferry them to Andrews AFB as soon as she's able to put the move to Washington together. G'night, Brick."

"They're going to be fine, Alex."

"Yeah. Thanks."

He hung up.

HAWKE HAD BEEN BELOW AT THE NAV STATION ON the radio with Brick perhaps ten minutes, if that. Yet when he emerged up on deck, he saw no sign at all of Crystal. It had stopped raining, and Pelham was removing and stowing the canvas awning he had so thoughtfully rigged for the evening.

"Ah. My dinner guest?"

"No longer with us, m'lord."

"So I see. Kidnapped, perhaps? Abducted at gun-point?"

"She left quite voluntarily, sir."

"Any message of farewell for the host?"

"Perhaps five minutes after you went below she took out her mobile and placed a call. Perhaps one-minute duration. Then she climbed up on the cabin top, stripped off her dress, and dove into the harbor. When last seen, she was swimming rapidly toward that large yacht out near the harbor mouth. *Celestial*, I believe she's called. Quite a good swimmer, too, I would say . . ."

"Was she . . . what's the phrase I'm looking for?"

"Naked?"

"That's the one. Was she naked?"

"No, sir, she was not. Madame was wearing a brassiere and a pair of panties. Both pink."

"Pink, you say? I see. I need to know these things, you understand. The . . . uh . . . details. It's my business. And, uh, God is in them, as someone once said."

"Certainly, sir. Seemingly meaningless details to

mere mortals such as I may prove of vital importance to someone in your line of work."

"Precisely. I'll be back in about an hour. Please don't wait up. Leave the dishes in the galley. I'll wash up when I return. You go to bed, old possum. Taking my motorcycle over to Shadowlands to have a little chat with Chief Inspector Congreve. Something's come up, you see."

"So I inferred, m'lord. As the chief inspector is wont to say, it would seem that the game is afoot once more."

"Do me a favor will you, old soul? Lock up tight and turn on the perimeter security system after I leave. Something about our guest this evening that didn't quite add up."

"I could not agree more." Pelham sniffed. "That woman smelled to high heaven."

"Perfume."

"I do not refer to the lady's perfume, m'lord."

"That's a bit stiff, Pelham."

"A gentleman never hurts anyone's feelings unintentionally, m'lord."

Hawke smiled.

"I imagine she'll be back."

"I would certainly hope not, m'lord."

"Well . . ."

"It is my belief that you dodged a bullet this evening."

"Metaphorically speaking, of course?"

"Indeed not. Literally."

"Crystal? Oh, please, Pelham. She's simply a gay divorcée out trolling for her next husband."

"If you insist, m'lord."

NINETEEN

THE NORTH COAST ROAD, WHICH TWISTED AND curved beside the dark and heaving midnight sea, was an oilslick with rain. Hawke wound up the revs. The vintage Norton Commando snarled up a steep and misty hill. Cresting it, he could see Congreve's home spread out below like a small and twinkling village overhanging the sea. The property had been in Congreve's wife's family for generations and the two newlyweds were seldom happier than the times when they were in residence there.

Hawke braked at the hilltop, took in the enchanting vision below, and accelerated down the hillside. A moment later, he roared between the large stone pillars and the massive wrought-iron gates at the entrance to Shadowlands.

"Ah, there he is, now, darling," Congreve said to his wife, Lady Diana. He put down his English newspaper, stood up, and bent to throw another log on the open fire. The couple always repaired to the library after supper, either for a game of gin rummy or quiet reading before bedtime. On a rainy night like this, there was nothing more conducive to a good night's sleep than quiet time by the fireside before retiring.

"Who on earth, at this hour?" Diana said, looking up from her needlepoint.

"Alex Hawke. Can't you hear his signature motorcycle growl?"

Diana made a show of looking at her wristwatch.

"Bit late for a social call, isn't it, darling?"

"It's not social, dear. It's business."

"Oh. Marvelous. What mayhem are you two up to now? You two have already engineered one bloody shootout on this island that practically destroyed his lovely cottage. Isn't that enough excitement on this little island for one season?"

"Apparently not. He rang when you were upstairs dressing, just before dinner. There's been another murder, apparently. Another spy bites the dust. Would you like to sit in and learn the gruesome details of the case or retire to the sanctuary of your boudoir?"

"Another murder? The latter, thank you. I'll leave you two boy detectives to your beloved cloaks and daggers. Please do apologize to that dear man and tell him he's invited here to dinner Thursday a week . . . I'm going up. Good night."

She folded her book, rose, and drifted upstairs just as the front door gong sounded throughout the darkened rooms of the ground floor.

"I'll get it!" Ambrose cried. No staff tonight, he'd given them all the night off as it was a Sunday evening.

"Sorry about the hour," Hawke said, soaked to the skin, shedding his sodden leather jacket and hanging it on one of the pegs in the hall. "Couldn't be helped," he said, using his fists to clear the water from his eyes.

Ambrose stepped aside, ushered his friend through the door, and shut it against the raging weather. "Come along, I've got a roaring fire in the library. Just the thing for you."

Hawke followed him down the wide hall hung with shadowy portraits of yore.

Ambrose plowed ahead, saying over his shoulder, "You know, it's odd. I was just thinking at dinner that we could use a little intrigue around here. Haven't told Diana, of course, but I'm coming down with a mild case of island fever. The floors are rising up and the walls are closing in. Even my beloved Sherlock Holmes is not providing the electric juice I crave."

Ambrose waved his friend into the room and went straight to the drinks table. "Sit down, sit down," he said and Hawke collapsed into the chair recently vacated by Lady Mars.

"I've got just the cure, Constable," Hawke said, crossing his long legs. "How does murder sound?"

"Murder? The mere mention of the word sets the sleepy neurons alight and shocks the dormant nervous system into vibrant life once more!"

"Few men on this earth would have quite that reaction, Constable."

"Well. More's the pity. Murder cures a host of ills, does it not?" Congreve said, smiling at his own small attempt at wit as he poured a glass of whiskey for himself. "Tell me. Who has murdered whom. And where? And why?"

"Start with where. The murder occurred less than twenty-four hours ago in Monte Carlo."

"Exotic locale. Good start. Who's our victim?"

"Russian. Some kind of KGB bigwig. A general, I believe. Putin's pal, apparently."

"That, too, sounds marvelous. Am I invited?"

"You're to be the lead investigator in the case. At the specific request of the president of the United States, if that name rings a bell."

"Really?"

"That's what Brick Kelly told me tonight. He wants your brain on the thing, apparently."

"President Rosow is second to no one in his ability to judge the capacities of his fellow man. How delightful! When do we leave?"

"Tomorrow morning, Hawke Air, 0700. Be ready at six, I'll pick you up. I wanted to brief you so you could sleep on it. That's why I'm here tonight. First stop, Washington. We're meeting with the president in the Oval Office tomorrow evening at six."

"Have a sip of something, Alex, you're still shivering."

"Rum, please. Gosling's if you've got it. Neat."

"Of course I've got it. Lightning in a bottle. Now. Pray tell. Why on earth is the American president even remotely interested in this little murder in Monte Carlo? Say when, please."

Hawke waited until the crystal tumbler was nearly full.

"When!" he said, and then Congreve handed him the drink. "And, thank you. . . . Because Vladimir Putin called the president, who called the director of the CIA, and specifically asked for you and me to investigate it. Number one. Brick immediately called me. And here's the crux. Rosow loves the notion of someone on our side getting cozy with the Russian leader at this particular moment. Tensions at a boiling point all around the world, as you well know. China, North Korea, Syria, Yemen, Iran, Saudi, Iraq, Ukraine, you name it. Frankly, I don't know how Rosow keeps them straight."

"With all due respect to the American president, Alex, I'm not so sure he does."

"What do you mean?"

"I'm uneasy about the position our American cousins seem to be finding themselves in lately. In fact, I would venture to say they are at their weakest state in a century or more. And Washington leaders seem to have trouble everywhere they turn, not all of it from their enemies."

"Self-inflicted," Hawke said, scratching the stubble on his chin.

"The military is practically being dismantled, Alex. The borders to the south are nonexistent, flooded with immigrants and spiced up with not a few terrorists. China is ascendant, Russia is on a real estate acquisition binge, the Middle East is aflame, and the Americans are setting free the worst of the worst al-Qaeda commanders from Guantanamo. I don't get it."

Hawke looked away, lost in thought. Then he sat forward and gazed directly at Congreve.

"You're quite right, you know. Putin's brazen invasions of his neighbors? Crimea and Ukraine being just the beginning? Troops massing at the Estonian border? Threatening Poland and the Czech Republic?"

"And zero response from Washington," Congreve said, nodding his head. "Nobody's got a hand on the tiller if you ask me."

"Other factors as well. Look, even my friend Brick Kelly at CIA can't bring himself to admit this. But if you don't think this is all about politics, you're not thinking straight. The president's poll numbers are in the tank and the elections are coming up. He can't seem to do anything right. Putin's walking all over him. According to Brick, Rosow believes that if you and I can solve this high-profile murder in a timely fashion, Putin will owe him one. Thus, saving his ass."

"A big solid, as the Americans say. Born of desperation, I'd say."

"Yes. But how the game is played, at least from President Rosow's perspective. Putin and POTUS will then host a show on the world stage that will make both of them look good, I imagine."

"Incredible game, politics."

"And we're just scratching the surface here. God knows what is really going on."

"So we go to Monte Carlo and nab the perp, hand him over to your pal Volodya, the newly self-elected tsar of Russia, and then what?"

Hawke took a swig of his rum and considered the question.

"Well, I'm just guessing here, of course. I'm a novice at duplicity on this level. But were it me, I would mass Russian troops and tanks on the bridge that joins Russia to tiny Estonia. Threaten imminent invasion over some trumped-up Estonian miscue or other. Maybe have my dupes fire on Russian troops. Set a deadline of twenty-four hours."

"Then what?"

"Then the American president calls an emergency meeting of the UN Security Council. He flies to New York, goes before the council, and gives Putin a very public tongue-thrashing over his recent violations of international law. Says this American president has had just about enough of it. Draws a line in the sand. That the U.S. and its NATO allies are prepared to send troops, tanks, and warships to help tiny Estonia to defend its sacred sovereignty."

"Gives Putin a deadline?"

"Exactly. Short and sweet. Make it tight."

"The whole world holds its breath? Edge of their seats?"

"Right again. The two of them go off the grid somewhere and meet in secret. Let's say, Malta. No word leaks. The press is going wild. For forty-eight hours, say. Then what?"

"Let me guess. Putin and Rosow emerge into the sunlight. They call a joint press conference somewhere, Zurich maybe, or Reykjavik, and announce that the world has gotten too dangerous for the two superpowers to push each other to the brink. Putin announces he is unilaterally pulling all his troops and weapons back from the Estonian border."

"Correct."

"Rosow salutes the Russian president," Hawke said.

"Exactly. They embrace for the cameras," Congreve said.

"Yes," Hawke smiled. "And then?"

"And then?"

"They kiss."

"On the lips?"

"Maybe."

"I look forward to our meeting with your Russian friend, the Great Dictator. But something tells me this dead KGB officer is nothing more than his idea of a honey trap," Ambrose replied. "Putin is no fool. I'm sure he has a wild card up his sleeve, Alex."

Hawke paused a moment and said, "Yes. I suppose we simply have to play the cards we've been dealt and see who leaves the table a winner."

The chief inspector expelled a long stream of blue smoke and said, "Hmm."

TWENTY

LONDON

FEW THINGS IN LIFE ARE MORE VISCERALLY TER-rifying than a child's screams in the middle of the night. Royalty Protection officer Nell Spooner sat bolt upright in bed, her heart threatening to explode and shatter her rib cage . . . instantly, another scream echoed down the long hall, this fresh cry wavering long and low before rising into a high-pitched and piercing wail of terror . . .

Alexei.

She switched on the lights, threw back the covers, and leaped from the bed, grabbing her service revolver from the nightstand and her bed jacket from the bedpost. The night was heavy with thunderstorms, electricity crackling inside the dark clouds hovering above London Town. Hawke's grand old mansion on Belgrave Square was cold and dead quiet, save for the quaking rumble of thunder.

Nell and her young charge were alone in the house. Her employer, Lord Alexander Hawke, was enjoying a brief rest at his cottage in Bermuda. This was a much-needed respite and recuperation stemming from his last mission to China and North Korea. Had he been home, he would have been racing up the wide staircase from the floor below, hurrying to his son's bedside . . . but he wasn't.

She ran.

She reached the nursery door, opened it, and flicked on the lights. Her eyes scanned the room in an instant, her pistol before her, gripped in both hands, looking for an intruder no matter how unlikely that was. There were two Scotland Yard officers positioned down on the street watching the house day and night, seven days a week. A third sat reading by the rear entrance.

Since the horrific events surrounding a coup in Moscow a few years earlier, one in which Alexei's father had played a major role, there had been at least three serious attempts on the boy's life. All courtesy of an extreme right-wing faction, retired agents of the KGB—seeking vengeance.

Sometimes, when MI6 picked up Russian intel or Internet chatter that warranted it, there were also two police snipers in position on the roof of the hotel across the street. As well as a heavily armed sentry standing duty just inside the front entrance to the house.

Alex Hawke's little boy had long had a price on

his head. It was Lord Hawke's sacred mission to remove that threat once and for all—and Nell had little doubt that one day he would do just that.

But, until then—they would all be vigilant.

The five-year-old boy was sitting up in bed, his face pale, his full head of hair, usually gleaming and black as a raven's wing, now plastered to his forehead, drenched in sweat. His blue eyes were wide, staring blankly toward the window to the left of his bed.

Nell sat on the bed and put her arm around his quaking shoulders. Night terrors at this age were fairly common but she'd no recollection of her younger siblings experiencing anything this extreme. She began whispering soft, soothing words, but Alexei's eyes never left that window and whatever he'd seen there that she couldn't see.

"Who's there, Alexei? Who do you see?"

Finally, he lifted his little head up and stared at her with wide eyes.

"The little boy," he said quietly. "The one in Hyde Park."

"The same one?"

"Yes."

"Your special friend, then. The secret friend. The one who looks just like you."

"Nell, I told you. His name is Tony."

"Did Tony come to the window and talk to you tonight?"

"Y-y-yes. A little." The boy took a long breath, glanced over at the window, shuddered, and squeezed the blanket to his chest.

"What did he say? What did Tony say to you?"

"He was crying . . . he was crying so hard, Nell . . ."

"Poor little fellow. Why was he crying?"

"Because the bad man was being mean to him."

"Being mean? How was he being mean?"

"He took away all the sticks."

"Sticks? What kind of sticks?"

"The sticks he gives us."

"A bad man who gives you sticks? Who is he?"

"The Snow King. You know, from the park. We don't know his real name."

"I don't think I've ever met the Snow King. Where does he live?"

"In the secret wood where we go."

"Oh. One of those. There are all sorts of meanies in the woods, aren't there, Alexei?"

"Not as mean as this one though."

"How is he mean?"

"He pinches us. On our cheeks, mostly. Sometimes on the arm. He does it when you or one of the other policemen are not looking. Then he smiles and says something funny in his secret language. His hands are so cold, Nellie."

"That is mean, pinching your cheeks. But where does he get the sticks?"

"They're inside his ice cream, silly."

"Ice cream?"

"The Snow King's ice cream. You know, the one I like. The Snowsicle. We always get that one, remember? Every Saturday after cricket practice."

"Oh, I see. You mean the ice cream vendor. The funny little man who wears a crown. So he calls himself the Snow King, does he?"

"Yes. But he's not funny, Nell. He's terrible."

"And you keep the ice cream sticks? I didn't know that. After you've finished the ice cream? Where do you put them?"

"In my pocket. I save them and later I hide them."

"Can you tell me where?"

"In the box under my bed. Wanna see them, Nell? I have so many now. They're magic, you know."

"Magic, are they? I'd like to see them very much indeed."

Alexei slid from beneath the covers and got down on his hands and knees as if to pray beside his bed. He bent down and peered underneath, using both hands to search for something. "It's gone, Nell, my box," he said. "He must have taken it. The King came and stole it."

"No, no. It has to be there. Here, I'll help you look."

Nell got down on the floor with him and flicked on the flashlight in her iPhone.

"Okay, scootch over a bit and let Nell have a closer look under there . . . I do see something . . ."

Her fingertips brushed against something solid.

"Here we go . . ."

She got a grip on it and slid it from beneath the bed. It was an old Cuban cigar box that Alexei's father had given him years ago. A picture of a voluptuous Latin woman and the words Hav-a-Tampa on the lid. Last time she'd peeked inside it had been full of various pebbles and stones, marbles, dried flowers, old crayons, and bird feathers . . . but now, apparently it was used for other purposes. The lid was taped shut and she pulled it open. Alexei had scrawled something on the outside of the lid: MAGICK STIX.

Inside, thin balsa wood sticks. A dozen or more of them.

"See?" Alexei said. "I told you."

"You saved all these?"

"Every one."

"Why?"

"The King tells us to."

"He's not a real king, you know. He's just fancies himself this Snow King. But he's just a silly old soul, don't you think?"

"Well, maybe. He does look silly, doesn't he?"

Nell ran her fingers through his curly black hair. "Why, yes, he does! He's just as round as a big balloon. With a tiny little head and tiny little feet. And scruffy black hair growing out of his ears, too!"

"And his nose! That's him. I've been telling you, Nell, he looks like a giant mouse!"

"He is a bit creepy, I'll give you that much."

"He's bad, Nell. And when he smiles, it's so scary because his teeth are all black."

"Why does he tell you to save the sticks, Alexei?"

"Because he says they're good for us. All little boys. Like vegetables, he says."

She looked at him very carefully. The dark circles around his eyes from lack of sleep. The sheen of perspiration on his pink cheeks and forehead, the lank shock hair, his thin little arms, pale as alabaster.

"Like vegetables? How? How are the sticks good for you?"

"The Snow King says that if I pretend to sleep, and wait until all the lights are out, and then when everyone has gone to bed, and I put a magic stick in my mouth and keep it there all night . . ."

"Why? Why does he tell you to do that?"

"Because if I do, I will grow up to be a real king. He says the sticks are filled with magic sugar that can turn little boys into anything they dream of being."

Nell put one of the sticks under her nose. No discernible scent. Nothing but a wet, woody scent, thank God.

"Does he say what else the magic will do?"

"Yes. The magic will make sure I have sweet dreams, every night. Instead of the bad dreams. But sometimes it doesn't work. Like tonight. I put the stick in my mouth and sucked on it forever. But he says one day, when I go to sleep, I'll have nothing but sweet dreams forever and ever."

"Forever? He said that?"

"He promised."

"We'll talk about him some more in the morning, sweetheart. Are you feeling okay now, kiddo?"

"Yes, Nell. I'm okay."

"You don't feel sick?"

"No, just sleepy."

"Want to sleep in Nell's room?"

"No, thank you."

"Call me if you wake up again."

"Okay."

She flicked off his bedside light, and the flickering shadows of cowboys and Indians projected by the lampshade stopped chasing each other across the nursery walls. When she was sure that Alexei was snoring softly and fast asleep, she placed her hand gently on his forehead. No fever. She pulled his favorite blanket up under his chin and tiptoed from the room. She'd left his soft yellow night-light on in case he awoke again in a panic while she was upstairs getting dressed.

Two minutes later, dressed for the foul weather, she hurried down the main staircase to Alexei's room. She gathered up the sleeping child into her arms. Then she retrieved the cigar box, and hurried down to the front door.

She unbolted the heavy door and dashed through the rain into the street. She was wearing rubbers on her feet and heavy rubber gloves she'd found beneath the sink in Pelham's butler's pantry. Then she made her way carefully down the rain-splashed steps and into Belgrave Road.

There was no traffic at this hour and she proceeded across the street.

Two Scotland Yard men in long dark raincoats stepped out of the shadows. They approached her as she crossed the street. After a whispered agreement, the three of them quickly walked a few yards on to the shelter of a large awning covering the entrance to a small maisonette sandwiched between two Belgravia mansions. "Please don't wake him," Nell said.

"Sergeant Spooner," the taller of the two plainclothes police officers said, doffing his hat, "I'm Detective Harrison. Now, please tell us what you've got there. Something about a possible poisoning?"

She'd immediately rung them up on her mobile, told them about her conversation with her young charge and her fears about the contents of the cigar box. She handed it to the detective and removed the rubber gardening gloves.

"I have no idea, to be honest," Nell said, "but I am concerned that the contents of this box may be toxic . . . or worse. Whichever of you two gentlemen is going to carry it back to the crime lab at the Yard, well, you should definitely be wearing those gloves."

"Yes, ma'am. We called ahead. The lads in the lab know we're coming."

"Good. This box is full of thin balsa sticks. Have them all run under a dosimeter. Every possible test for poison, toxicity, radiation, run the gamut, no stone unturned. Then call me at once with the results. If the news is bad, I may well have a very sick child in need of emergency medical attention."

At that very moment an unmarked black Rover sedan slid alongside the curb and waited silently, the man behind the wheel a hulking black silhouette. Nell recognized the car instantly. It was an unmarked Metropolitan Police armed response vehicle, and somehow it was immediately reassuring.

"Please tell that officer to pop the boot and stow the box back there. No reason for anyone to be any more exposed than they have to be. Also, please order a medical response vehicle to proceed here promptly and wait pending further instructions. The child's not vomiting, thank God, but he has had a fever and other symptoms that are deeply concerning. We may need to get him to a hospital in a hurry."

"We're on it," the tall officer said. "May I suggest that one of us remain with you and the child? Perhaps on duty inside the residence?"

"Perfect. Thanks for being here for us on this wretched night, gentlemen. Oh, and Detective?"

"Yes?"

"Do you believe in the power of prayer?"

"The wife does. Me? Not really, I don't suppose."

"You both do now," she said, holding the little box tightly as she dashed back across the street.

TWENTY-ONE

T HE BEDSIDE TELEPHONE JANGLED.
Nell snapped awake, realizing she must have put her head down on the pillow next to Alexei. He was still sound asleep and snoring softly. She felt his forehead. No fever. She must have dozed off. She reached over and lifted the receiver to her ear.

"Nell Spooner."

"Detective Harrison here, Sergeant. The lab came back with a positive hit on the sticks and—"

A dagger to the frontal lobe.

"Hold on, a positive hit?"

"I'm afraid so. Of the dozen sticks tested, ten tested negative. But two sticks showed minute traces of radioactive polonium-210. And the dosage is extremely low, almost undetectable."

"Are you at the lab now, Detective?" Nell got to her feet, slipping back into her rain shoes and raincoat, cradling the phone with her shoulder. She hadn't bothered to undress, knowing she might well be going out again. She looked out the window into the street. The Met's medical response vehicle was idling at the curb, smoke curling from the exhaust. She could have Alexei at hospital in less than five minutes. "Are you still there?"

"Yes, I'm here," the policeman said.

"Put the lab technician on the line, please."

"Certainly."

When the police tech picked up, Nell said, "I need to know one thing from you right now. Is this child in any danger, ANY danger, from radioactive poisoning based on your lab results? Do I need to get him to hospital right this second? I need an answer to that question, please."

"Has there been any vomiting at all?"

"No, thank God."

"That's good. Primary symptom of radioactive poisoning. Although it's not urgent, I think you should definitely take him to the hospital for observation immediately, Sergeant Spooner. But, at the very least I can assure you that he is not in any imminent danger. Based on the evidence, any amount he may have ingested would have been negligible."

"What exactly did you find?"

"Traces of radioactive polonium-210. Minuscule traces that I almost missed. Any symptoms of minor radiation sickness he's displaying now should begin to disappear within twenty-four to forty-eight hours. However, had you not discovered the presence of poison this early, it would have been very bad indeed."

"How bad?"

"Assassination attempts involving polonium-210 usually begin with extremely low dosages like this and increase gradually over time until they reach a lethal level. In order to avoid detection of course. The Soviet dissident Litvinenko was a classic case in point. He didn't learn of the presence of polonium in his body until it was too late. Polonium is an almost perfect poison from a sophisticated assassin's point of view."

"Is that it, then?"

"Your young charge has had a very close brush this evening. Do you have any idea at all who might be behind this?"

"I have a very good idea."

"Well, then, good hunting, Sergeant."

HALF AN HOUR LATER, NELL HAD CHECKED ALEXEI into the Private Children's Ward on the uppermost floor at St. John's Hospital. A room at the end of a closed hallway. His vitals were good and the attending physician said he could probably be released the next afternoon. There were two discreetly armed policeman sitting in the hallway to either side of the door to the child's room. No one was allowed into the hall except the night nurse.

"Is Daddy coming?" Alexei said.

"We're going to see Daddy soon," she said.

She bent to kiss Alexei on his forehead and left his room. The Rover was right where she'd left it at the hospital entrance.

"Home, Sergeant?" her Met driver said as she settled into the backseat of the black sedan. She was exhausted. She wanted nothing more than a few hours of sleep and a pot of steaming black coffee to get her moving next morning. At first light, she and the two armed detectives would drive to Hyde Park Zoo. There they would identify the man suspected of attempted murder and place him under arrest.

She yawned deeply and put her head back against the cushion. Could she even sleep on a night like this? She looked at the haggard reflection of her troubled eyes in the rearview mirror. There'd be no sleep for her this night. Not while the man who'd tried to kill her darling was out there somewhere.

She suddenly leaned forward and tapped the driver on the shoulder.

"I'm sorry. Change of plans. Do you mind taking me to my office? I've got some work to do, I'm afraid."

"Scotland Yard, ma'am?"

"That would be lovely, thanks. The underground entrance in the parking garage if you don't mind. Near the elevator."

"No problem at all, ma'am."

She sat back and gazed out the rain-streaked windows at the nearly empty streets. In two hours, dawn would begin to break over the ancient city. She couldn't shake the feeling that only the purest of luck had saved her Alexei this night. A nightmare had saved him, not Nell Spooner. How long would their luck prevail? Could she beat these odds forever? Could Alexei?

She closed her eyes.

"Here we are, Sergeant," the Met driver said and she realized they'd arrived at Scotland Yard.

"Oh, sorry. I must have dozed off."

"Will there be anything else this evening? Shall I wait?"

"No, no. I'll be fine. I'll get a car from the motor pool if I need one. Thanks so much, officer. Deeply appreciated . . . good night."

She climbed out of the rear of the car and headed for the elevator. After the warmth of the interior, the wet night air caught her full in the face, startling but refreshing.

Her troubled mind was suddenly pierced with a clarity that brought her life into sharp focus. She heard Alex Hawke's voice in her head.

This will never stop, Nell. These old men in Moscow won't quit until he's dead. I'll be next. But I won't stop either. I'll not sit and fret, waiting for the next attack. No. I will not stop moving. Not until I find them. And eliminate them. Because that is the only course of action that will end this nightmare of Alexei's.

She stepped into the elevator and pressed her floor number.

The weariness was gone.

It had been replaced by an adrenaline shot of sheer determination.

Nell marched down the long corridor, opened the door to her tiny workstation, and booted up her Metropolitan Police computer.

She typed in: "City of London. Vendor licenses, current, Hyde Park Zoo." She clicked "View" and isolated the ice cream vendors licensed to work in the park. It didn't take her long. Her "snow king" spoke only in monotones to her, deep and guttural. It came to her now that he was hiding his tongue, not wanting to betray his origins. She remembered hearing him in Hyde Park one day . . . yes . . . He was Eastern European, she knew that.

Czech, maybe, Polish or Hungarian . . ., she thought, scrolling madly down the screen.

Or . . . Russian.

A name floated up at her and disappeared.

She knew that name.

A name she thought she'd heard during one of their brief exchanges as she paid for Alexei's ice cream . . .

Her fingers flying on the keyboard, she retraced her steps.

There it was! She clicked on it, and his pathetic little file popped up.

Szell.

Jules Szell. Age seventy-five. Place of birth, Kiev. Emigrated to the U.K. from East Berlin in the late 1970s. Disgraced police officer. Political refugee from Soviet domination. Same address since arrival. No arrests. No political activity. A clean sheet.

The murdering bastard, yes, it had to be him.

There was an ID photo. Grainy black-and-white but it was him all right; Nell couldn't see it in the photo but she knew he was hugely round, five and a half feet tall, with a head the size of a medium-sized melon. His long grey-flecked hair resembled a writhing mass of black snakes—no wonder this guy caused nightmares—and an involuntary droop of his lower lip showed the blackened teeth that had so repelled her that day in the park. In the photo his skin had the texture of dimpled whale hide and—enough.

She removed her iPad from her purse and took a picture of the screenshot. As a precaution, she wrote his address down in her notepad. He lived in Whitechapel, of course, that lovely neighborhood celebrated down through history as the former happy hunting ground of Jack the Ripper. It was not a place Nell would normally visit with the sun not yet up. She stood and gathered her belongings and went to the motor pool. She got an official vehicle checked out and picked up the keys from the desk sergeant.

Her favorite was available and she had grabbed it. A forest green MINI-Cooper S with the high-performance engine. A good steed. It suited her and made her feel better about where she was going and what she had to do when she got there.

She dug the ignition key out of her big leather handbag, inserted it, and twisted . . .

"Oh, come on!" she said under her breath as the MINI's engine labored to start. She twisted the key again and again and on the third time, it finally caught. *Thank you!* She thought for a second of going back to the motor pool to switch out the MINI for something a bit more reliable, but there was no time.

She needed darkness for what she had to do.

And the sky was getting lighter in the east.

TWENTY-TWO

NELL TOOK THE A11 AND VEERED OFF THE EXIT at New Road just before she reached the massive complex of the Royal London Hospital. She was looking for a nasty little neck of the woods called Durward Street. Both sides of the street were lined with blank-faced and empty terrace houses, shuttered warehouses and factories, a place that had hardly changed since the Ripper's day. Dingy, grey, sad little windows looking out onto nothing at all . . . the streetlights fizzled and popped in the fog, the pale orange light reflected in the standing puddles on the greasy pavement below.

She caught a number over a door and glanced over at her notepad. She'd scrawled the address in large readable letters: DURWARD STREET, 117–118. She slowed to a crawl. It had to be coming up soon, she was nearly at the end of the road. A road, she noted, that ended in a cul-de-sac. Meaning there was only one way out of here.

There!

The number sign was hanging by its fingernails on the swing gate to a farther stable yard. She kept going about a hundred yards into the cul-de-sac, then turned the MINI around so she'd be facing outward if she had to leave in a hurry. Something she always assumed, no matter what. She cut the lights, pulled her service weapon out of the underarm holster, and placed it inside her oversized leather handbag. From here on she'd keep her finger on the trigger. She practiced firing through the bag constantly at the Yard's range and had gotten quite proficient.

As she stepped out into the damp and dreary street an almost palpable sense of dread seemed to surround her. It wasn't the fog and the low-hanging rain clouds either. No. All those Ripper nightmares she'd had as a child, she assumed, and she shook it off along with the cold wet air.

The gate squeaked loudly as she entered the filthy stable yard. The smell of it was awful, some beastly slop of mud and manure, dotted with rusty castaways and trash. There were gutters on all four sides of the yard, overflowing with a grey slime that bore no resemblance to fresh rainwater. Not a single light shone in the gloom back here off the street, yet she dared not turn on her flash.

Two doors were discernible beneath the overhang of the corrugated tin roof at the very rear, and she chose the one on the left to try first . . . Szell's a bloody hard-line Communist, right? Of course he'd be lying in wait on the left . . . a poor joke, she knew, but she was trying to keep her nerve up, after all . . .

She reached out and turned the knob.

Locked.

She knelt before the knob and applied the pick. Then she rose to her feet and twisted the knob again. The door gave way. She controlled her breathing and opened it inch by inch, now, holding her breath against the inevitable horror movie screech that would surely summon the hounds of hell, gnashing their teeth and leaping for—

Silence, as she stepped forward.

Nell found herself inside Szell's house, but *house* was far too solid a word. This was an enclosed space and nothing more. And it seemed to be decomposing in real time.

A small sitting room was full of dark shapes and shadows that resembled slowly collapsing furniture of different sizes and descriptions. She took small steps, the chambered round in the automatic pistol in her hand a comfort now. There were things on the floor, scurrying things, tiny teeth tugging at the shoelaces of her thick-soled boots, other things, too, things she'd rather not try to comprehend. The stench of the place was the biggest challenge, but she willed it out of her mind if not her nostrils. This was nothing new. Evil and the dead often smell bad, that's all. You deal with it.

She clenched her teeth, felt a fierce resolve welling up inside her mind, and despite her disgust, bent to remove her boots so as to make no noise at all. She then moved deeper and deeper into the gloom.

Ahead was a narrow corridor leading to the rear

of that awful house. The odor was even more powerful back here, and she had to make a huge effort to
stifle a gag. What the hell did the Snow King have
back here? A catacomb? A compost pile? An open
grave site?

The door to the single small room at the rear was
ajar.

A faint glow of light, perhaps candlelight, shone
dimly and spilled onto the filthy carpet outside the
room.

The scent emanating from whatever hell lay
behind that door threatened to turn Nell away in
disgust and horror. She moved toward the opening
one step at a time, her right hand seizing the grip of
her pistol as she hitched her handbag up into firing
position.

She took one step back and kicked the door
wide open. The first thing she saw was a huge six-
tiered chandelier hung from a rafter. It was studded
with guttering candles dripping wax on the scene
below . . .

. . . and the sight that now fully rose up into
her conscious mind made her reel backward and
wretch . . .

Jules Szell, deep within his lair.

The monstrous Snow King lay atop a vast,
shaggy grey bed that nearly filled the room.
Twisted within the dingy sheets and blankets,
churning and writhing on the bed, pale and naked
and hugely fat. He stirred at her approach, acres of
dead white flesh shifting and settling, twisting and
moaning in a low tone that sounded like nothing
human.

The monster's eyes were two black stones of obsidian almost buried in the folds of flesh, his head pressed against a torn and ragged pillow. She noticed something shiny in the candlelight from above. It lay atop his bloated, fish-white torso, an object suspended from a leather cord around his neck. The cord itself was buried somewhere in the countless fatty folds of what would have been the neck of a normal human being. It was a gleaming barber's straight razor.

The thing on the bed, grey and bloodless, giggled, stroked its great belly, and finally spoke. The Cockney accent was deep and guttural, tinged with street Russian.

"Well, looky-loo, Scotland Yard has come to call. Weren't expecting company, now, was I?"

Nell now had her pistol leveled at his head.

"Put your hands up where I can see them, Szell," she said, her voice surprisingly rock steady.

"Not bloody likely, dearie."

"You are under arrest, Mr. Szell. Suspicion of attempted murder."

"Are you going to arrest us all? The king and all his little princes and princesses?" he trilled in a high-pitched squeal. "They're all quite mad, you see, liberated by me from asylums and prison hospitals. All now trained petty thieves, under my tutelage. And, the odd assortment of murderers among them, of course. Mostly the girls."

"What are you talking about, Szell?" she said, seeing him alone in the room.

"My Imperial Guards, of course."

"You're obviously insane."

"I think you're going to have to shoot me, Sergeant Spooner. I'm not going anywhere. Besides, you'd have to shoot us all. My courtiers won't let you touch me."

"Don't tempt me. How do you know my name?"

"You work for the enemy, that's how. Ah, yes. Lord Hawke himself, that magnificent creature. It won't be long before you're looking for a new employer, Sergeant. First the boy, then the father. That is the plan, or so I hear from the powers that be where I come from."

"Whose plan? Who sent you here?"

"I'm just a messenger of death, dearie. My goodness. I don't know the names of the high and mighty. But surely you know who we are by now? This isn't the first time we've come after little Alexei. It won't be the last, either. No matter what happens to me. We like playing games with Alexei. We provide amusement for certain elderly gentlemen in Moscow. Did you know I've been videotaping him for weeks? At play in the park? Out and about? In Belgrave Square? No? I rather thought not."

"What sewer did you crawl out of, Szell? Don't tell me you're KGB. Even they couldn't stomach the likes of you."

"Now, now. No need to be nasty. Would you like some ice cream? The Royal Family and I were just having some."

"Enough talk. You're under arrest, Szell, on the charge of attempted murder. Get up. I'm taking you in."

Szell was waving his fat white hands about his head airily, bleached white hams whirling in space, not listening to a word she said. Finally, he spoke.

"And now it's time for you to go, Sergeant. Either on your own two feet . . . or carried out and thrown to the wolves by my little army of minions. Which would you prefer? I will warn you, they do bite, these nasty devils of mine. Some of them are even rabid. Nasty bat bites, I'm afraid. Bats, you know, can't seem to keep them out. Look at them all hanging up there with the boys and girls up in the rafters, all their beady little eyes on you."

"I order you to get out of that disgusting bed immediately. You are coming with me and—"

There came now a chorus of suppressed giggling from the dim gloom above. She looked up and saw the ragged horrors perched in the ancient wooden rafters that crisscrossed beneath the badly leaking roof. They appeared to be four or five older boys with filthy faces and matted hair, dressed in what could only be described as rags, sewn together slapdash by some mad seamstress. They leered down at her, two of them clutching their crotches and whispering obscene epithets.

At that moment the Snow King sat up and screamed, unleashing a torrent of filth in both Russian and English that seemed to galvanize the boys lurking above. They dropped to the floor, landing lightly on their feet, surrounding her, moving ever so slowly, never taking their eyes off her, baring their teeth, snarling like dogs. She could see it in their eyes; these savages actually wanted to rip her to pieces.

Nell turned and ran, the sound and smell of them hard on her heels as she fled out of Szell's bedchamber.

She screamed.

A small but strong hand grabbed one of her ankles and she went down hard, slamming her forehead on the stone floor. She felt the warmth of the blood filling her eyes.

She rolled on her side and turned to face them, saw their eyes gleaming as they emerged from the shadows, and knew they smelled blood.

"Get back, damn you!" she cried, waving her pistol at them.

It had no effect.

"For God's sake, you're just children, don't make me shoot you," she shouted at them, but on they came.

She had no choice now. They were too close. She started firing at them, or rather just inches above their heads, rounds chewing up the plaster above, and it slowed them down . . . but she knew even the pistol was useless. If she didn't move now, she was dead.

She scrambled to her feet and ran blindly for the front door, ignoring her boots and never looking back as she bolted barefoot into the muddy stable yard and ran for her life.

She could hear the demons behind her on the street as she raced through the rain and fog for the MINI, heard them shouting as she jumped inside and locked the two doors. She turned on the headlamps and leaned on the horn. For all the good that would do. The street was mostly deserted. The boys had moved into the street, arms linked, blocking her way. Two of them advanced toward the MINI . . . close enough now to slam their claw hammers onto the roof, denting it, and the bonnet . . . now the windshield . . . smashed! One leering boy leaned in close and ejected a gob of spittle through the shattered glass, missing her face by inches. She looked down.

The key! She still had it in her hand! She twisted it.

"Please start," she prayed aloud and again turned the key in the ignition. *Don't fail me now, okay? Please, please just start for God's sake!* She knew it was a mistake to come here alone . . . damn it!

It was the battery. It was fucking dead.

One more time, that's all I ask!

For a heart-stopping half second the machine growled halfheartedly, hesitated . . . then caught.

The one who'd spat was thrusting his hand through the jagged hole in the glass, reaching blindly for her face, his torn flesh bleeding from the effort . . .

She closed her eyes, gripped the wheel, stamped on the pedal, and accelerated away, her heart hammering as if to bursting. She saw the boys diving aside and kept going. She was vaguely aware of a few solid bumps and thumps beneath her wheels, but past all caring as she broke free. Two of the pasty white banshees were still standing, shaking their fists in her rearview mirror as she took the corner on two wheels, skidding and sliding and headed for the A11.

SHE FUMBLED FOR HER MOBILE, GRABBED IT, AND speed-dialed Alex at his emergency number. He picked up immediately and heard her nearly uncontrollable sobbing. It was barely audible over the screeching of tyres and brakes as she careened through the rain-soaked and darkened streets of Whitechapel, its inhabitants still asleep in the wee small hours.

"Nell! What is it? Are you all right? Has something happened?" Alex said, managing to keep his voice even. "Is everyone all right? How's Alexei? Don't pull any punches, Nell."

"Alex, listen carefully. Alexei is okay. Something happened to him, but he's in no danger. I'll explain it all once I'm back at home. Alexei is in the hospital. St. John's. But he's fine, I promise you, darling. Do not worry about him, please. The doctors have given him a clean bill of health and will release him first thing in the morning. I'm. . . . so sorry to be crying like this. It's just that I've been through something awful and . . . I'm okay. . . . I just need to get home and take a hot bath and—"

"Nell, did someone attack you and Alexei? Because by God if they did I will fly back there right now and—"

"No, darling, there's no need for you to do anything. He's not hurt. I'm not hurt, I'm just upset. Oh, Alex, it was so horrible that I cannot even begin to—"

"Nell, listen to me. Tell me this. Can Alexei travel?"

"Yes. He can travel."

"Good. You and Alexei are flying to Washington tomorrow to join me. My pilots are getting the plane ready right now. Heathrow FBO. I've arranged a place for you two to stay while I'm away on business. Just so you're not surprised, you're moving into the White House as guests of the president. For a few days only, maybe a week at most, that is if all goes according to plan. So stop talking to me and pay attention to your driving, all right? Deep breathing, remember? I'll call you in an hour. An MI6 driver will pick you up at the Belgrave Square address promptly at ten in the morning and take you both to Heathrow. Can you manage that?"

"Of course. We'll be packed and ready. We do need to get out of here for a while . . . oh, my Lord, we do."

"One hour. I'll ring you . . ."

"I love you."

"I love you, too. I'll be waiting at Andrews Air Force Base when you touch down . . . good-bye, Nell. Be safe."

TWENTY-THREE

SIBERIA

THERE ARE FEW BLEAKER OUTPOSTS IN THE TRACK-less wilds of the Siberian tundra than the tiny village of Tvas. It consists of two perpendicular and normally muddy streets: the Crossroads of No-where, some waggish early tsar once called it. There are, too, a number of crumbling one- and two-story cottages, a cobbler, a blacksmith, a rooming house, a pub of sorts. And one of the most spectacular former winter palaces of the tsars—now the secret KGB Headquarters.

There is also a one-room rail station.

The lord of this mostly forgotten realm is a relic of a stationmaster who has been there so long he seems more like just another piece of dusty furniture. His name is Nikolai Arsenyev and today, like every day, he is clothed in a grey Tolstoyan shirt of no particular shape, cinched by a broad leather belt, baggy grey woolen trousers, and worn felt shoes.

His snow-white beard usually reaches his knees before he thinks of trimming it, and hair falls down around his shoulders. Someone passing through once told him he looked like the fiddler on the roof, Tevye, but that traveler was met with a blank stare from the stationmaster. A fiddler? On a roof? Why? The outside world had been a lifelong mystery to him. He'd never been to the cinema, and television was only a rumor.

Nikolai, seated by his woodstove on this wintry summer day, peered outside the station house windows, marveling at the weather swirling around his barren platform. A freakish snowstorm slammed into the little village late last night. It hadn't stopped snowing all day long! He smiled. Summer in Siberia! Come to Tvas!

Summer's Winter Wonderland! Holiday Capital of the World!

Whoo-whoo! At the approaching sound of a train's mournful whistle, Nikolai instinctively looked up at the Soviet-era station clock gathering dust above the door. Five o'clock. He was expecting the legendary Red Arrow, a luxury train, one that only stops at this forlorn map speck when there are "special passengers."

Nikolai was almost always notified in advance. Some higher-up at the "palace." Administrative assistant, the bossy woman named Tania, called herself. Why she thought she could boss him—He paused midthought. He heard the old Arrow slowing as she chugged through blowing snow, coming up the steep grade of the final hill. He looked at his big pocket watch . . . precisely seven minutes past what the station clock said.

He knew that one of the passengers today must be very "special" because an unmarked white Sno-Cat from the winter palace arrived one hour ago. Two uniformed government police officers entered the station, drank every drop of his coffee, and left without a word of thanks or even hello.

For the last hour or so they'd been sitting in the warmth of the Sno-Cat, smoking and sipping from a shared flagon of vodka. He didn't begrudge them. It was warmer in the Sno-Cat. And the soft leather seats in the luxurious vehicle were vastly more comfortable than either of the two hard wooden benches that Nikolai could offer.

They were KGB guards, of course. And they had journeyed forth from the old country estate once owned by the powerful Korsakov family, the winter palace of the tsars. In earlier centuries, it was a vacation residence. It was now a top-secret military and police training facility for the Muscovy elite. And Eastern home of the secret police.

Nikolai well knew that KGB officers were not expected to be polite, but still . . . he looked up and saw that the two men had left the tracked vehicle. They were on the snowy platform, stamping their feet, their boots crunching in the snow. He noticed that they were slinging Škorpion automatic weapons from their shoulders, a sign that this was no ordinary diplomatic visitor from Moscow. Someone needed protecting—or arresting.

The old stationmaster, making what for him was a snap decision, stepped outside into the cold. He wanted a little fresh air and perhaps even some excitement. He could use a little, always, living the solitary life he did. The first robin of spring alighting outside his window months ago was still strong in his memory.

The long scarlet ribbon of train arrived, wearing a filthy mantle of ragged black ice. It pulled slowly into his station, screeching and snorting to a grinding halt. Immediately, the two frozen policemen began stomping up and down the platform, looking in every window for someone waiting to make an exit.

Nikolai stood in the cold in his front-row seat. This was what passed for dramatic excitement in his sedentary life.

Finally, a door at the rear of one of the scarlet-and-gold first-class wagons was flung open by a porter. A passenger, a very large man, appeared, filling the door frame. He was not Russian, not European, but rather some sort of Westerner. He stooped to retrieve something and then heaved a large red duffel bag out onto the platform. Nikolai saw that it was emblazoned with the symbol of a snarling black bear, a giant on its hind legs, gnashing its teeth. Some kind of big-game hunter, perhaps? What business would he possibly have with KGB bigwigs at the palace?

It was a place where men were taught how to kill—but not wild animals, of course.

One policeman bent to pick up the heavy duffel while the other stepped forward to greet the man as he stepped down from the train. To Nikolai's amazement, the Russian saluted the stranger.

"Colonel?" the KGB man said in heavily accented English.

"That's me," the big man said. No last names once he arrived; he and the Russians had agreed to that up front, just "Colonel" would do.

"I am Major Adropov," the husky Russian said. "Welcome. My superiors are anxiously awaiting your arrival. You've had a long train ride, Colonel. We have some refreshments waiting for you in our vehicle."

"Heavy," the other KGB guy said, hefting his bag. "What do you have in here?"

"Bricks," the American said. "Just in case I need to build a shithouse. You got any further questions?"

The stranger was tall and broad shouldered, thickly muscled, with long blond hair pulled into a ponytail at the back. Nikolai admired his beaded rawhide jacket with long fringe hanging from the sleeves. But, being a keen observer, Nikolai always looked at a passenger's shoes for any real clues to a person's true station in life.

He'd seen pictures of boots like these. A picture book of Texas cowboys he'd had as a child. But these red ones had jagged silver lightning bolts up the sides.

Nikolai got an odd feeling about him. Nikolai had never seen an actual Hollywood movie star, but he had a pretty good idea that this was exactly what they looked like. Big white smile when he wanted to flash it. He was handsome enough, but it seemed that if he were in a western movie he would be one of the men in the black hats, not the white ones. There was something in his dark eyes that made you want to avert your own.

So what in God's holy name was a movie star doing in Tvas? Nikolai could hardly wait to hurry over to the pub for his supper—it wasn't often that he had quality gossip of the very first order for his comrades at the old Hammer and Sickle. He'd already laid out his story. Hollywood had come to Tvas. One of the producers and a movie star were here to look them over. The movie was going to be called *Dr. Zhivago II*. Something like that, didn't matter much what, he'd make it up.

One of the two police officers brushed past Nikolai and spoke to the handsome visitor in English.

"We're glad you arrived safely, Colonel. Are you ready to go? Do you need to use the lavatory?"

"Matter of fact, I do. The only one still working on that damned train was clogged up and that foul-mouthed woman attendant was too damn drunk to fix it."

Hearing that, Nikolai rushed back inside the station house, grabbed the plumber's friend from the utility closet and went to work feverishly on the station's one and only commode.

Things are looking up around here, he thought to himself, whistling while he plunged. It wasn't every day you had a bona fide movie star make good use of your crapper after all. Next thing you knew? A bare-naked woman might come marching right through his door.

THERE WAS A REAR BENCH SEAT IN THE SNO-CAT. The two KGB men up front were silent, having exhausted their English vocabularies. Colonel Brett Beauregard spent most of the two-hour journey staring out the window at the undulating plains of snow and dense green forests painted white. He was a long way from Texas, where he kept his heart, but he found the vastness of the vistas beautiful. After about an hour, the plains gave way to hills and valleys leading to the south.

The snow had stopped, and shades of purple and gold tinted the hills in the fading light of the setting sun.

The erstwhile Texan was lost in his thoughts. His mind confronted whatever lay ahead with mixed emotions. He was pissed at the Russians, it was true. When his own countrymen, namely the White House Wienies and Congress Candyasses, threw his beloved Vulcan beneath the bus, the Russkies had been right there with them, step for step. Not as brutal as the Americans, maybe, but he and his men had plenty of axes to grind with the Kremlin. And if the brave men who remained with him after the shit hit the fan were good at anything, they were major-league axe-grinders.

There was one thing you just didn't never ever call a Vulcan warrior, especially in the *New York Times*. And that one thing was "traitor."

Putin himself was on his shit list too, right at the top, and they'd get around to his own personal payback sooner or later. There was one other KGB asshole he'd dealt with who seriously needed killing. Close friend of Putin, his guys told him, went by

the name of "Uncle Joe," and his death would send
Vladimir a message, that was for sure.

The backstory was what made this trip very
mysterious on the one hand, and very tempting
on the other. He had no idea who had invited him
to Russia, nor why. A private courier had delivered a package to his beach home in Costa Rica.
Inside were first-class airline tickets from Miami to
Moscow and then on to St. Petersburg. One night
in a suite at the Grand Hotel. A first-class ticket on
the Red Arrow to Tvas, and a packet of rubles the
size of a large brick.

A typed note, no signature, said only that a meeting had been arranged with someone very high in
the KGB who had an offer for him that would literally change his life. A name was used that he recognized, a high-ranking general, someone named
Krakov. A man he'd dealt with when the Russians
were one of his most prized and most profitable clients. His Excellency, General Krakov, the invitation
said, was very much looking forward to his presence
and he would find himself an honored guest at the
Siberian winter palace.

Was Putin aware that the Colonel was hell-bent
on revenge for the worldwide humiliation his boys
had suffered? Had to be. After the first few spy assassinations he'd executed around the world, Paris
and Maine, et cetera, it was no longer any great
secret among the world's intelligence community.
Maybe this whole deal was just a bogus setup, a
payback for another assassination. It didn't smell
like it. But, of course, at this level, it wouldn't,
would it?

Well, what the hell, he said to himself finally. Beat the hell out of getting fat and lazy in Costa Rica.

It wasn't in him to turn down an invitation like that.

And, besides all that, he was bored shitless living on a beach with two ugly whores and a ratty-assed dog.

AN HOUR LATER, HE WOKE AS THE BIG SNO-CAT shuddered to a stop. He lifted his chin off his chest, rubbed his tired eyes, and looked around, confused. Where the hell was he? Oh, yeah. Siberia. It didn't look the way you pictured it when you heard that word. Not at all. The sun was down now, a faint glow on the western horizon. He sat up and peered out the large window to his left.

The Russian Sno-Cat had come to a stop on a hilltop in a copse of hardwood trees. Below was a small valley with an elongated lake, gleaming silver in the strong moonlight.

Along its banks stood the magnificent white palace, ablaze with golden light glowing in hundreds of windows. From this vantage point it appeared to be three stories of gold and grandeur, the best of European and Russian architecture, with massive galleries and flanking wings that stretched along the lakefront for a good nine hundred meters at least.

"Is that where we're going, boys?" the colonel said, leaning forward between them. "Looks like something you might find in Disney World."

"The ancient home of the tsars," the driver said, his voice full of national pride.

"Mighty fancy place for this old cowboy. You fellas reckon I maybe should have worn me some different kicks?" He raised his right leg between the two front seats to let them eyeball his trademark lightning bolt cowboy boots.

The driver looked at the boots, then up at him, and then glanced over at the officer beside him, shrugging his shoulders as if to say, *Americans! Who the hell can understand these people?*

TWENTY-FOUR

THE WHITE HOUSE

A FEW THINGS ALEX HAWKE NOTICED IMMEDI-
ately when the president of the United States
strode into the Oval Office: he had the strongest,
longest grip in the long and virile history of male
handshaking. But his grey eyes seemed to wander
from your face when you were speaking. As if he was
casting about for someone else to talk to. It was odd.
Hawke's worst fears were immediately confirmed.
The focus just wasn't there anymore.

President Rosow was of medium height, fit and
trim, a man who obviously had a long and enduring
relationship with the rewards of the weight room.
But was he healthy? If Hawke had to make the prog-
nosis based on what he saw in the man's eyes, the

answer was no. The president of the United States was either ill or deeply troubled. And it was taking a toll.

The president and Ambrose Congreve had found each other kindred spirits and were already talking Sherlock Holmes. Rosow lit up; he clearly found whatever the renowned English criminalist was saying about the world's most famous detective riveting.

"And you are Lord Hawke," President Rosow said, turning to him with a ready grin. "Or Alex, I've been reminded. An honor to have you with us. Never again will I have to listen to your friend Brick Kelly over there saying, 'You *have* to meet this guy!'"

Hawke laughed.

"Alex will do fine, Mr. President. But it's a very great honor to see you as well. My men and I were deeply grateful for your support in our Chinese and North Korean actions of last year. That rescue mission would have been impossible without your personal efforts on our behalf."

"That mission was impossible under any circumstances, Alex, even with our help. But you and your guys did it anyway. And I want to extend my personal sympathy for your combat losses. I know you personally lost a good friend."

"I did, sir. Thank you. A French Foreign Legionnaire. His name was Froggy and he was one of the bravest men I ever knew."

"Our country remains in your debt. The true story of the rescue of Dr. Chase and his family will remain classified until long after we're all gone. But, around here, we know what you did. And how much it meant to the world and the cause of peace. At any rate, welcome to the White House, Alex. My wife, Jeanne, and I are delighted to have your handsome young son and Nell Spooner as our houseguests for a few days. I hope you found them well taken care of?"

"They're very comfortable, sir. Things are a bit spicy on the home front right now, and I feel vastly more secure knowing that they'll be safe here while I'm away. I want you to know how very much I appreciate it, Mr. President. I know it's not . . . I know it's an unusual request coming from someone whom you barely know."

"Not at all, not at all, Alex. You've been a friend of this old house and its prior inhabitants for many years. And certainly a very dear friend of my country. Did you know that the princess of Norway spent the entirety of World War II under this roof? FDR did it as a favor to her father the king after the Nazis invaded. It's something of a tradition around here, although we don't talk about it much. We'll look after Alexei and Miss Spooner, I assure you. I believe the Secret Service is giving them a tour of the place as we speak. Now. Shall we have a seat on the sofas over there and get down to business? Okay with you, Director Kelly? I think this is your meeting."

"Absolutely, Mr. President."

As soon as they were all comfortable, Brick handed them each a thick red dossier marked TOP SECRET

POTUS ONLY. The four men leafed through the dossiers quickly, already familiar with the up-front contents that had set the stage for this meeting.

Brick sat forward in his armchair to the left of the president.

"Alex, it goes without saying the president and I deeply appreciate your willingness to travel, especially in light of the recent near tragic events in London. And, Chief Inspector Congreve, we know how hard it is to take time away from your new bride and your lovely Bermuda."

"I assure you, Brick, there is no place on earth I'd rather be than sitting here in this room in present company," Congreve assured him.

Brick acknowledged the compliment and said, "I think it safe to say that all of us are aware of the peculiarity of this request from the president of Russia. Unusual, to say the least, you'll agree."

Hawke smiled and said, "Yes, Brick, I'd say Ambrose and I sailing off to solve an internal murder case involving the innermost power sanctum of the Kremlin and the KGB, is, as you say, rather 'peculiar.'"

Brick smiled.

"And were it not for the president's specific desire for you to gather intelligence and make close-up observations of the Russian leader at this very delicate moment in history, there is no way in hell we would have assented to his request. Mr. President?"

The president got out of his chair and walked over to the fireplace, resting his shoulder against the mantel.

"We'll get to the details of this KGB murder in Monte Carlo in a moment. But I would like to sketch a broader picture. First, the old post–Cold War era is over. Dead and buried. The old borders, treaties, mandates, and back-channel political dealings with friends and foes alike—none of that remains in play. The United States and Britain face two paramount common enemies in this still-new century. China. And Russia. One is ascendant, economically and militarily, and that is China. As Alex knows firsthand, they become more warlike with every passing month, it seems. The other, Russia, while in a slow decline on all fronts, is inimical to any hope of worldwide peace in the immediate future. It's ironic, isn't it, that, in its apparent weakness, Russia has become the more powerful, more immediate existential threat."

Brick said, "Alex, you dealt with a revanchist Russia during the Korsakov tsarist affair. You know how Putin, in fact how Russia, perceives its former client states and in fact, every state with whom she shares a common border."

"I do," Hawke said. "It's very simple. They want all of it, every square mile of that Soviet real estate, back under the Kremlin's iron fist. Crimea was the first to go. Ukraine, Estonia, and the rest will follow. And, unless we're willing to start a war over this, there's not a hell of a lot we can do about it."

"Exactly, Alex," the president said. "Precisely why you're here. We need some kind of goddamn strategy and we don't have one. 'Our hands are *tied*, Mr. President'; that's what everyone around here tells me. Maybe so, but what *can* we do? We can't sit on our hands and wait for the whole world to come crashing down around us. That strategy is not an option in this White House."

"With all due respect, Mr. President, I'm a spy, not a global strategist. But I certainly concede the point."

"Point taken. I'm not looking for you to come back with a strategy, Alex. I want you to come back with intelligence that can help me *formulate* a strategy. Because, for some very odd reason, this guy, our most dangerous foe, *likes* you. Putin respects you. Hell, Brick tells me Putin keeps asking you to come work for *him*! Comical in some spy movie, maybe, but ridiculous. And the most critical thing of all, for me, is that he's willing to talk to you, one-on-one, with no one else in the room. Apparently with no subject taboo or off the table. Is that right?"

"Depending on the hour and the amount of vodka consumed, I'd say that's correct, Mr. President."

"Could you just quickly fill me in on how the living hell you two came to be such bosom buddies?"

"My pleasure. We met in a Russian prison. A lovely little spot called Energetika, built on an island that was formerly the Soviet Navy's nuclear waste dump. Still off-the-charts radioactive. The kind of place where you check in but you don't check out. At the start of the tsarist coup, Putin was arrested and stowed in the basement. But he still had a lot of power. When I was arrested in Moscow for my role in bringing down the conspirators and assassinating the new tsar, they sentenced me to death at Energetika. I was scheduled for execution the morning after my arrival, death by impalement. Putin saved my life. He had me brought to his cell under his protection. We smoked cigarettes into the wee hours. He said he 'admired my work.' Truth is, we share a sort of weird satirical sense of humor, I think. Anyway, he had the execution called off, helped me escape, and here I am."

"Hear, hear!" Ambrose laughed and started clapping.

The president seemed nearly speechless at this fantastical tale, but managed to say, "Well, thank God you are. Now, Brick, we've got another topic to discuss. Some new information the CIA has picked up regarding the recent spate of killings involving high-level intelligence officers."

"Yes, sir. It seems this recent KGB murder is just the latest in an ongoing war against all foreign intel officers regardless of political affiliation. To recap, we, meaning CIA, lost Torrance in Paris, and our old friend Cam Hooker up in Maine, as you well know. Now this thing in Monte Carlo apparently involved a female assassin. Strikingly similar in appearance and modus operandi to the woman who picked up Torrance in the Hotel Bristol bar, murdered him in her suite. Some kind of pattern there we'd like Chief Inspector Congreve to look into. But this is where it gets interesting."

"Oh, it's already interesting, Brick," Congreve said.

"Well, get this. We can now account for at least three murders of high-ranking intel officers that occurred prior to Torrance and Hooker at CIA. Alex, you remember that one of your MI6 colleagues went missing while on assignment in Bangkok three years ago? Sir Miles Peele?"

"Yes, of course. I knew Miles well. Great officer. Case still open."

"We've recently uncovered evidence to suggest Miles was murdered by a woman he met at the Raffles Bar Singapore. The woman was arrested on another matter, we talked to her, and she confessed she'd been with Miles on the night he disappeared."

"You are kidding me," Hawke said.

"Not even a little. Next we have a victim from Delhi, Vidal Soong, retired head of station for India's National Intelligence Agency. The killers were never caught but again, the circumstances surrounding the murder have a familiar ring, to say the least. Honey trap, seduction, murder. And next the case of the Flying Dutchman, the head of the secret service in Amsterdam whose small single-engine airplane disappeared off the radar over the North Sea on a clear day. He never radioed a Mayday, just vanished. The body was recovered, traces of polonium in his blood. My point is obvious. That's six victims with a whole lot in common besides their job descriptions. And it begins three years prior to the murder by a female assassin in Paris."

Ambrose was literally humming with excitement. Now here was a case he could sink his teeth into. "I'm sorry, forgive me, but has anyone here ever heard of a film, back in the late '70s as I recall, with the title *Who Is Killing the Great Chefs of Europe?* It was quite amusing. And what you're describing,

Brick, sounds like a carbon copy of that screenplay. Am I wrong?"

"No. You're right. Only this time it's *Who Is Killing the Great Spies of Europe.*"

"Fascinating," the president muttered, thinking it all through. "You'd better make that *Great Spies of the World*, I think. This profile seems to be spreading far beyond Europe."

"Here's the question that occurs to me. Who the hell has a grudge against the whole world? It doesn't make any sense. Certainly not KGB, given this recent murder in Monte Carlo. Or am I missing something? Is there a lone rogue out there responsible? Or, perhaps more likely, someone highly organized with the resources of both men and money to pull off sophisticated hits on intel officers of different nationalities all around the world?"

"We've got to start with motive," Congreve said. "What is it that ties all the victims together? Aside from the fact that they were all spies in one capacity or another."

"He's absolutely right," Rosow said. "Motive will take us where we need to go. Brick, I want a dedicated team inside Langley to take this on effective immediately. With the chief inspector here available to them on an as-needed basis. And vice versa. Understood?"

Brick nodded in the affirmative and got to his feet.

"Well, I think we've taken all the president's time we've been allotted. But I do want to add something before we go in for dinner. Langley has been looking hard at your late friend Spider Payne, Alex. And he was a very busy boy before he showed up in Maine. We found a safe when we swept his so-called island fortress on a beach in Costa Rica. Fake passports, visas, receipts for travel, enormous sums of cash, et cetera. Guess where Artemis Payne spent six months of his life sometime before he came to Maine to kill Cam Hooker? Anybody?"

The president gazed out into the Rose Garden and shook his head.

"God knows," Hawke finally said.

Rosow said, "And more to the point, since our presumed spy-killer Spider Payne has been dead for weeks now, who the hell killed the top Russian spy in Monte Carlo two days ago?"

Congreve stood up, firing up his pipe. "I've no idea, Mr. President. It's a mystery," he said. "But I will tell you this. Alex Hawke and I shall not return here until we've found out."

"I very much appreciate your involvement in this case, Chief Inspector."

"I am flattered to be included, sir. I will give it my all, I assure you."

"Gentlemen, you'll excuse me but I've got another briefing," the president said. "I'll join you for dinner in my private dining room. But don't spare the whiskey on my account. Oh, and Alex, please tell that handsome boy of yours that I'd like him sitting next to the president at dinner this evening."

The meeting was apparently over.

TWENTY-FIVE

SIBERIA

His destination was plainly visible now, countless lighted windows winking back at him through the dark snow-laden forests. Ten minutes later, the Sno-Cat tracked across an arched wooden bridge spanning a swiftly running river, the water moving black below. For the last half hour, Beauregard had noticed endless miles of dry stone walls, small rural cottages inside neatly fenced fields of snow.

Suddenly, the big Sno-Cat swerved hard left and plowed forward under an arched entrance of stone and black wrought iron. The topmost part was filigreed ironwork surmounted by golden two-headed eagles. The aura of power and opulence grew as they neared the palace entrance, ablaze with light. The driver came to a stop inside a large cobblestone courtyard. At the far end, the colonel saw the entrance: a broad series of formal steps leading upward.

Armed guards stood at attention at the base of the steps.

The colonel climbed out the Cat's rear door, stomping his cowboy boots on the hard-packed snow, trying to get some feeling back into his feet. Then he grabbed his duffel and started for the door.

His new traveling companions escorted him up the broad marble staircase, and tall double doors were flung open to admit them. Suddenly he'd left the cold and dark of Siberia behind and entered another century in another world. He found himself standing in a gilded and black-marble entrance hall. The ceiling vaulted four stories above his head, upheld by fluted Corinthian columns the size of grain silos. Two curving white marble staircases floated up into the darkness and muted piano music could be heard coming from somewhere on the upper floors.

A liveried steward showed him upstairs and down an endless hallway to his room. It was surprisingly small, but the four walls were covered entirely in blue-and-white Dutch tiles, favored, he knew, by Peter the Great. There was a cozy fire crackling in the tiled dutch oven in one corner and a large four-poster bed that seemed to call out to him.

He pulled his kicks off, shed his buckskin jacket, and stretched out on the bed, reveling in the plush comfort of the deep featherbed. He looked at his watch. His meeting was in one hour. He lay his head back on the pillow for a little shut-eye. He could feel his exhaustion instantly melting away . . .

There was a sharp rap on his door a second later.

Beauregard sat bolt upright and looked at his watch. One hour had passed! He leaped up and quickly crossed the room to the door. Pulling it wide, he saw his old friend General Vasily Krakov standing there, beaming at him. He was splendidly attired in his full dress uniform and had two glasses of champagne in his hands.

"How do you like our Russian hospitality so far, Colonel?" Krakov said with a smile.

"You boys know how to live, I'll say that."

"You must rank very high on the Kremlin's list of VIPs."

"Why's that?"

"This room belonged to Peter the Great himself. It was the only room he would ever sleep in when he was using the palace."

"You gotta be kidding me."

"We have just enough time for a chat before I take you to meet your host. May I come in? Those chairs by the fire are very comfortable, if I remember. I, too, slept in this room on my first visit to the palace many years ago. I have happy memories."

"Please come in, Vasily. You want a real drink, I can tell. None of that local vodka shit. I've got us a bottle of best Kentucky bourbon in my satchel over there."

"Good! Good! We don't get good bourbon here in Siberia," Krakov said, settling into the nearest chair. "Come sit down. I need to prepare you a bit for this meeting you've come so far to attend."

"Be my guest. My curiosity is killing me."

"Nothing to fear. First, I will be with you the whole time. I will act as a translator for our host, who speaks very little English. You will let me do all the talking and—"

"Wait, let's start with the host. Let me guess. Putin?"

The general was overcome with laughter.

"Putin? Are you serious? He'd never set foot here. He's too busy conquering the world under the new Soviet banner for the likes of you, Colonel, with all due respect. He has no knowledge of this meeting, nor should he. This whole operation is compartmentalized. It can never lead back to the Kremlin, nor should it. This is the blackest of KGB black ops, pure and simple. Is that fully understood? This operation is never mentioned nor does it exist even on paper."

Krakov eyed him carefully over the rim of his bourbon glass.

"Hell, yes, it's understood," the colonel said. "I'm just trying to find my way here. Know what I'm dealing with kind of thing. You guys fucked with me once, you know. And once is once too often. Because I'm the kind of guy who fucks back."

"Now, now, Colonel, no need to get excited. You know I personally have had no involvement in Kremlin or KGB politics. I am strictly military. I do what I'm told. That unfortunate business regarding Vulcan all came down from the top, against my strongest objections. I am now, and have always been, in your corner. You are one of a kind. And I have made that plain to my superiors from the beginning."

The Texan was suddenly very, very tired. He chalked it up to jet lag.

"Fuck it, Vasily. Just tell me what in hell is going on."

"Tonight, you're going to be dealing with the Dark Rider. One of my country's most precious secrets. There has always been a Dark Rider in Russia, since ancient times. He arises in times of trouble to lead Mother Russia through the darkness. When she emerges once more onto the broad sunlit plain and into the light, the Dark Rider fades away, to be replaced by the Pale Rider, who cares for his people in a more benevolent fashion, let us say. Do you understand? It's just the ebb and flow of our history."

"What's his name, anyway?"

"He has no name."

"No name. We're off to a bad start already, aren't we, General?"

"Listen to me. I'm not joking. He literally has no name. Not that I or anyone here would know, at any rate. We call him Uncle Joe. You can call him that as well."

"This is some weird shit, pal. I'm telling you. Why Uncle Joe?"

"You're aware of Joe Stalin."

"Who isn't? The ugly little shit who succeeded Lenin. Crazy little pockmarked fucker who murdered millions and sent the rest to the Siberian gulags. Right?"

"Well, that's one interpretation. The great savior

of Mother Russia who defeated the Nazis and secured the Soviet Empire is another. Our new Dark
Rider got the name because he bears an uncanny
resemblance to the real Joseph Stalin. Same height,
five foot four inches, same blemished complexion,
same demeanor, et cetera. Hell, he even sounds like
the original!"

"Where'd you dig this hoary ghost up, anyway?"

"Let's just say his origins are clouded in mystery,
shall we, Colonel?"

"You say it. I don't really give a damn where he
comes from. So long as he pays his bills and doesn't
screw around with me."

"That will not be a problem."

"I hope not. So what's this Uncle Joe want to talk
to me about? Aside from apologizing for the fact
that his government stuck TNT up my ass."

"His vision, Colonel."

"His vision?"

"Yes. For a new and glorious Soviet Empire. One
destined soon to reemerge upon the world's stage
and dominate it. Rising imperiously from the ashes
of failure that have been Russia's fate after *perestroika*
and *glasnost* and all the trappings of democracy given
us by Yeltsin and Gorbachev in collusion with you
Americans. Two traitors who were responsible for
the unforgivable dissolution of the mighty Soviet
Empire. The greatest geopolitical disaster of the
twentieth century."

"I get it, I get it, spare me the histrionics. It's
good old empire building, that's all. So you already
gobbled up Crimea and the Ukraine. Estonia next?
That's just the beginning? You and your new boys

want it all put back together again, is that it? A massive land and power grab, no matter who gets crushed beneath the tank treads, right?"

"I will let Uncle Joe answer that question. I have no idea how much motive he intends to reveal to you. I know only that he thinks you can be extremely useful to implementing his vision. That is why you are here."

"So where is our boy Putin in all this? He's not the type to be sitting on the sidelines."

"Listen carefully, my colonel. Putin rules the old Russia. The Dark Rider rules the new Russia."

"And Putin is okay with that? Doesn't sound like the Putin we all know and love."

"Let's just say it's complicated and leave it at that, shall we? For your purposes, that's a very wise attitude to take when it comes to internal Soviet politics and—"

They were interrupted by the deep *thump-thump-thump* of a heavy helicopter descending overhead.

"He's arrived. We should make our way up to the tower. We do *not* want to be late."

"That big-ass tower by the lake? I was wondering about that? Only building with no lights on."

"It is his residence whenever he visits here. We call it the Dark Tower. There is a helipad on the rooftop. That's how he comes and goes."

"He doesn't like to be seen . . ."

"Correct. You yourself will not see him. He will be in the room with you and you will hear his voice . . . but you will not see him. No one does."

"This is all getting very mysterious, General."

Krakov laughed in his hearty way, "Yes, it is the

Russian way. You should know that after all these years."

The general stood, pausing to regard his appearance in the large gilt mirror above the fire. Satisfied, he tipped back his glass and drained the rest of the bourbon.

"Let's go," he said, motioning toward the door.

THERE WAS NO ELEVATOR TO THE TOP OF THE DARK Tower. The general said the tower was an architectural treasure, that it had been built in the sixteenth century and no one wanted to disturb its integrity.

"God forbid anybody screws around with this old treasure," the Texan said, taking a whiff of the cold dank air that poured down from above. The two men began climbing the worn stone staircase that wound upward. On every landing was a guttering candle stuck in an iron sconce providing patchy light. Not a lot of light, the colonel thought, minding his step, but enough.

"Which floor is he on, anyway?" the Texan asked over his shoulder, after they'd gained four or five.

"The top one."

"Of course. He's Uncle Joe, after all."

They trudged upward.

Ten minutes later, breathing heavily, they stood outside a heavy wooden door hung on iron hinges that looked to be centuries old. Two armed sentries stood at full attention on either side of the door, wearing fancy black uniforms that the colonel couldn't place for the life of him. If they were Russian, they were costumes from some earlier century.

"Good evening, General," one of the two guards

said, holding out a small thumbprint scanner. "If you don't mind, sir?"

"Not at all," Krakov said, pressing his right thumb on the touchscreen.

The two sentries stepped aside, allowing the general to open the wide wooden door. Inside, the room could only be described as a large cell of gloom. A high ceiling above where flags of the former Soviet states hung lifeless in a ring around the large desk below. There were two plain wooden chairs visible, clearly meant for General Vasily Krakov and the colonel. Between the chairs and the desk hung a black scrim. With little light behind it, it appeared as if the two chairs were facing a blank wall.

"Come in, come in!" a voice boomed, magnified and electronically modulated. The voice sounded as if it were coming from the bottom of a very deep well.

Colonel Beauregard was first through the door. He had to squint his eyes to see in the dim light. There was a worn Persian rug underfoot, barely covering the cold stone floor. There was a minimum of furniture, at least that he could see. And it was *cold*.

"Come closer," the disembodied voice called out.

And they did.

TWENTY-SIX

"GOOD EVENING," UNCLE JOE SAID.

The colonel heard a click, and a dim yellow light was illuminated atop the desk behind the scrim. Now was revealed the Dark Rider. A coal black silhouette, seated at a table facing outward, shoulders squared, head held high.

Trying to appear like a big man, Beauregard thought, *but in a little man's body.*

Two candles flickered in sconces on the wall behind him. A stubby candle or two on the desk shone light across the man's face but revealed no discernible features. Uncle Joe was sitting very erect, his hands folded together on the tabletop. That was about all you could see, just shapes.

"Good evening, Uncle Joe," Krakov said, a bit of timidity suddenly coloring his voice.

"Good evening. You look well, General. And

here is the famous Colonel Beauregard, I gather. Welcome to the Dark Tower, Colonel. It's over four hundred years old. And if these walls could talk . . . well, you would hear a lot of screaming."

Uncle Joe laughed at his own joke. A guttural, disturbing laugh.

The Texan was somewhat disquieted by that remark and shifted uncomfortably in his chair. If Uncle Joe meant it to be funny, fine. But, if he was serious? Fuck.

"Thank you for inviting me, sir. Mind if I call you Uncle Joe?"

"Not at all. It's my name."

"Well, then, Uncle Joe, this is quite a palace you have here, sir."

"Oh, it's not mine. It belongs to the people. To Russia. To the New Russia. *Novorossiya*."

"Sorry."

"Not at all. It is good to meet you, Colonel. I know you have come a long way. But I think you'll find your journey worthwhile. Let me say first that I have long been an admirer of yours. Vulcan mercenaries came to my aid when I needed you in Chechnya and again during the Georgian troubles. While I did not deal directly with you or your men, I have nothing but the highest regard for both."

"Thank you, sir. I wish I could believe that the Kremlin shared your feelings."

"Yes. As do I. Perhaps one day they shall. Their treatment of you was appalling after all you had done for the army, the navy, and what is now called FSB. I prefer the old term KGB and I would appreciate your calling it that as well."

"Always do. FSB never quite caught on down in Texas, Excellency."

"It will always be KGB to me."

"Yes, indeed, sir. Always."

"Now, Colonel, let's get down to the brass tacks. The very reasons why I wanted to have this meeting with you, agreed?"

"Please."

"I've studied your dossier at length. I know all about you. You are astute and politically aware. You know that there is a new Russia lurking just over the horizon. Rumbling over the horizon with the roar of a million battle tanks. Sometimes if you look in the right place, you can see the golden glow of destruction, heralding its approach. We owe a great deal to our forefathers just as you do in your country. Yet, for a time, Russia has turned its back on the past. I intend to rectify that. I believe that the collapse of the Soviet Union was the greatest geopolitical catastrophe of the twentieth century."

"A phrase I just heard from the general, Uncle Joe. I'm sure many of your countrymen would agree with you, sir."

"You've no idea. From the Soviet Union of our fathers we received a great legacy. Infrastructure. Industrial specialization, a common linguistic, scientific, and cultural heritage. To use this enormous gift together for our onward development is in our common interest . . . and also common sense. My wish is not to re-create the USSR. It would be naive to try to restore or copy that perfection which remains rooted in the past. But hear me now. A close integration of Soviet imperialism based on new values and a new political and military foundation is imperative."

"If I may interrupt, you speak of this 'New Russia.' What is your vision for it?"

"Good. You get to the point. Let me begin by describing the world in which we find ourselves early in the twenty-first century. In my view, our adversaries are weak and confused. In addition to proving himself spineless and without morality, the current American president seems utterly ignorant of the lessons of history. He has America in full retreat. Slashing defense spending, slashing military, slashing his own border protection. The entire Mideast has become a tinderbox with a hundred beckoning fuses. Our ISIS friends, for example. The fall of Syria and Yemen. The Boko Haram in Africa. We pushed your president in Syria, barely nudged him, and he folded like a house of cards."

Uncle Joe sat back, folded his arms across his chest, and continued.

"He is beset by enemies on all sides. He nearly went to war last year with China over the illegal expansion into the South China Sea, the use of North Korea as a surrogate bitch. Yet, when my country moved into the Crimea, what was his reaction? He ignored it. What does that tell you, Colonel?"

"I am an American and I find it disgraceful. But, for our enemies, it presents a huge opportunity. Historic, actually."

"Yes. You are exactly correct. This hollow man has the nerve to say that *my* country, Russia, is a 'local power that operates out of weakness.' Really? Weakness? Is he mad? I will only remind you Americans that Germany was once a local power operating out of weakness . . . that is, until Hitler came along."

"Exactly, Uncle Joe," the colonel said, liking where this was going. The little guy thought he was Hitler . . .

"Power, like nature, abhors a vacuum. A weakened American presidency, and, thus, a weakened America, presents us with a huge vacuum. The West underestimates us and that is good. Because I intend to fill that worldly vacuum, Colonel; I intend to fill it with the might and power of the New Russia! Do you understand me?"

"I do," Beauregard said, catching the fervor of the moment. "You think America is over. You think China lacks the nuclear arsenal to challenge you or even get in your way. You think the time is right for a new Soviet-style Russia to emerge as the world's new superpower, one that can challenge China or anyone else for world dominance. You want to return your borders to those you enjoyed before the fall of the Soviet Union. You want to—avenge your honor after the fall of your empire!"

The Dark Rider exploded with laughter.

"Yes! Precisely! General, you see that I was correct in my belief that the colonel here would grasp my vision?"

Krakov was laughing as well. "Oh, I think he more than grasps it, Uncle Joe. I think he grabs it by the neck and *embraces* it."

"Is the general correct, Colonel? Do you embrace my vision?"

"I'd say that's the understatement of the century, sir. Yes, I do embrace it. American leaders not only betrayed me, they are betraying themselves by letting Washington destroy in a few short years what has take two centuries to build. My men fought and died for the old America. I myself am a proud son of the American Revolution, the SAR. I wouldn't sacrifice even one of my glorious bastards for the new America."

"But you would let them fight for the New Russia?"

"I would indeed, sir. I would indeed."

"Excellent! It is the response I was hoping for, obviously. I welcome you with open arms."

"Please tell me how I can help you, sir. I don't know how much you know about Vulcan since our fall from grace."

"How many men do you have under arms?"

"I could raise an incredibly effective strike force of thirty thousand impeccably trained warriors."

"They are all still loyal to you?"

"Right down to their bones, sir."

"Weapons?"

"Armed to the teeth. The best combat armament in the field. In addition, at our facility in Texas and around the world, we maintain both aerial and naval assets that are the equivalent if not superior to that of any military on earth, including your own. We designed these things. We know how to fly them and we know how to sail them.

Surface vessels and minisubmarines employed in acts of sabotage. Sail into an enemy port and take down its power grid, for example."

"Good, good. We are on the same page, Colonel. Tell me more. Your intelligence assets? Still intact?"

"Intact and are ready to go operational on your signal. You have to understand something, sir. Our clients included just about every substantive government and intelligence agency on the planet. We know them inside out. Names, from top to bottom. Moles, who and where. Operations, both on the books and already in play. I can state unequivocally that there is no repository of the world's secrets on Earth that can rival this brain I carry around with me."

"You know all the world's secrets, don't you?"

"I do."

"Amazing. Do you know what we could do with that kind of knowledge?"

"I've been waiting for the right person to ask me that question for a very long time, Uncle Joe."

"What good is any intelligence service on Earth if the enemy knows all its secrets?"

"Worthless."

"Now I'm going to ask you a question you don't have to answer."

"Fire away."

"A number of high-level intelligence officers have died recently. Too many for coincidence in my view. Oddly enough, all seemingly of natural causes. A couple of deceased Americans, Brits, a French operative or two. Did you by any chance have anything to do with that?"

"Of course," the Texan said with a laugh. "How did you figure that out?"

"I simply looked at all the potential suspects to see which of them might possibly be at odds with the entire world. Yours was the only name on the list with a grievance sufficient to warrant such global retribution."

"Here's the deal, Excellency. These bastards, especially the American politicians and intelligence chiefs, thought they could shit all over Vulcan and its men and not pay a price. Hell, I haven't even begun to get even. You think I'm pissed off? You should talk to some of my warriors. I have to rein them in every now and then or you would see serious shit going down on Capitol Hill."

"Not an easy group to maintain control over, I would imagine."

"You've no idea, sir."

"You obviously have some very highly trained political assassins inside Vulcan."

"The best in the world, bar none. They're like ghosts. They can go through walls."

"Men and women who would be capable of systematically dismantling and eventually destroying certain agencies and their assets who are most troublesome to us going forward with our plans? Saboteurs who might take down the power grids of major cities without a shot fired?"

"Without question. Give me names and addresses. We'll take it from there. We're ready to start tomorrow."

The silhouetted figure sat back in his chair, appearing to ponder. Finally, he spoke.

"You're familiar with a man named Patrick Brick-house Kelly, I would presume."

"Brick Kelly, of course. Chief of the fucking CIA. He's the right bastard who found it convenient to throw Vulcan under the bus in the first place. Why?"

"A matter for another time, perhaps."

"Understood, sir."

The Dark Rider swiveled his chair to the left.

"General Krakov, it appears Colonel Beauregard and I are about to embark on a long and rewarding comradeship together. I will leave it to you to iron out all the logistics and compensation issues. I'm sure the colonel knows he and his men are going to be amply rewarded for their services?"

"I wouldn't doubt you for a second, sir. And I can promise you Vulcan will exceed your war-fighting expectations by a factor of one thousand. We will be worth every ruble."

"A pleasing scenario. I wonder. Could you please share your war-fighting modus operandi, Colonel?"

The American sat back in his chair, giving it some thought before replying. He said:

"I believe one must attack with a cold and unstinting fury. Leave the enemy whimpering and on its knees as quickly as possible. I believe in making the enemy at home scream out for their dead and wounded abroad. And I believe the suffering and pain of the bereaved left behind can be as effective as a fresh regiment in bringing a battle to a swift and timely conclusion. Teach them unalterable lessons about the horror of warfare. I consider myself not a warrior but a conqueror, sir. I learned these tactics studying another conqueror, General William Tecumseh Sherman, and his slashing and burning march through Georgia."

The Dark Rider was silent but nodded his strong approval of the colonel's remarks.

"Where is the bulk of your force currently located?" he asked.

"Scattered, for obvious reasons. I'm a nuisance, an inconvenience, for a lot of folks inside the Beltway. I myself live in a large fortified compound in Costa Rica. I have a skeleton force there dedicated to my personal security and the few regional ops we currently have under way. The bulk of my men have gone underground, waiting for me to notify them of an opportunity just like this one. I've got about a thousand men living and working at the old Vulcan complex near Port Arthur, Texas. And assets positioned around the world I communicate with via Skype and a dedicated satellite I had placed in orbit. Totally secure."

"How would you feel about relocating the entire operation in one place? All thirty thousand."

"No problem at all. Where do you have in mind, exactly?"

"Right here. I could begin construction of a facility to house and train your men immediately. A command-and-control center. Hangars for drones and combat aircraft. A landing strip that could accommodate your needs. Barracks and a dining hall for your soldiers. You would be adjacent to, but entirely separate from, the main KGB training and headquarters compound."

"Sounds pretty damn good to me, sir."

"I'm not sure our weather can compete with Costa Rica."

"Uncle Joe, let me assure you. Living on a mosquito-ridden beach with two fat ladies and a flea-bitten mongrel dog is not all it's cracked up to be."

The Russian laughed. He'd made the right choice.

"How soon could you mount an operation in, say, Washington? Or, just for argument's sake, let's say . . . Cuba?"

"Washington? That would take one phone call, sir. I have two of my very best assets in the capital. American, incidentally. Her late husband was former CIA, and his aggrieved widow is as good as they get."

"Excellent."

"Names?"

"In due time. But I already have one name for you to cross off my list."

"Consider him gone. Or, her, as it may be."

"Good. Another thing. You once worked with Fidel Castro in Cuba, I believe."

"I did."

"So you know El Commandante's successor, his brother Raúl?"

"Yes. We're on very good terms."

"I am mounting a critically important operation on an island called Isla de Pinos. You recall, perhaps, the old Soviet spy installation on that island. Twenty-four square miles. Fell into disrepair when we abandoned Fidel. Now, I could use your help in rebuilding it for twenty-first-century warfare in that hemisphere. In the early stages, I will use it as a base from which to mount sabotage operations against southern Florida."

"It's yours."

"Welcome to the New Russia, Colonel."

"Uncle Joe, I will say one thing. It is an honor and a privilege to be part of your vision, sir."

"I have one more question for you, Colonel, and then I'll excuse you. Was Vulcan ever considered for a contract involving the protection of America's national electrical grids? I believe I read that somewhere . . ."

"Did a lot of research on them that never went anywhere. The power companies provide all their own security. And they don't want the government or someone like me nosing around in their business. Sheer stupidity, but there you have it. But I knew more than just about anyone about those damn power plants before I was done."

"And that is still true?"

"Far as I know. A grid's a grid is how I see it."

"Very well. You will be hearing from me in the next few days. If there is anything at all you require, General Krakov here is at your service. I have assigned him to you for the duration of facilitating your incorporation into our existing KGB framework. Don't hesitate to let me know what you need, Colonel."

"Right now, Uncle Joe, what I require is a little vodka."

"So do I!" General Krakov said. The Dark Rider must have pushed a button or something, because in a heartbeat a white-jacketed servant was rolling a table into his office. On it were two bottles of some vodka called Feuerwasser, a large silver bucket of ice, and three glasses.

And the official meeting was over.

Beauregard savored the intense bite of frozen vodka on his tongue. He couldn't stop smiling. For better or for worse, the colonel was risen at last from the ashes. And what havoc he might wreak upon those whom he felt had betrayed him?

It was all yet to be seen.

TWENTY-SEVEN

WASHINGTON AND CAP D'ANTIBES, FRANCE

"DADDY! DADDY!" ALEXEI CRIED WHEN HIS father entered the White House nursery. "Guess what I did?" Alexei was sitting cross-legged on the carpet beneath a sunny window, his squirming dog, Harry, in his arms. Harry, who was now known officially as "Harry the Wonderdog." The little boy had regained his healthy smile and complexion and was a pink-faced picture of robust English youth once more. When the dog bounded away and made a beeline for Hawke, Alexei said, "Did you know there was once a president named Harry, too, Daddy?"

"Yes, I did, as a matter of fact. Harry Truman."

Hawke took long strides across the room, dropped his bulging Royal Navy duffel bag on the floor, and gathered the boy up into his arms. He raised him high above his head, saying, "What? What amazing thing have you done now? Nell tells me you two had quite an adventure this morning."

"Oh, yes! The Secret Man took me to the president's swimming pool! He's nice. He took Nell and I—"

"Nell and *me*."

"Nell and me swimming for two whole hours! Oh, Daddy, can we have a pool someday? Just like the White House one? Please?"

"The Secret Man? You don't mean Agent Sullivan, do you? Who works here for the president?"

"Yes! I do. And I went underwater all by myself!"

"Can the boy swim, Nell? Don't tell me he can already swim?"

"Yes! I can, Father!"

Nell laughed. "The Secret Man is a former Navy SEAL, Alex. He was working in the pool with Alexei for two hours. What do you think?"

Hawke laughed and threw his son up high and caught him.

"Do you and Nell like it here?" he said.

"Oh, yes, Daddy. Don't we, Nellie?"

"Oh, yes, Daddy, we do, we do," Nell said, grinning at Alex.

Hawke cupped his hand around her neck and kissed her lips. It lasted a little longer than it should have perhaps, but it was a good-bye kiss and they both attached a lot of importance to the kisses they shared whenever he flew off to put himself in harm's way again.

"Be safe, baby," she whispered in his ear.

"You, too, kid."

"Are you going away again, Daddy?" Alexei said, looking up at this father with a heart full of love in his adoring blue eyes. He had the same unruly black hair as his father, and Nell Spooner had finally given up trying to keep it under control.

"Yes, darling, I am. But only for a few days, I hope. And you and Nell will have lots of fun exploring the White House with the Secret Man, I'm sure. Just wait until you see the bowling alley."

"What's that?"

"You'll see," Nell said. "And this evening you're going for a pony ride, Alexei."

A small frown clouded Hawke's face. Nell and Alexei had a bad history with horses. Nell had almost died saving her charge from a man on a horse trying to kill them in Hyde Park one Sunday morning.

Hawke dropped to his knees and embraced his son, pulling him close.

"Now, listen very carefully. I want you to make me a promise, Alexei. You will do everything that Nell tells you to do while I'm gone. And everything Agent Sullivan says, too. No games. No running away. No hiding. No playing tricks on anybody. Do you understand me?"

"Yes, Papa."

"Are you sure?"

"I'll be the best boy. I promise."

"All right," Hawke said standing up. "I've got to go now or I'll be late. Good-bye, Nell."

"Good-bye," she said to him, quickly looking away to hide the tears welling in her eyes, those eyes that looked like two pieces of the sky.

"Good-bye, Alexei."

"I love you, Daddy, so much."

"I love you, son."

"Will you be back in time for my birthday?"

"Try and stop me," Hawke laughed, ruffling his hair.

"If your father can be here, he will be here, Alexei, don't worry," Nell added, knowing Hawke's schedule changed hour by hour.

Hawke turned and headed for the door, emotions swirling inside his heart and mind.

Time to go.

HAWKE LOOKED OUT THE AIRPLANE'S STARBOARD side window and saw Putin's bright red chopper's main rotor begin to revolve just as the U.S. government–issue G4 was making its final approach at Aeroport Nice Cote d'Azur on the coast of France. "Have a look, Constable," he said to Ambrose who was seated just across the aisle.

"At what?"

"Putin's chopper is painted the identical shade of red as his yacht. Don't you find that unbearably chic?"

"I'm worried about you, Alex. Seriously."

Hawke laughed.

"You think I'm no match for the old fox? You underestimate me."

"I certainly hope so. You know what I've been thinking about for the last hour or so?"

"I couldn't begin to imagine. Sherlock Holmes? Chess moves? King takes pawn? The famous 'King's Indian Attack' opening?"

"Please don't be clever. I'm thinking about what you told Brick Kelly. That something doesn't smell right to you about this whole scenario. This sudden invitation to go yachting."

"Yes. Do you smell it, too?"

"Perhaps. Here's the dichotomy you face, Alex. Putin is perhaps the most powerful bad man on the planet. Certainly the richest man on the planet. His resources know no boundaries. Forty billion is said to be conservative. I know you think he likes you. And you're rather fond of him in the most peculiar way."

"Not peculiar at all. I think he's amusing at times. He can be very funny, you know."

"Hard to believe."

"Not to mention that were it not for Volodya, I would have been impaled on a stake on an island prison and left to rot in the noonday sun. My child's mother would have died in front of a firing squad in Lubyanka Prison. And my son would have had his brains bashed in the moment he was born."

"Well. There is that."

"There certainly is that. Did you know he wants me to defect to Russia and work for him?"

"So I've heard."

"Don't you find that funny? That he would be so brazen about it? That's why I like him."

"Just be careful, Alex. Because as hilarious as you

seem to find this much-vaunted friendship with an evil dictator, it doesn't come without its downside."

"Such as?"

"He could turn on you in a heartbeat. If he felt for one moment that it would serve his purposes to take you off his chessboard, I have no doubt in the world that he would do it."

Hawke buckled his seat belt seconds before the plane touched down at Nice and began to taxi outward to the waiting Russian chopper that would ferry them on the short hop to Cap d'Antibes on the French Riviera.

He was thinking about what Ambrose had said.

And of course, as usual, he was absolutely right.

HALF AN HOUR LATER, THE THREE MEN WERE BASK-ing in the soft sunlight you only find in the South of France. A cool breeze came up off the sea and rippled the colorful flags that were rigged on the backstay from the masthead down to the aftermost cleat on the yacht's wide stern.

Tsar was moored within spitting distance of the Hôtel du Cap. It was Hawke's favorite hotel in the world and if it weren't for Putin's famous hospitality aboard the three-hundred-million-dollar ship, he'd be sleeping there tonight.

"Well. Good to see you, Chief Inspector. And you as well, Alex," Putin said, after the red-jacketed steward who'd served their drinks had withdrawn. "You look fit, old boy, well rested. Troubles me. I like to think we keep your side awake at night. That we get on your nerves."

Hawke smiled.

"Oh, you do that, too, Volodya. But the mere fact that the chief inspector and I are sitting here in splendor at your request would indicate that you're lost without me. Thus, my confident smile and easy manner. Right, Ambrose?"

Congreve was staring at the Russian when he said, "The whole world seems to find us indispensable, Alex, not just President Putin."

Putin found a laugh deep down inside, and there was sudden merriment in those light blue eyes that many who'd met him described as cold or ruthless. Ambrose was instantly aware of what forged this odd bond between one of Britain's greatest warriors and the man many thought of as one of the world's great villains. It was mutual respect. And, on some level, their intelligence found a connection through self-assurance, confidence, and humor.

"We were both sorry to hear about your untimely loss, Volodya. I understand you and the late general were very close."

"Thank you. Tragic. I shall miss that old soldier deeply. After hearing of your success with the Paris murder, I am eternally grateful that you both agreed to help me find his killer. In each of your staterooms you will find a dossier prepared by my office that contains everything we've been able to ascertain about what happened that night. You're already aware that he was killed aboard *Tsar* in the harbor over at Monte Carlo?"

Hawke nodded. "We are."

"I think it best if we wait until you have digested the contents of the file before we take up this matter in any detail. Is that agreeable?"

"Indeed, I was going to suggest it, President," Ambrose said.

"Good. I've got a reservation for lunch across the way at the Eden Roc restaurant. Hôtel du Cap. Best-looking women in the south of France. I know you like it, Alex; we've dined there before. Would either of you care for some water?"

"Water? It's delicious. What is it?" Ambrose asked, plucking a cold half-liter bottle from the icy champagne bucket. The bottle's bright red label proclaimed it to be a natural elixir called "Feuerwasser."

"Elixir?" Hawke said.

"Vodka," Putin replied. "We call vodka 'little water' in Russia. The 'Water of Life'"

"I'd be delighted."

"Ah, you'll like it, Alex. Very potent, shall we say. Our Russian specialty vodkas have become very chic, you see. This vodka is bottled for me in Germany. Worldwide sales, even in America. The manufacturer ships hundreds of thousands of cases each year. I was responsible for the first case served over here at Hôtel du Cap. Now they don't even offer Stoli anymore. I hate competition, as you know. Stoli doesn't know who it's dealing with!" He took a deep swallow and laughed.

Ambrose craned his head around to see what restaurant they were talking about. There was an extremely beautiful hotel perched on the edge of the rocky cliff, surrounded by manicured gardens studded with lovely old pine trees. A more modern wing stood atop the seaside cliffs.

"What is that place over there?" he said. "It looks marvelous."

"It is marvelous, Chief Inspector. That is the Eden Roc beach club. My launch will ferry us over. Say, one o'clock? Perhaps you'd both like to retire to your staterooms and freshen up? Your bags have already been unpacked."

Hawke caught Congreve's eye and winked. They both knew what *that* meant.

Putin got to his feet and smiled. He didn't need to say that he clearly had other matters to attend to. Hawke was struck by the set of his powerful shoulders and the jutting jaw as he turned away and strode toward the bow.

Say what you will about Vladimir Putin, he thought, *this is a man on a mission.*

ONE NIGHT, SOME YEARS AGO NOW, HAWKE HAD shared a prison cell with the then recently ousted Putin. It was most unpleasant: a dank, lead-lined hole in the dungeon of a horrific place, a fortress island called Energetika. Every square inch of the prison, every surface, every stone, every nail, and every denuded tree was burned ash black by decades of radioactive assault. The prison, not so ironically, had been built atop the mound of rock the Soviet Navy had used as a dumping ground for all its nuclear waste. Hence, Putin's lead-lined cell, provided secretly by his supporters inside the Kremlin.

Putin had that night given Hawke a peek into his soul that few if any other men had ever been made privy to. After a long night of cigarettes, Hawke had simply asked the infamous Russian leader what made him tick. And the floodgates had opened wide.

"I am a born patriot," Putin had begun. "My father and two brothers died defending our homeland, the city of Stalingrad. At the age of sixteen, I walked into the local KGB front office in St. Petersburg and tried to sign up. They laughed at me and suggested I go get an international law degree first, which I did, and come back later, which I also did. I was posted to East Berlin in the days before our wall came down. I spent most of my free time reading the history of my beloved country. At work? Well, there were plenty of Germans who deserved my undivided attention, shall we say.

"You in the West are deeply offended at my actions in Crimea, the Ukraine, Georgia. Let me tell you about the Ukraine. Countless Russian boys have lost their lives defending Kiev from invaders over the centuries. When Napoleon invaded Russia, he came in the Ukraine door. Likewise Hitler. And I knew that if I left that door open, sooner or later it would be some other rampaging horde streaming through the wide open gate of the Ukraine. So I closed it. That's all there is to it. It's Russian soil, damn it. My soil."

"You'd like to have back all your old Soviet real estate I take it, Volodya."

"You're damn right I would. What happened to my country was a criminal outrage. A deliberate humiliation orchestrated by the West. Well, the West better watch their fucking backs, Alex."

"Is that a threat? Do you want me to convey that message?"

"Listen to me. When I deliver a threat, I deliver it in person. I may be locked inside this prison cage of steel now, but it won't always be my home. I have time to think here. And all I think about is the future glory of my homeland. You can convey that if you want to."

In the morning, Hawke learned that his new friend had granted him a stay of execution.

TWENTY-EIGHT

PUTIN AND HAWKE BOTH ORDERED THE *SALADE niçoise*, so Ambrose did the same. Putin's new bride, Aliana, a stunning blond ballerina from Kiev, had specified Badoit water, no ice, and two aspirin, sliced, as far as he could make out. He had only a vague idea what kind of "salade" a "niçoise" might be, but he assumed that these two men of the world must have some long-standing appreciation of the menu, so why not follow suit?

When luncheon was served at last by a rather haughty and ill-mustachioed Gallic fellow, Ambrose was shocked to learn that his salad was nothing but a single large yellow-and-blue bowl containing carelessly tossed greenish leaves and the odd bit of tuna fish, parsimoniously gifted, and hard to locate among the weeds. He was obviously Putin's guest but he'd glanced at the menu. He damn well knew he was about to tuck into a hundred quid worth of tuna fish, if only he could find it.

A delicious Domaine Ott sparkling rosé was served at table and, across that white linen expanse, Putin and Hawke got right down to cases. Eye to eye, toe to toe, and nose to nose. The four were dining in a quiet, remote corner of the small private dining room overlooking the flashing blue sea. Most of the surrounding tables were occupied by KGB bodyguards, Ambrose was sure. You could tell. Big shoulders and small heads. They all had five o'clock shadows at noon.

Still, an air of tension and secrecy pervaded the sunny, flower-filled room.

There was very clearly an agenda here, set by the Russian president, and the murder of an overweight KGB man was just as clearly not on that agenda.

"Lovely meeting you, my dear," Congreve said, turning to the stunning Aliana with his near-perfect Muscovy Russian. He'd been a languages scholar at Cambridge long ago and it had come in extremely handy over the years, dealing as he and Hawke did with foreign agents of every hue and stripe. "I understand you're a dancer."

"Yes, I am. And you," she said shyly. "Are you a dancer, too?" She was quite young and exceedingly beautiful. No surprises there.

Ambrose laughed, "No, dear, not a dancer. Although I'm frequently mistaken for one."

She smiled and said, "You are a policeman?"

"Indeed, I am. Scotland Yard. Ever heard of it?"

She laughed. "Are you joking? My husband the president makes me read all the Sherlock Holmes books. Twice. Then he tests me. He is a stern professor. Woof! Ask me a question about *The Sign of the Four*."

"One of my favorites. The second Holmes novel, actually. So what exactly was 'the sign of the four' as depicted in the novel?"

She gave him a lively look and said, "A secret pact among four convicts during the Indian Rebellion of 1857. Something to do with a stolen treasure? Yes? Am I correct?"

"My dear girl, you and I are going to get along splendidly," Congreve said, heaving a huge sigh of relief. He had been agonizing all morning about what he and this young lady were going to be talking about, knowing full well Hawke would surely be sucked into Putin's orbit and leave him to his fate.

"That was the book where Holmes gave all of us coppers some good advice on solving mysteries," Ambrose lectured. "Holmes said, 'In any investigation, first eliminate all extraneous factors, and the one which remains must be the truth!' Remember that?"

"Yes, of course!" she cried. "So true!"

And they were off to the races.

Putin and Hawke had shoved their chairs back away from the table so they could look each other in the eye and communicate almost inaudibly. But they did so with visible and visceral intensity. Putin leaned in close and said, "So, Alex, you look well. No complaints?"

"Other than the fact that those bloody Tsarist

bastards took another run at my son, Alexei, no, nothing really."

Putin didn't flinch.

"Well. He's safe in the White House."

"How the hell do you know that?" Hawke asked, red anger flashing in his blue eyes. "How do you know where my son is safe?"

Putin placed his index finger upon his chin, fixed his stare, and said, "My dear friend, I know the exact thread count of the Egyptian linen sheets in the Lincoln Bedroom."

"I forgot about all that. Your state visit to the White House. The small problem with the sleeping arrangements you had so discreetly arranged. Your overnight guest, wasn't that the issue with the Secret Service? The lady from Baltimore. A dancer, as I recall."

"As well you should forget it. Permanently. Now, listen to me. You know I'm not one for idle chit-chats. I have some information for you. But it comes at a steep price."

"I'm listening."

"Not money, you understand."

"My God, I should hope not," Hawke replied, glancing out at Putin's bright red megayacht riding at anchor. With a rumored net worth of forty billion, it was hard to imagine Putin with his hand out.

Putin continued. "All I want from you is talk. What I need is your honest geopolitical appraisal as of right now. Today. Nothing beyond the boundaries of your Official Secrets Act, of course. I have certain questions about the disposition of different governments. And I respect your opinions, that's all. And, moreover, I feel lucky to have access to them. That's all I need in return for my information. A frank and honest appraisal of the strengths and weaknesses of the relevant pieces on the board."

"Well, I suppose my degree of honesty is somewhat predicated on what you intend to offer me. What are we talking about here, Volodya?"

Putin leaned back and smiled.

"I can give you the name of the man who recently murdered the U.S. president in his bed at Walter Reed Hospital. McCloskey's assassin. So far, CIA and FBI and all the rest have done a lousy job of finding him. I'd add MI6 to that list as well."

Hawke didn't blink.

"I'm listening. Tell me."

"A Chinese national. His name is Tommy Chow. Early fifties. He was a highly prized Te-Wu assassin from the Xinbu Academy in the South China Sea. Studied directly under your late unlamented friend General Moon. Still interested?"

"Please continue."

"We've chased him around a little bit. He is living now in Brazil under an assumed name. Ling Ping. He has a small casita directly on the sea. A little coastal resort town called Buzios. About two hours northeast of Rio. He works six days a week in the restaurant across the street as head chef. A trendy Italian bistro called Le Strega."

"How old is this information?"

Putin looked at his watch.

"About an hour and a half. The chef is preparing a paella right about now. A wedding party. Tables are being set up on the beach. Torches, too."

Hawke laughed.

"That's good."

"You want more, Alex?"

"Whatever you have."

"How about his motive?"

"That would be most helpful to us, Volodya."

"It was never any secret that General Moon wanted President McCloskey dead. There was a big Pan-Asian Conference coming up in Hong Kong, as you'll recall. Moon had sworn to his bosses in Beijing that McCloskey would be a no-show."

"Why?"

"They all hated McCloskey, those mandarins in Beijing. They thought he was a hard-liner. A cowboy who was quick on the draw and who'd always shoot first. They nicknamed him the 'Duke.' They wanted somebody more reasonable in the Oval Office. Someone more susceptible to flattery of various descriptions. Someone malleable. Moon put Tommy Chow in the White House kitchen to get rid of McCloskey and it worked."

"They wanted Rosow?" Hawke said.

"That's another story, but the answer is yes. The Chinese Communist Party much preferred having Rosow sitting on the Oval Office throne. Someone with a pressing domestic agenda to take his mind off international affairs. His primary goals, at least until the ISIS barbarians set fire to the Middle East once more, were sealing the U.S. borders coupled with increasing domestic oil and gas production. So. What do you think of my bargaining chip?"

"I'd say it was most impressive."

"Do you accept my offer?" Putin said.

"I do. Thank you. I shall convey that intel brief to MI6 and CIA at the first opportunity."

"Good. Now we can relax and talk realpolitik instead of political murder. Vastly more interesting topic."

"Sometimes certain governments have a hard time keeping them separated."

"Are you referring to mine? Hello Pot, meet Kettle. You of all people."

"I didn't say that, Volodya."

Putin pulled out his best sly fox smile and said, "Now, now, don't get your back up, Alex. It's only business. Let's get China out of the way, first, shall we? In China's case, I would like to say that the enemy of my enemy is my friend. But in this case I cannot. Beijing is our common enemy, yes. But they are not my friends, despite what you may read in the press. Secret treaties. A clandestine alliance against the Western powers. And all that rot. Big Russian and Chinese trade and energy deals made under the table. Bullshit. All nothing but someone's political currency to make my country look bad."

"I'm aware of that. Sino-Russian relations always run hot and cold. But I noticed the Chinese were on the sidelines, cheering you on in adventures in Crimea and the Ukraine. Not to mention, Cuba."

"The mandarins in Beijing and I share a common enemy, do we not? Why should they not enjoy the show we put on in what was, after all, Russian territory?"

"It's a complicated world we live in," Hawke said, looking away. There was something in Putin's eyes that he hadn't seen before. The cold blue eyes no longer looked clear and unclouded. There was a hint of something in them that Hawke couldn't quite put his finger on. As the day wore on, he later felt he'd identified it. A touch of madness had crept in.

Putin saw his stare and smiled, saying, "Right now, Russia is going through a rough patch. Economically, I mean. Oil prices, you know. The fucking sanctions and the falling ruble. Nothing I can't fix, you understand. But it will take time. Meanwhile, China remains globally ascendant. Political influence, raw materials and precious resources, hard cash on hand, masses of American debt, a huge spike in defense spending . . . I could go on and on but, frankly, it is too depressing. Just as Russia was finally getting its footing, China comes along and swipes our traction."

"Hmm."

"Agree with me so far?"

"For the most part, yes, I suppose so. From your point of view, of course."

"Well, it is the only one I have, Alex, just as you have yours. It is my mission to get Russia's traction back. And I will stop at nothing to do that. Nothing. I no longer care what they think in Paris, or Berlin. Or, London, for that matter. I've realized that I am a man of destiny. My legacy will be that I was my country's savior. I want to be remembered not as another run-of-the-mill politician, but as a twenty-first-century *tsar*. I want my Kremlin portrait to hang beside Peter the Great. You see my point?"

"I'm beginning to, Volodya."

"You've no idea how glad I am to hear you say that."

TWENTY-NINE

Hawke watched carefully as Putin sat back in his blue-and-white wicker chair. He saw the Russian appraising him through narrowed eyes. For perhaps the first time since they had shared a cell in the hellish Russian prison called Energetika, he believed Putin was recalculating his measure of the Englishman he'd happily called his friend for years. Calling into question his true motives for being here.

"I'm glad we understand each other, Alex. I think that's a healthy place for us to be, don't you?"

"To our continued good health," Hawke said, raising his glass.

Putin matched this gesture of goodwill and said, "Now. Your turn, Lord Hawke. I want to know what you think about the big players I've mentioned.

Where does the British government believe they now stand, politically, economically, militarily?"

Hawke said, "I agree with your assessment of Beijing. Fiercely militaristic and spending billions on defense. They're hell-bent on twenty-first-century world dominance, and only our two nations stand in their way. But you leave out North Korea. They are the primary wild card in China's hand. And Beijing will play that card as long and hard as they are allowed to. We are just as much to blame as you, of course. But my advice? You would do well not to play so cozy with those maniacs in Pyongyang, Volodya. It makes you look bad."

"Ah, Alex my friend. You bring up Babyface in Pyongyang. If someone could arrange for me to have five minutes alone in a small room with that mad dwarf, that's all I'd need. Unlike our Chinese friends, there is no love lost between Moscow and Pyongyang."

"I hear rumors that he's taken ill," Hawke said.

"Let's just say I'm working on that and leave it at that, shall we? So. China is ascendant, Russia has temporarily stalled, midair. What about the West? What about you Brits? More important, what about the Americans?"

"Descendant."

"Really? Tell me why."

"I'm sure I don't have to. It would be not only impolitic but borderline treason for me to discuss the difficulties of our closest allies at this moment in time."

"Then I'll discuss it for you. You don't even have

to nod your head, Alex. To be honest, I was sorry to see McCloskey go. Finally an American president with a good head on his shoulders. An understanding of realpolitik. And the stomach to adjust for a rapidly evolving world. There was mutual respect there, between the two of us, for a time at any rate. Now? This new president? None. Too many blunders in too short a time in office. Eyes off the ball, as it were."

"For instance?"

"For instance, the new American president pulls all the troops out of Iraq prematurely, despite all the sound advice of his generals to the contrary. Now, what? Now ISIS and the radical Muslim offshoots of al-Qaeda are knocking on the doors of Baghdad. The president fails to close his southern borders to thieves and murderers and empties the Cuban and American jails of the ones he's already caught. He defunds and cripples his military every chance he gets. And yet he draws red lines in the Syrian sand that he has no intention of backing up. Yes?"

"Go on."

"But, somehow, the Muslims, al-Qaeda, always get a pass. He opens the gates at Guantanamo and returns their most feared commanders back onto the battlefield in return for, what? A deserter? A single traitor to his own service and country. You tell me, Alex. Just what are we to make of such a man as this Rosow? A man who says *global warming* is his biggest fear?"

"You tell me."

"I will be glad to. He's in over his head, that's what I think. Despite all his promise as vice president. He needed a couple of more years of tough seasoning under McCloskey, but that was yanked away from him by the Chinese assassin. No fault of his own, of course, merely swept along by the tides of history. Rosow realizes it, but there's nothing he can do about it, is there? I think he's headed for a nervous breakdown. Or an impeachment. His enemies in Congress grow restive."

"You would appear to be pushing him in that direction, Volodya. Every chance you get you poke a stick at him. You completely humiliated him over Syria, and you're still kicking his butt around out there. Upping the ante in the Ukraine, Estonia. Next thing he knows you'll be marching into Poland, the Czech Republic, or Hungary. *Really* putting his feet to the bloody fire."

"Bullshit, Alex. You think I base my foreign diplomacy and policy on the latest transient to inhabit the White House? Don't be absurd. I have nothing against the man personally. Many people in Moscow find him quite congenial, very intelligent, even a brilliant statesman. I am simply pushing the agenda in *my* direction. If Rosow gets in my way, that's his problem."

"Bullshit, Volodya. Could it be more obvious? A weakened West is in your best interests. The weaker the American government and military, the stronger the Russian government and military. Especially in light of your need for ever bigger and better borders. New and improved maps of the motherland. And, more especially, in light of the newfound strength of your other quasi enemy. The Chinese. Are you quite sure you're not having this very same conversation with your little friends in the Red Army? Seems to me you're always hosting lavish receptions at the Kremlin for Li Xingping and his Communist puppets."

"No comment. You may sometimes forget that you are an English spy, but I do not. But I will say this, and you can take it for what it's worth. It's a poor dog that cannot wag his own tail, is it not, Lord Hawke? You once taught me that old American aphorism. Tell *that* to the American president. We'll continue this conversation later aboard *Tsar*. Now, what shall we all have for dessert? Aliana? What do you wish for, my darling?"

"*Nyet, nyet*," she replied and helped herself to another slice of aspirin.

AMBROSE PAUSED IN HIS CELEBRATION OF THE ALLURing Aliana for a moment and stole a glance at Vladimir Putin jousting with Alex Hawke. Here was, if ever there was one, a formidable adversary. Hawke might be somewhat charmed by him for the moment, temporarily under his spell, and that was dangerous ground. Putin had an odd air about him. A combination of paranoia and ruthless aggression that was a bit frightening to watch firsthand. At least Ambrose was here to keep an eye on his old friend if nothing else.

The importance of the KGB murder case in Monte Carlo seemed to be fading before Congreve's eyes. Nonetheless, he was very glad he'd come along. After lunch, Putin and Hawke were off on some kind of unlikely boy's own undersea adventure or other. A new toy of Putin's, a minisub that could accommodate three but which Congreve had wisely suggested might be more comfortable with two. Besides, he was anxious to get over to Monte Carlo and dig into the murder mystery. The case had grasped his attention despite the lack of urgency now displayed by the Russian president.

Already, he'd been informed by Putin's secretary that the president had made arrangements for a driver to pick him up at the Hôtel du Cap main entrance immediately following the luncheon. He was being ferried a short distance along the Corniche to Monte Carlo, to the morgue to be precise, to view the body of the president's murdered friend. He would then confer with the lead detective investigating the murder and an inspector from Interpol. Together, Ambrose told Putin, he hoped they could solve this mystery for him.

All this skullduggery sounded far more palatable when Congreve was informed that the Russian president had booked the Imperial Suite at the Hôtel de Paris in Monte Carlo for the chief inspector's stay. It was the most famous and luxurious hotel in town, the sight of much intrigue over the years, and Congreve had always been curious about it.

Hawke and the Russian president, it was quite obvious, seemed to have better things to do than investigate murder cases. For Congreve, however, criminal investigation was the soul and lifeblood of his being. His brain was already itching to go.

THIRTY

PUTIN, HIS WIFE, AND HAWKE HAD BID FAREWELL to Congreve, walking with him up the wide path from the beach club to his car. A sleek steel-grey Bentley was waiting at the Hôtel du Cap's entrance. The three of them, plus the security detail, then retraced their steps through the gardens to the docks, where they boarded the high-tech launch that would take them back to *Tsar*.

Once back aboard, Mrs. Putin, her makeup artist, and her hairdresser had retired to the owner's stateroom to prepare for that evening's cocktail reception up on the main deck. Alex and Volodya made their way to an upper deck where Putin maintained his offices and his private library.

It was a beautifully wood-paneled room, sound-proofed, and the place where Putin most liked to conduct meetings he considered too confidential for even the most private of everyday settings. He directed Hawke to one of the large leather armchairs beside the fireplace, and he took the second and more worn of the chairs. There were needlepoint footstools and worn Persian rugs underfoot and lovely eighteenth-century English and American furniture.

Hawke was admiring the famous equestrian portrait of Peter the Great hung over the fireplace when a steward knocked, then asked him if there was anything he would like. He was dismissed by the host, not rudely, but impatiently.

The man was in his strictly business mode.

Putin said, "I mentioned earlier today that, weather permitting, we might be going on a small undersea expedition this afternoon, did I not?"

"You did mention that, yes," Hawke replied, crossing his long legs, enjoying the simple beauties of the room. These lovely objects, paintings, sculpture, and objets d'art comprised what one member of the very richest of the richest on earth believed to possess great beauty. And, to a large extent, Hawke believed he was right in that belief. A little heavy on the epic battle scenes, but other than that . . . yes.

"Well, weather is permitting and I think you'll enjoy this, Alex. I've a brand-new three-man sub down on the aquatics deck. An SM300/3. This will be her shakedown cruise. I had her built by Lamor Subsea Ltd. to my specifications. I can be very specific, as you know."

"Oh, yes. You specified torpedo tubes fore and aft, one only hopes?"

Putin cracked a smile. "No. No torpedoes, sadly. But she's certified to a depth of three hundred meters seawater, is equipped with a fish feeder, digital video cameras, and a robotic hand manipulator. That thing takes a little getting used to, but I've been practicing as you'll see. She can accommodate two plus a pilot, but I'll be the pilot this afternoon. You're comfortable with that, I assume?"

"You've got considerable hours at this stuff under your belt?"

"Of course."

"Completely comfortable, then. Might I ask where we're going?"

"You may. It's a fascinating story. Some months ago, I was doing some deepwater archaeological exploration in the sub about a hundred miles offshore from Cannes. Late in the day, ready to turn for home, I came across a rather startling sight down there. A massive Russian cargo vessel, still mostly intact, sitting upright on her keel. Very deep, right at the edge of my sub's depth parameters. A thrilling sight, I assure you, Alex. Both of her two enormous stacks intact. World War II vintage, very probably sunk by a German U-boat late in the war. I maneuvered around to her stern and photographed her name and hailing port. Peeling paint and oozing rust, of course, but still visible. She was *Arkhangel* out of Sevastopol . . . nearly a thousand feet long and capable, I later learned, of carrying sixty-eight thousand long tons of iron ore . . .

"I had the navy look into it. No trace of *Arkhangel*

ever found, no reports of her sinking. She simply disappeared right near the end of the war. Took a couple of German Kriegsmarine fish low in the belly and sank with all hands, I suppose. I shot a lot of video of her recently, but I'll spare you that. We're going to see the real thing."

"Sounds like fun. Truly."

"Oh, it will be. But not for the reasons you may surmise."

"What then?"

Putin rose and crossed the softly lit room to a large equestrian portrait of Peter the Great posed atop a storm-battered mountain. He touched the heavy gilt frame and it rose silently up on a hidden track to reveal a wall safe. Putin entered the code on the keypad and the door popped open. He pulled out a small red leather container about the size of a cigar box.

Returning to his chair, he balanced the box on his knees and opened the brass latch.

"All very mysterious," Hawke said, amused at the man's theatrics.

"Oh, you have no idea."

"What the hell are those?"

Putin removed one of a dozen small glass vials that were kept stored in the green felt-lined box. Inside, a clear liquid could be seen. Putin shook it a few times and held it up to the light for closer inspection. Then he passed it to Hawke for examination. There wasn't much to see. It looked like plain water.

"What do you think?"

"Don't tell me. Some ridiculously rare vodka distilled beneath the polar ice cap for your private reserve."

Putin smiled briefly and shook his head.

"You can imagine I am a man of many secrets, Alex."

"Oh, indeed I can imagine that, Volodya."

"It is a measure of my trust and respect for you that I am about to reveal one of my most closely held."

"I'm honored."

"All right, Alex, I'll get right to the point. About ten years ago, I went in utter secrecy one snowy night to meet with a gathering of the top scientists at our defense research institutes. The ten most brilliant minds I could find at that time. I told them that it was my wish that they start from scratch and develop the most perfect explosive the world has ever known. And the most powerful. Work was to begin immediately. I gave them no deadline. No budget. They would work together in utmost secrecy. Something like the Manhattan Project, if you will. Share nothing with the outside world. I provided a small building inside the Kremlin walls. An old redbrick counting house, called Moskva House, disused for centuries."

"Fascinating, go on."

"'What should it look like, this substance?' they asked me. 'What form should it take?'

"'If you have to ask me that,' I told them, 'you have already failed.'

"'But . . . at least give us some place to start,' they said.

" 'It should be perfect,' I said, trying not to give them too much direction. For how should I know what it would ultimately be? I had no idea. I didn't *want* to give them any direction. Whatever I said would ruin the project before it got under way. 'Do it,' I said. 'I'll know.' "

"So, they began to work?" Hawke said.

"Yes. They were demons, slaving round the clock like Alan Turing's codebreakers at Bletchley Park. But the early efforts were not worthy of the objective. I rejected everything I saw. Came very close to abandoning the whole idea a few years into it. I realized they were like men driving in the dark with no headlamps. And finally, I don't know why, it all became clear to me. I saw that my very first words had shown the way. But none of us had realized it at the time, of course."

"What words did you use?"

"Just one. I had said it should be . . . *perfect.*"

"And somehow they knew what you meant?"

"Didn't know, perhaps, but were able to intuit. It should be like light, I had said. It should be like air. It should be like . . . *water.*"

"Something perfect."

"Yes. Look at it. What do you see?"

"It looks like water."

"So far, so good. Now. Unscrew the cap. What do you smell?"

"Nothing."

"Odorless. Even better. Taste it."

Hawke began to raise the vial to his lips but paused with his hand in midair.

"No."

"No?"

"It occurs to me that should I drink this and die here at your feet, I should go down in history as the most stupendously stupid agent in the history of British Intelligence."

"Why?"

"Why? A sane man who is ever so generously offered a cup of high explosive by his erstwhile enemy? And gladly gulps it down without so much as a second thought?"

"You don't trust me."

"Frankly? No. And, believe me, Volodya, you should take that personally."

"How sad. Here, hand it to me."

Hawke reached across with the opened vial.

Putin took it, said, "Cheers!" and downed half the contents in one swallow, without hesitation. Then he turned and smiled at his companion.

"Well? Look at me. Are my eyes bulging out of my skull? Am I gagging? Am I retching or turning blue? Writhing on the floor? No. It's an explosive, Alex, not *poison*, for God's sake."

"Is this all some overly elaborate joke?"

"Hardly. Taste it."

Hawke took the empty vial and sipped at it.

"What does it taste like?"

"Water."

"Water, of course. That's its genius. Now, taste this vial." He handed him another vial.

Hawke sipped. "Vodka," he said. "Bad vodka, but still vodka."

"Yes! Yes! I got the idea to flavor the explosive. A

clever deception when the situation calls for it, no? Send cases of it to one's closest enemies at Christmastime. Give the gift that keeps on exploding."

"Brilliant. May I have another? I sometimes have uses for such stuff myself, as you might imagine."

Putin smiled. Pulling a single full vial from the case, he gave it to Hawke, who promptly slipped it inside the breast pocket of his dark grey blazer and forgot about it.

"Do me a favor, Lord Hawke. Don't drink that stuff if there are ever any frayed electrical cords or thunderstorms with lightning striking nearby. Lethal combination!"

Hawke laughed.

"Perhaps you should call it 'White Lightning' in that case," he said.

THIRTY-ONE

PUTIN REMOVED ANOTHER SINGLE VIAL FROM THE leather box and placed it inside a thick felt pouch with a drawstring. He fastened the metal detonator screw top down tight and shoved the container back into the safe. Shutting the three-inch-thick steel Loc-Tite door firmly, he keyed in the security code once more to lock it. The framed picture of Peter the Great slid down to its original position.

Once he was satisfied that all was secure, they left the library and headed down the long corridor to the central elevator. It was quite a walk. Hawke kept forgetting that he was actually on something so mundane as a *boat*.

Putin walked very fast everywhere he went when he was in a euphoric mood, but Hawke's long legs easily kept pace.

"Question," Hawke said, matching him stride for stride.

"Go."

"What do you call that stuff, anyway?"

"There was a lot of debate about that inside Moskva House. Herr Schwenke, one of my German scientists, suggested the name 'Putinwasser.' Can you imagine such lunacy? My legacy is the world's most powerful explosive? Ridiculous."

"Firing squad would be too good for this Schwenke chap."

"Yes. But, in the end, it is I who came up with the perfect name."

"Well?"

"Feuerwasser. As the good professor would have it. Or, Firewater, if you prefer."

"Firewater. That's good. Even better than White Lightning. You probably didn't know this, but, firewater, that's what the American Indians called their—"

"Corn liquor? Please, do not insult me, Alex. Where do you think I got the name? I am a historian, you know. Captain John Crockett, Jamestown, Virginia, calls it that in his notebooks."

"Sorry."

Putin displayed one of his more enigmatic smiles.

"Show some fucking respect, Alex."

"It occurs to me that I'm walking next to a human bomb. You're not going to explode on me today, are you, Volodya? Down there on the bottom of the ocean at a thousand feet?"

Putin laughed.

"The only way to detonate Feuerwasser is a single charge of electricity passing through the fluid. Each vial, whatever the size, from a test tube to a fifty-thousand-gallon oil tank, is equipped with a suitable lead azide blasting plug. Or a simple cell-phone ring to the detonator will trigger the explosion."

"So, on the off chance that I zapped you with a stun gun right now, this whole boat goes sky high?"

"This whole fucking *harbor* goes sky high. The Hôtel du Cap, as well. Poof."

"Good Lord, Volodya. Are you serious?"

Putin didn't bother to answer that one. He was always serious.

They entered one of four polished steel elevators and Putin pressed the button for the lowest deck on board. He was bouncing up and down on his toes. Excited, like a little kid. This was a side of the man that few had seen, and few would have believed even had they seen it.

They emerged on deck into golden afternoon sunlight washed with salty air. There was a strong blow coming through the wide opening in the aft section of the hull. Hawke noted that the wind had really picked up while they'd been aboard. White-caps, seas running four to five feet. Not that it would be a problem down at three hundred feet. But on the surface? You might get the feeling you were Gus Grissom in the *Apollo* space capsule after the splashdown in the south Atlantic.

This was the aquatics deck. The crew on duty below, navy guys, obviously, all snapped to attention and gave the Russian leader the kind of salute he demanded and returned.

Here were all the toys one could ever wish for, including two matching Riva Aquaramas and a high-speed Pursuit speedboat with four Sea Hunter 557-horsepower motors hung on the stern.

But what immediately caught Hawke's eye was the bright yellow submarine dangling from an overhead hoist than ran the length of the launching bay. Sailors were all over the thing, making sure all was seaworthy for the boss. The articulating arm was folded into four ten-foot sections and mounted on the top of the hull. A halo of eight massive pieplate-shaped underwater halogen lights surrounded the entire structure. The thing was teardrop shaped with the bulge at the bow control station.

"As you can see by the name on her hull, I decided to call her *Sputnik II*. My romantic feelings about the glories of the old Soviet era are hard to shake, I suppose."

"Your fondness for all things Soviet is no great secret, Volodya."

"Titanium hull," Putin said, ignoring Hawke's gibe. "Twenty-five feet long, twelve feet high, nine feet wide. Propelled by five hydraulic thrusters. Equipped with an Israeli manipulator arm that can lift up to two hundred pounds as well as perform more delicate tasks."

"Impressive," Hawke said.

"All is in readiness, Excellency," a young seaman said to Putin. He held a stainless control box in his hands, cables running from the rear of the box to various input ports along the side of the sub's hull. The Russian president cast his eyes lovingly over his new acquisition, a predive checklist clearly going through his mind.

"Yes."

He motioned the boy to approach him, bent his head forward, and whispered something in his ear. Putin reached inside his breast pocket and withdrew the slender vial of clear liquid, roughly the size of a man's forefinger. He held it aloft so it caught the sun's rays and nodded to the young crewman, who took the vial and disappeared around the starboard side of the sub where more crew was waiting to launch the vessel.

"Lower away, now," another smartly uniformed blond boy called out to the man on the winch. "Steady as she goes now . . ."

The wind was really whipping through the tunnel now, and *Sputnik II* was yawing and twisting on the heavy suspension cable . . .

"Easy . . . easy . . . she's almost down!"

One crewman grabbed the bow while another steered the stern. The yellow sub slowly dropped until the hull nestled into a cradle on the deck. With a hydraulic hiss, two gull-wing doors to either side of the sub's hull rose up. Inside was a gleaming high-tech interior, a cross between a Ferrari and the starship *Enterprise*. There were two black leather seats, mounted abreast of each other and one pilot's seat mounted slightly forward, the center one, which gave access to the control panels and joystick.

"We'll communicate through headphones," Volodya said, slipping a pair of bright red Beats over his ears. Hawke did the same. He suppressed a laugh at what he heard being played over the audio system: the Beatles' "Yellow Submarine."

Of course. Putin was Putin, nothing more to it than that.

After Putin hit a button that caused the gull-wing doors to hiss shut and gave a thumbs-up to the crewman standing at the sub's bow, Hawke felt the sub lifting beneath him.

Slowly, suspended from the overhead track, the sub moved outboard until it was hanging about six feet above the wave-tossed surface of the sea.

"All buckled in?" he heard Putin say in his headphones.

"Affirmative."

Frothy seawater was soon washing up over the sub's bulbous forward plexi hatches, resembling nothing so much as the bulging eyes of a fly enlarged by a factor of ten thousand.

"You've been deep before, Alex?"

"Nothing like this."

Their descent seemed rapid, though without casting a glance at the depth instruments, Hawke really had no idea. He contented himself by peering out into the briny stew of life in the biosphere beyond his world and the thin web of pearlescent streams of tiny bubbles rising before his eyes. *String theory*, he thought, and it made sense in the state he was in . . .

Mesmerizing . . . hypnotic. Drug induced? He banished such thoughts immediately as to admit that paranoid notion into current circumstances would seriously . . . impair his ability to fight. . . . to resist whatever . . . besides, would Putin really go to this much trouble to simply dispose of him? Well—best not go there.

Sputnik II dropped into the abyss.

Occasionally his host would comment on what they were seeing.

"See that little goggle-eyed monster?" Putin said, out of the blue-tinged darkness of the sub's interior. "With eyes on the ends of his stalks?"

"How could I miss it?"

"For centuries scientists believed life was impossible down here. The total absence of light, extreme cold, the unbelievable pressure . . . all would have combined to extinguish any form of life. Or so they thought. In fact the reverse is true. We will be soon passing through the two-hundred-meter mark into the Mesopelagic wonderland. It's the 'Twilight Zone.' Faint sunlight but no photosynthesis. Most of the light you'll see will be nonsolar, bioluminescence."

"Life at this depth?" Hawke said, peering out into the murk. "I can't imagine."

"You have to learn to see with new eyes, Alex."

"Obviously. . . . What the hell is that?"

"I call it the 'Death Star Jelly.' Stunning, isn't it?"

"Hollywood couldn't come up with that monster if it tried."

"Alex, you may find this hard to believe, but the zone below two hundred meters is the most prolific home to organic life on the entire planet. It took the invention of machines like this one to make that discovery."

"Fascinating. Seriously, Volodya, I'm indebted to you for sharing all this with me."

He looked over at Putin and saw a grin split his mask of forward-looking concentration.

"As the American darkies down south say, 'You ain't seen nothin' yet' . . ."

They plunged even deeper into the abyss.

THIRTY-TWO

"Five thousand yards and closing," Alex heard Putin say in his headphones. "Let's light it up . . ."

Putin reached forward and flipped down four toggle switches on the main panel. The world outside exploded into pure white light as the sub's surrounding halo of high-intensity lanterns illuminated. Hawke instinctively leaned forward scanning his eyes back and forth, looking for the silhouette of the sunken *Arkhangel* waiting for him somewhere out there on the undulating plain of the seabed.

When Hawke finally saw it, it loomed up so suddenly that he feared *Sputnik II*'s impact was imminent. For some curious reason, they had come upon it at such a high rate of speed Putin had to haul back on the yoke and execute a steep vertical climb up the side of the corroded hull before leveling off and diving hell-bent between the two smokestacks, flipping the boat over onto one side to squeeze through.

"Fun, no?" Putin said, glancing over at him.

"Stunt like that would stiffen the back of a jellyfish."

"Ha."

By the look on Putin's face, Hawke believed the near miss had been intentional. Volodya was just having a little fun with the veteran flyboy captive in his jump seat. Even without visual contact with the freighter, Putin had been watching their rapid approach on his radar screen. He'd known exactly what he was doing.

"That was fun, actually," Hawke said mildly. "You enjoy all this, don't you, screaming around down here in the darkness all by yourself?"

"I do. It's as close as I'll ever get to flying."

"I suppose so. I must say doing it while getting shot at adds immeasurably to the fun."

Putin laughed. "I'm terribly jealous of all you combat flyboys. My eyes weren't good enough. I was good at judo, that's all. You had quite an aerial career, Alex. Some said you had a perfect genius for air combat."

"Owe it to my grandfather, I suppose. He flew Sopwith Camels with the Flying Corps over the Ardennes in the first war. There were plenty of trick flyers around in those early days, and plenty who knew more about the science of the new game than he did, but there was no one else with quite his magic for an actual scrap. The old fellow was as full of dodges a couple of miles up in the sky as he'd been among the rocks in the Berg. He knew how to hide in the empty air as cleverly as in the long grass of the Serengeti."

"What was his secret?"

"Secret? He was a right brave young bastard, not sure that he had a secret. But he had this theory he explained to me when I first set out to earn my wings. 'Every man has a blind spot,' he said, and he knew just how to find that blind spot up there in the world of air. The best cover, he maintained, was not in a cloud or a wisp of fog, but in the elusive unseeing patch in the eye of your enemy."

"I like that."

"Me, too. Somehow, I recognized all that talk of his for the real thing. It was on a par with his theory of the 'perfect atmosphere' and 'the double bluff' and all the other air combat principles that his queer old mind had cogitated out of his rickety military life . . . but it worked for him. And I guess a bit of it rubbed off on me."

Hawke's mind drifted off, watching Putin deftly maneuver the craft through, around, and inside the narrow crevices between the upper reaches of the giant ship's superstructure. When he tired of that game, he angled upward until they were floating a few hundred feet above the moldering monolith stretched out below.

Putin throttled back even more, and they hovered there above the sunken giant. She was remarkably intact, although submersion at this depth had done its best to eradicate her. Her hull was a deep iron red, and the superstructure appeared to be slowly melting toward the broad decks. Her railings were mostly intact and one could imagine what a prize she must have been as viewed through the periscope of an attacking U-boat.

"I'll give you a quick stem to stern tour, Alex. It's quite something to see, is it not?" Putin put the sub over to port and circled just beneath the bowsprit before cruising down the length of the vessel, remaining about twenty feet just off her port-side hull . . .

It was a sight. But Hawke could not imagine Putin would go to all this trouble just to show him a forgotten and rusty relic of the Second World War. Five minutes later, the tour was over. Putin slowly allowed *Sputnik II* to drift upward until they arrived amidships, hovering directly above the two towering smokestacks.

When he was centered about thirty feet over the forward-most of the two stacks, he brought the sub to a stop, setting the propulsion system to maintain their position against the strong and shifting currents. He got very busy all of a sudden, adjusting the angle of the halo lights, turning on all the sub's many sound recorders and video cameras and adjusting their positions—

"What's going on?" Hawke asked, although he had a fair suspicion.

"We've finally come to the demonstration portion of today's adventure."

"Let me guess. The Feuerwasser?"

"What else? Now watch closely. I'm going to engage the articulating arm nestled above our heads. You can see everything through the twin overhead portholes . . ."

Putin used the thrusters to maneuver into the

desired position, slightly above and roughly thirty feet from the forward stack. Only then did he take control of the forty-foot arm.

Hawke craned his head back and took a look. As he watched, the articulated arm slowly unfolded and extended itself upward and to the right. Putin used the most delicate of corrections until the small pincerlike mechanism at the very tip of the armature was where he wanted it. It was now positioned over the yawning black opening of the forward smokestack.

"Notice the object grasped by the pincers," Putin said.

In the fierce cold white light, Hawke could see the tiny vial of explosive gripped in the steel claws.

"Why here?" Hawke said, though he already had a pretty good idea. Bomber pilots had long tried to drop their loads down the stacks of enemy vessels at sea, because they fell all the way to the engine room and keel before detonating.

"It's a straight shot down to the bowels of the ship where the explosion will be most effective."

"So I can expect to see more than a puff of smoke rising from the stack?" Hawke said, not being able to help himself.

"Considerably more. We're a hundred miles offshore. Were we at fifty, the mushroom of water on the surface would terrify the pedestrians marching along the Croisette. As it is, we'll cause a blip on the undersea seismographers' screens comparable to a minor earthquake."

It was still difficult to believe that this substance,

in such a minute quantity of clear liquid, could have any such dramatic effect as Putin was describing. On the other hand, Hawke knew Volodya was not the type to drag him all the way out here to the bottom of the sea just to embarrass himself. Maybe, Hawke thought, the Russian scientists actually had created the perfect explosive.

"Oh, yes. I think you'll see a great deal more. Here goes—"

Putin carefully made minute adjustments that modified the articulated arm and twisted the slender pincers in a counterclockwise motion.

"That should do it," he said, a strong note of anticipation in his voice. Not until the explosive device was upright and dead center did he toggle the switch that released it. Not until just before the glass vial dropped out of sight, down into the bowels of the ship, did Hawke notice that some sort of tiny electrical mechanism had been screwed into the mouth of the tube. The fuse, no doubt. What had Putin called it? The lead azide blasting plug, whatever the hell that was.

The sub shot forward and away from the wreck.

"All right," Putin said, throttling up and giving a series of short bursts of the stern thrusters. "Let's get the hell out of here. The tiniest bit of electric leakage could trigger that little fucker and we don't want to be anywhere near *Arkhangel* when she goes up, believe me."

"You've done this before, I take it?"

"Blown up sunken ships? No, no. I didn't have to. I know exactly what my little love potion is capable of, Alex. In a few moments, so shall you. By the way, the French naval authorities are well aware that we're out here today. Not only do we have their permission, we are receiving some kind of official commendation from the Cousteau Society for creating a massive artificial reef to encourage more sea life out here. I asked that your name be inscribed on the citation of merit beside my own."

Hawke shook his head in wonder.

"You are really something, Volodya. I have to say that."

THIRTY-THREE

IT TOOK THIRTY MINUTES TO GET SAFELY OUT OF the *Arkhangel* blast zone. According to Putin, if they remained any closer, the explosion's pressure wave, and the resulting shock wave, would implode *Sputnik II* instantly. Underwater explosions, called UNDEX by scientists, were far more lethal than the equivalent aboveground. Underwater, the surrounding water doesn't *absorb* the pressure like air does, but *moves with it*. As a result, undersea explosions transmit pressure with far greater intensity over far longer distances.

There were two large monitors on the control panel and Putin was surveying the scene using the high-powered telescopic lenses. The picture wasn't crystal clear, but Hawke could easily make out the massive red freighter standing stolidly atop the vast undersea plain.

Putin was busy making sure all his photographic needs had been attended to: lighting, focus, all film and video cameras locked in on the impending scene of destruction.

Putin looked over at him, his face expressionless.

"Ready?" he said.

"Ready," Hawke replied.

"Well," Putin said quietly, "hold on to your hat, Lord Hawke."

With that, he reached forward with his index finger pointed at the "Fire Control" panel and pushed a single flashing yellow button in the middle.

There was a millisecond of hesitation before the whole undersea world was transformed into an ever-expanding field of white-hot light emanating from the disintegrating *Arkhangel*. The big red hulk had already disappeared from view on the monitors, but a dangerous glare remained inside *Sputnik II*'s tiny cabin and Hawke reflexively covered his eyes for fear of being blinded.

"Shock wave coming," Putin said. "Brace yourself."

It hit them hard.

The sub's bow was lifted straight up and flipped over on its back; thrown violently backward, the craft tumbled end over end inside the pressure wave, helplessly twisting and turning in the maelstrom of enormous shock created by the epic blast.

There was simply nothing for Hawke to do, except hold on to the handhold atop the control panel with both hands, trying to avoid a head injury if possible. Helmets? Why the hell hadn't they donned helmets?

Putin fought the controls, trying desperately to use the thrusters to regain stability. But it was hopeless . . . and getting worse. Soon, tiny jet streams of water began to spout, streaming from the edges of the thick glass portholes . . . and the fierce screeching noises of the hull being compressed to the breaking point were sufficient to cause Hawke to fear the worst.

And the most alarming part? They were in uncharted waters. A thousand feet down in a damaged machine that was out of control. He could remember a few times feeling this helpless, at the mercy of events, but not often. He cursed himself for allowing Putin to talk him into this insane experiment in underwater demolition. The sub was nothing but a hobby. And Putin had clearly not employed experts to predict the power of the heretofore untested new explosive.

Alex had had a niggling notion, an almost psychic premonition that Putin might try something stupid during this visit. He'd try to disable him or even take him out . . . but . . . a murder-suicide? No. This was just an utter lack of understanding of the surreal power of the explosive he was playing with at this ridiculous depth. And Hawke, well, he was simply unlucky enough or stupid enough to have gone along for the ride.

Putin's struggles continued for an eternity that probably lasted all of five minutes. But eventually he regained control of the systems. And, miraculously, he finally managed to actually right the ship. Once that was accomplished, he aligned all the thrusters on the same vector—out of the blast current—and he gave it one final blast . . . they shot forward . . .

And ended up in calm water.

"Jesus Christ," Hawke said, as soon as he could speak.

"I had no *idea*," Putin said. "Are you hurt?"

"No. But for God's sake, Volodya!"

"Do you want to return to the mother ship? Or go back and have a look at the debris field?"

"I want a bloody rum is what I want. But to hell with it. Let's go see what's left of the monster. Maybe the next guy will have a better idea what the hell he's dealing with regarding this stuff you've invented. Because you didn't, Volodya. You clearly had *no* idea."

"Yeah," Putin said, bristling. He was not a man used to criticism from any quarter, let alone a tall and good-looking enemy British intelligence officer.

Hawke said, "Look. I've got a son. I'm all he's got. As you well know, his poor mother's practically a prisoner in one of your KGB training camps. So, for better or worse, I'm it. He *cannot* afford to lose his father."

"You want me to apologize?"

"I want to see if you're man enough."

"I'm sorry, Alex. I made a stupid mistake."

Hawke made no reply.

THERE WAS A CRATER WHERE THE FREIGHTER HAD been.

Maybe a quarter of a mile across and a hundred feet deep. The ship itself was gone. Utterly obliterated. Tiny glittering bits of scrap metal were scattered for miles across the seabed for as far as they could see in any direction. There were a few objects of any size at all out there, only a smattering of crumpled hunks of metal about the size of a Volkswagen. But they were few and far between.

Most of *Arkhangel*?

Vaporized.

By less than a fluid ounce of something called Feuerwasser.

The two men spent the return voyage to *Tsar* in silence, each man alone with his thoughts about what he had just witnessed, and what it meant.

About ten minutes out from *Tsar*'s anchorage off the Hôtel du Cap, Putin broke the deadly silence inside *Sputnik II*.

"Quite an amazing achievement when you think about it, isn't it?"

"What achievement?" Hawke replied, stirred from a reverie about something else. Like his sudden unease around a man whom he'd come to believe he could trust, despite what all his colleagues had been saying for years now. C had told him, in no uncertain terms, to "watch his front, for when the stab came, it would not be in the back."

Putin continued his lecture.

"Aside from nuclear fission, isotopes, enriched uranium, which are the most easily detectible weapons ever invented, in Feuerwasser, you have one that is colorless, odorless, tasteless . . . virtually undetectable! Yes, in fact, it resembles nothing so much as the one substance that composes nearly eighty percent of the earth's surface . . . water!"

"Amazing."

It came to Hawke rather suddenly, then, an abrupt revelation, an understanding of what this weekend invitation of Putin's was really all about. It wasn't about the murder of some decadent and wasted KGB general who may or may not have been a close friend of the president's. Nor about someone roaming around the planet killing highly placed intelligence officers of various and sundry secret services. No. Not about that at all.

What this was *really* all about, Hawke now realized, was history repeating itself. What he had just witnessed was something much akin to Harry S. Truman's "Little Boy" A-bomb moment. It was the bombing of Hiroshima all over again, just without the victims. Truman's idea was to drop the big one on a major population center to let the Japanese know unequivocally that any further resistance to the Allied advance was useless. Send them an unmistakable signal. But when Little Boy fell on Japan, sixty-six thousand men, women, and children had to die to prove Truman's point.

Now, Putin had figured out a way to deliver the very same message of terror to his enemies around the world. And all he needed to do so was have one single solitary witness, one who would live to tell the tale.

All he had needed was Lord Alexander Hawke.

Hawke looked over at Volodya's profile, hazy in the dim reddish light of the instrument panel. He saw the military buzz cut, the stern set of his jaw, the keen focus of those pale blue eyes, the eyes everyone said were so "cold." He also saw the thin

line of a smile spreading across the face of the old
fox.

This, palpably, was a formidable enemy. This was
a man who was running rings around the American
president and half his allies. This was a man invading sovereign nations without batting an eye. This
was a man intent on doing whatever he damn well
pleased on this planet and God help you if you got
in his way.

Because Volodya now had an Armageddon Little
Boy weapon of his very own. But a weapon that was
virtually undetectable. It could be introduced anywhere, at any time, into any environment with no
one the wiser until a distant button was pushed and
it exploded.

The big question, then, was *why*? What the hell
did he intend to do with it? At some point before he
left France, Hawke had to find out. He now realized
fully why Rosow and Brick Kelly had been so adamant about him making this trip. Rumors of a new
Russian superweapon had been floating around the
American intel community for quite a while. They
were making a long-shot bet that Hawke could
ferret it out.

And Putin and the Kremlin didn't need the *Enola
Gay* and a whole goddamn air force to deliver their
new doomsday weapon. Hell, he could *ship* it to you,
FedEx! Deliver it at the doorstep of your country
in a million goddamn Stoli bottles and you'd never
even know it. That is, until he triggered all the little
metal screw caps that ignited the fluid. From the
mind-blowing destruction Hawke had just seen
with his own eyes, it was not a giant leap to the con-

clusion that a half-gallon of "tainted" Stoli firewater could take out most of lower Manhattan.

Message delivered.

Putin was now utterly secure in the knowledge that Hawke would take his message home, deliver it to the powers that be in the White House, in Whitehall, at Langley and MI6. That message was simple: BEWARE! Don't stick your fingers inside the Russian bear's cage. He bites but first he chews your fingernails.

And what then? Well, then would begin the long and arduous process of figuring out how the hell to stop a megalomaniac with a weapon like this. Because there was not a doubt in Hawke's mind that Putin's boys were shipping this stuff all over the world . . . and they were doing it right now. Stockpiles being created in Asia, in Latin American, America, Europe. Warehouses stacked to the rafters with this stuff, waiting for his signal to explode.

The man upon whose doorstep this clearly insurmountable problem would ultimately be dumped?

Well—unless he was badly mistaken—that would be none other than Alex Hawke.

Back into the bloody fray with you, Lord Hawke. And it all started right now. Here we go again.

Alex Hawke, saving the world, one madman at a time.

THIRTY-FOUR

―――

McLean, Virginia

―――

State Route 123 winds through the rich green Virginia horse country just outside of Washington, D.C. The sleepy little town of McLean, in Fairfax County, lies at the heart of things in this quiet corner of the world. Rolling green hills traced with gleaming white picket fences, long winding driveways leading to gracious brick homes in the Georgian manner.

Sleek thoroughbreds gambol inside the fences, sometimes keeping pace with a vintage convertible on the road as it accelerates briskly out of a sweeping turn and up a steep incline, braking at the hilltop for a school bus just beyond Hickory Hill, the old

Kennedy place, where Ethel and Bobby had raised their boisterous brood.

Old money speaks softly in this neck of the woods. *And the* really *old stuff,* the woman at the wheel of the genteel old station wagon thought, *that kind of money rarely speaks above a whisper.* She'd chosen the car carefully at the used car dealer in Tyson's Corner a few days earlier. She'd had her hair cut and dyed, pinned up in a chignon. She wanted to blend in. She wanted to be invisible.

Still, it was odd on that early summer evening to see a lovely old wood-sided Chrysler Town & Country station wagon doing over sixty in a speed zone marked for thirty. Witnesses said later the woman at the wheel was early middle age, very well dressed and coiffed. Some folks remembered good pearls and gold bracelets on the long tanned arm dangling nonchalantly out the driver's window, a cigarette pinched between her fingers.

"She did seem like a lady who was in a mighty big hurry," said a horse trainer who'd paused in the field to watch her whiz by.

Her name was Crystal Methune. And she was definitely not from around here.

But, to her credit, she certainly looked like any other well-to-do mother of two you might see strolling the aisles at Saks over at Tyson's Corner Mall. Late thirties, attractive if not downright beautiful, surely the product of Miss Porter's or the Madeira School followed by Barnard or Vassar. Even the car was perfect. McLean people didn't drive BMWs or Escalades; no, the car of choice would be that faded old station wagon that had been in the family since the '50s.

The sky-blue-and-white Town & Country slowed to a crawl. Crystal pulled off the road and onto the verge and stopped. For some reason she checked her lipstick in the rearview mirror, glanced at her newly done nails, took a very deep breath, composed herself. Then she accelerated back onto the two-lane highway.

Just around the next bend in the road she would come upon Burning Tree Farm, Virginia's answer to the legendary Calumet Farm in her hometown of Lexington, Kentucky. Burning Tree Farm was the home of America's Triple Crown winner, the prize stallion War Admiral, out of the Smart Strike mare Eye of the Sphinx, who had once commanded a $50,000 stud fee.

The sprawling horse farm was also the family home of Patrick Brickhouse Kelly, the current director of the CIA. The farm was certainly convenient, she thought, just down the road a piece from the CIA headquarters at Langley. Brick Kelly's great-grandfather, Ambassador Flynn Kelly, had seen Burning Tree through the glory years in the middle of the last century. Brick's beloved but troubled father, who had "health issues," had presided over its subsequent demise, finally filing for bankruptcy. But it was young Brick himself who had brought the old family place back to its rightful and proper place at the very top of the equestrian world.

Crystal had done her homework. She had a complete and thorough understanding of the daily schedules and workings of the farm. She knew when the owner left for his office and when he returned. But she also knew when the horses were fed, when the fields were mown, when the mail and milk were delivered. She knew the daily comings and goings of everybody and anybody who had anything to do with the stud farm. She even knew the Kelly dog's name.

Captain.

She rounded the corner and saw Captain trotting down the long and stately allée of maples that was the entrance to Burning Tree. *Good boy*, she thought, *good boy!* He was right on schedule, she knew, looking at her watch. It was just turning six thirty in the dusky gold of evening.

Captain was in his prime, a handsome purebred black Lab. Since the Kelly mailbox was located across the road from the property, Captain would pause, look both ways, and then race across the macadam. He would position himself beside the mailbox to wait for his master. He did this every day of the week, rain, sleet, snow, or hail. She knew. She'd watched him do it in every kind of weather.

And, today, she'd timed it perfectly, she thought, depressing the accelerator to the floor. Oh, yeah, Crystal thought, she had nailed it all right.

Captain was just halfway across the road when she clipped his hindquarters with her left front bumper. The dog was thrown some thirty feet into the air before landing in the tall grass beside the road. He hadn't even seen her coming, she thought. And there had been no one behind her, no oncoming traffic, no witnesses.

She pulled off the road, slammed on the brakes, and jumped out, sprinting to where the injured dog lay writhing in the grass. She knelt down to check his injuries. There was a lot of blood, but she had not killed him. She certainly could have, just by arriving a few seconds later. But that had not been her intention. Racing back to the station wagon, she opened the rear, pulled out an old woolen blanket, and hurried back to the animal she'd just run down in cold blood.

Somehow, Crystal managed to get the dark green blanket under Captain and gather him up into her arms so she could put him in the way back of the old Chrysler wagon. Once it was done, she backed up, and turned right into the unmarked entrance of Burning Tree Farm. She left a billowing wake of chalky dust behind her as she followed the snaking drive toward the main house with the dying dog whimpering in pain behind her.

THE ENTRANCE TO THE ANTEBELLUM HOUSE WAS suitably imposing. Columns, pediments, a true Palladian masterwork. A winding brick walkway through manicured hedges of boxwood and blooming white azaleas. Tall Corinthian columns and a massive front door in gleaming mahogany. Potted topiaries to either side of the door, perfect green obelisks. Crystal raised the door knocker, an old bronze horse's head, and rapped smartly three times. Less than thirty seconds later, an elderly black woman in a starched white apron and cap swung the door open.

The housekeeper's white smile was so radiant it

almost burned Crystal's eyes. But it fell away when she saw the blood-soaked blanket in the stranger's arms.

"Oh! Oh, my Lordy, what's happened, child?"

"Someone ran over him," the stranger said, crying real tears. "They didn't even stop!"

"That's not Captain, is it? Oh, no . . . please say it's not."

"I don't know his name. But he was hit out in the road right by your mailbox so I just assumed—"

"Hurry! Bring him inside quickly . . ."

"He's still alive," the stranger said, hurrying into the cool shade of the house.

The older woman turned and headed through the entrance hall and then into a beautifully appointed library. All leather furniture and illuminated English sporting pictures of horses and jockeys. Smelled of wood, old books, and wax furniture polish, Crystal thought, sniffing the air.

It was all she could do not to pause and admire a stunning oil portrait of the Kellys' famous 1937 Triple Crown winner, War Admiral, over the fireplace.

"Quick, child! Put him on that big leather sofa," the woman said, and Crystal did so, being as overtly gentle and caring and sad as possible. The dog was making a lot less noise now, just very rapid breathing and small cries . . .

"Ma'am, I just have to ask you . . . Why in God's holy name did you not take him directly to the Emergency Pet Hospital in town?" the housekeeper said as she pulled the blanket away and looked at

Captain's horrific injuries for the briefest moment before turning away in horror.

"I—I'm not from around here, you see. I live in Kentucky. In Lexington, near Calumet Farm. I brought him here because I just didn't . . . you see, I just didn't know what else to do! I couldn't just leave him out there, could I? Or stand by the road and wait for help?"

"No, no, of course not . . . oh, Lord, both his back legs are broken. Wait here with him, I need to get something."

She dashed into what looked to be a small powder room off the library and returned with fluffy white towels.

"Here, press this down on the wound in his hip to stop the bleeding. I'll try to stabilize his legs and—"

Crystal pulled her cell phone out of her bag. "Shouldn't we call the vet? I can do that, here let me show you . . . do you have a number for—"

"Yes, yes, ma'am. You stay with him. I have to run upstairs and get the phone number for the vet from Mrs. Kelly's address book. Are you sure you can handle this?"

"I used to be an E.R. nurse," she lied.

"Praise the Lord above! I'll be right back."

She rushed out of the room through the open double doors, and Crystal could hear her footsteps in the hall, then her huffing and puffing, pounding all the way up the curving staircase.

Crystal sat down on the sofa beside Captain and spied three crystal decanters on the bar. One of them had to be bourbon, she knew. Getting to her feet she went over and poured herself a stiff drink.

Calmer now, she considered her next move. After a few long moments, she got up from the couch and followed the housekeeper's steps up the stairs to the upper floors. She'd shed her heels and was walking on tiptoe to prevent the old wooden steps from creaking. She had a small, nickel-plated .38 automatic in her right hand, a silencer fitted to the muzzle.

HALF AN HOUR LATER, CRYSTAL HEARD THE SOUND of a car on the gravel drive out front. She looked at her watch. Perfect. He was right on time. She rose and went to one of the tall library windows to see a black Audi A8 slow to a stop. The driver, young, clean-cut, and unbelievably fit, was clearly Secret Service. He climbed out, looked around, spoke into the hidden mike in his sleeve. Then he went around the back of the car and pulled the rear door open.

She got her first good look at the director of the Central Intelligence Agency as he climbed out of the car and stood talking to his driver. One of them must have told a joke because they both were laughing. Even more attractive than his file pictures, he was. Tall, lanky, wavy dark red hair going slightly grey on the sides. He wore the Agency uniform, navy suit, pressed white shirt, red tie. It was Brick Kelly all right.

Goddamn, he was good-looking, which was too bad.

She sipped her bourbon, letting her eyes enjoy the view.

BRICK PATTED THE BEEFY YOUNG AGENT ON THE shoulder before the man got back behind the wheel of the Audi and pulled away from the house. A flash of chrome in the setting sun must have caught the director's eye. That's when he spotted the station wagon parked under the dark green maple trees some fifty to sixty feet away.

Odd, Brick thought.

They weren't expecting any visitors, at least that he was aware of. Jane had left yesterday morning, taking the three children down to Nags Head, North Carolina, to stay at her mother's beach cottage for the coming long weekend. He took another look at the car. It wasn't a car he recognized . . . but that wasn't saying much. Jane had a ton of friends and they were always coming and going. Ladies' luncheons, book parties, bridge, whatever mischief they got up to.

But Jane wasn't home.

It gave him momentary pause, but something about that lovely old blue-and-white car was reassuring enough that he brushed the feelings off. Probably some lonely widow neighbor, he thought, right, some bridge friend of his wife's, knowing Jane was out of town for a few days and come to call. She'd be dropping off a spicy Mexican casserole for the lonely weekend bachelor. Even now probably out in the kitchen with Hildy, telling her how long it should remain in the oven.

It wouldn't be the first time, he thought. And he resumed his walk up the mossy brick walk with a smile, remembering something his grandfather had said.

"Son, never let yourself stand in the way of a lonely widow with a casserole and an available bachelor."

THIRTY-FIVE

As Brick Kelly made his way up his brick walkway, the front door suddenly swung open. Expecting to see Hildy, he was mildly startled. Instead of his housekeeper of many years, there was a tall and very attractive blonde of early middle age. Big blue eyes and a pink Chanel suit that hugged her lush figure. The only sour note was her perfume. It may well have been expensive, but something about the smell was off-putting.

"Hello," Brick said, smiling. "I'm Brick Kelly."

He was off balance. He thought he pretty much knew all Jane's friends, but he couldn't for the life of him place this woman. She was extremely good-looking. He would have remembered this one, had he met her, wouldn't he?

"I'm terribly sorry to startle you, Mr. Kelly," she said in an accent that could only come from the

Deep South. She stepped back into the house so he could enter the foyer. "I'm Mrs. Methune. I'm afraid there's been a terrible accident."

"What happened?" Brick said, setting his bulging leather briefcase on the console table atop all the mail. He looked around, suddenly on edge for some reason.

"Is Hildy all right? Where the hell is Hildy? Hold on just a second, okay? Hildy? Where are you?"

Brick went first to the kitchen and emerged seconds later, heading for the central staircase.

"Hildy," he called out. "Please come down here. Right now." Getting no response, he went back to the woman waiting by the door. "Probably up in the attic," he said.

Crystal took a step toward him, her face full of tender concern. Her blue eyes brimming . . . for one insane moment Brick actually thought she was going to kiss him on the lips . . .

"Someone ran over your poor dog. Right out at the end of the drive. I came around the corner and saw the poor thing lying there in the road. It must have happened only a few seconds earlier. I saw the flashing brake lights of a car up ahead just before it disappeared over the hill."

"Captain? Jesus Christ! Where is he? Is it bad?"

"I would have taken him straightaway to the vet, but I'm a stranger here, just visiting friends in Upperville, and had no idea which way to go. I gathered the poor thing up in a blanket and brought him here to the house. Your very kind housekeeper and I tried to stabilize him until we could locate the doctor . . . but . . ."

"But what?"

"I am so very sorry."

"He's dead? Don't tell me that. Don't even—"

"He's on the sofa in the library."

The director tore himself away and raced down the hall and into his library.

She heard a cry of despair and ducked into the living room. There was a deep velvet wing chair by the hearth and she collapsed into it, her orange Hermès bag resting in her lap, the .38 automatic within easy reach when she needed it.

Timing was everything, as always. She needed to get the target out of the house as quickly as possible. Before he had time to question her about Hildy's whereabouts. She'd kill him here in the house if she had to, but that was the last thing she wanted to do. She wanted him out under the trees by her car. Where she could put a bullet in his brain and heave him up into the back of the wagon. Drive him back to Kentucky where she would dispose of him and the car as well . . .

"Where the hell is Hildy?" Kelly demanded, suddenly appearing in the living room doorway. He'd wiped away his tears, but the enormous grief was written all over his face.

"She's in shock, I'm afraid. Devastated. Poor old thing said she was going up to her room to lie down. I'm to let her know when you arrive and—"

"That won't be necessary, Mrs.—"

"Methune, Crystal Methune."

"I'd like to be alone now, Mrs. Methune. I'm sure you can understand that. I'm grateful for all your help. I know you did the best you could under the circumstances. Good Samaritans are as rare as rocking horse shit around here these days . . . and now . . . May I at least walk you out to your car? Least I could do, I think."

She took a tentative step toward the front door, paused, and looked over her shoulder. She said, "Oh, you shouldn't bother. I can find my way."

Crystal lasered the big blues on him as she pulled the door open.

"Well, then," she said, "I'll be going. But . . . wait . . . on second thought, it might help somehow if I described what I saw. The hit-and-run car up ahead, I mean. I only got a glimpse of it but I'm pretty good at that kind of thing . . ."

"Yes. Yes, that would be very helpful. I wouldn't mind having a little chat with that sonofabitch," he said, following her outside.

"Right. You of all people could probably find him. I mean—"

Shit, Crystal thought, her mind racing. Staring at that chiseled face, she'd lost her focus and put him on high alert.

"What the living hell do you mean by that?" he said, his eyes going suddenly dark and suspicious. "Why me 'of all people'? Do you know who I am?"

"No, of course not—I mean, whoever did it is probably a neighbor. Somebody close by. Someone you know."

He started at her hard, decided what she'd said was logical.

"Yeah. Probably so," Brick said.

"All right," she said, heading down the walk and

hoping he'd follow. She left her bag unlatched and hung it from her left shoulder the way she'd been trained.

He was a courtly sort, an old southern gentleman to be sure, trusted her because of her appearance and the old wagon. Men are all suckers anyway; she wasn't surprised. He'd looked like he wanted to kiss her back there.

He lightly took her elbow as they made their way out into the increasing gloom of evening.

"So, tell me, Mrs. Methune—"

"Please. Call me Crystal, won't you? And you are?"

"Brick will do. Just Brick."

First-name basis. *Bingo.*

"Well, Brick, the first thing I noticed was that there were no skid marks on the pavement. So, whoever it was, he didn't even bother to hit the brakes . . ."

"Christ."

Their footsteps were crunching on the pebbles now. Maybe thirty feet more to her car. She put her hand into her bag as if searching for her keys . . . covering her action by saying, "He was going very fast or I'd have gotten a much better look at him. Sorry."

"Definitely a he?"

"Definitely. Bald head."

"What else did you see? The car color?"

"Yes, it was red. Cherry red. No top. Some kind of sports car, I think. Very loud. Very low to the ground. Do they still make Corvettes?"

"Of course. A red Corvette. Wouldn't you just know it? Asshole."

They were very near the Chrysler now and she began to enter the semi-fugue state she went to in kill mode. Everything slowed way down . . . her fingers closed around the pistol grip, her index finger slid easily inside the trigger guard . . . and suddenly she went cold. He was no longer walking just behind her, he was matching her stride for stride . . . what was he doing?

He was stock-still, staring at the bloody front fender of her car.

All the blood! How could she not have seen that? How could she have been so stupid not to have realized—

"You lying fucking bitch!" he cried out, his rage given full vent in an explosion of curses.

She spun to her left, then to her right, pulling the gun as she did, knowing she had him now, swinging the muzzle up to where she'd heard his voice coming from.

He wasn't there!

No! Somehow he'd bounded up onto the hood of the wagon, and then leaped onto the roof.

She whirled again and fired, missing his head by inches. "You're going to die like your dog!" she said coolly, squeezing the trigger as she swung the gun around . . .

He wasn't there.

He was flown from the roof, hands outstretched, coming straight for her, getting his hands around her throat, his momentum slamming her to the ground, knocking the wind out of her.

He was on top of her now, his right hand going for her gun, his left tightening around her throat. His strength was just overwhelming, and she knew instantly that she'd underestimated her opponent—he was shutting down her esophagus and she had seconds remaining to put a bullet in his head. His hand was sweaty and she was able to twist the barrel away from herself and toward his heaving torso above her. He grabbed her gun hand with blinding speed.

Crystal squeezed the trigger and died in the same instant. At the last second, Brick had found the muzzle of her gun and pressed it into the soft flesh of her belly.

The woman would never know if she'd won that final battle and that was too bad, Brick thought, rolling off her dead body, because she'd goddamn lost that life, the murderous bitch who'd run his dog down in cold blood. His Captain. His beloved old Captain. He'd wanted to avenge Captain's life with hers and by God he'd done it.

He looked into her stone dead eyes and said, "He'll get a far better funeral than you will, you worthless piece of filth. You can bet on it. No one will even know you ever lived."

He lay there for a long time, watching the pinpoint stars pop into life in the blue-black heavens above. He mourned his dog then, letting the tears just flow, rolling hot across his cheeks, but not cried in vain.

He'd avenged the life of his old friend of many years. That was all there was to say now. He'd just have to live with the rest of it.

He left her lying there, dead on the gravel, and made his way back to his house. There were no lights on for some reason. It was full dark. Why hadn't Hildy turned on the—oh Christ . . .

He bolted up the walkway, through the front door, taking the steps three at a time. Hildy's room was up on the third floor, but it took him less than a minute to reach her door at the end of the hall.

He paused a second to catch his breath.

No noise from inside. No snoring. Perhaps she'd taken one of her "sleep tranquilizers" to shut down all the pain over Captain. Not only her own grief, but what she must have imagined Brick would feel like. Poor dear Hildy, with a heart bigger than the sky.

"Hildy," he said quietly, rapping softly on her door. "Hildy, it's me. I'm home. Are you asleep?"

Nothing.

Feeling a wave of nausea rising, Brick twisted the knob and pushed the door inward.

All the lights were off, but a new moon was flooding the room.

He walked toward her, already knowing what he was going to find, but unable to just turn and walk away without at least seeing her. He had to look away from her face. The stench of blood was overpowering. He bent down on one knee, taking her hand in both of his and squeezing it before bringing it to his lips.

"Oh, Hildy, I'm so, so sorry."

How long he knelt there in the streaming moonlight, holding her cold, dead hand he didn't know. Maybe forever.

But, finally, he realized that he'd seen far more than his share of death this night. He got up, profoundly sad and weary, and walked across the wooden floor, Hildy's whole room now turned silver by the rising moon. He picked up the phone on the hall table. First he called the McLean police, then CIA. Fighting tears, he descended the stairs.

He pulled the door shut behind him.

He went out into the moonlight. Everything looks lovelier by moonlight. He crossed the small stream and went into the barn to find his shovel. It was right where he'd left it, leaning against the wall just inside the door. He took it and stepped back outside, gazing across at the lovely pale blue countryside, his eyes finally coming to rest on one of his favorite places.

In the near distance was a grassy hillock overlooking the main paddocks, and he went there now. He made his way slowly to the top, seeking the solace he knew he would find up there. The night air was cool and sweet with a perfume that couldn't be bought for any amount of money, jasmine and honeysuckle.

A single apple tree stood atop the hill, now gnarled and twisted, but it had provided all the shade his family ever needed up there . . . high summer picnics, usually . . . but the children's swing he'd hung from the same limb where his father had once hung one for him. Everything made this a place close to heaven. In spring, it was covered with wildflowers; in summer, like now, with swaying green grass that was never mown. In winter, the gentle slope of the white hill was a paradise for children with sleds.

He found a perfect place at the base of the old apple tree and shoved his spade into the ground to mark the spot.

And then he went down the hill to bring the old Captain home to his final resting place.

THIRTY-SIX

MONTE CARLO

SUNLIGHT FLOODED THE EXPANSIVE LIVING ROOM of Ambrose Congreve's two-bedroom suite. Giant crystal vases of exploding pink and white roses bloomed on every table. He assumed the suite's second bedroom was in case of flower overflow. He had been booked into the ridiculously expensive Hôtel de Paris by the KGB Travel Department at the Kremlin, under specific orders from the big man himself. This famous old white hotel, this giant wedding cake of a building, overlooked the bustling harbor and the storybook palace at Monte Carlo.

He heard a faint bell tinkling from somewhere down a long hall.

"Hullo?" he'd called out. "Who's there?"

Room Service appeared like magic before him, two elegant uniformed staffers rolling in with an immaculate white table overflowing with so much china and so many silver platters, and even more flowers, that it was hard to believe this movable feast was indeed what one received when one ordered: "Breakfast for one, please."

"I'm sorry," the famous sleuth said, baffled, "I fear there's been some kind of mistake. I only ordered breakfast for one. There's only just me, you see. Not another half dozen waiting in the wings, as it were."

"*Ah, mais oui,*" the mustachioed captain said, taking in the table with a magisterial sweep of his arm, "*C'est ça!* This is the Hôtel de Paris, monsieur! *Voilà!* Le breakfast for one!"

"Really?" Ambrose asked, lifting one of the silver domes to appraise the contents of one of the chafing dishes. "Might I find a strip of bacon or a soft-boiled egg in here somewhere?"

"Where would you like the table placed, monsieur?" the waiter asked, all smiles.

Everyone in this damn hotel had been all smiles ever since he'd checked in the afternoon prior. Congreve wasn't stupid. He knew these blinding displays of perfect-capped white teeth did not reflect his star status as an English policeman. No, no. They were a reflection of the extraordinarily deep pockets and long-reaching power of his host, President Vladimir Putin, the new tsar of all Russia.

"You like it here by the windows, perhaps? Or over there, monsieur?"

Congreve sat down for a moment and contemplated the possible location of his breakfast table. Did he want the harbor view? A view chock-full of whirling white seagulls above a sparkling turquoise sea filled with gleaming megayachts?

Or, perhaps, the lovely view landward to the gentle foothills of the Maritime Alps with Prince Rainier and Princess Grace's fairy-tale palace in the foreground? It was a pleasant quandary, and Congreve took his time deciding, puffing away on his morning pipe.

"I think just over there by those two open French doors will do nicely, overlooking the harbor please. That fresh air coming in off the sea from all these windows is most salubrious," the chief inspector said, all perfectly accented in the language of the locals.

Congreve, a former language scholar at Cambridge before becoming a copper, spoke any number of them perfectly, but his idiomatic French was impeccable, really, and he rolled it out now, just to show these snooty Frenchmen that not all Brits were bumpkins from the boonies. The smiling captain, bowing yet again, was duly impressed, he was pleased to see. He adjusted the position of the table, making a few minute silverware adjustments until it was, as they say, *parfait!*

"*Mais oui, monsieur, c'est parfait, n'est-ce pas?*"

"*C'est genial, c'est très genial,*" Congreve replied as the waiter pulled out the chair for him. "*Le petit déjeuner, c'est parfait!*"

"*L'addition, monsieur,*" the captain said, bowing as he presented the bill with such pomp it might have been an historic treaty between their two nations at the close of the Napoleonic Wars.

Congreve signed the bill without a glance at the total, knowing that, even though it shouldn't, the vast sum would make him feel slightly guilty. His host may be worth forty billion dollars, but Ambrose was still making a modest stipend from Scotland Yard.

The two waiters bowed and scraped a few more times before finally leaving him in peace.

Congreve sat, inhaled the life-giving air from the sea, and spread his huge white linen napkin across his lap. What first? He lifted a cover and saw a rasher of perfectly cooked bacon. And here, eggs Sardou, and over here? Best not to know. He chose a simple croissant, knowing it would be flaky heaven, and anointed it with creamy butter you'd never find at Tesco. He smiled, lifting the delicacy at first to his nostrils so that he might inhale that sublime—

At that precise moment, the phone rang.

"Bloody hell!" he exclaimed, returning the croissant to his plate.

He looked across vast carpeted plains of the palatial room to where the offending instrument sat atop an antique walnut writing desk. Should he bother? He knew who it was, of course. Alex Hawke, checking up on him. Damn the luck. He poured a cup of steaming black coffee and went to answer the bloody phone.

"Yes?" he said coldly, putting the receiver to his ear.

"Am I disturbing you?" Hawke said, very chipper for this hour of the morning.

"You are."

"Working?"

"Dining. It is the breakfast hour, you know. One has to eat, after all."

"Sorry. I'll ring you back."

"No, no, don't be silly, Alex. It can wait. I've got my coffee. I'm just going to plop down on this delicious silken sofa where I can be comfortable."

"How's your room, by the way? Up to snuff?"

"Light-years beyond snuff, I should say. Almost embarrassing. Marie Antoinette might even find it a bit over the top. *De trop*, as we say *en France*!"

"That's our boy Volodya. When he goes, he goes big. By the way, did you make it to the morgue last night?"

"I did indeed. Saw the victim. The autopsy, forensics, the toxicology reports, and all the rest. I'll have copies for you when I return."

"How did he look, our late general? A rather large corpse, I assume. He was a bit of a jack-the-lad with some rather expansive habits, so I understand from Volodya."

"Hmm," Ambrose considered. "Let's just be kind and say one hopes the gentleman looked a good deal better alive than he does dead. I did a cursory examination to verify what I was presented with. No ligature wounds, no obvious trauma, no signs of poison either ingested or injected. I left the morgue at ten. I spent the balance of the evening inhaling secondhand smoke and drinking tepid coffee in the chief of detectives' offices at the *Compagnie des Carabiniers*. The vaguely charming man covering the case from Interpol in Brussels was there as well. Very interesting stuff."

"Progress, one only hopes?"

"Considerable. After viewing what seemed like countless hours of the casino's CCTV security tapes, we finally saw a match for the photo we had of the Russian general among the living. He was at the *chemin de fer* table playing baccarat with the able assistance of a comely blonde who did not seem able to keep her own considerable mammary assets within the confines of her evening dress."

"I know the type."

"I bet you do. Nevertheless, the happy couple were drinking masses of champagne and looking very chummy. The relevant footage was time coded just after midnight. After they left the casino, we picked them up again on the exterior security cameras, weaving arm in arm through the car park, arriving finally at a white Roller convertible, Russian plates, probably belonging to your pal. The local constabulary provided further footage of them arriving at the Yacht Club de Monaco and going inside for a nightcap. We got them on camera at the bar, too, thank heavens. Good close-up shots of the woman, which we posted on Interpol's worldwide alert site."

"Good news?"

"Yes and no, Alex. While we were studying the morgue photos at the bureau, I received a bit of a shock. Bernard Ledoux, the Interpol chap I mentioned, got a call from his counterpart in Washington. He was informed that there had been an attempted murder last night. It took place in the suburb of McLean, Virginia, and—"

"McLean?"

"Afraid so."

"Brick? Don't tell me someone tried to assassinate Brick Kelly!"

"I'm afraid so, Alex. The good news is the female assassin did not succeed. In fact, she herself was fatally wounded during the ensuing struggle with Brick over a gun."

"And Brick himself?"

"Unharmed."

"Thank God."

"But, as a ruse to gain entry to the Kelly homestead, the woman had deliberately run down Brick's dog in the road. She killed him."

"The bitch killed Captain?"

"Yes. Poor Brick is devastated of course. But he's alive. And she is not."

"How about Jane and the children?"

"A bit of good timing there. All were visiting the grandmother in North Carolina at the time of the incident. But, sadly, Brick's housekeeper of many years was completely taken in by the woman. For her troubles, she was murdered sometime prior to Brick's arrival back at the house."

"Hildy."

"I'm sorry, Alex. I know you're very close to the whole family. But . . . had the children been home? Well, it could have been a whole lot worse. This was a ruthless assassin and anything was possible."

"Does anyone have any idea who the hell this goddamn woman was?"

"No positive identification as yet. CIA and Interpol are all over it as you can imagine. But, thank God, there is some good news coming out of all this tragedy."

"What, pray tell?" Hawke said.

"On a whim, I requested that Interpol in Washington e-mail us autopsy photos of Brick Kelly's attacker, which we compared to the casino footage."

"And?"

"We can now tell Putin we know with absolute certainty who killed his KGB general aboard the yacht *Tsar* that night at the Yacht Club de Monte Carlo harbor. Our work here, frankly, is done."

"We can leave? Who the hell was it?"

"We don't have the name yet, but we know now that the woman who tried to assassinate the CIA director and the woman who murdered the Russian general were one and the same. We'll find out soon enough who she was."

"Good work, Constable."

"I've been cogitating. Don't you find it extremely odd that a female American assassin murders a KGB general in Monte Carlo without leaving a clue and then flies all the way to Virginia to gun down the director of the CIA in cold blood?"

Hawke nodded. "Beyond odd. She's not hanging out there all on her own. She's working for someone. These were complicated operations logistically. She must have substantial infrastructure behind her. But where's the motive? And, from a political perspective, who the hell out there wants both Russian and American intelligence officers dead?"

"China?" Congreve said, giving the only logical reply. "Russia?"

"I know you're joking, Constable, but it's not that far-fetched, I can assure you."

"Possibly, it is the same group who killed your CIA friend Cam Hooker in Maine. And the CIA chief of station in Paris, Harding Torrance. And, finally, almost you yourself in Bermuda. She was also a blonde, as I recall? The one you invited aboard for dinner? Pelham told me he believed you dodged a bullet that night."

"Crystal? She had something far less unpleasant on her mind. It was Spider who wanted me dead in Bermuda, remember."

"Right. But I think this vixen and Spider were batting for the same team. We find out who Spider and Crystal were working for, we find out who's responsible for the attack on Brick and the Russian general."

"Ambrose, Spider was working solo. He had gone rogue. He was royally pissed off at the Americans. But, to my knowledge, he had no beef with the Russians. Moscow was never part of his caseload, at least to my knowledge."

"Exactly my point. None that you know of."

"Point taken, Constable."

"So, all we need here, again, is motive. Figure out who had a reason to be royally pissed off at both the Americans *and* the Russians, right?"

Hawke said, "Now, you're getting somewhere. I knew that brain of yours had to kick in sooner or later. Volodya and I had a very frank conversation at our farewell breakfast up on deck this morning. I can't wait to tell you about it."

"Tell me something. You said, 'farewell breakfast.' Does this mean we can go home now?"

"Home? You'd leave your prepaid palatial suite and all that free caviar and Cristal champagne behind? All the topless Bardot wannabes and sunburned German hausfraus strolling the beaches below your terrace?"

"Alex, you of all people know how I feel about the French."

"So, it's only the hausfraus you'll miss?"

"I'd much prefer to go sit by my glorious window and eat my cold eggs Sardou. If you'll forgive me, I'll ring off now."

"D'accord. Je m'excuse."

"Alex, you swore you'd never attempt the French language again in my presence."

"Ah, so I did, so I did. So sorry. *Je m'excuse, mon ami!*" Hawke said.

"What's next?"

"I suppose our work here is done, isn't it? I've taken the liberty of having my London office book first-class passage for you home to Bermuda through New York. Is that all right?"

"Is that all right, did you say? Alex, you know I simply cannot abide the French for one more hour. I'm not too crazy about the Russians, either."

THIRTY-SEVEN

BERMUDA

"YOU LOOK EXHAUSTED, DARLING," LADY MARS said to Ambrose, taking shelter from the rain under the porte cochere of their Bermuda home, Shadowlands.

This upon the chief inspector's late arrival in the midst of a raging tropical rainstorm. Sheets of rain and ragged lightning lit the sky as a very bedraggled Ambrose arrived on his doorstep soaked to the skin. He felt as if he were washing up ashore like some poor drowned mutt.

Diana opened wide her slender alabaster arms, and her husband dove down into their welcome like a man drowning. He was extraordinarily tired, actually. The interminable transoceanic flight from

Nice, France, to JFK on British Airways, the bloody racing between terminals to make the last connection to Bermuda, plus all the indignities and myriad miseries of modern commercial jet travel had worn him down to the bare nubs. For dinner, United had served a small cardboard box full of stale crackers called "Tapas" in an attempt at humor.

Not to mention the intense hours he'd devoted to this latest mystery. The one he called, as he had now come to think of it, "Who's Killing the Great Spies of Europe?" The facts, skimpy as they were at this point, were straightforward enough.

The mysterious woman who'd killed the Russian KGB second-in-command, and the woman who'd killed the CIA director's housekeeper during a botched plot to assassinate Brick Kelly shared the same DNA. So. What on earth was the joint motive? Whatever did those two victims possibly have in common? Didn't make a scintilla of sense, as he'd told Hawke on their way to the Nice airport early that morning.

None at all. Absurd on the face of it. Still, Hawke was counting on him to solve this thing and by God he was going to do it.

His CIA informant within the hallowed halls of Langley had promised to keep him abreast of their ongoing investigation into the murder at the Kelly horse farm in Virginia. But, so far at least, he'd not heard peep one. Ah, well, he was too tired to dwell on anything anymore. Tomorrow he'd take his English newspapers down to his semipermanent chaise longue on the pink sands of his beach and—

"I missed you so, you old plodder," Diana said, squeezing him around his waist.

"I do not plod, I streak."

"Streak inside, will you, oh mighty Demon of Deduction? You look like you need a hot cuppa, boy."

"Oh, I sorely do, Mother mine."

He paused inside the door to gather her up into his arms. He nuzzled her warm cheeks, inhaling the clean sweetness of her neck and heavenly scent of her glorious mane of chestnut hair, and privately declared himself among the very luckiest of men.

"God, it's good to be safe home to my favorite Martian," he said, knowing how she delighted in his use of the old moniker he'd had for Lady Mars since the first days of their courtship many years ago.

Diana led him down the hall and into the library and there kissed him for a very long time on the lips, pushing him down into his cushy leather armchair by the fireside. A scotch magically appeared in his hand. His beloved meerschaum pipe and his leather tobacco pouch miraculously appeared, too, and—

His wife put her hand on his weary shoulder and said, "And how was our Mr. Putin behaving himself this time? Did he take his shirt off and strut about for you and his lordship? Full of the usual blood and thunder?"

"Ah, yes, indeed he did, metaphorically, at least. It was a sight to behold, I'll tell you that much. He thinks he's going to conquer the world, that one does. He's got the bottle to think we won't raise a hand to stop him. That no one will!"

"He's a bad boy, isn't he, darling?"

"A bad boy who certainly underestimates the resolve of Britain. The prime minister and Parliament can only be pushed so far. Putin just doesn't seem to understand the fact that we will not put up with much more of this bellicosity and . . ."

Ambrose yawned mightily and let his eyes wander over to the crackling fire, trying to let go his old worries about Hawke's sentimental belief in false friendships, something that might one day be the death of him.

His wife lowered herself onto his lap and began stroking his chestnut hair. Thinning a bit on the top but still there, by heaven, sixty years young and counting.

Half an hour later Ambrose and his wife were just finishing their supper in the dining room when someone pushed in from the kitchen and said to Diana, "Sorry to disturb you, Madame. There's someone on the line who wants to speak with Mr. Congreve."

"Who is it?"

"Would not say, sir. Said he was calling on a secure line. He said to tell him it was his friend from the farm in Virginia." She did so.

"Please tell my friend I shall be right with him, won't you? I'll take it up in my office," Congreve said, getting to his feet and placing his napkin upon the table.

"Who on earth is that?" Diana said.

"Business, darling. My new secret contact inside the CIA at Langley, Virginia. This shouldn't take too long, dear. Shall I join you for coffee back in the library?"

"Of course, Ambrose. Take your time. These secure line chats do tend to stretch out a bit."

"Congreve," Ambrose said, picking up the phone in his office, the salt-smudged windows overlooking the waves crashing in the dark below.

"Sorry to call you so late."

"Not at all, not at all. What have you got for me?"

"We've been working the suspect who killed Director Kelly's housekeeper. We've come up with a name. Not a last name, unfortunately; she had a list of aliases as long as your arm. But we do have a first name she's used in multiple assassinations for you. We got it both from the director himself and the bartender at the Bristol Hotel in Paris where the hit on Harding Torrance occurred. He was the station chief in Paris, remember?"

"Certainly do. He came up with the same first name, did he, this bartender of yours?"

"He did. Said she used the name 'Crystal' while she was chatting up Torrance at the bar. And Crystal's the name the killer gave the director when he came home to find her at his farm. So, same name used on both occasions."

"Crystal? I've heard that name before. Not the kind of name you forget. Where the hell was it? Let me think. I know—wait a second—yes, it was Pelham Grenville who used it. That's right. Pelham."

"And who is he?"

"Alex Hawke's eighty-year-old butler. And one of my very closest friends, by the way."

"What was the context, sir?"

"He was recounting a story about a woman

Hawke had asked to dine aboard his yacht at the Royal Bermuda Yacht Club. A week or so ago, I believe. Pelham didn't like her on sight. He said, 'One of us smelled like a tart's handkerchief. And it was not I.'"

"Don't tell me her name was Crystal, too."

"It certainly was. Hawke pooh-poohed any notion of villainy at the time, but Pelham was absolutely certain the woman meant to do him harm. And Pelham's instincts are always reliable, even at his relatively advanced age."

"This is good news, sir. We can now triangulate her movements. And we move closer to motive. She kills a KGB officer, she attempts to kill the head of CIA, and she takes a failed shot at an MI6 officer in Bermuda into the bargain. Who the hell wants to kill everybody? May I have permission to speak with Lord Hawke about the Bermuda incident?"

"Certainly. I'll give him your name and tell him to expect your call."

"Any woman who would deliberately run down a man's dog in the street is capable of just about anything. I'd say your friend Lord Hawke dodged a rather high-caliber bullet that evening in Bermuda."

"Funny. Those are almost the precise words my friend Pelham used."

THIRTY-EIGHT

—

THE WHITE HOUSE

—

NELL SPOONER CREPT SILENTLY INTO THE SUN-filled nursery, knowing full well her young charge had been lying in his bed, wide awake, for hours. His big birthday was finally here, and she'd had an awful time of it getting him to sleep last night. But it was going to be a very long day for him, and she felt he should get all the rest he could before the big celebration.

She and Letitia Smoot, the White House social secretary, had put a tremendous amount of effort into planning the birthday party. Nell, despite the possibility of rain showers, wanted to have the celebration outside on the South Lawn. She had invited her many friends at the British Embassy and their children, and she had wanted it to be American and old-fashioned in every way. The children would get to enjoy hot dogs and hamburgers, cake, Pin the Tail on the Donkey, bobbing for apples . . . the kind of birthday that would be memorable for all the English children. And the kind Alexei had never known in the mansions of Mayfair and the Cotswolds.

Nell went to the nursery windows and peered down at the wide green lawn and surrounding gardens. Fluffy white clouds in the bluest of skies . . . a picture-perfect late summer's day. Already balloons of every color were floating among the trees. A long white table festooned with flowers and more balloons was piled high with presents for the birthday boy.

During her recent tenure working diplomatic security at the British Embassy, Nell had been exceedingly popular. Most of her friends were young mothers with two or three children roughly Alexei's age, and now she had the very great honor of being able to invite them all to a White House lawn party.

When the pastry chef in the White House kitchen had asked Alexei what kind of cake he wanted for his birthday, he replied, "Every kind of cake, sir! All mixed up together!"

"I'll do it!" the chef replied with enthusiasm (for he really did like the idea). "But I cannot guarantee what it will taste like, you know."

"It will taste like everything!" Alexei beamed. "But better, sir!"

"So it will, so it will!" the pastry chef replied,

grinning with delight. He loved a culinary challenge, and this young fellow's birthday cake certainly fell into that category.

It hadn't taken long for the little boy to win the hearts of everyone who lived and worked in the White House. The Secret Service had adopted him immediately, making him the official K-9 officer in charge of canine hydration, making sure the guard dogs' water bowls were always full. He was a well-known figure down in the kitchen, usually helping out with the tasting of fresh-made brownies and licking the chocolate chip cookie dough from a wooden spoon before the cookies went into the oven.

Many mornings, when the president took his golden retriever, Fred, for his daily constitutional around the grounds, little Alexei was holding his hand. The child had been anointed the president's honorary companion. Rosow was also deeply grateful to the child's father for his help with the troublesome Russian leader; he felt taking Alex's son under his wing for a while was the very least he could do.

The recent, and nearly successful, attempt on the life of his CIA director had the president and everyone else at 1600 on edge. Were the White House and its inhabitants soon to be on the ISIS terrorists' hit list? Many of his Secret Service officers thought they already were. So did CIA, but the president kept that confidential to avoid a panic.

After Alexei had had his bath, while Nell was getting him dressed in navy blue shorts and a freshly laundered white-and-red cowboy shirt, she noticed that his lower lip was trembling as he regarded himself in the mirror.

"Alexei, what's wrong? Don't you like your birthday shirt? I thought it's the one you picked out of your drawer last night."

"Nell, I have a question," he said, tremulously.

"And I bet I have the answer," she said, wiping away a tear rolling down his pink cheek.

"Did my daddy come home last night?"

"No, darling. He's still in France."

"Is he coming home today?"

"He'll be back very soon. And, besides, he's going to call you today, remember? At twelve noon, just before your party starts. And he's got a big surprise for your birthday. He's bringing you a present all the way from France when he comes back."

"A pony or a fire engine, that's what I asked for."

"Maybe not that big a surprise, darling."

"Is Agent Buzzcut invited to my party? The Secret Man?"

"Of course he is! Agent John Sullivan. He can't wait. He's going to be handing out the presents for you to open."

"Is my friend Robby Taylor coming to my party?"

"Of course he is!"

"What about Johnny Eding and Larry Robins? Are they both coming?"

"Absolutely! I talked to their mommies just this morning. And you know what else? The chef told me the 'all mixed-up cake' came out perfectly! He says it's the best cake anyone in the kitchen has ever tasted. And the frosting is 'everything frosting,' too! Vanilla, chocolate, strawberry, caramel . . . everything all swirled up!"

Alexei wrapped his arms around Nell and squeezed.

"I love you, Nell."

"And I love you. Now, come on. The guests will start to arrive any minute now. First we're having ice cream and cake, then you'll open your presents, then we let the games begin! Which one is your favorite game?"

"The donkey one. Oh, and Blind Man's Bluff and Mother May I, too. I like those best."

"It's going to be a wonderful birthday. Oh! The phone is ringing. Go answer it, quick. I'm sure it's your daddy."

It was.

IT WAS A WONDERFUL BIRTHDAY. THE WEATHERMAN had cooperated and the rain clouds never appeared. The hit of the day with the children had to be the "all mixed-up cake," which looked like a giant rainbow building in the shape of the Jefferson Memorial with frosted green trees all around it. All the moms wanted the recipe, and Nell just laughed and said, "Ask Alexei, it's his very own secret recipe."

Nell, Alexei, and Agent Sullivan had moved to the long table covered with presents now, and she clapped her hands to get the children's attention.

"All right, everyone, it's time for the birthday boy to open his presents!"

Moms and children gathered close around the table in the shade of the spreading trees.

Agent Buzzcut was all smiles as he surveyed the

long table. "All right, Alexei, look at all these presents. I don't see a pony in there, but it sure looks like fun. And don't forget the old birthday rule: the best things come in small packages . . ."

He handed Alexei a small package, about the size of a deck of cards. The boy dutifully opened it and it was . . . a deck of old-fashioned Bicycle playing cards. Alexei smiled at his pal Larry Robins, who was teaching him to play Go Fish.

"And next?" the Secret Man said, reaching for another gift.

"I want the *biggest* one, please!" Alexei cried, in true six-year-old fashion.

"All right, Alexei, since it's your birthday you get to choose. Is this the biggest one? Or is *this* the biggest one?"

"That one is biggest! With the blue balloon tied to it!"

"Good choice," Sullivan said, handing the big box to the birthday boy. All the presents had been prescreened by the Secret Service, of course, and he knew what was in each box. This one he was sure the boy would love. It was a radio-controlled helicopter, one with four big blades, jet black and very high-tech looking.

"Can you help me open it, Nell?" Alexei said, tearing at the wrapping paper.

"Sure," she said, undoing the ribbon on top.

"What is it, Nell?" Alexei said, looking over her shoulder as she pulled the box top away. "Let me see it!"

"I don't really know, darling. Some kind of flying machine, I think. A stealth helicopter maybe. With a remote controller. Agent Sullivan will show you how to work it."

Sullivan got the toy out of the box and set it on the table, checking to see if the controller and the toy chopper both had batteries. They did. He picked up the RC controller first.

"Okay, Alexei, here's the deal. There are two joysticks. The one on the left controls elevation, making it go up or down. The one on the right controls which way it goes. Push the up switch and then the go switch in the direction you want to fly, okay? Got it?"

"Got it, sir."

"So it's switched on. The first thing you want to do is make it go straight up. Left side switch. Then, right side, very gently, to steer it anywhere you want to go. Out over the open grass would be good. Keep away from trees, that's rule one."

Alexei picked up the controller, and all the children gathered around to watch his maiden flight.

"READY FOR TAKEOFF!" NELL SAID.

"Easy does it, skipper," Sullivan added.

"I'm ready!" the boy said, gripping the controller with his left hand, his face flushed with excitement as he lifted off and nudged the joystick forward.

The flying machine rose slowly into the air. Whoops and cheers burst forth from Alexei's little friends as he slowly maneuvered the helicopter in a clockwise and then counterclockwise direction. He seemed to have an instant feel for flying it, surprising himself as well as Nell and Agent Sullivan.

"To go straight ahead?" he said, looking at Sullivan.

"Push the right stick straight forward."

"Here we go!" he cried.

The black chopper shot forward out over the wide patch of perfect green lawn. Alexei, instead of slowing the helicopter down or reversing it, chased after it, laughing with glee as the children cried out and ran after him across the grass.

And that was when Nell saw the strange face in the crowd.

She froze, unable to speak. It was the bloated white face of Jules Szell, the Snow King, leering at her from behind a group of happily chatting mothers just arriving from the British Embassy.

Nell grabbed Sullivan's arm and he turned toward her.

"Him!" she cried, pointing him out as Szell tried to disappear behind all mothers talking under the trees. "He tried to kill Alexei in London! Russian assassin!"

Sullivan sprinted toward the would-be killer, speaking into his mike, locking the White House down as he ran, other agents appearing out of nowhere and all converging on Szell simultaneously. She heard a shrill scream as agents knocked him to the ground and covered him, his hands immediately flex-knotted behind his broad, sweat-soaked back.

Nell instinctively ran toward Alexei. She had no idea how many potential assassins had managed to bypass the vaunted White House security. The birthday boy was about fifty yards away, nearing a copse of trees, and she cried out to him as he ran, but he was lost inside the group of shouting children.

She saw the black toy rising high above him. And then, it seemed to pause. Suddenly it was diving straight toward him. "NO!" Nell screamed as Alexei looked up smiling, ducking only at the last instant to avoid being hit in the face. He was terrified because his toy machine suddenly seemed to have a mind of its own! Now it was flying at full speed around and around him, the razor-sharp blades striking his arms, the top of his head . . . blood spouted from his forehead and filled his eyes. He cried out for her . . . it was trying to hurt him!

Nell's mind was racing, knowing everything now depended on her staying in the moment, steeling herself and saving the child she loved. It was the Snow King himself, Szell, who had wreaked this fresh havoc. Alexei's toy helicopter wasn't a toy at all. It was a weapon. Meant to kill him.

She dove forward, leaping up and snatching the speeding helicopter out of midair, landing on her feet.

"Run! All of you! Get away from me! Run as far away from this thing as you can! Now!" The children ran, in a blind panic, toward their mothers.

Nell herself ran, trying in vain to stop the spinning blades that were cutting her fingers to ribbons. She took off in the opposite direction of the children, racing toward Pennsylvania Avenue. Away from Alexei, away from the terrified boys and girls, away from the bewildered ladies gathered beneath the trees. She saw Agent Sullivan sprinting toward her on an angle to intercept her, but she waved him off. She had to get this thing away from everyone before—she looked back over her shoulder.

She was nearly fifty feet away from the children now, and she breathed an instinctive sigh of relief as she looked all around her. Alexei was safe. All the children and their mothers were safe.

No one was even close to Nell Spooner. She suddenly felt so all alone. But she knew that on this day she had done her duty. And duty, after all, was what she had dedicated her life to doing. She took care of the weak, protected them from the strong, those who would do them harm. Perhaps she was just an ordinary woman. But, by God, she felt the strong heart of a warrior beating in her chest. And that is when the helicopter exploded in her hands, killing her instantly.

THIRTY-NINE

—

SIBERIA

—

COLONEL BEAUREGARD'S ARMED CONVOY chugged through the main gate of the brand-new Vulcan complex at dawn. The sky was full black with a small band of orange and pink on the eastern horizon. In the months since his first meeting with the Dark Rider he had made huge strides in construction of training facilities and dormitories for his warriors, and amassing a weapons capability that would be the envy of any world power. Vulcan was rapidly approaching the allotted number of men under arms, the training processing, and the further development of radical weaponry that they'd had before Vulcan's downfall.

His men, all prior Vulcan personnel, had been re-positioned to hot spots all over the world. Working undercover in Iraq, Iran, and Syria. Working with their new Russian comrades to counter the West in places like Cuba and Mexico . . . all in the interest of furthering Russian interests under the express direction and beneficence of Uncle Joe.

At the center of the colonel's procession was an enclosed flatbed trailer truck. It was painted with camo paint and looked harmless enough to any nosy observers. But beneath the retractable roof was a newly developed weapon system that would strike fear into the hearts of Russia's enemies. It had been developed by Vulcan scientists and engineers from plans long on the drawing board but never brought to fruition. Now the mercenaries had the nearly unlimited funding necessary to create their next generation weapons of war.

The Vulcan support forces men involved had steeled themselves for the Trans-Siberian journey. It would take them into the most desolate regions of the Siberian wastelands. It would take them all the way, but not quite, to the northern border of China, their theater of operations.

Since the colonel's official arrival in Russia, General Krakov and the KGB senior staff had proved to be most hospitable to him and his entire support staff; they had accommodated Beauregard's every demand. Thirty-thousand Vulcan troops were well-fed, well-rested, and well-equipped at the winter palace. As the Kremlin moved ever closer to a war footing with their sworn enemies in the West, he'd been invited to more and more Kremlin briefings with the highest-ranking military brass under Putin's command.

Russia had rolled into the Ukraine like a tidal wave crushing all the Kiev-led opposition with Russian tanks, troops, and combat air support. The resulting world outcry was deafening, but a week later no one in the global media even talked about it anymore. They were focused like lasers on newly arrived Russian troops massing on the borders with Estonia, Poland, and Hungary. One hundred thousand men under arms, and the number was growing every day. Russian tank battalions and armored divisions were coming up from the rear.

For the first time, the phrase "boots on the ground" was being talked about on the Sunday-morning talk shows. American boots.

As the threat of world war loomed, the American in the White House was strangely silent. The political party in opposition was screaming for his head, but he was obdurate and immutable, noncommittal in his single press conference since the Ukraine disaster. There were increasing calls for impeachment in the media and on Capitol Hill.

Looking for leadership from Washington with rising hopelessness, the British prime minister, David Cameron, was beginning to believe he'd have to go up against Putin with only Australia, New Zealand, the Germans, and a few lesser EU members backing him up. America had suddenly and mysteriously retreated from its position of world leadership. Long gone were the days when President Reagan had told the Kremlin to "Tear down this wall!"

Without American strength, the world had veered into a very dark place.

TWO WEEKS EARLIER, IN AN OFFSITE MEETING OUT-side of Moscow, Beauregard had met with General Krakov and the highest-ranking members of the Russian politburo. All such high-level meetings were held at Rus, a secret KGB dacha deep in an ancient forest.

Drive one hour due north of Moscow, sticking to the primary roads, and you will find yourself tun-neling through one of Russia's great primeval for-ests. The *Belovezhskaya Pushcha* forest, the venerated Dark Forest.

If, like Colonel Beauregard's uniformed KGB driver and the armed security man seated beside him in the front, you actually know where you're headed, you will be looking for a secondary road, unpaved and overgrown with weeds and ferns, that veers off in an easterly direction.

That road is not marked, nor will you find it on any map.

Proceed through the dense wood in an eastward direction at thirty miles per hour for exactly twenty minutes. Stop and get out of your car. There you'll see a sign. It's very easy to miss but on the right side of the road stands a larch tree. High on the trunk is a small, hand-carved red wooden arrow. It points the way to one of old Mother Russia's most closely held secrets. So secret that the name is never uttered aloud or committed to paper with ink.

On that sign is painted a single letter. R.

Rus. A massive, rambling structure, deep in the Dark Forest, was built centuries ago of Siberian larch and without the use of a single nail. Prior to the Bolshevik Revolution of 1917, the ancient hunting lodge was used by the tsars. The Russian potentates would journey there from St. Petersburg or Moscow with their courtiers and assorted hangers-on, frequently with their mistresses, to carouse, drink, and shoot. But mainly, they would drink. They shot wild boar and duck primarily, but, not infrequently, blind drunk guests would angrily shoot each other.

The rough-hewn wooden lodge, with its massive porches, stone chimneys, and great dark green shutters, is situated atop a modest hill. Rolling green lawns sweep down to a large blue lake dappled with sunlight. In late fall, the docks still boast expensive sailing yachts and speedboats. There are also a number of fishing boats, fully staffed, for those who fancy an afternoon of stalking the finny denizens of the deep; or, simply sunbathing au naturel on deck with the odd lady friend or two.

In modern times the Rus Lodge has been the exclusive haunt of high-level Communist Party leaders. More recently, Russian presidents and prime ministers had been known to visit. Boris Yeltsin loved Rus and he went there to die. Cardiovascular disease and assorted other problems brought on by his beloved "little water," Russian parlance for vodka, had finally taken their toll.

In modern times, Rus and the surrounding forests had taken on a far darker cast. No longer do drunken kings chase golden-haired nymphs across the green lawns. Today, the woods were full of heavily armed security guards, and the single incoming dirt road from the outside world had been quickly landmined after the arrival of the last attendee, the American warrior for whom the Russians all had such high hopes. He could well be the man who made all the difference in the coming global conflict.

ON AN UPPER FLOOR OF THE LODGE WAS A ROOM known as the Eagle's Star Chamber. The rough wooden walls were hidden behind acres of bloodred velvet hangings. In the center of the room, beneath a candlelit chandelier that easily weighed over a ton, was a massive round table. The table bore the scars of use and had been hand-carved in the late Middle Ages. Many had supped at this table and many had died, having suffered unbearable torments and cruelties while bound to the *"Rus Stol,"* now known to the thirty men who sat around it as the "Circle of Life."

Carved deeply and long ago into the center of this great circle of oak was the ancient Russian motto: "The Wolves Must Eat Too."

It was an exceedingly warm day in early fall. Light breezes shivered on the lake and in the surrounding trees. And though the large leaded glass windows were flung open, it was oppressively hot in the room. Colonel Beauregard swiped at his brow with his sopping linen handkerchief. Wanting to keep his wits about him for this important meeting, he had been fastidiously abstaining from sampling the contents of the cut crystal vodka decanters that were ringed around the table, one for every two attendees.

Krakov got to his feet, perspiring heavily inside his old Soviet uniform, the ceremonial attire he always donned while at the dacha regardless of the season.

"I would like to respectfully propose we warmly welcome to our table a great soldier of fortune. His name is Colonel Brett Beauregard. He has an army of exquisitely trained warriors, political assassins, and professional killers. Male, female, young, old. An *army* of them, do you hear me? With weaponry of his own design and, in many cases, far more advanced than most of the military superpowers, including our own. He is here today because of our impending offensive in the Caribbean and elsewhere in the weeks and months to come."

The heavyset man sat back down and said, "Let the record show that Brett Beauregard and his Vulcan Corporation shall be placed on the list of honored members of this tribunal."

"So moved," said the secretary and all hands went up in support of the colonel.

The ranking general then gave a brief presentation, outlining the plans for the next phase of what was now being called in the world press "Putin's Soviet Reintegration." He stated the obvious need for some sort of "distraction" to cover the coming Russian offensives in the West. And he reiterated the tribunal's motives for choosing Beauregard to provide the mother country that cover before formally giving the American the floor.

"Comrades," the colonel began, eliciting knowing smiles around the table. "My team on the ground in Tvas was humbled by your choosing us to come up with a pivotal component of Operation Sword and Shield. We have been hard at work. But what we have conceived and built is a weapon the likes of which the world has not seen before . . . I call it . . . 'Avenger.'"

A flatscreen monitor was suddenly filled with the image of a flatbed-mounted mobile launch system. The ground-to-air weapon's design was so radically unlike anything any of them had seen before, they had no idea how to react.

"Tell them what it is, Colonel," the general said, his eyes full of admiration.

"The Avenger Missile Delivery weapon is completely autonomous. It has self-contained radar and satellite mapping and geotracking. Capable of downing military aircraft from a remote location, obviously. But also sinking a destroyer. And taking out enemy spy satellites at surveillance altitudes. A one-weapon air force, manned or unmanned. Capable of covert high-speed transport to remote locations, firing, and then withdrawal. Nobody will even know Avenger was there. Any enemy satellites overhead will already have been destroyed."

There was laughter and applause around the table. One man cried out, "Let's send a few of those into Poland!"

THE INTENSE DISCUSSION OF DIVERSIONARY TACTICS wore on into the evening until the subject had been exhausted. Krakov said he would announce their decision on Colonel Beauregard's proposal the next morning. He needed to get the Kremlin in the loop. The general rose, weary, and went to the windows.

Was Putin right? Could Russia really do this? Would no one fight? Not even the Americans when pushed to the limits? Would no one obliterate his beloved Moscow in retribution? Who had the answers? He felt in his gut that Putin and his right-hand man, Uncle Joe, were leading them all down a path fraught with equal measures of opportunity and existential danger. A rocky road that could lead to a rebirth of the new Russian spirit. Or the end of Russia as he had known and loved it.

He looked to the window.

The moon was yellow through the gnarled black trees.

He whispered a silent prayer for his country.

FORTY

MIAMI

STOKELY JONES JR. HAD THE TOP DOWN ON THE GTO crossing MacArthur Causeway. Not so much for the blue sparks zinging off the wave tops to either side, or the salt air and the South Florida sunshine, as for the throaty exhaust note on his precious metallic black raspberry 1965 Pontiac GTO.

If this wasn't music to beat the blues, he didn't know what was. He downshifted to third, whipping back the shiny 8-ball atop the chromed Hurst shifter and double-clutching, just to hear the street-legal deep burble and pop of the heavily modified bored and stroked V-8.

"Sweet," Sharkey said, dark eyes straight ahead. "And street legal!"

"Ain't it just, brother?" Stoke said, looking over at him and smiling his trademark megawatt white smile at the little guy. Not that Luis Gonzales-Gonzales, a.k.a., the Sharkman, was really all that little. Besides, he was a tough guy, wiry, but wires of woven steel. But, still, when you personally tip the scales at three-hundred-plus pounds and stand over six foot seven like Stoke did, *everybody* seems little.

Sharkey, a one-armed Cubano, formerly a fishing guide down in the Keys, was Stokely's sole employee over at his small office across the water in Coral Gables. Tactics International, founded and funded by Stoke's best friend in the world, the British espionage cat named Alex Hawke, was a cover operation. They pretended to be helpful to companies planning to shift operations overseas, mostly to Latin America. But what they really did was travel to the four corners looking for bad guys and playing whoop-ass m'lady all day.

Once located, Stoke's mission was to blow their shit to hell and do it completely off the radar. His number one client, and the bane of his existence, was his partner. He was a CIA field officer, name of Harry Brock. Harry, who caught a lot of shit from Stoke for growing up in a gated golf community in Southern California, was one of those guys who was absolutely convinced he was the toughest and funniest white man alive. The fact that he was neither never seemed to occur to him. Still, if you're a small operation, pretty much running on a shoestring, the U.S. government and the CIA are pretty good clients to have on your roster.

But, hell, save that stuff for Monday. Here it

was Friday evening and they'd had a tough week at Logistics. Some enterprising young Colombians had set up a meth factory to hell and gone out in the Everglades. Los Hermanos, they called themselves, the brothers. They were hooked up with MS13, baddest of all the Latin drug gangs in the country. Pretty bad bunch of gators, Stoke had warned his man Sharkey while they were suiting up in their ass-kicking gear.

Miami Dade PD, another VIP client, had hired Tactics to go out there at night and do their dirty work for them. Go in there in the wee hours aboard two airboats with mounted .50-cals and shut those boys right down. What the local cops had failed to ascertain was that these hombres had built a damn fort out there, surrounded by barbed wire, and they had a thirty-foot-high lookout tower with a few of their own damn .50-cals mounted on top.

That he and Shark had survived that bloody and noisy rumble in the jungle was one thing. That they'd shut the operation down for good was another. To celebrate their newly extended life spans, Shark and Stoke decided to stop at their favorite watering hole, the Mark, for a couple of cold ones on the way home. He'd called his housekeeper on the cell, saying to tell his wife he'd be a little late getting home. Mama ain't happy, ain't nobody happy, rule one.

STOKE AND HIS WIFE, FANCHA, A FORMER MIAMI Beach nightclub chanteuse and now a famous torch singer with a number-one hit single, lived in a palatial Key Biscayne estate right on Biscayne Bay. Most Friday nights Mr. and Mrs. Jones invited Sharkey and his wife, Maria, over for Stoke's world-famous BBQ poolside cookout.

The Mark, short for Marker 9, was a notorious gin joint just off the causeway near the Fisher Island ferry. Once a mob spot and then a hangout for dirty cops, it was smoky and smelly maybe, but maybe that's just the way they liked it. They parked the GTO in the last available spot and made their way through the muggy tropical heat that hung over Miami. Didn't bother either of them. Stoke, born and raised on 196th Street up in Harlem, loved all of it. Heat and humidity, skeets and sunshine. Bring it.

"After you, amigo," he said, stepping aside so Shark could enter first. The kid looked good. Rocking a lime green porkpie hat and matching loafers, he rolled in on a tide of smooth. Stoke smiled. He was in the man's debt. One of the Colombian brothers in the 'Glades had gotten the drop on Stoke while he was busy shooting with a couple of the other brothers. Sharkey, who could use a fillet knife with lightning skill, had dropped the guy before he could pop a plug into Stoke's brainpan.

Stokely was about to enter the joint when his cell vibrated. He pulled it from his pocket and checked the ID. It was Fancha. She never called this number, ever, unless it was something serious.

"Hey, honey," Stoke said.

"Hey, baby," Fancha said. "You going to be late?"

"Yeah. Just stopped at the Mark to buy my coworker a cold one. Won't be long."

"I hope not. I've got a surprise waiting here for you."

"Aw, baby, don't do that to me now. Hold that thought, okay?"

"Not that kind of surprise."

"What then?" he asked, smiling, her making him wait for it.

"Alex Hawke just showed up at the door."

Stunned silence and then Stoke said, "No way! Hawke? Here? Are you kidding me?"

"You think I could make that up? He's here all right. Going to be staying a few days, too. He brought Alexei with him."

"Well, damn. Tell him I'll be there in five. Lemme go get the Sharkman before he orders for us, okay?"

"Something bad happened, Stoke. He didn't say what. But I can tell. See it in those baby blues of his. Man's in trouble, honey."

"I'll be right there."

THE GTO PULLED UP AT THE BIG WROUGHT-IRON gates of Casa Que Canta seven minutes later despite rush hour. Stoke hit the call button, identified himself, and the heavy gates swung wide. He drove up the narrow drive through a lush jungle of every kind of tropical vegetation, dense, green, and almost dripping with humidity. There were tropical birds twittering away in an old aviary near the house, many of them purchased by Fancha on her recent Latin American tour.

"You got it made, amigo," the Sharkman said. He was never able to quite register Stoke's rich and famous lifestyle as that of someone he actually knew.

"Nobody's ever got it made," Stoke said quietly. "Ever. This all goes up in smoke in a heartbeat. Everybody's hanging by a thread, you understand that?"

"Yeah. You right, brother. Sorry."

"Didn't mean to bust your balls, rocket man. I'm just worried about my friend, Alex, that's all. Hop out, we'll leave the car here at the front."

Fancha kissed him at the door and led them down a long tiled corridor to the sunny bay side of the sprawling house. Stoke paused in the doorway and saw Hawke down at the pool, swimming in the shallow end with Alexei.

"He say anything yet?"

"No. He's waiting for you, I think. You guys go put on your bathing suits. I'll go down there and tell him you're here."

"What's for dinner?"

"BBQ. It's Friday night, remember?"

"Oh, yeah. I forgot," Stoke said, and headed up the wide curving marble staircase that led to the second and third floors of the mansion. "Come on, Sharkbait, get your suit on, son! Last one in is a dead Latino."

SHARKEY AND FANCHA STAYED IN THE POOL, teaching Alexei how to play Marco Polo. Stoke and Alex Hawke took a stroll across the wide green apron of manicured grass that ran down to the white-ruffled bay. A long white dock there extended about fifty feet out into the blue water. Bobbing on her lines at the end was Stoke's speedboat, a vintage Cigarette painted a fiery red. Her name, *Lipstick*, was painted on the stern.

"Tell me," Stoke said, not looking up, but wanting to get the bad news over with.

"They're getting close," Hawke said.

"Who is?"

"The Russians. They smuggled a bomb into Alexei's White House birthday party, for God's sake! C-4 packed inside a toy helicopter. If it hadn't have been for Nell . . . Alexei would . . ."

"Nell," Stoke said. "Is she all right?"

"She's dead, Stoke. The thing exploded in her hands and blew her . . . blew her . . ."

"Don't say it. Shake it off, boss, shake it off."

"What the hell am I to do, Stoke? They killed Nell! If the two of them are not safe at the bloody *White House*? I mean—where the hell do we go?"

"Listen, boss. We're not going to let them get close ever again. No matter what it takes."

"How? How on earth do we do that? He's not safe, I'm telling you . . . he's never been safe since the day he was born. They stole his mother and now they've killed my darling Nell!"

"I know how much you loved her. And I'm working on it, Cap'n. The old Stoke ain't ever let you down yet, has he?"

"No."

"And he ain't about to start now."

Hawke turned and looked back up the sweep of close-cropped green to the pool. He could hear Alexei's distinctive laughter.

"Hear that, Stoke? That's the first time I've heard him laugh since I got back to Washington. He doesn't speak, doesn't eat. He's lost without her. And frankly, so am I."

"You want to go for a boat ride?"

"I don't really know what I want to do."

"Listen. Did you fly down here in your plane?"

"Yeah."

"From where?"

"A little strip out in Bucks County. Lumberville. Alexei and I drove there after the memorial service for Nell at St. John's this morning. He cried for most of the trip."

"Drove straight from D.C.?"

"Right."

"Who knew where you were headed?"

"No one. Not even the pilots. Not even the president or the Secret Service. I didn't tell anyone because I intended to decide on a location on the drive north. I had the pilots circle over Princeton, New Jersey, until I chose a remote field that could accommodate the Gulfstream."

"Who drove you to Princeton?"

"Me. Hired car from Hertz. Low profile. A grey Kia sedan. Random taxi here."

"So no one has a clue where you are at this exact moment. I mean, including Pelham and Ambrose Congreve. Nobody?"

"No one."

"That's a good start."

"Stoke, Nell died for my son."

"I know, I know. I am very, very sorry for your loss. She was a hero and a fine woman. And she gave her life, not only for your son, but for all those other children at the White House that day."

Hawke looked away, his eyes shining. "There was love between us. We talked about getting married. She knew that being married to me was dangerous. But how many people close to me have to die, Stoke? How many?"

They were at the end of the dock now.

"Hop in. I'll drive," Stoke said.

"Let me get the lines."

"Just get in the damn boat, boss."

Hawke climbed over the gunwale and settled into the bucket seat on the starboard side, strapped himself in. A minute later, Stoke was in the boat and cranking up the twin 400-horsepower engines.

"Hold on," Stoke said, his hand on the throttle.

"Believe me, I am holding on."

And Stoke could see, the Hawke man really was holding on. But just barely. And for his life.

FORTY-ONE

CASA QUE CANTA

"YOU WANT A NIGHTCAP, BOSS?" STOKE ASKED Hawke. Standing at the railing overlooking the wide bay lit by pinprick stars, he turned to look at his old friend. Hawke had no reply.

"You okay?" he asked Hawke.

"I will be."

"Yeah, I know that. Future tense. Present even worse. Past debatable."

Hawke smiled. A line from Congreve? He couldn't remember for the life of him.

After a sunset supper spent in the golden light of Stokely's upstairs porch, Hawke had excused himself. Had to put Alexei to bed. He'd promised Stoke he'd return, but he had spent a long time getting Alexei to sleep.

Stoke waited at the table outside, gazing at the silvery lights on Coconut Grove glimmering across the bay. Normally, it was a view that gave him a lot of pleasure, but not tonight. Tonight, for the first time in a long time, he was afraid.

Hawke was in trouble. He had a look in his eyes that Stoke couldn't quite find the right word for. And then he did. He looked . . . he looked haunted.

Fancha had given Alex two third-floor bedrooms that adjoined so the child would not feel far away from his father. After finally coaxing his son into bed, Hawke read him a story by E. B. White. It was one that the little boy never tired of hearing. *Charlotte's Web*. When, after twenty minutes, his son still couldn't go to sleep, Hawke simply sat on the edge of Alexei's bed with a hand on his shoulder, reading softly, until he finally did.

Now the two men sat outside, staring at the carpet of stars over the dark and shining bay.

"He finally go to sleep?" Stoke asked.

"Yes. Poor little guy. He's brokenhearted. It's going to take a long time for him to get over the loss of Nell. If he ever does."

"I figured that much. But listen. Alexei's safe here. Nobody knows where he is. And we've got world-class security around the clock."

"Why's that, Stoke? Don't tell me you're expecting trouble, too?"

"Somebody stalking Fancha got over the wall one night. I have a night watchman, but the guy was asleep. Stalker got all the way up into our bedroom, standing by the bed looking down at her when I woke up. Unlucky for him."

"That's when you got serious about security?"

"Damn straight. When we first got married, I upgraded the security. Cameras front and rear, bulletproof glass in every window, steel-frame doors on the ground level—nothing startling. But. All this you see and don't see now? Serious shit. I even had a sign up out at the gate said: INTRUDERS WARMLY GREETED WITH GUNFIRE.

"But that was before Fancha made me take it down. You talk about Casa Que Canta today—you talk about the House That Sings? Man, it's a fortress, boss."

Hawke looked out into the night. The windy bay, the small waves rolling ashore on Stoke's white crescent of beach.

"What about the approach from the water?"

"Armed night watchman lives on the top floor of the boathouse down there. Night-vision goggles, security cameras, heat sensors in the sand, motion detectors covering the approach from the bay out to a thousand yards."

"I wonder. Would you mind if Alexei stayed here for a while? Just until I can take him back to England? Or, a bank vault in Switzerland."

"Of course, Alex. It's safe. He's known me since he was born. And Fancha, she loves that little kid like he was her own. You see them playing together in the pool this afternoon? Man."

"Stoke, no offense to what you've already got in

place, but the president has kindly offered to provide Alexei with two DSS agents to be on duty round the clock. One's a guy I know named Chris Kopeck; works with SO14, Royal Protection Branch, who covers Prince Charles."

"Cool. What is DSS, again?"

"Diplomatic Security. You got room for all these people?"

"Look around you, boss. We got *rooms* that have rooms. Rooms nobody's ever even seen. They can stay downstairs in the boathouse. Two bedrooms, one head, and a kitchen upstairs."

"Perfect. Thank you, Sir Stokely, for your generous hospitality."

"When can they be here? These protection guys?"

"Tomorrow."

"Done. What about that nightcap?"

"Yeah," Hawke said. "Got any Gosling's rum?"

Stoke smiled. "That question is not worthy of me."

Hawke laughed. "These bloody Russians must be getting to me."

"Maybe its high time we should begin getting to them," Stoke said, dead serious.

"You know what's most worrisome, Stoke? Putin. Alexei used to be under his protection. Hell, the guy invites Congreve and me aboard his yacht for four days in the south of France. And, somehow, he knows my son is staying at the White House! What the hell? And then this human nightmare, Szell, Jules Szell, appears at Alexei's White House birth-

day party? The very same KGB assassin who tried
to poison Alexei in London. And when that failed,
the bastard follows him to Washington? How does
that happen, Stoke?"

"You think Putin's behind that? After all that's
gone down between you two during these years?
Boss, you're friends with the man, right?"

"If you'd asked me that a month ago, you'd have
gotten a different answer. Hell, I don't know anymore. Szell is a low-life renegade KGB killer. So
maybe he's off Putin's radar. Working for those
retired KGB guys who're still pissed off at us for
taking out their beloved Tsar Korsakov."

"I'm not sure anything is off that man's radar
anymore, boss. He seems to be calling the shots
worldwide these days."

"You know what, I'm starting to agree with
you. He was acting very strangely during that stay
aboard *Tsar*. Ambrose had the same reaction to him
in France. Beware the wolf, he told me."

Hawke took a deep breath and expelled it slowly.

"He wants the old USSR back, Stoke. The glory
days he remembers so fondly. And I can tell you
that he sincerely believes no one has the guts to stop
him. Not France, Germany, Britain, and certainly
not the United States of America."

"Damn. He's got that right."

"He practically admitted his primary objectives to
me. Going back to the old borders. Fairly amazing."

"It's weird all right. Good move on the White
House's part, right? Taking all those missile defense
systems away from the Poles and Czechs. Stoning

NATO back to the Stone Age. Those folks in Eastern Europe must be shitting bricks right about now. You heard Russian troops are already moving in that direction, right? War games, the Kremlin says. Ain't no game about it, way I see it."

"Worse than that. He sees a new world order. Beginning with a new European Empire with Moscow as the capitol."

"You're talking Hitler, now, boss. That's how he envisioned Berlin. *Templehof*, you remember, that was going to be Europe's airport."

"I honestly think that's how he sees himself. The new Hitler. It's that classic sociopathic narcissism run completely amok. He believes someone needs to rule the world, and he has no question but that he's the only man for the job."

"Wheels coming off the damn world, you ask me."

"That's an understatement. Listen, Stoke. I had another reason for coming to Miami. Brick Kelly at CIA is flying down tonight. He wants an offshore meeting with me first thing in the morning. Aboard a Coast Guard cutter."

"What's up with that?"

"He wants to debrief me on my visit with Putin. I'm going to tell him what my gut told me. Vladimir Putin is right on the verge of going to a world war footing and he doesn't care who knows it. Brick would like you to be there. He's got an assignment for Tactics that's apparently urgent. Black ops. You, Brock, and, ultimately, whatever local CIA resources you need. Involves travel. A nighttime insertion into an armed facility. You know the drill."

"Yeah. Where we drilling this time?"

"No idea. We'll both find out in the morning. Is Brock in jail yet or is he around these days?"

"Oh, yeah. He's around all right."

"Tell him you're meeting with his boss, Director Kelly, bright and early tomorrow morning at the U.S. Coast Guard HQ. That you thought he might want to be there so you don't bad-mouth him any more than is absolutely necessary."

"All due respect, boss, what do you need us for? I'm talking 'big picture' kind of thing."

"Somebody's going to have to figure out how to stop the newly combatant Russians before this thing spirals *completely* out of control. Brick thinks I have as good a chance at doing it as anyone. At least I've got an inside track. Maybe so. As long as you've got my back. Or standing in front of me or right by my side."

"You got that right."

"Call Harry now. Tell him to be at USCG Station Miami at 0530. Come aboard the USCG *Sentinel* at 0600. I'll be waiting for you both on board. There's a big clock in the sky and it's ticking like a goddamn doomsday bomb right now. Tell him that."

THE DAY HAD DAWNED TO LIGHT RAIN AND DRIFTING patches of fog. Aboard *Sentinel*, Brick Kelly had welcomed the attendees at a full breakfast served in the officers' wardroom. A lot of navy brass were down from Washington—some of whom Hawke knew—plus CIA, plus God knows who else. Brick would make sure Alex met whoever he needed to meet before the voyage was over.

Hawke had been trying to follow a conversation he'd been having with an elderly American admiral on his right, but the old fellow was feeling poorly and had excused himself. Hawke turned to Brick Kelly seated to his left at the wardroom table.

"I noticed we're not just swimming in circles out in the Atlantic this morning," he said to Brick.

"You noticed? Yeah. We're bound for Cuban waters. Should arrive on station any moment now."

"Any particular reason?"

"I got sat intel that a vessel I'm interested in will be departing Havana harbor today. I plan to intercept her. I need you guys to see up close and personal what we're dealing with now."

"Which is?"

"Putin has entered into a secret agreement with El Presidente, Raúl Castro, to rebuild the old supersecret Soviet spy base at Isla de Pinos, an island just off the Cuban coast. The compound was built in the 1960s to eavesdrop on U.S. communications from Miami to all points south. The largest espionage installation in the Western Hemisphere. Twenty-eight square miles. Fifteen hundred KGB and GRU military intelligence officers manning an array of antennas and electronic surveillances systems back in the day."

"Good God," Hawke said.

"Yeah."

"But hasn't that old technology been superseded by spy satellites and NSA-style eavesdropping from space?"

"Yes, precisely why I'm interested in it. Russian freighters and supply ships have been arriving and departing Havana and Isla de Pinos on a very regular basis lately. If they're not building a new spy station on that island, then what the hell are they building?"

At that moment, a young naval officer appeared at Brick's side and said, "Director, the captain asks that you and your party adjourn to the bridge. We have the target vessel in radar contact. Visual contact expected in . . . twenty minutes."

"Tell Captain Wick we'll be right there. Thank you, Lieutenant."

FORTY-TWO

AT SEA, OFF HAVANA

MOST OF THE INVITED BRASS STOOD INSIDE THE warm, dry bridge where U.S. Coast Guard captain, Mike Wick, was describing the impending operation. When Stokely Jones and Harry Brock had arrived on board, they had been quickly escorted up to the bridge to join Hawke.

A fast-moving storm front up from Jamaica had brought sudden wind gusts and rapidly dropping barometers to this region of the Caribbean. Brick Kelly and Alex Hawke, who had donned regulation USCG foul-weather gear, had stepped outside to the exposed bridge wing deck, where they could speak privately.

Both men stood in the driving rain, staring out to

sea. Both focused their attention about ten degrees off the port bow, waiting for a ghost ship to appear out of the mists. An old Russian warship descended from a war they'd thought ended fifty years ago. Hawke was peering through the fog, eyes squinted against the slanting rain. Brick had very sophisticated pairs of naval binoculars.

"So. Putin," Brick said out of the corner of his mouth. "Time to talk Putin."

"Putin. What about him? I wouldn't even know where to start."

"Five words. Any order. Don't even pause to consider. Go."

"Terrified."

"Why?"

"He's terrified that his big dream is dying, and that means so is he."

"Next."

"Delusional."

"Because?"

"He thinks he can stave off his own inevitable end through mass murder. And by taking down the world piecemeal through genocide. Hell, maybe he thinks he's Hitler. I *know* he thinks he's Napoleon. No, he's *convinced*. They've got a couple of words for it in Russia now, as I'm sure you know. They call it 'Putinism.' Nearly 90 percent approval rating. And '*Novorossiya*,' the New Russia. Compare Vlad's poll numbers with Rosow's latest numbers when you get a chance. Very enlightening."

"But with the precipitous fall of the ruble, the plummeting price of oil, the world's starting to close in on him. His people are hurting. And so is he," Brick said.

Hawke went on. "As long as he keeps feeding the citizens the line that it's all America's fault and they've been through worse and come out stronger? That their suffering is for the greater good of the motherland? He hangs in there."

"I agree. But our people see a possible regime change just over the horizon if he's not careful. And what's number three?"

"Paranoid. He thinks the wolf is at his door. He doesn't know the wolf no longer thinks he's worth eating."

"Good. Four."

"Morally bereft."

"Tell me."

"He has a new weapon capable of killing millions that is completely undetectable. A tasteless, odorless, colorless liquid explosive. He's ready to use the stuff without warning at the drop of a hat. Just because he can."

"Holy crap. And you believe him?"

"I certainly do. He gave me an eyewitness undersea demonstration off the coast of Cannes. He used a thimbleful to vaporize a huge sunken Russian freighter."

"You think he'll use this stuff on us?"

"Yes. Now that the U.S. has kowtowed to the Castro brothers and opened up relations with them, Putin's forging ahead with creating an offensive base ninety miles from Key West, for God's sake. Tell me, Brick, what's the difference between what

Putin's doing now and what Khrushchev did to Kennedy with the Cuban missile crisis?"

"No difference. Couldn't agree more. Last one. Five."

"Two words. Vicious and merciless."

"Why?"

"He seeks revenge for what he sees as Russia's humiliation by the United States. The last thing he said to me before I left for Washington was, 'You tell your American friends this, Alex. I alone possess the sole nuclear arsenal in the world that can turn all of North America into a radioactive parking lot. Give me a good enough excuse and I will not hesitate to do it.'"

"You are shitting me Alex. Holy crap!"

"Nope. He thinks there's something far worse than nuclear war, Brick. Soulless surrender of the dreams of Soviet glory. The slow and relentless decay of the Putin myth if he doesn't fight like hell against it."

"Jesus," Brick said, dropping the binoculars to his chest and using his fingertips to massage his temples. He felt like a brick wall had collapsed on him.

"Worse than your guys thought, right, Brick?"

"Somebody shoot me."

"Yeah. One piece of advice, not that you need any from me. Something my father taught me when I was still in short pants."

"Yeah?"

"Never corner a rat. He has to bite you to get out."

"Right. I'm glad I sent you over there to France to take the new tsar's temperature, Alex. All the goddamn intel in the world doesn't have one-tenth the juice of what you just told me. Do you know there are still sentient beings inside the Beltway who believe Putin bemoans the fall of Communism? Putin never gave a crap about Communism. He thought it was a joke. What he misses are the power trappings of imperial greatness."

"You got it, Brick. And—"

Three short horn blasts sounded from a speaker bolted to the underside of the overhead. Now the two men heard the captain speaking via VHF radio to an approaching vessel still hidden in the fog. A few seconds later they saw the ship's running lights fast approaching in the mist.

FORTY-THREE

THE COAST GUARD CAPTAIN'S TRANSMISSION TO the Russian warship went out over the ship's PA system.

Mike Wick said, "Vessel located position 22 degrees north, 79 degrees west, steering course bearing one-seven-zero, speed seventeen knots, this is the United States Coast Guard vessel *Sentinel* approximately two nautical miles off your starboard beam, standing by on channel 16, over."

"We read you loud and clear, Coast Guard. This is the Russian Navy vessel *Viktor Leonev*, over."

"Uh, vessel *Leonev*, this is Coast Guard, request you switch to channel 22, over."

"We're going to 22, over."

"Coast Guard standing by on 22 . . ."

"Go ahead, Coast Guard."

"*Leonev*, maintain course and speed. We are sending over a boarding party . . ."

"Negative, Coast Guard, we are a military vessel sailing under flag in international waters. We are proceeding."

"Captain, this is Captain Michael Wick, U.S. Coast Guard. I have in my hand a signed international search-and-seizure warrant for your vessel. You have two choices. We believe you are in violation of certain long-standing U.S. maritime treaties and rules of international law. Now, you can allow my men to board and search peacefully. If you are not in violation, you may proceed without delay. If you refuse my boarding order, your vessel will automatically be seized and escorted to the nearest U.S. port at Guantanamo Bay. You've got five minutes to contact Russian naval command and verify my legal right to board."

"You think he'll buy that crock of shit?" Hawke asked Kelly.

"You think he wants to start World War III all by himself?"

"I thought it already started," Hawke replied, studying the Russian warship through the binocs from stem to stern.

A moment later: "Coast Guard, this is *Leonev*. We are maintaining course and speed. We are preparing to receive your boarding party. Standing by on channel 22."

In less than a minute, an orange-and-white CG chopper rose rapidly into the air from the stern helipad, dipped its nose, and headed straight for the Russians.

Stoke's guys called themselves "Stokeland Raiders." Hardened combat veterans especially chosen for this mission by Stoke, Hawke, and Director Kelly. Mostly ex–U.S. Navy, snipers and frogmen, who'd deployed all over the Gulf region and wherever else they were needed. Many of this proud new squad were well into their late thirties or early forties; men who had remained steadfast friends with the CIA director and Stoke long after they'd all retired from the military.

Kelly and Stokely now kept every one of the Raiders' cell numbers in a pair of encrypted iPhone 6s they called the Batphones. This was the first time these men had gone into action as a unit. But something told Brick it would not be the last. Now, Brick Kelly looked at Hawke. "Stokely Jones is aboard that chopper, Alex. My guy Agent Brock is with him, too. An honorary Raider."

"I was wondering why you wanted them out here all of a sudden. What's going on, Brick?"

"Cuba, of course. Ever since we were ordered to 'normalize' relations with the Castros, I've had a lot of young Cuban CIA undercovers working construction at the spy base site. From what I hear, the Castro brothers' desire for normalcy includes them working with the Russians on a way to take down their brand-new Yankee allies without launching a missile."

"Jesus, Brick. Who the hell is running your ship? Sounds like Washington has gone down the rabbit hole."

"Who said anybody was running it?"

The Coasties' big orange H-65 helo was now hovering just above the Russian warship's stacks.

The Stokeland Raiders would now commence fast-roping down to the *Leonev*'s rainswept decks.

The first man out the door? Fast-roping down to the pitching decks of the Russian missile-cruiser?

Stokely Jones Jr.

"Stoke's still got it, hasn't he?" the director said.

"The man is a speed-burner, Brick. What else can I say?"

FORTY-FOUR

SIBERIA

THE COLONEL KNOCKED BACK A SLUG OF VODKA from his canteen, then swiped the back of his hand across his mouth. It would be dark in a few hours. The only thing separating the black sky in the west from the black earth below was a narrow ribbon of pink where the horizon should be. Standing at the side of a muddy road, he looked out across the rolling tundra, south, as far as he could see, across the last few hundred miles he had to cover.

Godforsaken hell-on-earth of a place, he thought, thoroughly sick of this endless, mindless journey to nowhere. He hadn't seen a tree in over a week. Just mile after mile of muddy dirt and skimpy patches of sedge grass frosted with ice. And the wind! Constant, always blowing, sometimes gusting to sixty miles an hour. He pulled up the hood of his bear-skin parka, just at the thought of it.

For, make no mistake about it. Siberia is, literally, *nowhere* in any language. And nowhere is fucking *cold*.

He parked his butt against the front fender of the crap Russian-made jeep. It ran okay and it had a brand-new .50-cal. machine gun mounted where the rear bench seat would be. Might come in handy someday. Beauregard jammed an unfiltered Russian cigarette in his mouth, fired up his old Zippo, and lit it. He stood there smoking and watching the chaotic scene unfolding below him with disgust.

A small army of peasants and their flyblown mules were struggling to pull his tracked command vehicle out of a deep fucking ditch full of mud, hacking through the layer of permafrost. First they'd had to clear all the rotten and broken timbers of the bridge that had given way under the weight of his command vehicle. The bridge his Russian recon map boys had assured him was crossable.

Now the convoy was going around the ravine, bumping and grinding over open ground. Two hours lost, at least, he figured.

If he wasn't so damn pissed off, he'd be laughing at the whole thing. The peasants and soldiers were whipping their mules and screaming at them to pull his behemoth out of the ditch. "Heave! Heave!" they shouted. The Russian foot soldiers were whip-ping the peasants and screaming at them, "Heave! Heave!" Screw it. The chances of either team having any success extracting his ride were slim to none.

This whole mission was beginning to look like a classic goatfuck, that is, if it wasn't one already. When your command and control goes into a ditch, it can ruin your day. The new vehicle was jam-packed with radar and tracking technology and he'd have a near impossible time completing the mission without it.

And his destination? The shining city on a hill waiting at the end of his magical wanderings in the vast Siberian wilderness? Well, it wasn't exactly Disney World, now, was it? No. It was the Chinese-Russian border, an imaginary line that ran through thousands of acres of heavy forest. Apparently there were vast shantytowns built in the depths of the forests. Home to countless thousands of Chinese who'd crossed illegally into Russia and homesteaded, all in order to harvest stolen timber and schlep it back to the Chinese lumber mills south of the border.

The situation was far too remote for the Kremlin to care about it. But the Russian peasants who'd depended on the lumber for their survival? They were forming armed militias of local peasants and attacking the Chinese settlements at night, slaughtering them in their beds with swords. The Russian fighters had all flocked to a giant of a man they called Ivan the Terrible. Guy wore two short swords at his waist and had two bandoliers of ammunition across his chest. A Heckler & Koch machine pistol in each hand. Good guy. If the colonel ran across him, he aimed to hire him.

Because, if Beauregard didn't have enough crap to

worry about, this operation he was mounting would take place in a guerrilla war zone. Think Custer and the Lakota Sioux at Little Bighorn.

Christ!

Endless days trekking beneath a brutal and unforgiving sun, wind, and rain took its toll on man and machine. Heat prostration. Overheated diesel engines. And then the torrential rains. And then the torrential mudslides that took out what passed for roads around here. He did a mental calculation of what he figured Siberian real estate would go for on the open market these days. Didn't have oil, didn't have water, didn't have grass, didn't have shit. Negative value. Except for the huge forests on the border to the south, and the valuable lumber Chinese peasants were stealing on the Russian side of the border. Any rate, you'd have to pay some poor rube a fortune to grubstake this territory.

Oh, and you haven't lived until you've had to spend a whole goddamn day going door-to-door to recruit local farmers and their mules to pull a half-million-dollar tracked vehicle out of the Siberian permafrost-impacted mud—and then sit around with your thumb up your butt until—

Beauregard hadn't even seen the old crone approaching him. She shuffled along, looking like some kind of evil Snow White character, dressed in tattered, filthy rags, long greasy grey tresses hanging down to her waist, and a huge beauty spot on the tip of her pointy nose. She was hobbling toward him, a rough carved staff in her right hand for support. She was clicking right along, kicking stones out of her path, making a beeline straight for him.

By the set of her craggy jaw and the look in her hooded black eyes, she was definitely a woman on some kind of a mission. Russians. The colonel thought, *Where do they come up with these kinds of people, for crissakes?* Centuries of some very backward inbreeding shit was the only answer he could come up with. Too much cousin humping, like they had down in Appalachia, he figured. What was that movie with the pig-oinking scene in it? *Deliverance*, that was what you had around here all right.

When the hag got to within two feet of his personal perimeter and he could smell the stench pouring off her, Beauregard raised his hand and shoved it within an inch of her face. "Stop," he said.

Apparently this was considered impolite in her social circles because she started screaming her bloody lungs out, her thin little mouth stretched wide revealing her teeth, or rather the rotted black stumps that were all that was left. He leaned back, sucked on his cancer stick, and smiled at her, waiting for her tirade to subside. When she paused to catch her breath, the colonel smiled and said, "Could you please repeat that, ma'am?"

And she did. Word for word at an even higher decibel level.

Motioning to one of the young Russians assigned to protect him, he said, "Come here, soldier." The boy raced over, snapped to attention, and saluted. He had strong eyes and enormous black bushy eyebrows.

"Yes, sir!" he said in good English.

"What's your name, partner?"

"Tolstoy, sir, Corporal Grigory Tolstoy."

"Any relation?"

"Yes, sir!"

"What's this old bitch going off about, son? I speak pretty decent Russian, and I haven't heard a word I know yet."

"Is ancient Tatar dialect, from the old Cossack days, sir. She says this is her land and that we're destroying her ditch like we destroyed her bridge. We have no right to be here. Her many sons have rifles and horses. If we don't leave now, she's going to get them to come shoot us."

"How do you destroy a ditch?" he said. But the kid just shrugged his shoulders.

"Well, that's a problem ain't it? What I'd like you to do, in the most polite way possible, is to inform her ladyship that your commanding officer, me, would like her to hightail her ugly ass out of my face and go back over that hill to whatever hole she crawled out of. You got that?"

"Sir! Yes, sir!"

"In the nicest possible way, of course."

"Of course, my colonel!"

The young boy leaned in close to the old woman so she could hear him and began speaking very quietly in her ear. Then he listened to her hoarse reply and turned to face the colonel.

"She says 'Fuck you.' And she put a curse on you. A hex that will bring your days to a quick end."

"Is that right? Well, how about that?"

A second later, with surprising strength, the hag shouted out an oath and shoved the young soldier away. Then she swung on the kid with her stout wooden staff. The kid tried to duck, but the blow was unexpected and she caught him squarely above his right ear, opening a large bloody gash. The unconscious kid went sprawling in a muddy puddle, and she began kicking him viciously in the face with her hobnailed boots.

She clearly intended to kill him.

The colonel thought about it for a couple of seconds, then pulled out his sidearm and put a neat black hole in the center of the witch's forehead. She didn't even twitch much. He looked down at her thinking the old wretch gave a whole new meaning to the phrase putting somebody out of their misery.

He stepped over her corpse and knelt to attend the young soldier, using his handkerchief to stanch the kid's blood. "I'll get a medic to clean that out and stitch it up for you," he told the wounded soldier whose eyes now fluttered open.

"Thank you, sir," he managed to say.

"You all right?"

"Just dizzy, I guess."

"Son, tell me, do you feel well enough to drive that jeep there?"

"Yes, sir. I do."

"Good. You work for me now. Get on your feet and go fetch me some troops to offload my personal gear and supplies. Take them from the command vehicle and stow them in the back of this jeep. You and I are leaving this scenic paradise forthwith and driving this jeep to the Chinese borderlands. I hear they have trees there. If I don't see a tree within the next twenty-four hours, I'm liable to shoot myself after I shoot you. Tell your captain, what's his name, Koczak, what I said. Tell him we'll be waiting for him at the exact time and coordinates we've agreed to. If he wants me, use the radio. You got all that?"

"Yes, sir. No problem finding trees in that region of Siberia."

"Good to hear. Tell Captain Koczak if he's a minute late to our rendezvous on the Chinese borderlands, his ass is mine, understood? We got ourselves a date with destiny and we can't be late."

"Understood. Sir."

"Then get your skinny ass moving, cowboy. Time to saddle up."

"Yes, sir! Will do, sir!"

The smiling young Russian soldier turned to run in search of the captain.

"Hold on a sec, Corporal Tolstoy. If they ever do manage to get my command vehicle out of that ditch? Tell them to throw that raggedy-ass old carcass there in the hole before they fill it back up. Oh, and stick some kind of cross in the ground to mark her grave. She may have been mean and ugly as sin, but I'm sure in her prime she was a fine Christian woman. Hard life out here. For anybody."

The colonel watched the still woozy corporal march away, thinking what a fool he was for not coming up with this plan hours ago. Just thinking about pitching a tent and getting a little campfire going in the deep woods cheered him right up. Let Koczak worry about getting the damn vehicle out of the ditch and getting the troops and the whole support convoy to the site on time. You want to succeed in this world, you got one option and one option only: if you're not the lead dog, you spend your whole life looking at the wrong end of the dog ahead of you.

Delegate your ass off.

The colonel allowed himself a brief smile. His capacity for resilience in the face of adversity was legendary.

"Sometimes you find yourself in the middle of nowhere," he said to a young Russian sergeant standing idly beside him. "And sometimes in the middle of nowhere you find yourself. Remember that, son."

The young soldier looked up at the American with reverent admiration and a total lack of understanding.

FORTY-FIVE

At sea, off Havana

First thing Stoke and his black-clad Raiders did aboard the *Viktor Leonev*, CCB-175, they assembled all the ship's Russian Navy officers up on the bridge and Stoke laid down the laws. How the boarding and search would be conducted. What they could expect and not expect. How the law demanded they behave during a lawful boarding. How he, Stokely Jones Jr., demanded they behave, law or no law.

The message behind his message?

Don't fuck with me. Don't fuck with my crew.

Expecting the Russian crew to be hostile, Stoke was prepared for anything. Got some dark looks and some evil eyes, but everyone kept their damn mouth shut and called him "sir" when they spoke to him through the team translator and SEAL warrior with the Florida cracker name of "Gator" Luttier. The Russian captain behaved himself too, doing as Stokely ordered: going on the PA system to inform the entire crew that they were to cooperate with the commandos now aboard and commencing a search of the vessel without hesitation.

Harry Brock and Stoke were up on the bridge along with Gator. Had an HK automatic weapon slung over his shoulder. Gator was sheer badass material, and he was just itching for some Russian dipshit to give *him* some shit.

He'd gone to the University of Florida on a football scholarship, majored in Chinese and Russian as an undergraduate, graduated from Florida law school, tried being a divorce lawyer in West Palm for a while before going to SEAL school out at Coronado, ending up as a UDT explosives specialist.

Gator had eventually tired of wading into rich people's shit, their messed-up marriages, listening to either side of their sad little stories until he just couldn't freaking take it anymore, no matter how lucrative his family law practice was becoming.

"Lieutenant White, gimme feedback," Stoke said to the Coast Guard leader in his lip mike.

"Cleared forward and amidships and heading aft. Collecting arms. No resistance," Ryan White replied. White, a former U.S. Coast Guard skipper, had driven USCG frigates before being wooed away by Hawke Industries' Marine Division to helm *Blackhawke* whenever the captain was away from the bridge. He was also a headbanger who liked to shoot bullets.

"Say your location."

"Port side, amidships, sir, on the rail."

"Thirty seconds," Stoke said, looking at Brock and Gator. "Gator, Brock, and I are coming down to finish this Easter egg hunt. You cool, Lieutenant?"

"Born cool, Skipper," White replied.

"I know that, son. Those Russkie boys start misbehaving? Just give the Stoke a shout-out."

"Aye-aye, sir!"

"Can I borrow one of your guys?"

"Aye-aye, sir!"

Stoke smiled. This new generation of hard-ass navy men showed the ones who'd gone before some respect. They knew the old Stoke had done three SEAL combat tours and honored guys who'd served in the shit and—Never mind about all that; time was a'wastin'. There was bad crap aboard this Russian rust bucket—Stoke knew it in his gut. He nodded in the direction of the two former navy guys covering the officers with their MP5s.

"Okay, you fellas got the conn. Gator, Mr. Brock, and I are taking over what's left of this search. Anybody makes a move on you, you shoot first and apologize later. Law of the sea, understand?"

"Yes, sir!" they shouted in unison.

STOKE, BROCK, GATOR, AND A LANKY KID THEY BORrowed from White named, oddly enough, Fat Jesse Saunders, a skinny blond-haired boy from Waycross, Georgia, descended the steep flight of aluminum steps down into the bowels of the ship.

Saunders was packing a double-slung submachine gun with a pistol grip he could get at in a big hurry if need be. Fat had the kind of loose-limbed confidence of someone who could make good use of any kind of weapon at all, including his hands and feet.

When they got to lowest deck and moved aft, they came to something they hadn't encountered aboard this vessel before. Stoke had borrowed a SCAR H-CQC machine gun with the short thirteen-inch barrel. "What have we here, gentlemen?" Stoke said, eyeing the two gorillas standing in front of a thick steel door.

A locked door, most likely. A locked door with two armed Russian military policemen positioned squarely in front of it, automatic weapons at port arms. Some stenciled Russian gibberish was written in red on the right-hand door, Stoke noticed. Heavy, steel doors. And the two guys were wearing Russian Army uniforms.

Army? On a naval vessel?

Gator turned to Saunders and said, "Fat?" But Saunders's gun was already up and trained on the two Russkies.

"What's the sign say, Gator? Ask them that," said Stokely. Gator asked the question in slow but sure Russian. The two guys looked at each other before one of them answered the question.

"He says this is KGB HQ aboard the vessel, sir. Their military intel unit. No admittance."

"Seriously, Gator? No admittance? Is that what he said? Well, hell. Do what you gotta do, Fat," Stoke said.

In the blink of an instant, Saunders made a

blindingly fast move forward. In one fluid motion, he leaned into the two guards, his two hands out like twin pistons, seizing both weapons and whipping them away from the Russians.

Stoke said, "Thank you kindly, Fat. Now, Gator, tell those two boys to stand aside before I perform rifle-butt dentistry on their asses."

"Yes, sir," Gator said, shouting an order. The two angry young men stood reluctantly aside.

"You see that palm plate access doohickey on the wall there, Gator? Tell one of them to put his hand on it. We're going in there."

Gator told them. They both glared back, shaking their heads in the negative.

"Tell them if they refuse again I'll cut one of their fucking hands off and do it that way."

To make his point, Stoke pulled out the assault knife sheathed on his right leg. "Tell them to open that goddamn door!"

Like magic, it was open sesame time in the KGB kingdom. Fat Saunders soon had the two military cops facedown on the deck, cuffing their wrists behind their backs.

"Gator, stay out here and keep these two boys facedown on the deck, got that?"

"Bet yo' ass."

"I don't bet. Fat, you're coming in with us."

"Wouldn't miss it for nuthin', Skipper."

Stoke stepped through the opening first. It wasn't KGB; it was storage. The ship's hold was cavernous. Lit only by a smoky blue light that swirled around like ground fog on a moonlit night. Nobody home. No personnel, no desks, no communications, nothing. He signaled his guys to follow and moved deeper into the mist.

"Shit!" Stoke cried out in the swirling mist. He felt like he was walking into a void. And then he slammed into something solid, and it startled the living bejeezus out of him.

FORTY-SIX

B ROCK WAS BY STOKELY'S SIDE IN AN INSTANT, HIS
weapon up, peering into the gloom.

"What the hell?" Brock said, waving his free
hand to clear away the swirling wisps of bluish fog.

"What is it?" Stoke said, looking around.

"It's like a damn pool hall in here," Fat an-
nounced.

"Pool hall?" Brock said, incredulous. "Did he say
it's a pool hall?"

"Damn straight," Fat said. "Pool tables, or something similar, stretching out as far as you can see in
the dark. Only there's something on top of them."

"Like what? If you say billiard balls, I'm shooting
you first," Brock said. "This is not a pool hall."

"Like a . . . I don't even know what."

"Turn your damn light on, maybe?" Stoke asked,
he and Brock moving toward Saunders.

Fat flicked his LED assault light on, and all three men looked down in amazement.

"It's like a tiny city," Fat said, bending down to peer at the table, wolf whistling his amazement. "See what I mean?

It was a large model of a city, Stoke saw now. Incredibly detailed and realistic.

He flicked a switch he'd seen on the side of the heavy table. The whole damn town suddenly lit up. Streetlights, window lights in hotels, apartments, skyscrapers. Lights on the bridges and ships in the port, even on the interstate cloverleafs. Even traffic lights sequencing through red, yellow, and green. Any kid would go nuts over this. But what the hell was it doing on a Soviet spy ship leaving Havana and headed home?

Perfectly detailed, Stoke saw, bending down to look more closely at the thing, perfect in every way, right down to the cracks in the sidewalk. Right down to the *doorknobs*. And then he noticed something else.

THE MIST HAD DIMINISHED. MAYBE THE NOW opened aft hold door behind them had sucked out a lot of the cold foggy air. But, whatever the reason, Stoke could now see similar tables stretching away to the bulkhead at the aft end of the room. Cities large and small, but all with something in common he couldn't put his finger on. Not yet, anyway.

And there was yet another steel door back there.

"Fat, do a recon on the rest of these tables. Light 'em up. See what you see. Use your GoPro camera and record everything. Look for patterns.

My bet is they are all American cities, but I may be wrong. See that large door aft? Mr. Brock and I are going back there and see what's behind it. C'mon, Harry."

They made their way through the maze of cities and stopped before twin doors of very solid-looking steel.

"Locked," Harry said.

"How do you know? You haven't tried it yet."

"You want to bet money, Harry? I recognize a locked door when I see one."

"I bet you do. With your background and all."

"What's that supposed to mean?" Stoke said.

"Nothing. I was talking to your boy Sharkey about you a while back. At the Versailles Restaurant in Little Havana."

"What about?"

"Your checkered past, that's all."

Stoke looked at him.

"Is that right? You must have found that very interesting, you with your checkered present. What did he tell you?"

"Oh, I dunno. Just that he saw one of your files one day in the office. It said you had a criminal record."

"He said that? Sharkey? My one and only employee?"

"Uh-huh. He did indeed."

Stoke looked at Brock and smiled.

"Of course I had a criminal record, you idiot. I was a criminal!"

"Well, there you go."

"Tell me. What kind of a criminal worth a shit doesn't have a record of his greatest hits to show for it?"

"Don't get defensive, Stoke."

"I'm not defensive. I'm laughing at you. Open the door, Harry. Now."

Harry grabbed one of the two handles and pulled.

"I can't."

"Why not?"

"It's locked."

"No shit, Sherlock," Stoke said. He laughed and stepped forward toward the door, brushing Brock aside with the back of his hand, a hand about the size of a Smithfield ham.

"Nothing a little Semtex can't fix," Stoke said, packing the puttylike explosive into the seam between the doors. "You might want to step your skinny white law-abiding ass back a few feet."

He stuck a fuse in the explosives, lit it, and moved away.

The Semtex blew, loud as hell in the closed space, and when the smoke cleared, the right-hand door was hanging from one hinge, revealing what looked like a large storeroom beyond.

"Can you imagine what kind of a criminal I could have been if I'd had Semtex, Harry? Back in the day?"

But Harry was already through the opened door.

"What the hell?" Harry said. He was staring at the stacks of cardboard liquor boxes lined against the wall. Some boxes had been opened, some were scattered empty around the storeroom.

Each box was filled with bottles, Stoke saw, reaching down to pull one out.

It was vodka. And not Russian vodka, which would have made at least a scintilla of sense. No, hell no, it was *German* vodka, according to the label. A Russian boat delivering German vodka to a spy listening post? No. No sense at damn all.

"Looks like vodka," Harry said, holding a bottle aloft and shaking it.

"Because it is vodka," Stoke said, taking the bottle away from him. "Now why in hell would these Russkies be carrying German booze back home from Cuba?"

"Maybe they delivered most of it to the Cubans, and stowed some of it for the trip home."

"Delivering vodka to Cuba, Harry? Really? That doesn't make any sense. Cubans don't even drink vodka. They drink Cuba libres, right, they drink sugar cane rum. And, besides that, it's not even Russian vodka. Look at this label. It says 'Made in Germany.' German vodka? Who ever heard of that?"

"Feuerwasser," Brock said, reading the name on the bottle. "What's that mean in German? You did a tour there."

"I dunno," Stoke said. "But I'm sure as hell going to ask Gator. Grab a couple more bottles and let's get out of here."

"Roger that."

"And don't say 'Roger that.' How many times do I have to tell you?"

"It's navy. Why not?"

"It's a cliché now, Harry. Tom Clancy ruined that phrase for everybody."

"So what do they say instead of 'Roger that,' then?"

Stoke started to say something but stormed out of the storeroom, muttering something unprintable under his breath. Harry, Harry, Harry.

He was anxious to get off this barge and back to the mother ship. Any of this crap he'd found in the bottom of the ship make any sense? Not to him anyway.

FORTY-SEVEN

The Chinese Borderlands

THE CAMPFIRE WAS STILL BURNING IN THE DARK heart of the forest. Night had fallen swiftly beneath the canopy of tall timber where they'd pitched camp. Above the treetops, the moon blazed in a blue-black bowl of Siberian skies studded with sharp white stars. After sunset, the temperature had dropped to near freezing, and the sounds of the dense forest were amplified by the cold. The colonel threw another log on the fire, shuddered, and suddenly went very still.

Then he bent down and picked up his automatic weapon.

"Tolstoy," Beauregard said, "you hear that?"

"Yes, sir."

"What the hell was that?"

"Wolves."

"Wolves? They got wolves in this forest?"

"They do."

"Well, the hell with them. Let's eat our supper. You're hungry, aren't you?"

"I guess I am, sure."

In the waning hours of sunlight, the colonel and Corporal Tolstoy had pitched a two-man tent over a soft cushion of pine needles, then cleared a spot for a fire to keep them warm and cook their supper. They talked little, both men exhausted from the rough passage overland to the Chinese borderlands. Both men, alone with their thoughts, ate the meal of spit-roasted chicken and cornmeal porridge in silence.

After the feast, the older man sat back, wiping the grease from his lips and jamming a cigarette in the corner of his mouth. Lighting it, he leaned back against the trunk of a mammoth evergreen and watched the sparks from the fire rise on a column of smoke and hot air. They rose high, only to disappear in the dark tangle of branches high above.

"Tolstoy," the colonel said, sitting up and tossing a chicken bone into the fire. "You hear what I'm hearing?"

"Yes."

"That's howling, I believe. I don't like wolves howling nearby."

"No one does. Especially here."

"Now, why is that, do you suppose?"

"Fear, sir. Too many Hollywood films, maybe.

The sudden leap from the shadows, the snarl, the tearing rip of those razor-sharp teeth. I don't know. But that fear is a human survival instinct."

"You trying to scare the old colonel, roughrider? Telling ghost stories around the campfire?"

"I sometimes wish they were ghost stories, Colonel."

"Meaning?"

"I grew up in Eastern Siberia, sir. Wolf attacks on remote settlements were not infrequent. Mine was attacked one night."

"How many of them?"

"Maybe two hundred, someone said. No one could believe the size of that pack. Maybe it was a number of packs that had joined forces for some reason, or just decided to work together for their own good. Maybe it was just the ominous light of a full moon overhead. Like tonight."

"Is that common? Packs hooking up like that? Attacking a village."

"Well, normally, as I said, they'll kill horses or dogs, or babies if they find one unattended. You have to understand, sir. These are animals that can crush a human skull and snap thighbones like sticks. Got a bite twice as strong as a German shepherd and that's no lie. But nothing had happened like what happened that night. Nothing. It was like a horror movie only worse. Women and children were screaming so loud you could barely hear the wolves."

"But wolves like to stay away from humans normally, right? You're saying these Siberian wolves seem to have lost their fear and . . ."

"They're not afraid of us anymore. No, sir."

"The wolves in this forest. They scare you?"

"Not yet."

"How many you figure are out there?"

"A pack, maybe."

"But it could be larger?"

"Cooperation among some wolf packs is very common. Usually, packs are small. A nuclear family with waifs and strays of some ten to twenty animals."

"You seem to know an awful lot about wolves for a young soldier, Tolstoy."

"Yes, sir, I do. Most of my village was wiped out. Torn to shreds. I'm the only one in my own family to survive. I dove into a well. The wolves knew I was down there at the bottom, a big she-wolf in particular. I could see her in the moonlight, up above at the mouth of the well, looking down at me, snarling and gnashing her teeth. Very frustrated, I'm happy to say. They can hear your heartbeat from six meters away, you know. Uncannily powerful hearing. They even judge the moment when the prey is most petrified—that's the moment they go in for the kill."

"Jesus."

"Oh, God, sir—watch out!"

Beauregard saw it happen in slow motion. The black shadows, maybe twenty, maybe more, leaping from the darkness into the light . . . circling cautiously around the perimeter of light thrown by the fire, their heads lowered, their teeth gleaming white in the firelight.

They drew closer.

The old man tried desperately to slow his heartbeat, knowing wolves can hear fear. He cradled his weapon, his finger inside the trigger guard applying gentle pressure.

"Tolstoy," he said softly. "Where's your weapon?"

"Inside the tent."

"Shit. We're going to need two weapons at least . . ."

"Yes, sir, we will."

"I need to do something, okay? These bastards have picked up our fear scent . . . Think you can make it across to the jeep? To the .50 cal.?"

"Maybe, sir."

"I won't order you to try."

"It's our only chance, Colonel. I'm fucking petrified and they know it. Look at them!"

"Wait, I'll try to distract—"

But Tolstoy was already on his feet and running for the jeep at the edge of the clearing. He got maybe twenty yards. In the blur of a second he went down, buried beneath four or five of the frenzied beasts, the boy's screams silenced as the wolves ripped him apart in chunks . . . a frenzy of blood and snapping bones.

"Leave him alone, goddamn you!" the colonel cried, leaping to his feet. He had his weapon on full auto and he cut loose on the animals attacking the young soldier. Because of the intensity of his focus he didn't see the rest of the pack. Didn't see the wolves slinking around and coming up on his blind side until it was almost too late.

"Oh, no you don't," he said to them, whirling around and eyeing the jeep's .50 cal. on the far side of the clearing. Wolves were advancing right toward him. He was now the sole focus of their attention and he knew he couldn't possibly kill them all.

On they came. Their eyes were fiery red in the firelight, their bloody teeth gleaming white with loopy saliva hanging from the jawbones. Coming for him from both sides of the campfire now, more of them than before it seemed, their heads low to the ground now. Waiting for an opening. Beauregard whipped his head around and looked behind him, seeking an escape route. Nothing but dense columns of tree trunks forming a wall behind the tent.

Nowhere to retreat, you have to advance, his military mind yelled at him.

He squeezed the trigger and started spraying lead at the startled beasts as he ran straight ahead into the fire.

"You've got me surrounded, you poor bastards!" he cried out to the encircling wolves, flames licking at his boots.

He ran right through the burning embers, straight for the jeep. In the clear at last, two of them snapped at his trousers, but he already had one foot planted inside the vehicle. He grabbed the swivel-mounted fifty and started spraying at everything that moved. He killed and killed, and still they came. More wolves emerged into the clearing, new arrivals attracted by the noise and the smell of blood and the fear. They leaped up at him and he dropped them in midair with quick bursts of concentrated fire.

And still they came.

Worried that his ammo was running out, he

grabbed his sidearm and started firing with that, too . . .

And just that quickly, it was over.

Dark humps and blood-soaked piles of dead wolves lay everywhere he looked around the campfire. He climbed down from the jeep and surveyed the scene. The ones who'd survived now slunk off back into the forest. Would they rally the troops and mount another attack?

He looked at his watch.

Another two hours till daylight. Colonel Beauregard lit a cigarette, smiled grimly in the darkness, and reloaded his weapon. In the morning he'd bury Tolstoy. Then he'd crank up the jeep and cross the border into China. Captain Koczak would meet him at the rendezvous coordinates and they'd begin deploying the Vulcan weapons system.

Meanwhile, he'd developed a taste for wolf blood. He heard some movement two or three hundred yards away. He jammed a cigarette between his lips and lit up, smoking furiously to get the nicotine rush.

"Bring it, you bastards," he said softly. "Bring it."

FORTY-EIGHT

Miami

I T WAS A DAY THAT WOULD LONG BE REMEMBERED as the calm before the storm.

"You sure you didn't forget to pack anything, boss?" Stoke said, peeking his head inside the door to Hawke's guest room.

"Just my heart," Hawke said, turning to smile at his old friend.

"Your heart?"

"A joke, Stoke. Just trying to say thanks for taking on boarders at such a tough time for Alexei. Fancha has been an absolute mother to him. Precisely what he needed, what we both needed. So, thank you, is all I'm trying to say. Thank you, Stoke, for everything you've done for us."

Stoke smiled. "You're welcome anytime, you know that. And, by the way, you picked a good time to check out, I'm telling you that, man."

"Really? Why's that?"

"Power just went out in the house. Not just this property, either. Apparently the whole damn neighborhood is without power."

"What happened?"

"Some kind of explosion is all I know. Very faint, but I heard it boom. Couple of transformers, I guess."

"Yeah, that would do it, all right. How long will the system be down?"

"Couple of hours maybe. Maybe longer. They're not really saying much on the emergency radio, which is a little weird."

"Bureaucracy, Stoke. Withholding information from the public makes petty bureaucrats feel like big shots."

"You got that right, brother."

After a lengthy visit, Hawke had no desire to wear out his welcome. And, besides, Hawke's yacht, the enormous *Blackhawke*, had arrived the night before and was now safely berthed at the Port of Miami, made fast to American soil once more.

After this was all over, Alex and his young son would take an extended world cruise, visiting random ports of call so no enemy could detect a pattern. He was going to look for the safest, most inaccessible location on the planet to stake his flag. Perhaps Switzerland. At some point, Hawke would return to his country home in England. But he had chosen to wait until final security arrangements were completed by crews from MI6 and Scotland Yard at Hawkesmoor.

On board *Blackhawke* was a fair-haired young Scotland Yard detective inspector named Tristan Walker, a highly respected officer of the Royalty Protection Branch, SO14.

Effective immediately, Detective Inspector Walker would assume the duties long held by Alexei's beloved and sadly missed Nell Spooner. *I will never forget her, Papa, not ever!* he would say every night, following his evening prayers. Hawke, who seldom showed emotion and tended to keep his deepest feelings within himself, would hug his child and say a small prayer for them now that this woman he had come to love was gone.

"YOU WANT THE TOP DOWN, ALEXEI?" STOKE asked. "Drop the boot or whatever it is you say over in England?"

"Can we, Daddy?" the boy asked his father, craning his neck around. Alex had climbed into the backseat of the beautifully restored 1965 Pontiac GTO so his son could sit up front with his hero.

"Lower away, Captain Jones!" Hawke shouted as they wound their way along the curving drive through the green jungle of lawn to the road. Casa Que Canta was located on a small island off Key Biscayne called "Low Key." It was hidden, just the way Stoke liked it. He lowered the top, and salt air flooded the interior and sunshine beamed benevolently down.

"How do you like this car?" Stoke asked his co-pilot.

"I like it, sir."

"Your daddy tried to win it from me one night in a poker game in Manila. Guess what. He lost."

"Daddy cheats," Hawke said, laughing.

"It's beautiful, sir. May I ask what kind it is?"

Hawke leaned forward between the pleated white leather seats.

"Oh, no, Alexei. Don't even get him started."

Stoke tousled the boy's shaggy black hair and said, "Pontiac GTO, son," he said. "Nineteen sixty-five vintage. Custom metallic black raspberry paint job, rolled-and-pleated hand-sewn white leather interior, bored-and-stroked V-8 mill with Edelbrock headers, full race cam, Hurst shifter . . . I'll tell you what, son, she'll blow the doors off anything you've got in the standing quarter mile and yet she's totally street legal, little brother. Street legal! What you going to say to that?"

Alexei furrowed his brow. "Golly, I hardly know what to say, Mr. Jones. I don't even know what *you* said!"

In the backseat, Hawke threw back his head and laughed out loud.

FORTY-NINE

Twenty minutes later Alex Hawke was back aboard his beloved *Blackhawke* once more. Hawke had gone up to the bridge to have a word with his new captain, an American woman named Geneva King. She wanted to discuss matters regarding their departure for Jamaica first thing next morning. And about security once they had moored in Montego Bay.

But Hawke wanted to talk to her about Cuba.

Hawke had a keen desire to get a good sense of the topography of a particular island off the south coast of Cuba that they would pass en route south. And he'd asked the captain to have sat photos, marine charts, and topographical maps printed out for him when he came aboard.

The Russians' newly rebuilt spy compound was located on a twenty-eight-square-mile island just off Cuba's southwestern coast, the Isla de Pinos. A green island in a blue sea, it was suddenly sprouting enormous white radar domes like giant mushrooms in a rainforest. Alex needed to see those charts in order to memorize the island's coastline, and to understand the geography and topography completely for future references.

Stoke and Alexei, along with the boy's black Scottie, Harry, trotting along faithfully behind, went forward to the main saloon. There they would find the Scotland Yard Royalty Protection officer, Detective Inspector Tristan Walker, waiting for them, along with his colleague, an armed bodyguard with the name of Sergeant Archie Carstairs.

Holding hands with Alexei (who was understandably nervous about meeting his new male nanny), Stokely descended a broad set of mahogany stairs to the grand saloon below. Filled with sunlight, glass on three sides with a retracting ceiling above, and boasting a shiny black ebony concert grand piano, the movie-set saloon overlooked an expanse of ship-shape teak decks and the imposing thrust of the ship's great bow.

Beyond the windows were members of the crew, all wearing sharp-creased white trousers, white sneakers, and navy polo shirts. They seemed to be moving about like a troupe in a chaotic ballet, making sure all was ready for the impending voyage south to Jamaica.

Stoke couldn't help but smile at the image Hawke had ordered embroidered on the breast of the crew's new dark blue shirts. The infamous skull and crossbones flag depicted above the vessel's name in red below. The Jolly Roger, in honor of Hawke's notorious pirate captain ancestor. He was the yacht's patron saint and namesake, the pirate who wore silver skulls woven into his great mane of a beard and whose name struck fear into the hearts of the Brethren of the Coast: the fearless and fearsome scourge of the Spanish Main, "Blackhawke" himself.

HALFWAY DOWN THE WIDE MAHOGANY STAIRCASE, Stoke saw that a tall blond man with a deep tan, pale green eyes, and very white teeth was now racing up the steps toward them with his hand outstretched. He had to be pushing fifty, but there was something incredibly youthful about him. He was wearing a white polo shirt and white shorts and seemed like a guy who got waylaid on his way to play a few quick sets of tennis.

Stoke shook his hand, liking the grip.

"Allow me to introduce myself, sir. I'm Inspector Tristan Walker, Scotland Yard," he said with gusto, pumping Stoke's hand as they all paused on the stairs. "And you must be Stokely Jones Jr.! Awfully good to meet you. I've heard so much about you. Very much an honor indeed, Sir Stokely."

Stoke smiled, liking the man already.

"Inspector, let me tell you something. If I ain't Stokely Jones? Then, we're all in big trouble. Just how many other black dudes my size you see messing around this big old stinkpot today?"

"Point well taken, indeed, sir. There would certainly appear to be little room for confusion."

"Damn right there isn't any room, because I take up most of it. One other thing, Inspector Walker, please. We'll probably be seeing a lot of each other going forward. Given your new responsibility in the family and all. So do me a favor. Don't call me 'sir.' Just call me 'Stoke,' okay? I only use that 'sir' title when I'm back in England, having tea and crumpets with the Queen at Buck House or up in Scotland at Balmoral Castle, tossing the old cricket ball around with her two grandsons. You understand what I'm saying?"

"You and Her Royal Majesty are tight, Mr. Jones?" Walker said with a flashing grin. "Ever since you and Lord Hawke saved her family up at Balmoral."

"Damn straight."

When Walker smiled, it lit up his whole face. "Stoke it is, then," he said, and he pumped the big man's hand again.

Stoke instantly felt good about this guy. He'd been worried sick about this meeting all morning long. What kind of guy this would turn out to be. How he would feel turning Alexei over to a stranger. He'd been pretty sure about one thing. That he'd know instantly whether or not this new protection officer was someone he believed might be capable of stepping into the shoes of the late great Nell Spooner. Or not.

But the inspector's large green eyes were strong and clear, and, more important, sincere. Nothing phony in his face or posture or big white smile. And his grip was very, very powerful, although you'd never guess it to look at him.

This was no nanny nursemaid at all. No, sir, this was a warrior, a former British Army Ranger captain, a man who'd won the Victoria Cross for his bravery in the face of an implacable enemy in the mountains of Afghanistan. A man who had now chosen to dedicate the rest of his life to protecting the loved ones of the Royal Family and their friends.

"Inspector, please say hello to my young friend Alexei Hawke, here. He's all excited to meet you, jumping up and down all morning. Right, Alexei?"

Alexei looked up at Stoke and grabbed his hand, puzzled, not understanding what he'd said at all.

"Alexei," the officer said, going down on his knees to look the boy in the eyes, "I am so very, very glad to meet you at last. I've heard all about you. And this is your dog, Harry, isn't it? A fine black Scottie, isn't he? Good boy, Harry, look, I've a treat for you! And here's something else, Alexei. I do believe you and Stoke know Chief Inspector Ambrose Congreve, don't you?"

His warm manner seemed to relax the little boy, and he smiled at the stranger.

"We do know him very well, sir. Mr. Congreve is my godfather. But he's more like my grandfather, really, since he's old. He's my very best friend in the whole world. Except for my friend Pelham. He's the best."

"I'm sure he is. And, I hope one day you and I will become best friends, too. Would you like that?"

"I guess so."

"Well, we will have a lot to talk about this morning. I have another friend and colleague with me named Archie Carstairs. Sergeant Carstairs will accompany us on all our many splendid adventures, Alexei. He's very happy to be meeting you and is waiting for us down there on that white sofa by the windows. See him waving? Won't you and Mr. Jones come down and say hi to Archie?"

The man stood up and waved. Since he was to be Walker's backup armed bodyguard, Stoke was pleased to see that he was a squat square of a man, very powerfully built. Walker was also armed, Stoke knew, as the Yard's protection officers all wore a pistol in the small of their backs when on duty.

"Can we go down to meet Archie, too, Uncle Stokely?" Alexei asked. Stokely smiled, took the boy's hand, and started down the steps. But at that moment, Stoke became aware of a man in a white steward's jacket racing down the wide staircase toward the three of them.

"Hullo, there, gentlemen!" the nervous young steward said, taking the steps two at a time. "Hold hard a minute, will you?"

Stoke and the inspector paused and turned to look up at the fresh-faced English steward.

"What is it, Gibbs?" Walker asked the young man.

"Yes, yes, thank you, Inspector. I'm sorry to disturb you both at this very private moment, but I am afraid Lord Hawke wishes you all three to come up to the bridge. Er, at once. He said."

"What's this all about, Gibbs?" Stoke asked, worry suddenly coloring his voice.

"Lord Hawke will tell you, sir. But . . . I'm very much afraid that there's been some kind of explosion, sir. In North Miami Beach. I'm afraid it's not good at all. A large number killed or wounded."

Stoke flashed on the column of black smoke he'd seen rising over the beaches of North Miami while they were en route to the port.

"What's the fastest route up to the bridge?" Stoke said.

"That elevator right down there at the foot of the staircase, sir. Straight to the bridge."

"Let's go."

FIFTY

$B^{\scriptstyle LACKHAWKE'S\ NEW\ SKIPPER,\ GENEVA\ KING,\ HAD}_{\scriptstyle already\ downloaded\ a\ real-time\ satellite\ photo}$
of the explosion by the time the three of them
reached the bridge. A pretty woman turned and
smiled at them. The ship's new captain was a very
attractive American woman, with dark red hair and
bright green eyes. Tall, rather stunning in her white
uniform, she stood watching the sat photos spit out
of the printer.

Suddenly, seeing Stokely Jones appear in the elevator with his son, Hawke strode across the sunlit
bridge deck to gather the little boy up into his arms.
To Alexei's enormous delight, his father lifted him
up and placed him astride his shoulders.

"And you, sir, must be Tristan Walker, unless
I'm very much mistaken," Hawke said, extending

his hand to the stranger he'd heard so many good things about.

"I am, indeed, sir," he said. "It's a very great honor to meet you, sir."

"Well," Hawke said, looking a bit anxious, "here we are. So. How are you and Alexei getting on, Tristan?"

"Very well, I would say. Would you agree, Alexei?"

"I miss Spooner, Papa," he said, burying his face from sight in his father's curly black hair.

Tristan's eyes softened ever so briefly with compassion for the bereft child now in his care. He placed his hand on the little boy's shoulder. "I'm sure you do, Alexei. We all miss Nell terribly at the Yard. Nell Spooner, in addition to being the sweetest soul alive, was a magnificent woman, a courageous woman in every way. One of my closest friends."

Alex set his son back down on the deck as he said, "Alexei, I want you to shake hands with the inspector and tell him how much you appreciate his coming along to help watch after you. Will you do that for me?"

"I suppose so, Daddy."

The little boy raised his hand, his eyes cast downward at his feet.

"Look a man straight in the eye when you shake his hand, son. Just like I've taught you. Firm grip."

"Awfully glad to meet you, sir," Alexei said, every bit as manfully as his father could wish as he put out his hand.

Stokely approached, holding sat photos in his hand. He held one up for Hawke's inspection.

"Any news on whatever the hell happened?" Hawke said, taking the picture in his hand.

"That smoke we saw in the distance on the way over here? Big explosion at Florida Power & Light. The primary Miami-Dade station."

"Bad?"

"It's gone."

"Gone?"

"Look at this sat shot taken earlier, before the thing blew sky high."

"It's a massive complex. The whole thing went up?"

"Evaporated. That's before; this shot is another satellite pass after the event."

"Jesus Christ. Obliterated. Cause?"

"Brock has been on the phone with CIA Miami. At first they thought it was electrical, because all the main transformers blew. Now, it's different. They're starting to say it's terrorists. Some FP&L employees were shot by intruders just prior to the explosion."

"How bad, Stoke?"

"Bad. All Miami is down, all Dade County. South to the Keys, north to Fort Lauderdale. The whole damn grid has gone dark, boss. And it'll take months to get it all back up and running. I hate to think of the chaos we're in for, months of darkness and no power. A nightmare for people. Big trouble. Big damn trouble, I'll tell you that for sure."

"Harry?" Hawke said, looking over at him.

"It's bad. Nobody saw this one coming. No threats. No Internet chatter, nothing. Clear out of the blue."

"Any early ideas?"

"The usual suspects. We're looking at ISIS, Cuba, AQ, homegrown terrorists, but . . ."

"But what?"

"The explosives. It was an instant controlled blast, judging from the force parameters and the look of it. But . . . my guys on-site can't find any trace of C-4, Semtex, Demex, or any satchel charges. Nothing. We don't know where to start looking at this point."

Stoke spoke up. "Harry, I think it's about time you showed him the pictures you took with your iPhone when we boarded that Russian spy boat."

"Okay. First, here's the military sat shot taken of Miami Beach very early this morning. Right before all hell broke loose. The angle from above and the composition looked vaguely familiar to me. I knew I'd seen this aerial view before. And guess what. I had. Aboard that Russian ship, believe it or not. Here's my iPhone shot."

Harry handed his cell to Hawke. The small screen displayed the scene down in the hold of the spy ship.

"Right," Hawke said. "You showed me some of these when you returned to the CG cutter. Didn't make a whole lot of sense at the time. You shot this down in the aft hold?"

"I did. In the 'billiard room' as we called it. The whole space was filled with pool-table-sized plat-forms, each one with a different model American city. They all looked sorta alike at first glance. But this one? That's Miami, all right. Including the central FP&L power station right there. Only now, it looks like this."

Hawke looked at the second, postattack photo.

"Remarkable. Scorched earth."

"There's nothing left but twisted steel. At least a square mile of blackened earth," Stoke said.

"Unbelievable, isn't it," Brock said, nodding his head. "What possible kind of explosive could cause that much destruction and not leave a trace?"

"I was just thinking about that," Hawke said, looking away and clearly concentrating.

"Stoke," Hawke said finally, "you mentioned something about another locked compartment down there."

"Yes, boss. Way in the back. Nothing much there. A couple of cases of German vodka, some of the bottles opened and half empty."

Hawke looked over at him. "I don't recall you saying anything about any vodka."

"Well, it just didn't seem all that important, boss," Stoke replied, troubled by the look in Hawke's eyes.

"I did grab a couple of bottles as souvenirs," Brock jumped in.

"You did?" Hawke said, his eyes lighting up.

"Sure did."

"Tell me you didn't drink that stuff, Harry," Hawke said sharply.

"Me? No. I only drink scotch. That stuff's rotgut, right? Jet fuel, that's all I know."

"Something like that," Hawke replied, his mind suddenly racing, putting two and two together.

"Where are those vodka bottles? Right now?"

"In my apartment. Over in Coconut Grove."

Hawke, excited, took hold of Brock's shoulder.

"Call CIA Miami, Harry. Now. Tell them about

the vodka you found when you searched the Russian ship. Tell them this is all somehow related to the power station bombing. National security priority. Tell them I said so. Got it?"

"Got it."

"And tell them not to let any agents go anywhere near those two bottles. I want the bomb squad to remove them. Under no circumstances should they break the seals of the metal screw tops until they've spoken directly to me. Do you understand the urgency in my voice, Harry?"

"Yes, sir, I believe I do."

"Get them on the phone. Now."

"A bomb squad, boss?" Stoke said. "For a couple of bottles of vodka?"

"Not exactly vodka," Hawke replied, watching Brock make the call and listening to every word he said.

FIFTY-ONE

THIRTY MINUTES LATER, HAWKE'S MOBILE RANG. He looked at the screen. It was area code 305, Miami, but routed through the primary switchboard at MI6 on the Albert Embankment in London.

"Commander Hawke," he said, after punching the button.

"Commander, I have Sentient Stormchasers in London calling. I'm going to be putting the call through to you on a secure line. It's a Miami call. CIA station there. All right if I put them through now?"

"Please."

Hawke listened for the familiar yet still mysterious echoes of whizzes and clicks from far across the sea. And then a voice.

"Commander, this is Special Agent Sheffield, Miami station, calling you on a secure line."

"Thank you. Go ahead, please, Agent Sheffield."

"We are currently located at the Miami address in Coconut Grove. We've just completed evacuating the entire neighborhood. Bomb Squad is on-site for removal."

Hawke said, "Have you found the two vodka bottles?"

"Two squad members completed a thorough search of the premises, sir. They are reporting a recent forced entry of Brock's residence and a burglary. However, electronics, TVs, computers, et cetera, were left behind. So far, we can find no trace of the two bottles of German vodka, Commander. Is Agent Brock with you?"

"He is."

"May I speak with him?"

"Certainly. Harry, here, take the phone."

Harry took the phone.

"Hello? The vodka? Yeah, right, it's there all right. Two bottles of German vodka. Has a red-and-black label with the German word *Feuerwasser*. I left them both on the stainless-steel counter next to the fridge in the kitchen. Just stuck them in among all the other hooch bottles, sir. What? Really?"

Harry handed the cell phone back to Hawke.

"He says they can't find the vodka. Seriously? Why the hell would someone knock my door down to steal a couple of bottles of vodka?"

Hawke was about to reply. He looked around at the officers and crew now on the bridge. This was his yacht, and every last soul aboard it had been vetted and revetted with MI6 background checks that went back to birth certificates, and prior generations. For some reason, at that particular moment, all that just wasn't enough.

He turned to Stokely and Brock and motioned to them to come closer. He said, "You two gents ever seen my ship's library? No? Six thousand volumes. Knowing what a big reader you are, Harry, I should think you'd find it fascinating. Couple of Danielle Steels down there I think you'd enjoy."

"Is that a slam? I am a reader. Huge fan of Danielle's. Ever read her? Phenomenal. I've read every one of her books. Twice."

Hawke just stared at him in disbelief. Nothing about the man could amaze him anymore.

"Inspector Walker, will you take my son down to the galley? The pastry chef promised to teach him how to make brownies today."

ON A LOWER DECK, HAWKE, STOKE, AND HARRY found big red leather chairs standing before the large, lozenge-shaped portholes in the library bulkheads. Hawke plucked a cigarette from the lacquered black holder on the coffee table and then offered one to Brock. A steward came by to see if he could get them anything and Hawke ordered coffee.

"So, Harry," he said, lighting up a Morland's and expelling a thick blue cloud, "this may surprise you, but I think I know who stole your hooch."

"You're kidding."

"I don't kid. How big a presence would you say the KGB have in South Florida today, Harry?"

"Hard to say. The Russian mob, as we all know, are huge in Miami these last few years. Megayacht millionaires, boy billionaires, you name it, buying up mansions everywhere. Mob's wholly infiltrated with KGB officers, you can bet on it. You remember that Russkie birthday party we blew up in South Beach? The night we met Stoke's friend 'Urine Yurin'? That whole group was the tip of the iceberg. I'd say at any given moment we've got eight or nine senior KGB operatives under surveillance down here. Why do you ask?"

"When we're done here, I want you to get your chief of station in Miami over here to the boat. Sheffield, that's his name. He and I need to have a serious discussion about your robbery this morning, Harry."

"What's up, boss?" Stoke said, hooking his columnar left leg over the arm of the chair.

"It's a long story, but I'll make it short. Putin's developed a powerful new explosive. Looks and tastes like vodka."

"The Russians blew the FP&L station, am I right, boss? Cubans or Russians or both. Maybe using this untraceable vodka stuff to do it?"

"Yeah. Firewater," Hawke said. "The name fits, all right.

"Okay," he went on, getting to his feet and pacing back and forth in front of the small fireplace. "Putin demonstrated this new stuff to me. He wanted me to see Feuerwasser in action for a reason. He wanted me to see the full reach of his global power now. Why would he do that?"

Stoke said, "Because Congreve was right. Putin was setting you up in France, man! Hell, yes, he was! He's got something major up his sleeve. He is getting ready to roll the planetary dice big-time and he sure doesn't want the Americans getting all up in his face about it. That's why. Florida Power was nothing but a threat. What he did here in Miami, he must be able to do anywhere in the world, what he's saying. He's probably already shipped out a few million cases by now. Pretty good threat."

"A don't-fuck-with-me message," Brock said, getting into it now. "Of course! That's exactly why Putin blew the power station. But this little pissant Miami explosion? Shit, ole Vladimir's just getting warmed up! My bet is he's getting ready to make his big moves in Europe. Probably moving troops across the bridge into Estonia or Poland or somewhere as we speak. Hell, he's out to rule the world, we know that. Man like that? He needs distractions to cover his actions. He's got to take the Pentagon and the White House's eyes off the damn ball before he rolls tanks and heavy artillery across sovereign borders in Eastern Europe."

Stoke said, "Yeah, blowing up Miami, London, or Los Angeles would be a pretty good distraction."

Hawke nodded. "If you'll excuse me, I've got to go back up to the bridge and have a word with the captain."

"What's up, boss?"

"I'm changing our travel plans, boys. All you buccaneers aboard this pirate ship just got a brand-new destination."

"Cuba," Harry said, giving a wolf whistle. "Setting sail for Spy Island! Hot diggity dog damn!"

Stoke said, "Calm down, Harry. We need you to

get your CIA station chief's ass over to this damn boat, right now. Boss is heading into dangerous waters here. I don't want us getting in over our heads before we know what the hell we're doing. Or informing CIA of our various theories and what the hell we plan to do about it."

"*Hooahhhh!*" Brock shouted.

"Calm down, Harry," Hawke said.

"Are you kidding? I love this shit," Harry said. He was actually jumping up and down in his chair. "I mean I *really* love it!"

Hawke and Stoke just looked at this wild man. Stoke said, "You're something else, Harry. You're like some caffeinated kid at a Midwest carny."

Harry paused midjump, his arms supporting his weight.

"Really? Excuse me all to hell, Sir Stokely. You mean like all us plainspoken grassroots types unlike you who haven't yet been knighted by the Queen?"

Stoke looked at Hawke and then back at Harry.

"*Grassroots?* That what you said, Harry? Yeah, the grass of ten thousand country clubs maybe."

Hawke laughed.

"Too bad you didn't get to drink that German hooch, Harry. You'd *really* have gotten a lot of bang for your buck there, soldier."

FIFTY-TWO

The Chinese Borderlands

Waking after a restless night, Colonel Brett Beauregard rose from his cot and ventured outside the tent and into the clearing. There, he added some wood to the still-glowing embers of the campfire that had probably saved his life the night before. Not until he bent to pick up the first piece of fallen timber did he see he still had his assault knife clenched in his hand. He'd realized his MP5 would be useless if the beasts got inside his tent while he was asleep. That knife would be his only chance at survival. Or so he had reassured himself, drifting off at some unholy hour.

The damp, deep forest air outside the tent was deeply cold. He was stiff as a board, having barely slept a wink all night. The goddamn howling in the wee small hours! The wolves, he imagined, had been teasing him, playing with him by making noises close by one minute, retreating deeper into the forest the next.

He swung his long legs over a fallen timber, sat down, and looked at his watch, a relic from his days of glory. A Rolex Daytona he'd bought in Lucerne. Those were the days. Fat Rolodexes and fat Rolexes and a seat at the table with the Big Dogs.

It was nearly 0600.

No time to dillydally thinking about what used to be.

After three cups of piping black coffee and two hard biscuits, he went about the surprisingly emotional business of digging Corporal Tolstoy's grave. He had a good U.S. Army camp shovel and he made short work of the roots and stones and the ice-hard soil. Before going to sleep, he had gathered up what remained of the young soldier. He carefully wrapped his remains in a dark green tarp. Now, he placed the boy at the bottom of the fresh grave. Saying a prayer over the corpse, he began to shovel the dirt.

A quarter of an hour later, he'd packed up camp. His jeep was following the muddy, deeply rutted timber road shown on his map. A winding river that had no name snaked through woods and meadows toward his rendezvous with Captain Koczak. They were to meet at 0800 in the foothills of a mountain range located a good fifty miles to the south. Fifty miles on the wrong side of the Chinese borderlands. The Chinese side.

The seldom used unpaved road was rough and

jarring, and Beauregard had to mind the twisty trail
lest he put the jeep on the wrong side of the river-
bank. He was going far too fast for conditions, he
knew, but he'd overslept and he had a reputation for
never being late for a military rendezvous, and this
was no time to start.

He careened over an old covered wooden bridge
and crossed into China. Then he drove exactly fifty-
three miles deeper into the blasted wasteland that
was northern China. A few minutes later, his overheated jeep crested a stony hilltop. He saw his team
spread out down below. They were already pitching
camp and establishing a defensive perimeter to keep
out Chinese raiders looking for Russians to kill.

In the center of the concertina fence line was his
command-and-control vehicle. God only knows
how the boys had extracted it from the runoff
ditch. But they had, and he accelerated down the
hill toward them, happy to be back among his men,
his fighters, once more. He saw the Russian captain
huddled with a few of his men outside the newly
pitched field operations tent. Koczak huddled over
the map table, studying their escape route once the
mission was accomplished.

"Welcome, Colonel!" he said, not looking up.
"We got your e-mail about poor Tolstoy. We are
only thankful that you survived the vicious wolf
attack."

"Captain Koczak, good morning! How long until
the Avenger radar is operational?"

The captain whipped his head around and said,
"Avenger Team SAM is saying we need three hours,
Colonel." The two men had an uneasy peace. The

seasoned Russian Army officer resented having to report to an American mercenary.

"Look at your watch, Captain. Inform them they've got two."

"Yes, sir."

"We have system power up? Are the Avenger generators online?"

"Soon."

"Now."

"But of course, Colonel. I will order them to double their efforts."

Beau looked up at the broad expanse of clear morning sky, noting the position of the sun. And then at his watch. They would be ready, all right, come what may. He knew there were roving bands of heavily armed Chinese peasant militias carrying bazookas and mortars. Like the Huns, they preyed on the weak and lost. Russian peasants who unwittingly crossed the border into China and made camp for a few nights had zero chance of survival should they fall prey to the vicious marauders from the mountains.

The colonel had surrounded the Avenger launch site with a steel cordon of heavily armed soldiers with orders to shoot on sight anyone coming within a thousand yards of his operation. Two people had been shot and killed a little after daybreak, after straying inside the colonel's no-man's-land, the captain had informed him. They turned out to be two starving women who had been scrounging the barren land in search of food.

He ordered that the corpses be removed from where they had fallen and given a proper burial.

AND LESS THAN AN HOUR LATER, THEY INFORMED
the colonel that all generators were online, all offensive combat systems were powered up and running. Team Avenger, along with their Russian
Spetsnaz "advisors," were ready to execute the mission. Spetsnaz had long been the umbrella term for
all Russian special purposes forces. These were elite
units operating under the command of the GRU, or
Main Intelligence Directorate, Russia's largest foreign intelligence agency. The two Spetsnaz techni-
cians, who had designed, maintained, and prepared
to unleash the American Avenger system weapons
control were seated in the tracking cockpit of the
tracked SAM carrier. The Dark Rider had demanded in a recent memo that one of the Spetsnaz
officers must pull the trigger once the target had
been acquired.

Avenger had been developed at Vulcan's Port
Arthur, Texas, weapons lab; it was a highly modified version of the truck-mounted Buk Russian missile system. The design and implementation and
the combined Russian and American mercenary
warfare training teams had been led by the colonel
himself.

The target aircraft, Beauregard knew, would be
traveling at roughly 965 kph, or 600 miles per hour.
It was now flying at a mandated altitude of 33,000
feet at a heading of 180 degrees, SE.

The old Russian SA-11 Buk surface-to-air system,
and likewise the newer Avenger, were find-and-
follow systems. The colonel's new launcher, though,
was a vastly more sophisticated variant of the much
older design. It was designed to track a target with

radar long before interception, and then throughout the flight of the missile until it detonated.

Once launched, the target's radar data were transmitted continuously to the missile, guiding it toward the target. Avenger could find and follow targets at altitudes up to 70,000 feet. But it was not without its drawbacks. For instance, it couldn't distinguish between a military transport plane and a large passenger aircraft, or even a heavy bomber. The team Beauregard had put together knew only the coordinates of the target and the approximate time the airplane would be within range.

The eighteen-foot Avenger air defense missile carried a high-explosive warhead that would detonate, not upon impact, but within a preset distance from the moving target. A blast field of bolt-sized shrapnel would perforate the engine nacelles, the cockpit, the entire fuselage, causing the aircraft and anyone aboard to simply disintegrate in midair. However successful the Avenger was, the results on the ground were not going to be very pretty. Death rarely was.

The colonel looked up at the towering blue skies and donned his headset. He and the rest of the men scanning the heavens through powerful telescopes did not have long to wait.

Six silent minutes had ticked off the countdown timer display when a voice cracked the stillness.

"Target heat signature acquired, sir," the Spetsnaz commander said in his headphones. "Radar tracking initiated . . . and, uh . . . yes . . . we now have radar lock, sir."

"Radar lock. Roger that," Beauregard said. He

could see the crew inside the plexi-bubble cockpit high atop the tracked carrier, both giving him a thumbs-up. The entire bubble and its occupants were now swiveling in a clockwise direction as they tracked the invisible target high above.

He heard a scratchy noise in his headphones, and then this: "Target flying at 37,000, range is 90.5 nautical miles uprange and closing. All missile launch and radar component systems are a go. And . . . we are now approaching optimum launch parameters, sir."

The colonel replied, "Thirty-seven thousand altitude at 40.5 miles and tracking, roger."

"Avenger missile is armed . . ."

Beauregard raised his binoculars even though there was nothing visible at that altitude and said, "Missile armed, roger."

He suddenly heard the launch commander say, "And . . . on my mark . . . and . . . Mark. Five . . . four . . . three . . . two . . . ONE! Launch sequence initiated . . . and . . . *Launch!* Avenger is away . . . onboard missile systems now tracking target . . . and . . . okay, we are approaching optimum detonation parameters . . . looking . . . uh . . . looking good . . . climbing through 10,000 . . . 15,000 . . . our airspeed is maxed at Mach 4.6 . . . missile climbing through 20,000 feet . . . 25,000 . . . 30,000 feet now . . . we, uh . . . we have critical . . ."

A brilliant flash of white light exploded in the skies almost directly above the colonel's head. He looked up at the sound of an enormous *c-r-a-a-a-ck* from on high.

Then he heard Captain Koczak screaming.

Debris from the target was thudding into the rocky desert just shy of the mountains surrounding them.

ALMIGHTY GOD, THE COLONEL THOUGHT, WHAT *have I done?*

He ran ahead a thousand yards toward the spot where a giant piece of engine nacelle had just impacted the ground. Captain Koczak was right on his heels. Within minutes the two men were standing just outside a vast and growing debris field. But what they saw next shook Beauregard to the core. It was raining people. Bodies, and pieces of bodies, were plummeting from the sky . . . even severed heads thudding to earth all around him. Bodies fell, still trapped inside their seats. Luggage, clothing, newspapers, a Raggedy Ann doll . . . it was hailing death.

Captain Koczak looked away, grey and stricken, as two small corpses, children, landed within a hundred feet of his position. By some miracle, they were still holding hands. The Russian officer clearly had no idea what was happening now. Or even how to assimilate this civilian human carnage into what they had all been told was to be a strictly military mission.

The captain and all his men had been led to believe they were taking down a military transport plane. And the colonel as well had been led down that same fabricated road himself.

"Good God, Colonel!" Koczak cried out. "There's been a terrible mistake! It's a fucking passenger plane, Colonel! We've just shot down a civilian airliner!"

Beauregard remained silent. He watched the still-flaming engines and torn wings full of jet fuel as they slammed into the mountains a half mile away, burning every tree and bush in sight, scorching the earth black.

"Colonel, you need to see this," a young soldier said.

One of the troops had approached the colonel. He had a charred piece of the disintegrated A-320's fuselage in his hand. It was pockmarked with jagged holes that Beauregard recognized as damage inflicted by high-energy particles. In other words, shrapnel from the warhead of the Avenger missile.

Emblazoned on the lower right-hand corner of the plate-sized fuselage piece he held in his hand was a red, blue, and white emblem. The flag of the Russian Federation! Beauregard went rigid at the sight of it.

He'd just shot down a Russian passenger plane.

Uncle Joe had fucking lied to him.

Since the very inception of this mission, and all the subsequent training of his Vulcan crew and battle support troops, the colonel had been led to believe he was tasked with bringing down a Chinese air force military transport carrying troops en route to Beijing. But he had not done that. No, no. He had not done that at all.

Hell, it was an Aeroflot jetliner, the flagship carrier of the Russian Federation, for fuck's sake. Russians shooting down Russian passenger planes? Way beyond the pale, even for a man who had seen it all. This was a KGB black op of the very blackest persuasion. Why in God's holy name were the Russian secret police now committing mass murder against their own citizens? Beauregard had done a lot of very bad things in his life, but this nightmare was indisputably evil.

He walked away from the Vulcan site in a fury, fists clenched, shaking his head in disbelief, storming across the blood-soaked ground toward his mud-spattered jeep. He wanted to be alone. He climbed in and sat behind the wheel, pulling out his cigarettes and lighting one.

He saw Koczak striding angrily toward him. He looked like he felt he'd been betrayed by the colonel himself. But then the captain saw the look on Beauregard's grief-stricken face, stopped abruptly, turned and walked away. He had seen that the American was in shock, clearly just as shaken about what had transpired as were he and his men.

Beauregard sat there in that open jeep for a long time. Preparations to depart were almost complete. He thought back to his initial meeting with Uncle Joe, the so-called Dark Rider, in his tower office at the winter palace, parsing their entire conversation, word for word. He had a knack for remembering conversations, a mental vault where he stored the valuable ones. He'd made no mistake. Uncle Joe, the very spooky reincarnation of Joseph Stalin, and God knows how many of his new employers, namely, the freaking Kremlin, had duped him. Set him up and played him like a freaking patsy right from the bloody beginning. Betrayed his trust, like many another client had done before them, in the bad old days.

He'd believed he was making a comeback here in Russia. Put all his foolish mistakes and misplaced confidences behind him. And *yet*. And yet, here he was, thrown right back under the goddamn bus again. The one place he'd sworn he'd never find himself again.

Fuck.

Had the whole damn world suddenly gone crazy?

What the hell was going on?

FIFTY-THREE

THE OVAL OFFICE

THE PRESIDENT OF THE UNITED STATES WAS IN his office, alone with his thoughts. The barrage of worries that had buffeted him all year long was not mitigated by the Washington weather. A hard rain beat against the windowpanes. It seemed to Rosow that it had been raining for months. Even now, heavyweight thunderclouds were coming out of their four corners and sparring in the skies above the White House; jagged spears of bright white lightning appeared to strike closer and closer still to the storm-whipped bushes out in the Rose Garden.

He let a quiet sigh escape his lips, then turned away from the windows and opened the center drawer in the Resolute desk. Pulling out a crumpled pack of Marlboro Reds, he struck a match, and lit one up. The sharp nicotine bite was instantaneous, and he drew the smoke deeply into his lungs. Oh, yeah. That was definitely better.

Nicotine and caffeine were the only ways the besieged president could manage the stress these days. One wave of crises after another, it seemed, each one roaring toward the shoreline almost before its predecessor had a chance to begin to recede.

He certainly couldn't play golf during these dark days. No more buddy-boy foursomes at Congressional, not after the media beating he'd taken during his latest summer golf vacation on Nantucket earlier that year. Christ, they'd killed him. Nothing left to do now but hunker down, ride out the storm, and—

His door was pushed inward. His long-suffering secretary, Maura Murphy, also under siege, stuck her head tentatively inside the door.

"They're here for you, Mr. President," Maura said, somewhat nervously. She knew trouble when she saw it. And, from the overheard whispers among those waiting out in the hallway, she knew one thing. This meeting was not going to be easy for the boss. She'd long feared for his health—now she feared for his sanity. He'd made a brave start, tried his best, but now the world had conspired to kill him.

"Already, Murph?" he said, glancing at his watch.

"It's just gone ten, sir," she said in her clipped upper-class British accent.

"You're right. Show them in, please, Maura."

She said over her shoulder, "Gentlemen, the president will see you now."

The president, seated behind the famous Resolute desk, rose to his feet and stiffened his spine. He'd been dreading this morning's first scheduled appointment all week. *All you have to do is get through it*, he reminded himself. *Just get through it. And move forward.*

He stood there smiling warmly and watched them enter.

First through the door was his CIA director, Brick Kelly. Next, the chairman of the Joint Chiefs, Admiral Charlie Moore. Then, in quick succession, the new secretary of state and his old Florida golf buddy, Will Matthews, and the visiting director of the British intelligence agency MI6, a tough old bird named Sir David Trulove.

The president smiled broadly at his colleagues' solemn entrance and went around his desk to greet them all. Once everyone had been seated, and the steward had served coffee and poured tea for Sir David, the president took the big winged chair to the right of the fireplace and the famous porthole portrait of General George Washington hanging beside it.

"Well, gentlemen, let's get down to business. I know you've all got a lot on your minds, so let's hear it. Brick? You look bright-eyed and chipper this morning. Why don't you go first?"

Director Kelly had had a lot of coffee that morning and his brain was humming. He leaned forward, putting both hands on his knees and waiting until he was sure the commander in chief was giving him his full and undivided attention. Kelly began.

"Thank you, Mr. President. We'll try not to take too much of your time today. I hope you don't mind if I attempt to summarize the concerns of the group? Might be easier, sir."

"Absolutely. Everybody okay with that?" the president said affably.

Everyone nodded in the affirmative.

"All right, then. Your meeting, Brick. What's up, guys?"

Brick stood up, took a quick look at his colleagues, squared his shoulders, and said, "Mr. President. It may come as no surprise to you to learn that we here in this room find ourselves deeply troubled. We've lost our way. As a nation. All of us. We believe the whole world is coming down around our ears. We simply cannot continue to hide in the shadows hoping that all this will go away."

"Excuse me. All this?"

"With respect, sir, yes, *all this*. Allow me to elaborate in broad brushstrokes, the status quo. Russian-backed troops have now taken the capital of Kiev. When all of Ukraine falls, and it soon will, Putin will quickly move to reabsorb it into the renascent empire we at Langley now call 'Soviet Union II.' Even as we speak, Russian T-90 tanks, armored divisions, and ground troops are massing preparatory to a surge across the bridge over the Narva River that marks the Estonian-Russian border. Resistance and bloodshed around the capital of Tallinn will be heavy, but futile. The prime minister of Estonia, your friend, Taavi Roivas, and his military command are hunkered down for a fight . . . but they are extremely anxious for a strong signal of support from this office."

"I'm not unaware of Russian aggression toward its neighbors, Brick."

"I understand that, sir. Here's my point. What we're now facing resembles, to me at any rate, the domino theory in Southeast Asia back in the 1970s, Mr. President. And what we believed then was that once one domino tile toppled, the other tiles in the region would soon follow. That's why we at CIA have been monitoring Estonia so closely since the fall of Crimea and most likely the Ukraine. Continue to sit on our hands and a single bridge is all that stands between one of the great democracies and horrendous bloodshed. I will state the obvious. Every one of our allies in Eastern Europe is now feeling Russian heat. Poland, the Czechs, and all the rest are very nervous about our response here . . . if there even is one."

"With respect, Brick, I am not the one generating the heat. The heat these capitals are feeling is coming from the Kremlin, not this White House. Let me be clear. Americans know this. They know that no one is more passionate about the right of sovereign nations to remain free than I. Do we understand each other?"

"Unfortunately, I'm quite sure we do, Mr. President," Kelly said, and sat down.

Admiral Moore leaned forward, lasering in on the president.

"With all due respect, Mr. President. This administration began by betraying existing American commitments to Poland and the Czech Republic. Withdrawing their missile defenses as a sop to

Putin, from whom we got absolutely nothing. And leaving our allies and vulnerable borders unprotected. Followed by undermining Israel's position in the Middle East. Basically throwing them to the wolves and courting our worst enemies, the Iranians! Now we're about to leave Ukraine twisting in the wind, refusing to give them the weapons to defend themselves."

The president managed a smile.

"Go on."

"Let's not forget our recent deal with Cuba," Kelly said. "We gave the Castros every single thing they demanded and got only a hostage or two in return."

The president glowered at his CIA chief with such intensity that everyone was silent for a moment. Finally, Admiral Moore, Chairman of the Joint Chiefs, spoke up once more.

"I think Putin has got this whole damn administration hornswoggled is what I think, sir. Look at just one incident. A few days ago, the Russian army shoots down a Russian passenger plane full of Russian citizens. Why? Who the hell knows anymore. White House took their eye off the ball? And what does the administration finally do? Express moral outrage and demand a full investigation? No, sir. We call Putin up and express our condolences and sympathy for the families! I'm speechless, Mr. President."

"Let's just say we agree to disagree, Charlie. Okay. Anyone else? I can see this is going to be an all-cards-on-the-table kinda day around here. So. Who else wants to play their hand?"

"I seem to have a full house, Mr. President," Secretary of State Will Matthews said, getting to his feet. "So I'll go next."

"Fine, Will. Go ahead."

"En route to this office from State just now, I received a call from the Florida governor telling me in detail about a newly developing nightmare in South Florida."

"*Nightmare?*" the president said, staring at his newly minted cabinet officer as if he found this outpouring of more bad news from a friend of his own party hard to believe. "Is that what you said?"

The president suddenly seemed very weary, shaky, unsteady in his movements, and many in the room feared he might even collapse. But Matthews had the floor now, and he was determined to press on whatever the cost might be.

"I think one could safely call the situation in South Florida a nightmare, sir. I realize you have a very full calendar, but I'm saddened and somewhat surprised you've not already been briefed by your own staff."

"Don't apologize. Just tell me what the hell happened."

"No apology on my part is called for, sir. I personally put in a call to you at five-oh-five this morning. It's logged on the White House phone record. With the intention of informing you that shortly after dawn, a huge explosion rocked North Miami Beach. The primary FP&L power station located there on the coast, the one that fuels the entire South Florida grid, has been leveled. We already have reason to suspect terrorism."

"Terrorism."

"Yes, sir. Terrorism, by any other name, is still terrorism. Sir David Trulove here and I have spent the last two days chairing the Global Terror Crisis panel at the Carlisle Barracks at the War College in Pennsylvania. He's been on the phone with Governor Brian Burns offering help with the investigation. Perhaps he can shed additional light on this situation in Florida. Sir David?"

"I can do that," Trulove said, rising and looking directly at the president. "Mr. President, first, I want to say how delighted I am to be here in Washington and how deeply I value the friendship between our two countries. I've also been on the wire this morning with Alex Hawke, sir, one of my senior MI6 officers whom you may recall from the enormously successful Operation Lightstorm in China and North Korea last year."

"Of course. The rescue of Dr. Chase and his family from a North Korean death camp. Brilliant action. Lord Hawke and his son were recent guests in this house."

"Yes, sir. Hawke's in Miami now, recuperating in the wake of that recent tragedy right here on the White House lawn."

"Dreadful, just dreadful," the president said.

"I have asked Lord Hawke to look into this matter, as he is already pushing a link to Cuban terrorism."

The secretary of state rose to his feet, joining Sir David in addressing the president.

"Commander Hawke is already quite certain that

Russian-backed Cuban terrorists from an island spy base came ashore somewhere in the Keys. Then made their way surreptitiously up to Miami and used a wholly new Russian explosive to obliterate South Florida's entire power grid."

"Jesus Christ, Will. Didn't we just normalize relations with the Castros and Cuba? The ink's hardly dry on the treaty."

"We did indeed, Mr. President," Secretary Matthews replied. "Apparently, this is the new normal."

FIFTY-FOUR

Rosow waited for the British intel chief to proceed, but he seemed to have nothing more to add. By now, it was apparent to all that the president had retreated to fight his corner. He was on the ropes now, just suffering the body blows, not truly engaged, hanging on by his fingernails and yet another cup of coffee.

The silence lingered on. Trulove looked around for guidance from his colleagues, found none, and sat back down. The old spymaster closed his eyes and focused on his breathing. He could not remember being in a more tension-filled room in his entire life. It seemed as if they were all sitting around having coffee and discussing the end of the world.

"Anything else?" the president finally muttered, his voice colored with exhaustion and tinged with sarcasm.

Brick Kelly was quick to speak up.

"Mr. President, here's what we're trying to say. I can't emphasize this enough. We are going around the world creating power vacuums. Like the one that gave rise to ISIS in Iraq. The isolated political space America now occupies vis-à-vis both our friends and enemies around the world is untenable. Shaky ground at best. We need to return to terra firma, sir, and we need to do it right now. We need a strong hand on the tiller. We're out of options."

"What the hell are we supposed to do, Brick?"

"Show some strength, for God's sake. Some guts, some backbone. Some goddamn courage. Some goddamn leadership."

The truth was finally out in the open. And it hurt. Not only the president, but every man in the room. A deep silence pervaded the Oval Office. Everyone seemed to be staring at their shoes. After an eternity, the chairman of the Joint Chiefs, Admiral Moore, seemed barely able to contain his anger as he got to his feet.

"He's right, sir. We're knee-deep in the shit, if you'll pardon an old navy saying. You asked us if there was more. I'm afraid there is a great deal more. Kelly's right. Because the White House failed to follow my suggestion and leave a force multiplier of marines behind when we pulled out of Iraq, ISIS has now moved to within mortar distance of Baghdad and closing. Because we have failed to subsequently augment air strikes in Iraq and Syria with boots on the ground, ISIS is rapidly gaining ground and territory. Even Yemen has fallen to them. They are hell-bent on conquering the Arab world."

"Now, just a damn minute. Are you saying you and Secretary Matthews now disavow any State Department role in these goddamn decisions?"

"I'm saying, Mr. President, that I personally cannot and will not take public responsibility for the loss of that historic city to barbaric terrorists. Cities, like Tikrit, Mosul, and Ramadi, that we paid dearly for in blood and treasure. Add that to the copycat homegrown terrorists now beheading our citizens in the streets of the Midwest and—need I really go on, sir?"

No answer.

The president seemed to have wilted. He slumped back in his chair with his hands clasped quietly in his lap. His greying head was back against the tufted yellow cushion and he was staring at the ceiling; soon tears were running down his cheeks. His visitors were aghast. This man, who once seemed so charismatic, so much bigger than life that he was bulletproof—now he was shrunken and shrinking, disappearing inside an empty suit.

No one dared speak.

After a while, Rosow seemed to summon strength from somewhere. He looked across at them and spoke.

"You know, it's funny. My father used to say something to me back when I was knee-high to a grasshopper. Made a lot of sense, the old guy. He'd say, 'Son, always surround yourself with folks who come to you with solutions, not problems.' And that's what he always said, you know, when I went to him with one of my problems. So how do I respond to this—to this laundry list of problems? How? You tell me. You're all here now. Tell me what—tell me what to do."

"Mr. President," Kelly said, "would you like a glass of water? Some more coffee, sir?"

"No, thanks, Brick, I'm fine."

"May I make a suggestion, sir?"

"Please do."

"I know we've given you a lot to think about. But I think it prudent to deal with the closest problem to home first. The incursion and sabotage just carried out by Russian-sponsored terrorists in South Florida."

"Go on."

"Sir David and I drove over here from Langley together. We had a chance to talk about this in the car. I think we're very fortunate in one respect. We have personnel already on the ground who are best equipped to remove the current threat from Cuba. Sir David, will you tell the president our thoughts on Cuba?"

"Mr. President, as was mentioned earlier, Alex Hawke witnessed the explosion firsthand and was in touch with CIA station, Miami, in the immediate aftermath. If I may go off the record for a moment, I will reveal some highly classified information. I will tell you that Commander Hawke has a personal and long-standing relationship with Vladimir Putin.

"It's actually a friendship, as bizarre as that may sound, but it's been of some benefit. A couple of months ago, Putin gave Hawke a demonstration of a new Russian explosive called Feuerwasser. Virtually undetectable and more powerful than anything we've got by a factor of ten."

"Hawke thinks the Russians are behind this Florida outrage?"

"Think it through, Mr. President."

"One more remark like that and I'll have your ass sent packing on the next thing smoking, Sir David," the president said, barely concealing his mounting rage.

Trulove, aghast, looked around at his friends for support before continuing. He was determined not to let the American president's bizarre behavior intimidate him.

FIFTY-FIVE

Hawke is absolutely certain the Russians are behind this attack in Miami," Sir David said. "And in retaliation, it is Hawke's intention to mount a joint strategic assault force and destroy the rebuilt Soviet espionage facility in retaliation. Director Kelly and I are prepared to view this sabotage on American soil as an act of war. And respond accordingly."

The president said, "For Christ's sake, Sir David, you're talking about World War III here. I'd be very careful with your choice of words in this office, Sir David. You're going down a road you may not want to go down."

"Let me rephrase that. Certainly, I would posit that we stand on the *brink* of war, sir. Commander Hawke's idea is that his action in Cuba will send a very strongly worded message to the Kremlin to back the hell off. If we don't respond at all, it's my personal belief that we most certainly will be sliding into global confrontation with President Putin."

"Assuming your assessment is correct, and that's a big assumption, what's the next step in your view?"

"Great question, sir. Let me help you out there," Admiral Moore said. And he proceeded to lay out the rationale they'd all agreed upon.

The president paid attention, nodding in the affirmative at the conclusion.

The men who were present that morning breathed a collective sigh of relief. The most powerful man in the world seemed to have at last begun to grasp the enormity of the forces arrayed against him around the planet. And the challenges the Western world would soon have to grapple with if it was to survive.

Sir David was quick to respond to Rosow's question of what must be done. "Twenty minutes ago I was on with the prime minister at Number Ten Downing. I informed him about the Florida situation, just as I've informed you. I asked his approval for an immediate British-American assault force to be mounted, a joint operation between CIA and MI6, under the command of Alex Hawke, an active officer in the Royal Navy."

"And?"

"The PM gave his swift approval to proceed, Mr. President. As did Secretary Matthews and Director Kelly. All we need now is your agreement to do the same, sir. And Director Kelly and I will take all appropriate actions in coordination with CIA and the

Pentagon to bring the perpetrators of this outrage to swift justice."

They waited for a response. And waited some more.

"Approved, Sir David," Rosow finally said, getting to his feet. A bit of color seemed to have returned to his cheeks, and he had mustered a somewhat more confident demeanor.

"I have worked with Commander Hawke before, as you all know. Tell him my prayers go with him . . . So. I see I'm running out of time. Will that be all, gentlemen?"

They all stood up at once, some relief much evident on their faces.

"Thank you very much, Mr. President," Secretary of State Will Matthews said, speaking for the group. "We deeply appreciate your not only listening to us this morning, but hearing us as well."

They all began to file out.

Admiral Moore was lingering as the others headed for the door, filing past Murph.

"Got a minute, sir?" Moore said.

"Of course, Charlie."

"I do have one more thing to say, Mr. President, on a personal note. I had a guy in my office at the Pentagon early this morning. Navy fighter pilot, a major, 301st Fighter Wing at NAS Fort Worth. Big-time hero. He wanted to see me because something bad had happened to him and he didn't know who else to tell. This guy's on Facebook, see, and two days ago, ISIS posted his face. And the face of his nine-year-old son, Lucas. And the kid's *dog*.

They wanted people to know where this guy and his family *lived*. Then they wanted them to show up at his house and slaughter them. The whole fuckin' family. Now, Mr. President, I am deadly serious about this. If you need a bigger wake-up call than that? Hell, I think it's high time I tendered my resignation as the chairman of the Joint Chiefs. That's all I've got to say. Sir."

He started to walk out, but the president stopped him.

"Believe me, Charlie, I hear you. I count on all you guys to tell me the truth. If we hang together, I believe we have a very good chance of not only getting through this difficult time, but coming out the other side on the side of the angels."

"I hope to God you're right, Mr. President, I sincerely do. Because if you're not, the only option left on the table is a great white nuclear flash of freedom out there in the Iraqi and Syrian desert. Turn those goddamned ISIS safe havens into charbroiled landfill."

Moore turned away and headed for the door.

"I hope it doesn't come to that, Charlie," Rosow called after him. Moore stopped dead in his tracks and turned around to face the president.

"You do? Really? Why?"

"Humanitarian reasons, that's why. I got elected for my convictions in that regard."

"A few minutes ago you told us a story about your father. How he didn't like problems. Well, I'll tell you a story about my father. Rear admiral in the Second World War, a submariner. They called him

'Boomer.' Know what old Boomer told me? He said, 'Son, when you take an oath to defend, you also make a promise to yourself . . . No retreat. No surrender.' You might want to try listening to my old daddy for a change. He was pretty smart too."

STANDING OUT OF THE RAIN AT THE SOUTH PORTICO, waiting for their respective cars and drivers, the four men were speaking in lowered voices.

"Well, that was fun," Admiral Moore said.

"*You're going down a road you may not want to go down?* Is that what he said to Sir David? *Put his ass on the next thing smoking?* Are you kidding me?" Brick Kelly said. "Funny, I thought we were all on the same side, just doing our goddamn jobs."

"On the side of the angels, as it were," Sir David Trulove added with a wry smile. He was still in a state of shock at the way he'd been treated by an American president.

Secretary Matthews said, "At any rate, if we all get fired, at least we finally got his attention. Maybe."

"He can't very well fire me," Sir David said, raising his pale blue eyes to the troubled heavens.

"Good thing, too," Moore said. "If he fails to act on this Cuban crisis thing, Sir David? You and that magnificent bastard Hawke, you sail Royal Navy destroyers right up into that *Cubano* harbor all by your lonesomes and you kick yourselves some serious Commie ass."

"Rather colorful, Charlie, but I admire the sentiment."

The Four, as they'd nicknamed themselves, fell

silent then, watching their black cars moving slowly up the drive in the punishing rain; each man wondering if he'd ever be standing on this exact spot again. At that moment, every member of the Four considered that prospect to be highly unlikely.

But, at least, they thought, individually and collectively, they had done their duty by their country.

FIFTY-SIX

COTSWOLDS, ENGLAND

"GOOD MORNING, DARLING!" AMBROSE CONGREVE trilled, practically bouncing into the sunny dining room of his country home, Brixden House.

Lady Diana looked up from her exquisitely tiny portion of perfectly poached eggs, kippers, and toast. It was early on a brilliantly sunlit Sunday morning. The French polished George III sideboard in the Adams dining room was groaning with piping hot goodies *pour le petite dejeuner.*

"Wait!" she said, gazing sternly at her husband. "Are you actually *skipping*, Ambrose Congreve?" she said.

"Am I? Well, I suppose I am, aren't I?"

The portly old fellow hopped over to the cook's vast sampling of delicacies arrayed beneath a large sporting oil of Diana's late and unlamented grandfather, the Earl of Airlie. Ambrose, as was his wont, winked at the Earl and poked his forefinger at his belly. The old bastard was seated aboard his favorite hunter, Redhead, surrounded by his hounds.

Congreve heaped his plate with cheese-scrambled eggs and crumpets and Irish butter and a generous dollop of Mackays Three Fruit Marmalade. He filled his old mug with piping hot coffee and made his happy way around the long, long table to where his lovely wife was seated.

"What *are* you on about this morning, darling?" the lady of the house asked, patting her lips with crisp white linen.

"Well, for one thing, it's a glorious day. Have you not bothered to look out the windows? God's in his heaven and all's well with the world, you cannot deny it." He dropped his knife on the floor and bent beneath the tablecloth to retrieve it. "There you are!" he exclaimed, as if he'd found the mythical needle in the haystack.

"Really, Ambrose, wherever are your manners? This is not a rumpus room. Please, do try to compose yourself."

"I shall, I shall. May I sample your eggs?"

"Don't be ridiculous. Sit down and shut up."

"Now, now, *mon petite bijou*, try not to be so crab-appley on such a splendid day."

"What has gotten into you? Why on earth are you dressed like that?"

"Like what?"

"Conflicting plaids of dubious shades."

"Well. Where to start? Number one, we have left that drear idyll of ours on Bermuda far, far behind us."

"Are you referring to Shadowlands?"

"I am."

"I'd really prefer you not refer to a lovely old Bermuda home that's been in my family for six generations as 'drear.'"

"Duly noted. And, two, I have returned at long last to this . . . this royal throne of kings, this sceptered isle, this earth of majesty, this seat of Mars, this other Eden—this—"

"Seat of Mars? You got that right!" Lady Mars said, squirming on her well-rounded bottom and giggling.

"My curvy little Martian!" the husband exclaimed.

"Got that right, buster. And don't forget it."

" . . . this blessed plot, this earth, this realm, this . . . England!"

"Are you quite finished?"

"A little Shakespeare never hurt anyone. Pass the *Times*, please."

"There you are. Read, and weep. The world markets have tanked because the Russians are invading Estonia. All of NATO is up in arms. Happy?"

"I am, I am."

"You're happy? How can any sentient being possibly find joy in the ruthless, jackbooted invasion of a sovereign nation full of free and happy people?"

"Oh, I have my reasons."

"Care to enumerate one or two?"

"I certainly can. One, I have the Russians at a distinct disadvantage, you see."

"Really, dear? Poor old Russians. And what might that disadvantage be?"

"They have no idea that the celebrated Demon of Deduction is hot on their trail."

"Completely in the dark, are they?"

"Utterly. And, two, I've donned my cloak and dagger once more. The game is afoot, you see. Well, there you have it, dearest. I cannot tarry, I fear. Headed down to Cambridge after breakfast. Taking the Yellow Peril. Going to see an old friend."

"Male, one only hopes."

"Indeed. You remember Stef Halter."

"The history professor. Magdalene College. You were at Cambridge together."

"Correct. Dr. Halter and I are set to have a very interesting day of it."

"Picnic by the Cam? Punting, just you two and a blanket?"

"Don't be clever, Diana. This is serious business. Halter, Alex Hawke, and I have enjoined our mighty forces once more. We are well into the fray, I'll have you know."

"What fray?"

"Hawke's erstwhile friend, Vladimir Putin, the second and third president of Russia, has been acting very much the naughty boy lately. Eating countries like popcorn. We three valiants are going to put a swift stop to his gluttony."

Diana looked up and gazed deep into the middle distance.

"My God, he's serious," she said, putting down her heavy silver fork.

"Deadly serious."

"What has our Mr. Putin done now?"

"Blown up Miami Beach, for starters."

"*He* did that?"

"Alex and I certainly believe he did. Using Cuban proxies, but yes. Saboteurs, you see. That's why Professor Halter and I are meeting. Prove he did it. Stef and I can wrest the truth from the mire of lies, if anyone can."

"This Dr. Halter. He's a Russian scholar, is he?"

"No, my darling, he's a Russian spy."

"For whom?"

"MI6 for one. KGB for the other. A double agent. You might want to keep that bit under your hat."

"A mole?"

"Hmm. The longest-serving double in the history of British Secret Service. Man's a veritable genius at playing the Great Game. Not always one move ahead, more like nine. When he's not teaching the unteachable at Cambridge, he's lurking about deep in the labyrinthine wonders of the Kremlin. Together, the great Halter and I shall uncover who exploded Miami Beach. And who brought down that Russian passenger airliner. One and the same chap is behind it, I think. Major acts of military sabotage of epic proportions with civilian casualties. Quite unlike the typical fingerprint of a KGB operation. Stef thinks it may even be an outsider. Someone Putin keeps in the shadows, you see."

"I'll save you a trip. The Chinese brought that airplane down, Ambrose, not the Russians. Murdered all those poor souls. Even I and the BBC could have told you that."

"Not necessarily true, Diana. Stef has some very good friends inside the uppermost echelons of Mandarin society in Beijing, you see. The crème de la crème of the Chinese Communist Party. And the inside poop is that the Chinese had nothing to do with that horrific act. It was the Russians."

"Preposterous. Even *they* are not capable of killing three hundred of their own."

"Ah, but they did."

"So you say. Why, for heaven's sake?"

"A feint. A dodge. A distraction. Putin is hellbent on re-creating the former Soviet Union. He's decided it's his legacy to history. Despite how all the denizens of the free world may feel about it being overrun by Russian tanks. Unconfirmed reports have him mobilizing Russian troops on the Czech border, the Polish border, Hungary, and God knows where else. All under the cover of war games. Stef and I aim to uncouple the Russian words for 'games' and 'war' before we're through."

Diana paused, put down her napkin, and stared far into the middle distance. There was a pretty starling in the Japanese cherry beyond the windows. Then she turned her worried countenance once more upon her husband.

"You really *are* going up against Putin, aren't you?"

"Yes, Diana. I am."

"I don't like it. Not a bit of it."

"Why?"

"Why? Because he's incredibly dangerous, that's why. You could get yourself killed."

"Goes with the territory, darling. I'm a copper. It's what I do."

He tried to caress her hair, but she pulled away, her eyes glistening.

"What you do is scare me to death sometimes. I simply could not face life without you, you know."

"Nor I without you."

"And yet, off you go again."

"Because I must. It's my duty. My honor."

"Well, go on then, damn you, and do what you must. And, for God's sake, please be careful. I don't relish the idea of you driving among all those lorries on all those motorways in that little bright yellow toy car of yours. Why don't you take my Range Rover? You just might find that Boz Scaggs CD you've been searching high and low for in the audio player."

"I'll be fine. The Yellow Peril is unmatched when it comes to sheer roadability."

"So you say. You're not wearing that horrid yellow jacket and yellow tie to meet with a distinguished Cambridge don, are you?"

"What's wrong with them?"

"Well, they're both equally hideous, for starters."

"Match my car, do they not? The old Growler?"

"Try matching your big blue eyes. Always a better strategy."

"I vastly prefer yellow."

"That's because, unlike you, my darling, I was endowed by our Creator with impeccable taste."

"You're not opposed to this cap's sprightly young check, I don't suppose . . . are you?"

"Your red driving cap? No. By all means wear it. Maybe we'll all get lucky and it will blow off . . ."

Ambrose got up and headed for the staircase.

"I'll be off as soon as I change, then. I do love you madly, dearest."

"And I you. Will you be home in time for supper?"

"Maybe a little late, depending. Could you ask the kitchen to leave me a roast beef sandwich on the sideboard? Rare with Dijon mustard? With crisps and cornichons? Be a good chap, will you, and leave something out?"

"Oh, all right. Consider it done," she said, following him upstairs and going up on her tiptoes to kiss his rosy cheeks.

Too soon, he was away. In a moment, his little yellow Morgan roadster had disappeared round a bend in the sweeping drive. He was lost within the fold of deep green woods surrounding Brixden House. Despite her heroic and stoic intentions, Lady Mars suddenly found herself bereft and in desperate need of the solace of flowers and the red and gold of fall foliage.

So there she remained, bathed in the golden light streaming down through the Gothic library windows. And, long after Ambrose's lovely little lemony putt-putt was gone, she remained there; gazing out into the garden, thinking of a summer to come when the grounds would be dappled with O'Hara roses, Sweet Avalanche, Veronica, and *Lisianthus* showing the softest pale grey foliage . . .

Her dear old knight errant, off tilting at wind-mills once more, convinced he was saving the world once and for all. God, how she loved that man. She knew he played the fool for her sometimes, just to see her smile. But she also knew that the crystalline mind he'd inherited from his mother was his diamond.

Clear, hard, and brilliant.

And, really, who knew? Perhaps he was well and truly off to save the world and perhaps . . . She sighed, and then bent down to gather up her needlepoint and needles from the seat of her favorite chair. She then moved outside to her shady bench in the garden. Glancing at her busy hands in the warm sunlight, she found herself much heartened by the brief but brilliant flash of her precious engagement ring, nestled beside her wedding band.

A solitary diamond he'd given her long ago on the beach at Pink Sands in Bermuda, the one that had belonged to his dear mother, Charlotte. The precious stone suddenly caught fire in the sunlight, like a distant explosion, though it was only inches away from the tip of her nose.

A lone tear had escaped her eyes, and she brushed it away with a flick of her wrist.

Charlotte's son, Ambrose, had, after all, been his mother's solitary diamond, too.

FIFTY-SEVEN

CAMBRIDGESHIRE, ENGLAND

IT WAS, AMBROSE THOUGHT, DÉJÀ VU ALL OVER again.

The former chief inspector had been behind the wheel of the Yellow Peril for hours now. And the Peril was no easy beast to rein in out on the open road. So it came as some relief to find himself finally nearing the little hamlet of Haversham, on the distant fringes of Cambridge proper. When Professor Halter had rung him up earlier that week, Stefan had told him he'd recently bought a country house somewhere around this quaint ville.

Why move? Ambrose had had to ask himself at that point. *Leave Cambridge Town?* Why should someone of sound mind leave all the charm, the mystery, the architectural splendor that was that brilliant lovely old market town of yore?

As Congreve drew near the crossroads at the town center, he knew Halter's choice could not be for the charm of this garden spot, Haversham. A drear little map speck, with nothing but a couple of dingy pubs, a sad, ill-lit curry house, a forlorn fish and chips, and a decaying petrol station to recommend itself.

Ambrose stopped at the one and only traffic signal. With both man and machine forced to sit idle for a moment or two, Congreve found himself gazing up at the red light dangling overhead. It called to mind a snippet from a Sherlock Holmes adventure: A manually operated gas-lit traffic signal, the first ever to be installed in London, figured as an alibi in Conan Doyle's brilliant mystery. The incandescent Holmes, the great hero of Congreve's life, had determined that the newfangled traffic light had exploded moments before the crime and thus exonerated the innocent suspect!

The old Sherlockian now looked down at directions he'd scrawled on the back of an advert. Halter had said Ambrose would recognize the place when he saw it, but the famous criminalist had only been in this sad little ville once before. And that visit had been on a dark and moonless night in hot pursuit of a female murderer.

He read his scrawl aloud to himself: "Left at only traffic signal, continue on dirt farm road for one mile, go right at milepost sign just after wooden bridge . . . thick birch woods straight ahead . . . iron-gated entrance on left . . ."

The light went green and he quickly engaged first gear and "hung a looey," as his good friend Sir Stokely Jones Jr. was so fond of saying, and proceeded merrily on his way.

By now it was midafternoon, and the sun fell softly on the fields and meadows in this quiet corner of rural England. Here, the aforementioned rutted cart path wound through white-fenced pastures where flocks of Leicester sheep grazed peacefully. Birds flitted about in the sprays of richly hued autumn leaves overhead. Congreve and his Morgan Plus 4 bounced along at a prudently slow speed until he braked just shy of the shaky-looking wooden bridge over a narrow stream or brook.

Mighty Caesar had crossed the Rubicon.

Here was the white mile-post marker peeking up from the grass verge. He turned right as directed. The road instantly went from dirt to some very welcome macadam and he sped up. Ahead loomed the great stand of white birch he'd been promised. It was under darkening skies, with a cooling breeze upon his cheeks that he entered the ancient wood.

It was all starting to look vaguely familiar as a distinct sense of déjà vu suddenly came over him.

And then he came upon a large gated entrance of blackest iron and—it could not be! Oh, yes! Mental flashbulbs popped, and the thing was suddenly crystal clear. He'd been here once before, all right. And it had been a night to remember, indelibly imprinted in the cortex. A most unpleasant evening was putting it mildly.

In trying to arrest the woman who had just murdered Lord Hawke's nanny and nearly killed his son, the noted criminalist had been physically assaulted and nearly tortured to death on the vile grounds of this very estate. Yes, there was the sign—

Ravenswood Farm!

Rounding a bend, the imposing vine-draped edifice hove into view. If you didn't know this relic from antiquity was back here, buried deep within a primeval forest, you would not believe your eyes should you stumble upon it. Almost Disneyesque. The soaring stone towers, the many chimneys, the crenellated stone walls covered in *Hedera helix*, a dense ivy, the mossy domes and flying buttresses, the countless mullioned windows lit by the fire of very old and bubbly glass . . .

This was the former palace of the Bishop of Ely, now known as Ravenswood Farm. Congreve shivered at the nightmare memories stirring in his suddenly fevered brain. He had nearly died here on that cold night last year. He had been beaten to within an inch of his life and nearly pecked to death by countless killer ravens. All the while locked inside the cage of a Victorian aviary he could see peeking above the stables.

Ravenswood had been home to a monster.

The Gothic pile had then belonged to a deranged female sadist known as Dr. Chyna Moon. Moon had been a well-respected professor of Chinese studies at Cambridge once. That was until she had been outed as a Chinese spy and colonel in the Te-Wu, or Chinese Secret Service. Her late father, General Moon, was an avowed enemy of Alex Hawke. And the general's number one daughter, Chyna, and her student accomplice had been given the very challenging task of murdering both Hawke and his small child in an act of vengeance.

She had failed miserably, thank God.

One night, after breaking into the nursery at Hawkesmoor, Chyna's surrogate's botched attempt at the murder of Alexei had resulted in the death of his then nanny, Sabrina Churchill. Congreve had raced out here to Ravenswood to confront and arrest the evil woman's live-in accomplice, a beauteous Cambridge graduate student named Lorelei Li. Miss Li, a conniving bitch of the very first order, had escaped from Ravenswood on her motorcycle minutes before Congreve had arrived.

But not Chyna Moon.

Congreve had seen to that. He had put her in a maximum-security prison, and there she remained to this day. Rotting in hell, one hoped. But most likely using ancient Chinese torture methods to bedevil her fellow inmates for her amusement. The whereabouts of Miss Li, sadly, remained unknown to this day.

So what the hell, he wondered, advancing into the forecourt between two large stone ravens perched on matching pillars, was the good Professor Halter doing here? Receiving houseguests in this haunted manse? Congreve proceeded slowly into the bricked car park, finding a spot of late-afternoon shade and parking the Peril beneath a spreading elm.

He extricated himself from the bucket seat, adjusted his new blue twill tie, and made his way

across the brick pavers to the formidable entrance
to the joint. It was quite chilly now, the light was
going gold here in the damp forest, and he would be
glad of a lovely tumbler of Halter's marvelous Tal-
isker and tap by the fireside.

He rapped the bronze lion's head on the oaken
door. It creaked a bit, then swung open almost in-
stantaneously. Congreve almost gasped at the towering apparition before him.

There in the doorway, where an aged butler
might well appear, stood an enormous TV wrestler
known by the name of Optimus Prime.

Prime had been Chyna Moon's butler cum bodyguard during those dark days of the Moon Dynasty.
The night Ambrose had come to arrest Chyna, the
infamous "Mauler from the Midlands" had nearly
snapped his neck in two on the faded Aubusson carpets of the library. Dr. Moon, who cheered Optimus
on from a nearby sofa, had called for Prime to finish
him off.

He'd felt himself a wee gladiator going up against
the biggest lion in the Coliseum that night. It was
an experience he'd rather not see repeated tonight.

"Yes?" said the wrestler, then coughed a sticky
wet bark full of whiskey and cigarettes accented
with phlegm.

"Hullo, there!" said the weary visitor with forced
jollity, pretending not to recognize the brute guarding the portals. "Ambrose Congreve here to see
Professor Halter. I'm expected, you see."

"You will find him in the library, sir," Optimus
Prime said, nearly as full of as much pomp and cir-

cumstance as any butler on *Downton Abbey* worth his salt could muster. He seemed deliberate in not remembering that awful night of one year ago.

"Thank you," Congreve said, squeezing past, "I know the way." He barely refrained from adding the unspoken phrase, "My good man."

HALTER, DRESSED IN A THREE-PIECE SUIT OF NAVY worsted and a Brook Club tie, was seated in a comfortable red leather club chair by the fire. He rose immediately and went to embrace his friend and colleague as Ambrose entered the capacious room. It smelled of dust, of old leather books, cigarette smoke, beeswax, spilled liquor, and, faintly, the lingering scent of the Dragon Lady herself: Opium, by Yves St. Laurent.

Halter, a very large, robust, and enthusiastic man, said, "I see you made it down in one piece, you old specimen. My directions sufficed?"

"So it would appear. Listen, I am quite in need of a largish alcoholic beverage of some kind. I am a bit shaken up. Unless I'm very much mistaken, I was just greeted at your front door by a formerly famous TV wrestler!"

"Ah, Optimus Prime. Yes, yes, he came with the house."

"You allowed him to stay?"

"So it would seem."

"Is he ill? He seems ill."

"Nothing but a cold. He was out all night in the freezing rain chopping wood for the fire."

"Ah. A health nut."

Halter laughed out loud as he made his way over

to the drinks table, noisily dropping cubes of ice into a pair of crystal tumblers. "And, pray, why not? I could use a little celebrity glamour around here."

"Celebrity glamour?"

"You disapprove?"

"Disapprove is a bit mild. The fiend is as tightly strung as Venus Williams's tennis racket."

"He's a bit intense on first meeting, I'll grant you that. You need to get to know him, that's all."

"Sadly, this is not our first meeting."

"What?"

"I know him. He's psychotic."

"Has he offended you in some way? Was he rude?"

"Quite rude, I daresay. He tried to kill me on that settee over there."

"What?"

"Oh, never mind. I'll tell you later."

"Come, come, let bygones be bygones. Do have a seat by the fire. I am delighted to see you, Ambrose. You look splendid, old fellow, marriage to someone far above your station clearly agrees with you. And I do love the headgear. Nothing screams Ambrose Congreve like a perky lemondrop driving cap. It has been an age, has it not?"

"Far too long. Look here, Stef," Congreve said, lowering himself into the chair and looking around the room. "I'm a bit confused. You're renting this monstrosity? Where evil lurks? I thought you were happy in your cozy apartments at the college, views of the lovely Cam Bridge, as I recall."

Halter handed him a tumbler half full of whisky and water and joined him by the hearth.

"I was happy. Then I saw a four-color advert in *Country Life* and simply couldn't resist. Bought the place at a fire sale."

"*You actually bought it?* How interesting. Do go on."

"Well, here's the thing, you see. After you and Alex Hawke provided the evidence that put Dr. Moon in jail, Ravenswood Farm fell rapidly into disrepair. Weeds as high as the chimneys. Our favorite lady spy stopped paying the staff. Groomsmen in the stables, gardeners, butlers, cooks, the whole lot up a creek. Optimus was the last one standing when the realtor showed me the place. I begged him to stay on if I ended up buying it. And luckily he agreed."

"Luckily?"

"Hmm."

"Why him?"

"Simple, really. I desperately needed someone who knew how to maintain the house and grounds, and how to staff the place, et cetera. Whom to call when one was desperate for a good chimney sweep or plumbing specialist. You must know the drill, living as you do in a place as gargantuan as Brixden House. It takes a village, no?"

"The village of the damned, apparently. Does he still keep his killer ravens out in the aviary?"

"Ravens? What ravens?"

"Oh, never mind."

"Oh, come on. He does come off as a bit of a brutish fellow, our Optimus Prime, I do agree. But you never know when someone with talents like his may come in handy, especially in our particular . . . line of work."

"Stef. Listen. It all came out at the trial. The man tried to kill me in this very room, I tell you. Locked me in a cage where killer birds almost pecked me to death. He's insane."

"He's filled with remorse. I told him you were coming, and he was horrified by the idea of facing you. Did he say anything at the door?"

"The monster was silent."

"Well, I'm sure he's only waiting for an opportunity to beg your forgiveness. At any rate. How are you, Ambrose? Missing Bermuda? Happy to be back in England?"

"Ecstatic," Congreve said, casting a worried glance at the library doors and whoever might be lurking beyond. "But, I must say, it's a little disconcerting to see you in this . . . this unique setting. However. It may well be of no particular consequence. Whatever made you decide to move out to the countryside?"

"Ah, but I've always wanted to be the country squire, you know. Devoured every issue of *Country Life* for decades now. When I saw their advert for Ravenswood some months ago, I jumped on it. I'd come into a little money and decided, you know, what the hell. We're both running out of runway rather quickly, you know."

Ambrose drew on his pipe and looked around the high-ceilinged room.

"I must say the old dump looks better without all the stuffed crows on the walls. Mangy bear heads.

Good for you. I'm sure it was a bargain and now you've got some room to roam around."

"Thirty of them."

"Mmm. Pull down all these heavy velvet curtains soon, will you? They're held together with the dust of centuries. And you need more light in here, Stef. The whole house is a bit tomblike, if that's the phrase I'm looking for. The word 'macabre' comes to mind."

Halter nodded agreement and said, "How is our mutual friend, Lord Hawke? I'm so sorry about all the horror and sadness he suffered in Washington. Poor Nell Spooner. What a brave soul. I shall miss her."

"As will I. You know, Stef, I'd say that, all things considered, he's doing fairly well. He's finally seen the light with his quasi-friend Putin, thank God. I was worried he was under some kind of evil Cossack spell."

Congreve paused a moment, then knocked back the remains of the reviving potion and leaned forward.

"I had a meeting with C in London right after Alex got back from his visit to Washington and—I say, may I freshen your drink?"

"Please do. More whisky, less water this time, Stef. I'm suddenly in the whisky mood. Abject terror at one's dire surroundings is oft mitigated by strong drink, I find."

Halter got his large frame extricated from the chair and made his way once more over to the drinks table.

"Buckle your seat belts, we're in for a bumpy

night," the rotund professor said, smiling as he poured a topper libation for his old friend. They were two kindred spirits, after all, each doing what he loved, donning the blackest cloaks and snatching up the longest daggers. And this was precisely what the two co-conspirators conspiring by the fireside happened to be very, very good at: *spoiling other people's fun.*

FIFTY-EIGHT

As I was saying," Halter said, collapsing ever more deeply into his chair, "I went down to London to meet with Sir David immediately upon his return from the States. Behind closed doors in his office at MI6. Trulove said he'd been witness to a rather grueling White House session with President Rosow, but he had managed to come away with U.S. approval to forge ahead with Hawke's Cuban operation."

"Yes, I got the very same message. I was on with Alex in Miami early this morning. Preparations for the joint naval operation are nearing completion aboard *Blackhawke*. Switching gears for the moment, Stef, please tell me what the hell is going on in Moscow. That singular town of yours lies at the heart of danger, now, it does seem to me. All that's dire. Save the murderous thugs establishing an unholy caliphate in Iraq, Syria, Libya, and Yemen, of course. Any chance of getting Putin to put more pressure on Assad and Syria to assist the Kurdish militia in efforts to stand up to the ISIS savages?"

"None. Putin's insistence on keeping Assad's government intact is couched in a reading of the conflict in Syria far more cold-blooded than the views of those in Washington. It's merely engaged in an ancient religious war as far they're concerned."

"Bottom line?"

"Western attention has shifted dramatically from the murders carried out by the Assad regime to those carried out by Islamic terrorists. Simply another sign of the overwhelming complexity of this new multifront Middle East war."

Congreve paused to digest this. Sometimes his friend adopted a more professorial tone in his locutions, and one had a bit of a time of it putting two and two together.

"What a nightmare, Stef. I often feel like the man falling from a building and saying something to a chap in an office window on the way down. We are going to war with Russia, you know. Any day now. Unless you and I manage to do something brainy in a hurry."

"Indeed we must, Constable. And the very best thing we can do at the moment is not let this attack by Russian-sponsored Cubans on the American homeland stand without answer. It will only encourage the Kremlin's ambitions in North America."

"It just doesn't feel like Putin somehow. Attacking America with the foreknowledge that the West will retaliate against Cuba in all likelihood. Has the real Vladimir Putin finally emerged from the closet of statesmanship and shown his true colors?"

"That's why I invited you to Cambridge, Ambrose. I don't know the answer to that question. Haven't a clue, in fact. Perhaps we can cobble together an explanation for all this."

"You said you believed this may be a Kremlin outsider of some kind. What do you mean by that?"

"I'm not sure. It's purely a gut feeling. There is certainly nothing subtle about shooting down your own passenger planes. If indeed, Putin was responsible. And yet that's just what he may have done. If it was him, of course."

"Who else could it be?"

"There are rumors within rumors, worlds spinning within worlds, as you of all people know best. Nothing new within the ancient walls of the Kremlin, of course. But still. There's substance enough to be found in there somewhere, if we dig deeply enough. A power behind the throne, perhaps."

"Go on, Stefan," Ambrose said, tossing off the remains of his whisky. This, now, was the reason he'd driven all this way to Haversham.

"Mmm. I wonder. You will perhaps recall a remote KGB outpost in the frozen tundra of Siberia. Near a small railway outpost called Tvas. It was the former winter palace of the tsars before the late Count Korsakov acquired it. Know what I'm talking about?"

"Of course. Hawke's beloved Anastasia is currently imprisoned near there. He's visited once or twice, the last time to bring home his son. The boy's mother, I believe, is held captive by the KGB. The mother of his only child. Awful situation for her. And him."

"She's no captive, Ambrose. She is there of her own free will. She married the old officer who's in charge there. General Kuragin was his name, as you remember."

"*Was* his name?"

"Probably dead. I never see him in Moscow anymore. There are rumors about him, too, of course. That he fell into disfavor. That Putin had him assassinated using polonium-210. Same stuff used to take out Litvinenko in London, you'll recall."

"Alex never told me Anastasia had married."

"I hardly blame him for not wishing to speak of it. It fractured his heart. It was their cherished secret."

"What made you think of looking at Tvas in the first place?"

"Something is going on out there, Ambrose. I hear things, seeping from beneath closed doors. There are KGB black ops within ops. Black sites. And then there are KGB black holes. This is the latter."

"A black hole, huh? Putin behind it? He'd be at the top of my list."

"I can't run it back to him. No matter how hard I try, I can't stick Putin with a damn thing. That's where I've hit the wall. For the life of me, I just cannot. Unless, of course, Putin has acquired a proxy bully to protect him in the court of public opinion."

"Interesting concept. Tell me, Stef. Unless you *can't* tell me. Did Sir David ever ask you to keep anything from me? Or even Alex?"

Halter shrugged. "He has done. But, no, not this time."

"Good."

Halter got to his feet and went over to the broad Georgian desk. It stood solidly beneath a huge canvas depicting the Battle of Stalingrad. Ambrose, looking at the painting, thought, *Is it a constant reminder of the motherland Halter is betraying?* That would certainly be in keeping with his ability to survive on both sides of the game. Alliance to all, allegiance to none.

Congreve wondered about that, Stefan's true allegiance. To one or the other. And not for the first time, either.

FIFTY-NINE

HALTER RETURNED A MOMENT LATER WITH A red-and-black leather TOP SECRET folder. Congreve noticed the faded sword and shield symbol of the old KGB embossed on both sides.

"What's that?" Congreve said as the professor sat down and began leafing through the pages in the secret file.

"Everything I've managed to nick from my Kremlin office regarding developments out at Tvas. The remote KGB headquarters for Eastern Affairs. Here are some aerial photos, sat photos, et cetera, all pertaining to a recent construction project nearby . . . come have a look . . ."

"Good heavens," Congreve said, flipping through the stack.

"Amazing. Look at this one. You see, right here, this very large structure is the winter palace itself.

Built sometime around the middle of the last century. It's where General Kuragin and Anastasia maintain their residence. And where Alex's son spent his early youth. Here is the pond where his mother taught him to ice skate . . . So sad, no?"

Congreve nodded, feeling a wave of pity for the boy, separated from his mother for all these years. And now, threatened with death everywhere he turned. It was utterly untenable. Alex Hawke forced to retreat to the shadows to protect his son? No, that simply could not stand.

"And look here, Ambrose. All this area to the south of that existing residence is where new work is taking place. Or, was, at the time these photos were taken. I'm sure it's all practically completed by now. Notice it's surrounded by three layers of security fencing, concertina wire, a broad no-man's-land with kennels for the guard dogs to roam here. And with an unobstructed field of fire from these six guard towers here, here, and . . . here. Three more to cover the western approach through the forests."

"Incredibly dense forest from the looks of it. What's it called?"

"Czar Nicholas called it the *Schwarzwald*. Black Forest. After the German hunting lodges he frequented with his father as a child, in Baden-Württemberg on the Rhine. It was his happy hunting ground."

"And what's this? Looks like a landing strip was just being completed over here."

"Five thousand feet. Sufficient runway provision for the heaviest troop-transport planes."

"Makes sense. How about these large parallel rectangles? I count sixteen of them. Barracks, maybe?"

"Barracks, all right. Twenty, thirty thousand personnel, easy. Maybe more. Huge."

"And this steel and glass cube in the center of the compound?"

"CCC. Command-and-control center. Completely self-sufficient. And separate from the primary KGB HQ to the north."

"And, here, a row of hangars?"

"Perhaps. Wondered about that myself. Aircraft? Drone storage maybe. Who knows, at least until we get a peek inside."

"Peek inside?"

"Rudimentary, my dear Congreve. Simply time on task. We need to get eyes on this thing."

"Yes, but, 'we'? What do you mean by 'we'?"

"I'll complete that thought in a moment. Listen, Ambrose, I don't like the looks of this at all. I've heard rumors these several months. The creation of a wholly new KGB unit. Independent. Composed of mercenaries, soldiers of fortune from around the world. Under the putative command of the cream of the Spetsnaz officers. But more likely by Putin. Or his surrogate."

"I've been ruminating on the subject prior to your arrival," Halter said. "Why *not* base such a force out here in the middle of bloody nowhere? Airlift troops and materiel on an as-needed basis. As far from prying eyes, above and below, as you can possibly get. Wouldn't that make sense to you, Stef?"

"Indeed it would. What still does not make any sense, though, is why the hell KGB or Spetsnaz, or any units under their control, would even need such an isolated base camp. Especially since they've already got one almost next door to this monstrosity. What's the distance separating the two?"

"Three or four miles, max. With this dense forest separating the two. My question remains. Why an isolated base camp when you've already got one right next door?"

"Right. Unless the new one was designed from inception to be completely off the books," Halter said, scratching his grizzled chin, his concentration and focus almost giving off heat.

Congreve nodded vigorously. He said, "A surrogate leader. A surrogate army. A surrogate air force. Every bit of it off the books. Invisible and . . ."

Ambrose continued, "An army that answers to no one. A distinct new unit . . . to complement . . . and . . . compete with the KGB. A new combat entity that can't be traced back to the Kremlin. Not the dumbest idea I've ever heard of. Putin seems to be full of ever more ingenious ways to rule the world these days, does he not? But, listen. What kind of man would he put in charge of such a new army?"

"Not one that I'm aware of, at any rate. I have no idea who could be put in charge of this . . . hybrid army. His existing officer ranks within FSB/KGB wouldn't do it. Does he go outside? Hire that mini-Putin I spoke of earlier?"

"Hmm. I wonder. Let us speculate about that topic, my dear Halter. Alex Hawke used to talk to me about someone in Russian history called the Dark Rider. Who was the 'Dark Rider,' Professor? I mean, in history or mythology?"

Halter explained, "He who rose to the highest pinnacle of power. Uncommon strength, uncommon valor, uncommon virtue at a time when the country had veered in the wrong direction. He who would alter the course of the state set by those weak sisters currently in power. In ancient times, such weak leaders were known as the 'Pale Riders.' Considered weak, lazy, unpatriotic. I could go on. Yeltsin was one, for instance."

"That doesn't sound much like our boy Volodya."

"Definitely not Putin," Halter said. "He's the living definition of a Dark Rider. So who is the man in the shadows?"

"Doesn't make any sense, Stef. You're now talking about *two* Dark Riders? Operating as one? Or set against each other?"

"It's Putin. It's not supposed to make sense. It's a black op like nothing I've ever witnessed. Not only is it stranger than you believe, it's stranger than you *can* believe."

"Who, then? Someone in opposition to Putin's reign?" Congreve said. "Mounting a challenge?"

"Men like that don't live long enough to oppose anything or anyone. Whoever the hell he is, we know one thing. Putin is well aware of whatever the hell is going on here. I will tell you, knowing Putin as I do, that once this fellow has fulfilled the mission he's been given, he finds himself in the cemetery business."

"But he's vital to Putin. For the nonce, anyway."

"He is. We need to find out why."

"And we need to find out *who*."

"I think we're on the same page, Ambrose."

The growing excitement between the two old colleagues could be felt in the room.

"Oh, we're totally on the same page," Congreve said. "What next?"

"We dress up like gypsies, get a wagon and mule, and begin the long trek across Siberia to the remote outpost of Tvas. Are you game?"

"My wife won't be thrilled. She's already going to be miffed I'm late for supper this evening."

"I'm happy to do this all by myself. I told C some of what I've just revealed to you. At first, he wouldn't let me even think of going out there. Afraid I would not come back, I suppose. I am his valuable asset, let's be honest."

"Or, at minimum, you'd be exposed as a double agent and thus end your enviable record of clandestine aid to British intelligence. Groveling naked on the stone floor of some prison, begging for a bullet."

"Thanks for that image. If I end my career or my life in this effort, I shall have no regrets. It has been my life's work, and I do believe I've made a difference. At any rate, in the end Sir David and I were in full agreement. We both agreed that the ends justified the means. This will be an MI6 operation, start to finish."

"Would the old bastard balk at my tagging along?" Congreve said.

Halter laughed. "Why, Ambrose, I'm surprised at you! Use that big brain of yours. Why do you imagine you're here? Who do you think suggested this visit?"

"This whole thing was C's idea? Very devious of him, I must say."

"He's a *spy*, for heaven's sake, Ambrose. Remember?"

"How could I forget? Well, there you have it. I suppose you and I are back in the Great Game at last, my old friend. The 'Cambridge Two,' I suppose the history books will call us. No?"

Halter looked away, lighting the cigarette that had been dangling from his lips for the last half hour. Congreve saw his eyes come to rest on the painting of Stalingrad hung above his desk.

"With only the whole world hanging in the balance . . ." he murmured quietly. Having moved on to one of his other worlds within worlds, Ambrose surmised. Halter, a true genius, was nothing if not a complicated man. Ambrose had the strangest sensation. He suddenly felt as if the man had left the room.

"I must be getting home," Ambrose said.

"I suppose so . . . yes."

"We can and will win, you know, Stef; with God's help, we will," Congreve said, rising from his chair and stretching his back out. He was tired, and he had a long drive homeward on a dark night.

"God's help?" Halter murmured, lost in thought. "Is that what you said?"

"I'd best be getting home," Congreve repeated.

"What? Oh, yes, of course. I'll ring for Optimus and have him show you out."

Halter sounded odd, as if something, some looming dark cloud, was sliding over him. A premonition, perhaps. And Ambrose got the impression he'd perhaps overstayed his welcome. Not an auspicious beginning to a very dangerous travel plan.

"Please don't bother Optimus, Stef," Ambrose said quietly, making his way to the door. "I know my way out."

SIXTY

KEY WEST

The yacht *Blackhawke* was now under constant twenty-four-hour guard at Naval Air Station Key West.

The impending Cuban mission, code-named Operation Rumdum, was now an official CIA/MI6 combined combat operation. It was felt this hurriedly put together spec op had but two possible outcomes: it could either avert war with Russia; or it could initiate the commencement of worldwide nuclear hostilities. A black cloak of secrecy surrounded Rumdum. Hawke, his crew, and the land-side support teams were all operating under a strict code of silence.

Blackhawke, no longer deemed a private yacht and

now officially considered an active U.S. warship
by the Pentagon, had departed the Port of Miami
forty-eight hours earlier. She'd been provided with
a protective navy destroyer escort for the short
voyage. She was now moored down south at NAS
Key West on Boca Chica Key.

Located just four miles east of downtown Key
West, the naval air station had originally been
built to combat piracy in the Caribbean. It was
now located on a small, low-lying island covered in
thick mangroves. A giant white sphere, the massive
radar station, loomed up out of the thickets, along
with other white, low-lying buildings.

Primarily a state-of-the-art training facility for
air-to-air combat fighter pilots of all military services, the base also supported operational and readiness requirements for the Department of Defense
and Homeland Security (Coast Guard) and was
host to several tenant commands, including Strike
Fighter Squadron 106, Fighter Squadron Compos-
ite 111, and the U.S. Army Special Forces Underwater Operations School.

Strike Fighter 106 command was now on full
alert. Should the new warship encounter an unfore-
seeable degree of hostility en route, or when engaging in combat operations, pilots would be aloft in
under five minutes.

Blackhawke was taking on stores and ammunition
for the naval assault operation now under way. She
was undergoing a complete combat-readiness refit.
Certain modifications to her hull, superstructure,
and armaments, and minor glitches in her defensive radar systems were now either fixed or being

repaired. In addition, her offensive and defensive air missile systems were receiving a substantial upgrade. This, in order to defend her against attacking enemy fighter aircraft or land-based SAM systems surrounding the enemy objective. And eliminate threats from enemy installations.

What no one had witnessed, at 3 A.M. that morning, was an unmarked black truck with blacked-out windows arriving at the gangway ramp leading from the docks up to the ship's main deck. Sixteen hand-picked commandos, the baddest of the bad, emerged from the vehicle quickly and in single file boarded the boat. In less than thirty seconds all the men in black had disappeared inside *Blackhawke* and the black truck sped away under cover of darkness.

Three veteran crew members from Hawke's "yacht" had been assigned to prevent any incursion from the sea, above or below the surface. One of them, an ex-SEAL Team 5 UDT demolition expert, named Scott McBain, patrolled underwater in the one-man sub. Scottie's job was to prevent swimmers or enemy minisubs from attaching explosive devices to her hull.

The other young crewman who'd pulled sentry duty was Lieutenant Sam Kennard, a plainclothes counterterrorist warrior with long brown hair, dressed in a Hawaiian shirt, zipping around the harbor surrounding *Blackhawke* on a Jet Ski like an off-duty sailor after a few beers.

U.S. Navy security personnel ashore were also heavily involved in preparations. Some would be on board and on duty for the duration of the big yacht's brief layover at Key West. Teams of armed and uniformed U.S. Marines patrolled the docks and secured the land-side approaches. The main gate to the air station, and all other entrances, had been secured. While Hawke's boat was moored at NAS, no one was allowed within a thousand yards of her docks without official government ID and signed documents stating their reason for being there.

At noon on the day before they would sail their boat into harm's way, Alex Hawke, his son, Harry Brock, and Stokely Jones were en route from the ship to the Key West International Airport. A second government vehicle trailed right behind them. Inside were Alexei's new protector, Tristan Walker, and Archie Carstairs, the new bodyguard.

Stoke was at the wheel of a blacked-out U.S. Secret Service Chevy Suburban, armored, with blacked-out windows. Brock was up front with him, cuddling Alexei's beloved dog, Harry (named after him, maybe?), and staring out the window at the endless mangrove swamps.

Alexei and his father sat in the rear. Alexei had jumped out of bed very excited about a ride in his dad's new airplane, and Hawke wanted it that way. He knew his son was being extraordinarily brave about not having his dad around to protect him right now, and only the prospect of a great adventure had kept his spirits as high as they were.

At home in England, dear old Pelham Grenville would make the little boy feel loved and safe again.

"Alexei, are you listening to me, son?"

"Yes, Daddy."

"What did I tell you to do the minute you get back home to England and Hawkesmoor?"

"Find Pelham. Tell him I missed him. Hug him."

"No. Those are the next things you do. The first is to show Tristan our house. Show him where everything is. Your room. His room, Archie's room, Pelham's room, things like that. The kitchen. The attic. The gardens and the big lake. It's his home, too, now. His and Archie's. They're both your new friends now, am I right?"

"Archie is my best friend. And I'm his best friend, too. He's funny. He showed me a comic book about him when he was just a kid. His best friend's name was, Jughead!"

"He is funny. Well. Good. We're all clear on that subject, are we, sonny?"

"The kid's all over this, boss," Stoke said, "nothing to worry about."

Harry Brock, in his own little world and hoping to see an alligator cross the road, looked over at Stoke and said, "Does anyone else beside me think this new Scotland Yard babysitter, Tristan, is secretly gay?"

"Shut up, Harry," Stoke said. "Seriously, man, stuff a sock in it." Glowering angrily, he added, "There's a little kid sitting back there, remember?"

Hawke had already leaned forward, grabbed a handful of Harry's left shoulder, squeezed, and said, very softly, "One more stupid remark like that, especially in front of my very young and very impressionable son, and I will stop this car and make you get out of this car, out of my life. Do you understand, Harry? Say no if you don't. Right now."

"Sorry," Brock said. "Jesus, I didn't mean anything by it. I like gay people."

"Says it like he means it, doesn't he, boss? Man doesn't even know the meaning of the word 'sorry.'"

"There are countless words Mr. Brock doesn't know the meaning of, Stoke. But if he says even one of them, stop the car."

"Aw, shit," Harry said.

"Watch it, Brock; you're only one more word shy of a long walk under a hot sun on a bad road."

That shut him up for about five minutes. As they neared the town of Key West, Harry lowered his window and said, "You know it's hot outside when you stick your hand outside and it's hot."

"Shut up, Harry," Stoke said.

They rode the rest of the way to the Key West Airport in silence.

SIXTY-ONE

THE SLEEK, NAVY BLUE GULFSTREAM 650 THAT would ferry Alexei, Detective Inspector Tristan Walker, and Sergeant Archie Carstairs across the Atlantic and home to England was fueled and ready on the baking tarmac at the private aviation FBO. Stoke drove the Suburban through the gate and out to the waiting airplane, parking twenty feet from the port wingtip of the bossman's pride and joy, gleaming in the tropical sunshine.

Hawke emerged from the rear of the Chevy Suburban, carried his son up the steps to the plane, and quickly ducked inside to the cool cabin air.

"Welcome aboard, sir," his chief pilot, E. B. "Smitty" Smith, said. "We're all set, whenever you're ready. How's our young passenger this morning?" The former Montana sheriff reached over and playfully tousled the boy's curly hair.

"Alexei, you remember Captain Smith, don't you?"

"Hullo, Smitty," Alexei said, thrusting out his chubby hand.

"Good morning yourself, Hawkeman! I've an idea for you today, if it's all right with your daddy. How'd you like to sit up front? Sit in my lap and fly the plane?"

"Can I, Daddy, can I fly the plane? Please!"

"Why not? I was allowed to do it by my father . . . And, Smitty, these two fine gentlemen just boarding are Detective Inspector Tristan Walker and Sergeant Archie Carstairs, both from SO14, Scotland Yard Royalty Protection. I e-mailed you about them last week."

"Nice to meet you, gentlemen," Smitty said with a tip of his black cowboy hat. "I'll give Alexei a tour of the cockpit until you're ready to go. There's no rush . . . what's your puppy's name, Alexei?"

"Harry. Like the man who Daddy just told to wait in our car. Harry said something bad and everyone is mad at him."

Hawke looked away, an embarrassed smile on his face. "Let's go aft," he said to Walker and Carstairs.

The three men took seats in the richly paneled aft seating area, three large overstuffed armchairs in dark navy velvet. Hawke had decorated the airplane in a very nautical way, a teak and holly cabin sole, blue upholstery with white piping, framed pictures of eighteenth-century warships starring the Royal Navy. It was a bit unusual, he would admit. But he liked it, and that was that.

His go-to London interior designer was the

lovely Nina Campbell, whose clients included the Duke and Duchess of York, Ringo Starr, Rod Stewart, and Hawke's club in New York, the Brook.

"Tristan," Hawke said, hooking one long leg over the arm of the chair, "how comfortable are you with current security arrangements at Hawkesmoor?"

"I'd say very comfortable, sir."

"And you, Archie?"

"Very much the same, sir."

"I'm glad to hear that. Because we're going to need it. I waited till we were on board the plane because I can't afford to trust any other location right now, not anyone, frankly."

Tristan said, "You're talking about Cubans, sir? The Cuban American civilians working around the docks?"

"No, Tristan, I'm talking about Russians working around the docks."

"Please explain, sir," Archie said. "We need to know as much as we possibly can going forward."

"Archie. Here is the thing. We are about to take on the most dangerous man on the planet. Vladimir Putin. And he knows it."

"His every move seems left unchecked," Walker said.

Hawke nodded. "Right. But I think I can stop him. With a little luck and a little help from above, I will stop him. But I'll pay a price for whatever I do. And the one price I am not willing to pay is the life of my son."

"Please explain, sir," Tristan said, leaning forward in his seat, his clear green eyes full of an intensity Hawke welcomed.

"Putin and I know each other well. Or at least we used to. But recently I've faced the hard truth. He's not the man I used to know. I was vain enough to think he admired me and just wanted my friendship. I was wrong. He has been using me since some years ago when we met in a Russian prison. Now, because of recent events, I know we're mortal enemies, and I believe he feels the same way. And my enemy has limitless resources and power. He also knows the only possible way to slow me down, or even shut me down, is that little boy up there in the cockpit. With me?"

"Indeed we are, sir," Archie said. "Just tell us what we can do."

"I know Alexei is in good hands. You and Tristan would not be aboard if I didn't think that. I also know there are unintended consequences to every action. As soon as I sail my boat into that Cuban harbor, it's game on. Putin will know I'm coming for him. He knows it's going to be no retreat, no surrender. And he will do everything in his power to take me off the board. He thinks my weakest flank is my son. He will attack me there. I'm putting my faith in Scotland Yard and you two men to prevent that."

"Archie and I are honored, indeed, sir. And, I assure you, we will guard him with our very lives."

Hawke paused for a long moment's thought before he spoke. "No assurances necessary, Tristan. You have my complete confidence, both of you."

"Thank you, sir."

"Now, please listen very carefully. This is critical. As soon as you arrive at Hawkesmoor, I want you examine every layer of security, every line of defense. The CATV, the motion sensors, all of it. Take notes. Either fix it or e-mail me anything major you think I should be aware of. Walk the perimeter daily with the MI6 officer in charge of the detail there. Take notes, stay in touch. Carefully explain to your Scotland Yard colleagues my concerns about a possibly imminent attack . . . tell them I expect you and Archie to identify any holes anywhere, and plug them. Anyone gives you any crap, or looks at you sideways, have them escorted off my property, under my orders, and reported to their superiors as suspicious, or unfit for duty. Is that clear? Archie? Tristan?"

"Could not be clearer, sir," they said in unison.

"Archie, what kind of weapon do you and your concealed weapons team ordinarily carry?"

"Glock 226 pistol, sir. And the HK MP5 machine gun. Inspector Walker, the same."

"That's good. I have one of each myself. And another thing, Archie. You're the point man. Never *ever* let my son out of your sight. I want one or the other of you on duty sleeping in the room adjacent to his every single night until my return. Archie, when that child sets one foot outside the established lines, I want you glued to him. Right?"

"Done," Archie said.

"Good on you, lad. Now. Here's the real reason I wanted to deliver this speech in complete secrecy . . . I have a backup plan. And no one on Earth save the three of us sitting here has any idea of what I'm going to tell you."

"We're listening, sir."

"In the event you even *suspect* a perimeter breach, or an impending attack on Hawkesmoor, by land or air . . . or even if someone is suspected of giving the dead wrong answer to a vital question, then I want you two to grab Alexei and Pelham, go up to the helipad above the stable rooftop, and you four get the hell out of there.

"I've got a helicopter. It's armed. Two Sidewinder AIM missiles mounted in the undercarriage and a .50-cal. machine gun in the nose. All gassed and ready to fly. If it takes you longer than four minutes after the alarm bells go off, it's already too late. So rehearse that escape a few times. Time it. From the second things go bad until you lift off from the rooftop. Get it under four minutes. Are we clear?"

"Clear, sir."

"I know you're both qualified combat helo pilots. I don't care who flies the damn thing. You'll be flying due north. Up to an island in the Outer Hebrides, in the north of Scotland. Isle of Skye. Only access to it is by air or water. I still maintain an old family hunting lodge up there. My great-grandfather built it in 1900. It's called Drum Castle. Empty now, most of the year. But it's well stocked with food, weapons, provisions. There's heat, power, and cords of firewood in the cellars if the power goes out. It gets very cold at night up there. It's remote, as I said. Once you land on the property, near the main house, use the ATV and immediately tow the helo into one of the barns and out of sight. Remember this always, the skies have eyes. Enemy satellites."

"Damn good plan, sir," Tristan said. "I'm only

sorry I didn't think of a backup myself. Should have done."

"I hope to hell you don't need it. Pelham is my dearest friend. That boy up there is my son. They are all the family I've got. Thank you."

Hawke put his hands on his knees and began to rise from his chair. The pilots had lit up the engines. He needed to get back to the boat and finish his prep.

"Hold on. One more thing. There's an old caretaker up at Drum Castle. Known him since I was Alexei's age. A good friend of mine named Frank McPhee. I call him Laddie, always have. Don't let his advanced age mislead you. Laddie McPhee is a crack shot and tough as a blacksmith's barrel of nails. I've told him about you two. That you might drop in out of the blue one day. Know what he said? He said, 'I hope I never have the pleasure of meeting those two gents, m'lord, fine as they sound. But I'll welcome the sight of that fine little boy.' That's Laddie, for you. Here's his mobile number."

Walker took the card and said, "We will immediately coordinate all our security measures with him, sir."

"Laddie's still got eyes like a hawk. He'll watch the water approaches from an observation tree platform he and I built when I was twelve. There's a pair of Kawasaki ATV vehicles in one of the garages you can use to cover more ground on patrols. Air is another story. No radar up there, I'm afraid. Like I said. Keep your eyes to the skies."

"Aye, sir," Archie said. "We will indeed. You've left no stone unturned, sir. We won't let you down."

"I've left a good many stones unturned, I'm afraid. But I've run out of time. The good news is, I remembered Drum Castle up there at the top of the world. There's no one alive save Laddie and Pelham who even know it exists anymore. Alexei's been up there once or twice with me. Loves exploring it. If you and Archie have got to make a stand somewhere, do it at Drum Castle. God knows how many sieges and battles it's withstood over the centuries, and it's as good a place to hold fast as you're going to get. Are we clear?"

"Perfectly, sir," Walker replied.

"Good. This envelope has everything you'll need to know about the house and grounds and terrain. GPS coordinates, weather for the month. Laddie's mobile number, as I said. Call him soon as you're airborne en route to the castle. He'll be waiting for you out at the pad near the main barn. Square, are we now?"

"Square, sir."

"Have a safe flight back to England. I'm going up to say good-bye to my son."

Tristan Walker watched Lord Hawke make his way forward to the cockpit. As relaxed as he seemed, he had the coiled energy of a stalking lion on the Serengeti plain. The inspector felt he now understood why the man had the burnished sterling reputation of a great warrior. And Tristan was proud that Royalty Protection was able to help such a fine man in his time of greatest need.

SIXTY-TWO

Tvas, Siberia

LESS THAN TEN DAYS AFTER THEIR GAME-changing meeting at Ravenswood Farm, the two old spies found themselves shivering at the edge of a dark Siberian wood, hunkered down against the chill in the night air. But, as the Englishman politely reminded his Russian *confrere*, it was Siberia after all. Was that not a word synonymous with freezing one's balls off?

The Cambridge Two were wholly exhausted. They had endured a long and perilous trip. The journey to the back of beyond had been an exhausting chore but they had prevailed.

Traveling incognito, dressed as wealthy businessmen, the two men had flown from Heathrow to Moscow. Then, having safely gotten past airport security, it was on to St. Petersburg, sitting in the back of the 1950s bus. Disembarking, they caught the Red Star Trans-Siberian train with seconds to spare, and began the endless journey to Tvas.

Once aboard, shivering in their beastly compartment, they made their way overland to the tiny rail station at Tvas. Somehow, they managed to secure a pair of stout horses for the arduous cross-country trek across the bloody tundra to the winter palace of the tsars. That had taken the better part of the day and now, when night had fallen, they knew the temperature would surely plummet like a stone.

In the lone canvas duffel bag they'd shared were food, ammo, weapons, and two heavy bearskin coats. These were coats Halter used when he was at his home in the Swiss Alps, and they were undeniably warm. Halter's coat fit; Congreve's did not. It brushed the tops of his gum boots and proved very difficult to walk in. However, it had been a godsend while they were traveling in high winds on horseback.

They were now shut of their traveling clothing, and beneath the bearskin coats each man was wearing a black KGB officer's uniform from Ambrose's carry bag. Halter had secured these from his tailor in Moscow for their impending operation. These, along with serviceable identification and both men's fluency in Russian, were the only hope they had of getting inside the heavily fortified compound.

But Congreve wasn't so sure. His spoken Russian, while technically correct, was not nearly so idiomatic as Halter's. But, he reassured himself, perhaps it was good enough. He felt he looked preposterous in the ill-fitting KGB uniform and voluminous bearskin rug, but who in God's name knew what the reaction of the guards might be to this apparition.

Ambrose saw Halter looking at him in an odd way.

"What?" Congreve said.

"The trademark moustache, I'm afraid."

"What about it?"

"It won't serve, that's what. It needs shaving. No one, I mean no one, in the officer ranks of the KGB wears a moustache. You'll have to lose it."

Ambrose, a chap in a perpetual state of moustache, was stunned.

"*Lose it?*" he said, clearly terrified.

"Here. Use my knife. Don't bloody cut yourself, either."

A light and misty rain had begun to fall, adding to the chill and filling the forest with shadowy plays of light as Congreve removed every trace of facial hair without use of a mirror.

They had managed to get their horses inside the dense thicket of woods sight unseen. From there, they had made their way to a serviceable hiding place at the edge of the forest proper. Their concealed position was perhaps a thousand yards from the main gate.

It was staunchly defended. Guard towers manned by machine-gun-toting soldiers every fifty feet, a broad no-man's-land occupied by roving Dobermans, and armed sentries on high alert around every searchlight tower.

It occurred to Ambrose that such redundant se-

curity didn't make much sense out here in the uncharted realms of Siberia. Unless, of course, you
were expecting unwanted company after the out-
break of recent hostilities in Florida. Or perhaps the
arrival of some deity from Moscow had upped the
ante?

"Are you quite done with those binoculars?" a
slightly nicked but freshly shaven Congreve asked.
They'd only managed to secure one pair of night-
vision optics when they really needed two. The
misty glare from the mammoth searchlights atop
each guard tower made seeing clearly all but impossible, only adding to Halter's apparent frustration with what he thought merely an expensive
gadget.

"Just a damn minute, will you? I think I actually
see something," Halter said out of the corner of his
mouth. "Movement in the vicinity of the command-
and-control center entrance. A small motorcade is
arriving. A fancy black Audi in the lead has just
pulled up in front. Kremlin cars, I'd recognize them
anywhere. Two KGB men getting out of the front.
Someone climbing out of the rear seat . . . yes. Has to
be bigwig whose helo has just landed from Moscow
and he's . . . he's standing out in the cold, talking to
two or three officers who've come out from inside
the gate . . ."

"Recognize him?"

"No. Can't make out that much detail at this
distance. Short. Squat. Has two security brutes
in close attendance. They're all chatting like mad
about something. Odd. A high-level meeting in the
middle of the night? Here, have a look."

Halter handed Congreve the high-powered NVGs.

Congreve first turned them over in his hands, scrutinizing the optics.

"Ever used these before?" he asked Stefan.

"Not really. No. Why?"

"Your settings are all wrong, Professor. You need enhanced filtration in these wretched conditions. There we go. That should do," Congreve said, raising the glasses to his eyes and peering through them. He looked hard for a few moments before exclaiming, "What? No, no, that cannot be. I think I'm going stark raving mad, Stef!"

"What is it? Let me see . . ."

Congreve held on to the device.

"Hold on a tick . . . yes . . . unless my poor eyes deceive me . . . here . . . have a look and tell me what you see. Maybe I am crazy after all."

"All right, what am I looking at?" Halter took the bloody things to have another look, swinging them back and forth.

"Zoom in, Stef. Get a very close look at the short chap in the middle of the group. Turn the big knob underneath . . ."

"What? Oh, yes. Good God. I don't believe it. That's impossible . . . astounding likeness, really . . . however, I do think . . . but, still, I mean, really."

"It's Stalin, isn't it, Stef?"

"Well, it's obviously not Stalin, now, is it? Uncle Joe left us to fend for ourselves in 1953, remember?"

"So who the bloody hell is it then?"

"I've seen hundreds of hours of film of Joseph Stalin. Yet, for all that, I would swear on my mother's grave that the fellow I'm looking at was him," Halter said, handing the NVGs back to his comrade.

Congreve peered through them and said, "The ghost of Joe Stalin is now entering the building. Time to make our move, agreed?"

"If we've got but one life to live," Halter said, "let us give it now. We've really no alternative at this point, old fellow. Let's go cause trouble!"

THE TWO SPIES RETRACED THEIR STEPS THROUGH the heavy wood, the rocky ground now sodden with rain. They saw their tied steeds where they'd left them, stamping their hooves and snorting steam in the frigid air of the small clearing. They mounted up and made their way out of the woods to the stony, now muddy road they'd found earlier. The one that eventually wound its way around the perimeter of the forest and back to the main gate of the KGB compound.

Congreve could feel a thousand eyes on him as they approached the brilliantly illuminated guardhouse next to the heavily gated entry. Two men with machine guns instantly emerged from it and called for them to halt and dismount. Not a request, an order. Halter nodded agreeably and nimbly dropped to the ground. He then walked smiling toward the waiting muzzles of the dozen or so guns now pointed in his direction. It had been decided on the way in to let Stef do the talking. Ambrose would mutter a few appropriate words when challenged and show his ID when asked.

Halter was accustomed to real power inside the

subtle but deadly political minefield that was the Kremlin and most of Mother Russia. His name was known and feared inside the Kremlin walls, and his imposing presence could knock down any door that was closed against him.

One guard stepped forward while the other took the reins of Halter's black steed.

"Identification, please, General," the man said, holding his hand out.

Halter presented his KGB and state papers. The man perused them with great care, nodding his head. Congreve felt a wave of relief. Stef must have pulled it off. The two guards actually seemed in awe of his friend who, had, after all, legitimate credentials. But then they shifted their focus to him. At least, the two brutes didn't seem in the mood to shoot him where he stood as they approached. Even his horse was visibly nervous.

"Papers, Captain," the larger of the two demanded in harsh language.

Congreve muttered back in a strong Russian dialect intended to convey the tone of a seasoned KGB officer with a strong sense of power, command, and entitlement.

"Of course, Sergeant."

The man had a sturdy flashlight and studied his papers in the brilliant white beam. These gentlemen, he noticed, had helmets with a bit of flash. They appeared to be made of steel, polished to a mirrorlike finish. And their sharply tailored black uniforms reminded Congreve of nothing so much as Hitler's infamous SS "Death's Head" outfits.

"What is this here? No stamp? Why is it blank,

the space, Captain?" the fellow said, staring at him suspiciously. Congreve's mind went blank for a terrifying moment while it searched in vain for a satisfactory response.

"Well?" the big man said, with deliberate menace in his voice. He unsnapped his leather holster and grasped the grip of his pistol.

Congreve froze.

SIXTY-THREE

WHAT SEEMS TO BE THE TROUBLE HERE?"

It was Halter, thank God. Somehow, he was suddenly at Congreve's side. Congreve snapped out of it, affected irritation, and told Stef the problem.

"Missing a stamp or two, it appears, General Halter," Congreve said. "Sorry, sir. I don't know what happened. Some bureau idiot forgot to—"

Stef turned to the guard. "My man missing a stamp, is he?" he said, glowering at the younger of the two guards.

"Well, General, it does appear that his interdepartmental transit sticker is missing and also his—"

"I am his transit sticker, you bloody idiot! Do you have any idea whom you're speaking to?"

Halter held his opened KGB ID folder an inch from the man's frozen nose.

"Well?" Stef asked. "Can you read?"

"First Chief Directorate . . . Foreign Intelligence Service, sir. You have my deepest apologies. I'm sorry, sir. We were not informed of your impending arrival. And this man is your . . . your—"

"Captain Georgy Molotov is my aide-de-camp! And, as you can plainly see, he may be missing a sticker, but he is also wearing the fucking Gold Star of a Hero of the Russian Federation on his chest, for Christ's sake! Now, you will please escort us through the HQ entrance immediately. I want no further trouble out of you men. The captain and I are arriving late because our flight from St. Petersburg was diverted due to engine troubles. We had to ride for hours on bloody horseback just to get here."

A few minutes later they were standing just inside the imposing building. A decorated officer shook Stef's hand.

"I'm very sorry about the inconvenience, General. Please follow me. The meeting has already started, I'm afraid, but just a short time ago. All seats are taken save a few at the rear. You and the captain will have to be seated at the back of the room. Unless you want me to disturb them and inform them of your late arrival? Perhaps you'd rather be seated at the very front?"

"No, no. Won't be necessary, Sergeant. Just show us inside the room. We'll take it from there."

"Of course, General Halter. Again, my apologies. And to you as well, Captain Molotov. If you gentlemen will just follow me? The captain of the guards will then escort you into the meeting room."

And so he did.

Halter's one great fear now was that he himself might be recognized. Recognition meant the end of his life, whether he was executed immediately or not. There was little chance he could talk his way out of this one; he had known that all along. Putin would have his head and that would be the end of it.

So be it, he said to himself, and forged ahead.

He wore his cap low over his eyes entering the hall, and that, combined with the collar of his furry overcoat up around his ears seemed, at least so far, to be working. Should they be discovered, he also knew Ambrose Congreve would be tortured endlessly, months in Lubyanka Prison perhaps, perhaps more.

And then Ambrose Congreve would be shot for a spy—

Halter shook such thoughts of impending doom out of his mind as they settled into the two remaining seats.

STEFAN WONDERED IF THIS SPUR-OF-THE-MOMENT mission to Siberia had not been ill-advised. But he decided he'd been in much tighter situations and always survived. He was doing his duty. What he was doing could change the course of history. He had it in his power to save the Motherland. It was that simple. And he decided to let whatever was coming his way, come. Alas, if the worst should happen . . .

He and Congreve could see a raised podium. Six ramrod-straight KGB officers in jet black uniforms, glittering with gleaming decorations and combat ribbons, sat facing the audience below.

In the center of all this militaristic magnificence was an apparition. The living ghost of Joseph Stalin was in the center seat.

His face was bright red and contorted in anger. He was screaming at a big John Wayne of a man standing at attention. His gnarled hands were clasped firmly behind his pressed-khaki-shirted back as he stood a few feet below and facing the raised platform. An American, obviously, Halter thought.

At that moment, he saw Stalin glance over at him. He brushed it off. He'd never met the man and the chance of recognition was minimal.

The two imposters sat and listened as if fate had put them in this room. And, indeed, it had. Their fate would be determined this night.

"And what do you have to say for yourself, Colonel?" Stalin said to the defiant man looking up from below. The American was equally belligerent.

"You pay for my military advice and then you tell me what to do, for crissakes. This is not what I came here to do."

"I tell *everyone* what to do, you fucking idiot! Now, it seems that even our famous American mercenary has qualms about civilian casualties. This, while leading a tank battalion into the outskirts of Prague. I ask you once more, Colonel Beauregard. Are you refusing to lead your men across the Czech border? Your answer will decide your fate, I warn you now."

The man began to speak, reconsidered, and paused a moment to reflect on his options.

"American mercenary?" Congreve whispered, not turning his head toward Halter.

Halter placed his lips near Ambrose's right ear. He whispered:

"Beauregard. The famously disgraced founder of Vulcan. Our suspicions and Kremlin rumors are true. Meant to divert attention away from Putin's own actions. Shh. Listen."

And the American continued.

"Uncle Joe, listen here, I'm giving you a stern warning, not refusing a goddamn thing. I am questioning the military wisdom of marching into a NATO capital at a time when tensions are higher than at the height of the Cuban missile crisis. I don't see how you can avoid a preemptive nuclear strike on Moscow from the United States or Britain or any nuclear power.

"The U.S. is sworn to protect its NATO allies," Beauregard continued, "and the Pentagon will choose to fight, I promise you people. I know the chairman of the Joint Chiefs, Admiral Moore. He is a hawk of the first order, severely disappointed in the White House. And he won't wait for a weak president's approval before launching his big missiles, trust me. You want World War Three? You got it, Uncle Joe. Your call."

Uncle Joe smiled, a cat with a flurry of canary feathers stuck to his lips.

"Thank you for that lesson in political science. Do you really believe that we have not considered the ramifications of every single move we are preparing to make? Are you insane? Any threat to attack us will result in our country going to a war footing. And the destruction of more American cities like Miami, only exponentially worse. Our network of KGB saboteurs in the U.S. will put a quick end to any military threats resulting from the invasion of Estonia, Poland, and the Czech Republic. Now I ask you. Do you wish to follow my orders? Or resign your commission and face the consequences?"

"Give me a date and time, Uncle Joe. We will march into Prague and we will take no prisoners."

"Good! Finally, he comes to his senses!"

"May I be excused?" the Colonel said. "It's late. I have a lot of work to do if we're to be ready to start moving troops into theater in one week, sir."

"Yes, of course. Go. See to your men. Now . . . what's next?" Uncle Joe said, his lidded eyes roving around the audience. "Oh, yes. I'd like to call upon the two gentlemen in the rear of the room . . . yes, yes, the two who just arrived. Please stand and be recognized."

Congreve felt Halter go rigid, his hand suddenly clenching Congreve's knee painfully. *Heart attack*, Congreve thought. "I've been recognized," Stef whispered fiercely. "It's over."

"Gentlemen," Uncle Joe repeated, "I've asked you to stand."

"No, Stef, wait—"

"When I get up," he croaked under his breath, "leave the room. Now. You have to get out or we both die . . . go!"

"No! I won't leave you! You cannot—"

Halter stood up tall, and all eyes were riveted on the big man.

"I am General Stefanovich Halter. Some of you here may know me. Sorry, we were unavoidably delayed. My adjutant, Captain Molotov, and I are here at the express order of President Putin. The president asked me to convey his compliments and ask that you—that you—sorry, I feel a bit—"

A dry and strangled cry rose up from Stefan's throat.

Halter suddenly clutched at his chest with both hands and uttered a loud scream of pain. His face turned tomato red and his eyes bulged as he stumbled backward to the floor, knocking over his chair. Congreve, who'd first thought his friend had suffered a heart attack, now thought he might have been shot. Calling out for a doctor in Russian, he knelt down beside his fallen comrade. He leaned down and spoke rapidly into his ear as pandemonium broke out in the crowded room. No one knew quite what to do.

"Stef! What is it? What's wrong?"

"Heart attack," Stef croaked with a grim smile. "Go! Get the hell out while you still can, Georgy. Run. Don't look back. Warn everyone you can. Tell them what you saw and heard here tonight. Imminent invasion. Keep moving, say you're calling General Halter's doctors in Moscow—now, don't argue. Get to your horse while you still can. *Go! Go!*"

AN HOUR LATER, AMBROSE CONGREVE WAS GALLOP-ing across the rocky tundra through the frigid night air, his great bearskin coat flapping wildly behind him. He was using the stars to navigate, headed for the little train station at Tvas. Once there, he would wait in the shadows, watching the tracks from the shadows. If no one came to kill him, he would try to catch the next train headed west for St. Petersburg. If he could evade capture by watchful KGB thugs sure to be waiting for him at the rail stations, he hoped to find his way onto a Swissair flight to Zurich. And from there a train or two northward to Calais; finally, a ferry across the English Channel and on to London.

That was his plan, at any rate.

An hour passed, then two. He'd almost grown comfortable with the snorting and sweat-soaked beast beneath him. The secret, he learned, was to focus only on holding on, boots taut in the stirrups, one hand on the pommel, the reins in the other.

He couldn't shake the feeling that as desperately bad as things were for him, they were no doubt far, far worse for his friend Halter. Stef was either lying dead of a heart attack or, if he'd survived that, being interrogated by brutal KGB agents.

Ambrose whispered a silent prayer, knowing full well he owed his life to his friend for aiding and abetting his escape, even in that dire moment when Halter most surely knew himself to be lost.

Congreve had to survive at least long enough to honor what was perhaps Stef's last wish. *Go back. Tell everyone what happened here.* He'd already decided that as soon as he got safely home to London he'd go directly to Number Ten Downing. There he would tell the prime minister about everything he'd both seen and heard at the secret KGB military facility at Tvas. And the little man who would be Stalin.

As he rode on, Congreve was unable to shake off the heavy sense of grief over his old friend Halter. He'd long known there was heart trouble. But Stefan Halter was a force of nature. Perhaps he'd beat the heart attack into submission. If he wasn't dead, he'd prove a hard man to kill, that much was certain.

But what then for poor Halter?

Ambrose put the spurs to his steed, having decided not to even think about what those monsters in the black SS uniforms might do to his friend before they killed him.

SIXTY-FOUR

ABOARD *BLACKHAWKE*

H AWKE COULDN'T SLEEP.

He was tossing and turning again, chasing sleep. A bad habit of his that only made the nightmare worse. He cursed aloud, rolled over, and squinted one-eyed at the little red Hermès travel clock he always packed when traveling. Just gone five. He turned over on his back, placed his hands behind his head, and tried the meditative breathing exercise: three in, three out. A little trick his darling Nell Spooner had taught him once when he first began battling insomnia.

He pressed a button on the overhead. A flatscreen monitor that mirrored the instrument panel up at the ship's helm station slid down. He tapped the touchscreen and it flared into life. He angled it toward him for a closer look. All systems looked good: propulsion, weaponry, ship's comms, air and sea defenses.

The big boat was currently making twenty-two knots over the bottom, holding true on a corrected course of 188 degrees, SSE. To the casual observer, or even the not-so-casual one, she was on a line drive for the southwest coast of Cuba.

Hawke stared at the dim bulbs glowing softly in the overhead. He turned his thoughts to the impending sea battle. The owner's stateroom was dark. Faint pink light was showing through the large oval port lights on the eastern side of the cabin. Far below and aft, the engines were throbbing away, a deep, rumbling rhythm present as always. He tried an old trick, trying to put his body's machinery in sync with his big diesel engines.

Breathe in . . . hold . . . exhale. Breathe in . . . hold . . . exhale. Breathe in . . . hold—hold on.

Someone was rapping at the door.

Hawke got up, grabbed his navy blue dressing gown off the bedpost, and went to see who the hell it was. He pulled the door open.

It was Stokely. He said, "Hey, it's me."

"Stoke, right? Thought I recognized you."

"I come in?"

"Yeah, what's up, man? Have a seat."

"I know it's early. I know how much you hate somebody waking you up when it's still dark. But this is important."

"Come on, Stoke, no worries. I was already awake, man. Never can sleep on the eve of battle.

Sit down over there by my desk and I'll get us some coffee."

Hawke walked over to the small bar where a Nespresso coffeemaker stood. "Coffee?"

"You got a Diet Coke in the fridge somewhere? Don't bother, man, I know where the damn fridge is."

Hawke sipped his coffee and stepped into his all stainless-steel head. He stared at his bleary blue eyes in the mirror over the sink and splashed some cold water on his face. It was beginning. He could tell by the look on Stoke's face that whatever it was he had to say, it was serious business.

He went back into his stateroom and dropped down into the upholstered chair opposite his old friend. "Tell me this is good news, Stoke."

"It's just news, bossman. I'll leave it to you to decide."

"Fair and balanced."

"I was up on the bridge, talking to the skipper about what she could expect in the way of, uh, excitement when we get near the island later on today. Death-from-above kind of conversation, you know how that goes. Geneva King is one cool dude, though. Not her first rodeo."

"Why I hired her. Decorated naval combat veteran, first in her class at Annapolis. So what's up?"

Stoke could tell the boss had gone into full attack mode now, had the bone in his teeth again and didn't want to waste any damn words.

"Brick Kelly called the boat earlier. Comms guy tossed it to me. Brick said you needed your sleep, he

could tell me what he had to say. Here's what went
down in Cuba last night. Two Puerto Rican CIA
guys, posing undercover as construction workers
on 'Spy Island,' inspected the three big waterfront
warehouses on the port. They got caught, unfortunately, and there was gunfire exchanged. One guy
didn't make it. Head shot. The other guy managed
to get outside with a couple of bullets in his shoulder, dove into the harbor, hid under the dock for a
while, and then swam to safety. When Brick called
me, he put the guy who'd made it out on the line."

"And?"

"I talked to him. Guy said they found vodka. I
mean, cases of that damn vodka in the warehouses.
It was that German vodka, the one Harry took off
the Russian spy ship. Stuff was stacked up to the rafters in those warehouses. CIA guy said he estimated
the total count at over ten thousand cases, twelve
per. So over a hundred thousand bottles with those
Feuerwasser labels. I made the CIA guy describe
them in detail."

"Warehouses full of vodka."

"What the man said."

"Logistics operation," Hawke said. "Okay, this is
good stuff. That Russian spy ship offloaded its ship-
ment at Isla de Pinos. The enemy is obviously going
to be mounting all sabotage attacks on the eastern
U.S. from that port. Meaning there are more attacks already in the works. Hell, they've got enough
firewater ninety miles from America to take down
the whole state of Florida. But here's where it gets
really good. We can now tie the power grid sabo-

tage in Miami right back to Cuba, Stoke. That's very good news. Because that means we'll have conclusive evidence of Russian complicity in an unprovoked attack on U.S. soil."

"Which means?"

"It means Putin can't weasel out of this one. We pin the Miami sabotage directly on Putin and he goes from offense to defense overnight."

"Putin. He's everywhere we look. Getting in people's shit."

"Yeah. Which is good because it'll make it easy for me to find him when I go looking."

"What do we do about all that hooch in the harbor at Isla de Pinos? Stuff is dangerous to deal with, man."

"Destroy all three warehouses," Hawke said. "Need to figure out a sensible way to do that. By that, I mean without blowing up Cuba and the state of Florida. I'm glad you got that former navy UDT explosives team guy along for the ride. What's the kid's name again?"

"Gator Luttier."

"Yeah, Luttier. We're going to need Mr. Luttier to level that installation in a controlled detonation. Do me a favor, Stoke. Go aft to crew quarters. Wake up Gator and the SEAL team captain. Tell him you and I need a little powwow with both of them at 0800. In the ship's wardroom. Got it?"

"I guess it *was* good news."

"You bet, Stoke. Thanks. Anything else?"

"Two things. Ambrose has decided to go trekking in Siberia. And—"

"Wait—What did you just say?"

"Brick says Ambrose is in Siberia. He and that Cambridge pal of yours, Halter. Two of them didn't bother to tell anybody at the CIA or MI6. Just took off. Trying to find some secret KGB base out in the middle of nowhere, Brick says."

"What the hell, Stoke? Ambrose is in no shape to do anything like that. Siberia? I can't believe he wouldn't talk to me first. I would never have let him go."

"Probably why he didn't talk to you first."

"Damn it to hell. He'll get himself killed. Does his wife know about this?"

"I couldn't say, boss."

"All right. I'll call her. What else?"

"Big storm brewing. On a collision course with us, blowing up from south of Jamaica. Could be the first hurricane of the season. Tropical storm Annabel. This rain and wind we've seen the last six hours is the leading edge. NOAA Key West is watching it for us. They're saying it may veer northwest and head for the Gulf of Mexico, but nobody's calling it yet."

"We'll deal with it. We always do. You and Gator better be on top of this explosive situation. Dig huge holes in the floors of the warehouses and let all that stuff run into the ground before they light any fuses. I don't know. Whatever."

"On it," Stoke said, realizing the boss had just solved a huge problem for him.

HAWKE HAD THE PHONE IN HIS HAND, PUTTING through a call to Lady Mars. He'd try to assure her about Ambrose although he felt like he could use a little assurance himself. What the hell had gotten into Ambrose? Whatever it was, it was likely to get him killed and—Hawke had to do something and do it fast—the call was going through.

"Hullo?"

"Diana, it's me, Alex."

"Oh, God, Alex, I've been so terrified. Thank you for calling. I didn't know where to turn."

"Where is he, Diana?"

"Russia, I guess. I've no idea. Three days ago he left for Russia with a knapsack slung over his shoulder and a lilt in his step. Your friend the professor told him about some kind of secret KGB base in Siberia. Next thing I knew, he was gone. The two of them."

"Did he say why? What did he think he was going to do about it?"

"He said they were training a non-Russian army there. Foreign troops and weapons to give Putin plausible deniability for his imminent invasion of sovereign NATO countries. He and Halter planned to expose the whole thing before war started."

"Ambrose planned to stop an entire army? God save us all."

"That was his idea when he walked out the door seventy-two hours ago, Alex. Off to save the world, he said."

"Good Lord, Diana."

"Can you help him, Alex? You have to do something!"

"I'll do whatever I can, I promise you. I'll start our people looking right away."

"Move heaven and earth if you have to. If I lose him . . . sorry . . . I . . . I've lost everything."

"So have I. You have my private number. Call me the second you hear from him. Try not to worry, he's incredibly resourceful."

SIXTY-FIVE

OFF THE COAST OF CUBA

THE SHIP'S WARDROOM, WHERE *BLACKHAWKE'S* officers normally met for briefings and dining, had been turned into the ship's "war room" for the duration of the Cuban mission. There was a round carbon-fiber table in the center; various rectangular liquid crystal maps, embedded in the crystal clear surface, could be accessed using touchscreen technology. All nine screens were multilayered with real-time radar, weather radar, thermal imaging, live sat passes, almost every aspect you needed to fight the boat in a combat situation.

At eight A.M., Hawke entered the room to find everyone already standing around the table, poring

over various maps and layers, whiteboarding a final
battle plan for the impending attack. Ship's officers,
the sonar/radar officer, fire control, and other key
Blackhawke personnel were there. And the Stokeland Raiders were represented, not just Stoke himself, and the incorrigible Harry Brock, but also a
few new leaders who'd emerged, younger guys with
names like Gator and Fat and 12-Gauge.

Chatter around the table ceased as they all turned
to greet the ship's owner. He looked well rested and
his white smile was full of positive energy and determination. Hawke wished everyone a good morning and got right down to business. When he asked
them who wanted to go first, they all looked at each
other, waiting for the other guy to go.

"Okay, I'll go," Hawke said. "Number one. You
cartography guys figure out where the Russian
combat-ops blockhouse is located yet?"

"It's here," Brock said, touching his finger to the
central map screen and highlighting a mountain
location on Isla de Pinos. "On this hilltop in the
jungle overlooking the port operations. Two stories,
concrete block bunker-type building. Cuban army
patrols, twenty-four seven. Defenses include SAM
missile emplacements hidden here, here, and here,
in the jungly terrain above and below the bunker.
The only viable ground approaches are trails located here . . . and here. Overgrown jungle trails
that haven't been used in decades. All you need is a
good machete from the looks of them. Element of
surprise, whichever trail we go up."

Hawke looked at Harry. "Those trails look

too good to be true. You'd better assume they are booby-trapped or mined, Mr. Brock."

"You're right. Hadn't considered that."

"You found the bunker, you take it out, Mr. Brock. How many troops do you need to go up the hill?"

"Me and Gator could maybe handle it. Just give us a couple of M60 heavy machine guns and some jiffy-bang Semtex explosive charges. I don't anticipate a lot of resistance."

"Nothing's easy, Harry, you should know that by now. Stoke? What do you say to Mr. Brock's plan?"

"Yeah. I looked at it. Gator Luttier over there and Harry ought to be able to handle it. We can spare 'em."

Hawke said, "What else?"

Stoke said, "Our primary commando force will have its hands full dealing with perimeter defenses containing the three explosives stockpiles. That, and the port-side defenses. Guards, concertina wire fences with machine gun towers and searchlights all over the damn place, boss. Look at these thermals and sat images during yesterday's guard changes on the fence line. See these troops marching here, and over here? Black uniforms. They ain't Cuban militiamen, that's for damn sure."

"Russian Spetsnaz forces," Hawke observed.

"Yeah," Stoke agreed. "Storm troopers. The toughest of the tough. Up to you, boss. We've got two primary objectives. Destroy the combat-ops bunker. And meanwhile take out those three vodka warehouses. Mr. Brock's got the bunker. I'd like to go in there with the six-man SEAL squad and eliminate the threat of the explosives. Everybody else is a shooter."

Hawke nodded approval. "Do me a favor, Stoke, when you breach those warehouses. Get at least one intact case of that explosive safely back here to the boat for analysis."

"One case of joy juice coming right up."

"All right. You men know what we have to do, so go do it. I'll stay right here on board and keep the chili warm down in the galley," Hawke said with a smile.

Everyone laughed because everybody knew the owner would have more than enough to keep him busy just fighting the harbor air and shore defenses. A drone would be launched from the foredeck of *Blackhawke* once they entered the harbor. That would give them a solid picture of what they were up against. Resistance, it went without saying, would be heavy. The Cubans had the might of battle-tested Russian forces behind them.

On land. And from the sky, MiG 35s.

Pentagon sat shots downloaded the evening before had revealed an airstrip with perhaps an additional squadron of older Russian Sukhoi Su-35 fighter jets. Those fighters, Hawke anticipated, could be airborne seconds after Cuban radar saw the big boat make a drastic course correction and veer to the east, headed on new course as straight as a frozen rope, directly toward the mouth of the harbor.

Hawke left them to it and made his way down to the primary gun deck and some fresh tropical air. Dark clouds, swollen with rain, towered up in the south. He looked out across a sea of whitecaps marching away to the horizon. The wind whipped his foul-weather jacket around him. He was about to go to war. And the sky all around him had an eerie greenish cast that spelled trouble.

There were a lot of logistical issues remaining, and time, such as it was, was running short. Hawke immediately decided to visit each of the four on-board 23mm cannon turrets. Two were located on the foredeck and two aft. These formidable weapons systems, in addition to the ship's SAM launchers, would be the principal defenders of the boat when the shooting started.

HAWKE'S FIRST STOP WAS A VISIT WITH THE COM-mander of all four turrets. His home was the forward-most turret on the foredeck. In peacetime, all four of the boat's gun turrets were concealed under specially designed bulkheads, which gave the ship the profile and pacific appearance of a gentle-man's megayacht, not a lethal warship. In combat configuration, it was another picture altogether, bristling with armament.

Now that all four of *Blackhawke*'s turrets had been exposed, even Hawke was impressed at the sight of the big guns. Ironically enough, they were Russian-designed cannons. He'd recently had them installed while they were in port in Key West. He was extremely curious to see how the powerful guns performed in battle today, as each turret represented one of the four cornerstones of *Blackhawke*'s defense measures.

The ZSU23-4 23mm antiaircraft liquid-cooled guns were capable of acquiring, tracking, and engaging low-flying aircraft and featured a folding radar dish that could be retracted to the chassis. The cannons were also capable of firing at land and sea targets while under way in rough seas. This was because of a highly sophisticated integrated gun/radar stabilization system.

Each main turret was also equipped with a day/night camera and a laser rangefinder. Mounted above the radar/sensor pod was a layer of six fire-and-forget surface-to-air missiles, to complement each of the four main cannons in combat situations. Each gun crew consisted of a gun commander, gunner, and radar operator, all stationed inside the turret, afforded a comforting degree of protection by the 8.9mm thickness of the turret's steel armor.

Blackhawke now presented a formidable naval foe. But, still, for her owner, the big question remained unanswered as the boat neared the coastline of Cuba. Would *Blackhawke* now prove her worth in combat? And when he attacked the heavily defended harbor of Isla de Pinos, could she simultaneously fight a threefold attack from the air, land, and sea?

And another unknown. Hawke was carefully keeping a weather eye on meteorological events now approaching Cuba from the south. The strong hurricane was unleashing its early fury on the coast of the island at the moment. The eye of the storm would provide a window for his assault. As soon as it passed over the mainland and headed out over warm water, the boat would be making its escape. Would that weather, too, become a factor?

He would find out soon enough.

Hawke was still up forward talking with the young commander of the number one gun crew when the war started. He looked at his watch and noted the time to be used later. It was now 1830 hours, Zulu time.

The number three turret radar operator was first to disturb the false calm.

"I've got a contact, sir," Hawke heard in his headphones.

"Go ahead, Sparky, what have you got?" Hawke said.

"Radar showing four fighter aircraft approaching our stern out of the east-southeast, sir, altitude thirty-five hundred feet, speed Mach 1.14, range nine miles and closing . . ."

"Four bogies?" Hawke said.

"Four total, roger. Three bogies now breaking formation and shedding altitude," the gun commander said. "Looks like they may intend to get on our stern quarter, sir. Lead airplane now climbing new course south-southwest and . . . uh, climbing through forty thousand . . . and . . . diving now . . . he's on us."

"Take them out, gentlemen," Hawke said, climbing down from the turret and getting the hell out of their way. He dropped nimbly down to the deck and headed back up to the bridge where he naturally belonged when in combat.

The turret behind him instantly rotated forty-five degrees as the Gun Dish locked in on the single approaching Cuban fighter. Hawke, headed aft, could actually feel the deck shudder beneath him as the crew fired a burst from the 23mm cannons. Looking back over his shoulder as he made his way up the steps to the bridge, he saw the muzzles spouting flame as they recoiled in anger.

Hawke was racing upward, taking the steps two at a time, when he saw the solitary Su-35 diving on them. The single-seater fighter had a brown-and-grey camouflage paint scheme and Cuban flags on her fuselage and wings; her two thrust-vectoring turbofan engines were screaming as she maintained her descent and opened fire on *Blackhawke*.

As he bolted up the last few steps, Hawke saw the Cuban fighter's single 30mm nose cannon blazing away at his bow turret, rounds zinging off the steel, a multitude of geysers erupting in the stormy seas around the boat.

As he watched, he saw the forward turret swiveling, her guns locking in on the approaching enemy airplane as the antiaircraft crew opened fire with a vengeance, throwing thousands of frag rounds in the face of the oncoming fighter.

When Alex pushed inside the bridge, a loud cheer went up from his officers. Not for him, but celebrating the sight of the flaming, disintegrating carcass of the Russian-built Su-35, just missing the bow and trailing a flame of burning jet fuel before impacting the hard and unforgiving sea.

Hawke took a quick look at his navigator's air combat radar display and said, "It looks like that guy's three friends are no longer all that sure they want to mess with us at the moment . . . The other three bogies now peeling off and appear to be high-tailing it back to sunny Cuba, land of enchantment."

"I'd say round one goes to us, Commander," the ship's new skipper, Geneva King, said. "Now comes the hard part."

SIXTY-SIX

———

HAWKESMOOR

———

BING CROSBY AND LOUIS ARMSTRONG. HE'D never forget it. The two crooners were singing that lovely old duet "Gone Fishin'," from the 1940s. Pelham Grenville would later recall that, when he first heard explosive gunfire erupt beyond the kitchen windows, it was playing softly on his old radio. And Satchmo was singing . . .

"You gone fishin', you ain't got no ambition . . ."

It had just gone midnight. He was perched on his stool in the butler's pantry, finishing the needlepoint Christmas belt for Alexei, singing right along with the two crooners:

Gone fishin' by a shady, wady pool
I'm wishin' I could be that kinda fool

And then it started. Bombs. Explosions. A terrific fusillade of gunshots ringing out in the night as, outside on the lawn, the heavily armed Scotland Yard Royalty Protection officers defended the house. They were up against a sudden and devastating ground attack. Pelham shook off the shock and *moved*.

He dropped his needlework and ran for the main hall. The exchange of gunfire rapidly grew in intensity and volume out on the lawns. His sense of terror grew. It was quickly turning into a pitched battle with the Scotland Yard and MI6 defenders; and it was edging nearer to the house now, much closer than when he'd first heard the single shots ring out. He raced into the darkened main hall and switched off all belowstairs illumination, his mind suddenly reeling at what he next heard.

Was that noise coming from upstairs?

Distant echoes of gunfire could be heard from somewhere inside the house! The intruders must be inside now! Had someone gotten in through a blown-out window up there? Had an exterior door been breached in another wing? Racing up the winding marble staircase, Pelham called out to Inspector Walker and Archie Carstairs. Pelham shouted, "Walker! Carstairs! They've gotten inside the house! Shooting over in the west wing and getting closer. Turn around! Go grab Alexei from his bed and head for the roof. *NOW!*"

He continued to shout at the top of his lungs over and over as he climbed. Perhaps Tristan and Archie had been firing upstairs, probably shooting from their windows overlooking the entrance to the main house. But now he heard shouting and gunfire in the Great Hall below. No more doubts; gunmen were in the house now. He almost made it to the top floor.

"Is Alexei all right?" Pelham cried out to Detective Walker. The boy's room was to the left of the stairs. When they emerged, Walker cradling the boy in his arms, Alexei appeared to be unhurt.

Walker said, "Yes! He's fine, but we've not a second to lose. Russian paratroopers with mortars, a bloody invasion. We counted a dozen or more on the south lawn—they're about to breach the main entrance to the house—every second counts!"

There then came that rumble and explosion, the deep roar of it rolling up the staircase, the mammoth oak doors blown off their hinges, gunfire on the night wind howling inside. And that sound was soon overwhelmed by the horrific chatter of automatic weapons being fired indiscriminately into the dark chambers of the massive old seventeenth-century pile. More shots on the first floor, ricocheting off the marble floors, ripping up art and centuries of priceless old masterpieces of furniture and woodwork and portraits of Hawke ancestors.

There was not a second to grieve. This legendary country seat of the Hawke family had been through fire, pestilence, and war, time and time again down the centuries; and yet here it still stood. And it would survive this invasion, too. Somehow. But a dozen or more armed foreign invaders, intent on murdering the heir to the Hawke throne in the sanctity of his home?

Not if he had anything to say about it.

Pelham's white-hot anger at the enormity of this outrage mounted second by second. He was filled with a strange energy, almost a felt force, that inhabited his very being. He would deny them their young and innocent prey or he himself would most certainly die trying.

Reaching the top of the stairs, Pelham eyed a towering mahogany armoire standing on the landing of the third floor.

The ancient piece of furniture was almost twelve feet high and as broad and as heavy as two grand pianos. But, if you could somehow manage to just tip it forward enough, it would go careening down the three flights of marble steps all the way to the ground floor, killing or gravely injuring anyone in its path and . . . perhaps even stalling the assault long enough for them to reach the . . .

"They've breached the front entrance!" Pelham shouted to the two guardians. "They're coming up the staircase. Detective Walker, you've got to get Alexei up to the roof *now*! Archie, come down here and help me topple this wooden behemoth and we'll send those who dare ascend a little present. It might buy us a few minutes . . ."

In an instant the brawny bodyguard was beside him and throwing all his might and muscle against the thing. It creaked loudly and then started to pitch forward an inch or so. Pelham, with his newfound power, also put his shoulder into the thing at the critical moment, and it leaned over well past the recovery point. Over and down it went, like a runaway freight train careening down a steep mountain slope.

He and Archie could hear the screams of men ascending the staircase being crushed as they saw it coming. They tried vainly to get out of the way of the mahogany hurtling toward them.

Pelham and Archie then turned and raced up stairs to the topmost floor. There they found the opened door and narrow stairway leading up to the roof. Pelham called out to the inspector.

"Have you got him, Inspector Walker?" Pelham cried out. "Are you out there?"

But there was no answer.

DETECTIVE TRISTAN WALKER SWUNG OPEN THE heavy iron door onto the roof. The yellow moon, scudded with dark clouds, was nearly full and he could see the dark silhouette of Hawke's black helicopter waiting for them amid the maze of chimneys. He held Alexei in one arm and gripped his automatic weapon in his right hand, scanning the skies for more descending paratroopers as he and his young charge raced across the rooftops toward salvation.

All was still across the vast black sea of ancient tarpaper and towering brick chimneys, some dating back hundreds of years.

Tristan was nearly halfway to the helo when a black figure jumped out from behind a tower of ancient brick and fired at him twice, point blank, then turned and ran for the chopper. Walker had been completely spun around when one of the rounds found his left shoulder, missing Alexei by an inch or so. His upper arm erupted in pain, and he saw his blood had spattered the boy.

He ignored the burning wound and set the child down on the tarpapered roof. Then he bent down and said, calmly, "Wait here for a moment, Alexei. Don't move, all right? We're going to be fine. Pelham and Archie will be here to get you in a second. That bad man wants to destroy our helicopter. I've got to stop him . . ."

"He shot you . . ." Alexei said through tears.

"Mosquito bite," Walker said, kissing the top of his head. "Happens all the time." Then he turned and ran toward the escaping Russian militiaman, firing as he ran.

A moment later, Pelham, having heard the gunfire on the roof, was on his knees with his arms around the boy. He was shocked by the amount of glistening blood on Alexei's face and in his hair and feared for the worst.

"Are you hurt, Alexei?" he said, fear pumping madly inside his poor old heart.

"No, sir, not me. Inspector Walker is. He ran over there, where the helicopter is."

"I'll take him, Pelham," Archie said, bending down to gather the boy up in his arms. "Chopper's over that way. Let's go!"

They ran through the chimney forest, startled at the chatter of an automatic weapon nearby. They saw the detective now, hiding behind a large pipe and firing his machine gun. At that moment they saw another man, dressed in black from head to toe, dart out from behind the helicopter. He was running soundlessly, racing toward Walker from his blind side, his gun up, unseen . . .

The Russian raised his gun to fire and . . . suddenly screamed and twisted, then collapsed to the roof, still and silent. Pelham saw that Archie had fired his pistol, dropping the assailant on the run. Now, the bodyguard called to them as he raced to the aid of his wounded comrade, Walker, crouched in the shadow of the waiting chopper. Pelham was right on his heels.

"Let's go, Pelham," Walker cried. "They'll reach the roof at any second!"

Archie had started the chopper's motor.

Pelham took Alexei's hand and they raced toward their only hope of escape. Its large blades beginning to rotate slowly beneath the unblinking white stare of the cold and oblivious moon.

SIXTY-SEVEN

Isla de Pinos

THE WIND HAD INCREASED DRAMATICALLY. THE big ship was pitching and yawing in heavy seas, towering waves of green water crashing over her bow and superstructure. A hard, slanting rain hammered the bridge, so hard you could hear the thrumming through the steel bulkhead above. Every now and then a jagged spear of lightning would crack nearby, lighting up the night outside the forward bridge windows, illuminating the rain so brilliantly that it looked like a solid wall. One they somehow penetrated as the ship steamed on toward the mouth of the island harbor.

Hawke looked at the Chelsea barometer up on the bulkhead and was shocked to see how quickly and how far the thin red needle had fallen. Masses of dark purple thunderheads were stacking up on the southern horizon, and the sky was now the color of a nasty bruise. Cuba was directly in the path, soon to get slammed by Hurricane Annabel.

Unless, as sometimes happened, the storm changed its mind. Veered west-northwest for the Keys and the Gulf of Mexico. But that was a very big maybe.

Hawke remained on the bridge, watching for any early skirmishes at the outset of the coming battle. The relatively moonless night and increasing dark clouds provided good cover for combat operations tonight. But the approaching tempest was putting severe pressure on the mission timetable. In his head, Hawke now advanced every aspect of his battle plan and made mental notes to keep his crew abreast of these critical changes as they happened. He was one of the few naval officers ever to graduate from Dartmouth Naval College who could hold an entire battle plan within his mind.

Everything was now dictated by the changing course and speed of the storm bearing down on them.

When the real battle commenced, former SEAL snipers with IR scopes in full camo, having taken concealed positions on the ship's highest deck, would take out any uninvited waterborne guests who happened to make the serious mistake of getting too close to the bizarre yacht they'd declared war against.

Or, onshore, his navy snipers would handle enemy soldiers advancing on the Stokeland Raiders' defensive position once they were safely ashore. And, finally, they were tasked with taking out all the enemy searchlight towers looming over the harbor compound to enable Stokely's guys to breach the perimeter and attack their targets.

For now, the boat proceeding at dead slow, all calm aboard. Minutes passed . . .

The peace was soon shattered by the sonar-radar operator's warning booming over the PA system. Two thirty-foot Cuban coast guard high-speed patrol boats made a fatal error as the strange vessel steamed into their harbor. Despite *Blackhawke*'s stern radio warning to their skippers to give the big yacht a wide berth, and come no closer than a thousand yards, the Cubans chose to come charging out into the harbor, engage, and open fire; each with two deck-mounted .50-cal. machine guns.

Hawke endured this pestilence of bee stings for as long as he could before giving the four turret commanders the "Engage. Fire at will" order to silence all that infernal buzzing. Suddenly, *Blackhawke*'s fore and aft 23mm cannons opened up, all four turrets swinging around, blazing away in tandem. The fire had a horrific effect on the lightly armored patrol boats and their crews; the barrage of incoming rounds was causing serious damage to the two enemy vessels. But, either bravely, foolishly, or both, on they came.

"Enemy vessels closing to within one thousand yards, Skipper," said the voice on the PA system heard throughout the bridge deck. Hawke acknowledged as he spotted the approaching enemy blips on the nearest radar screen.

"Enough of their crap," Commander Hawke told his gun crews. "Attention, two and three. Send those two bastards to the bottom where they belong."

Gun turrets two and three immediately whirled and tracked and locked onto the two closing targets. Both turrets belched fire as two deadly antiship missiles were launched. The perfect twins arced into the deep black sky en route to their targets. Leaving a billowing plume of orange and white smoke trailing in their wakes, the pair of Hellfires raced upward, reached the apogee, and dove, screaming downward. They closed on the two zigzagging Cuban attack vessels, both captains now effecting desperate evasive maneuvers and hoping to escape.

But any hopes the Cubans had of avoiding catastrophe were instantly dashed. Two missiles struck each boat simultaneously, instantly turning both vessels into twin balls of hellish fire and death. Black smoke and flame rose up some fifty feet into the air while spilled fuel oil raged on the roiling surface of blackest water.

"On we go," Hawke said.

THE BATTLE WAS JOINED. THE YACHT *BLACKHAWKE* had just made a spectacular and very noisy announcement of her arrival in port. And she had plainly demonstrated her further intentions as she stormed deeper into the enemy harbor, all guns blazing. A half-dozen Cuban navy patrol boats buzzed around her, but the fire from their deck-mounted machine guns had negligible effect and they were dispatched to the bottom forthwith.

Commander Hawke was back on the bridge and his blood was up. Captain King was standing at the helm, watching him bark orders, as she witnessed what was for her a miraculous transformation: the kind and courteous man she'd only recently come to know had been replaced by a modern gladiator with an air of utter invincibility. Steel true. Blade straight. The cowardly saboteurs ashore would soon begin to feel his true heat.

Come on out you bastards, come out and fight.

Hawke glanced up at the mission clock above his head, the minutes relentlessly ticking down. It was 2 A.M., Zulu time. The entire assault team had by now completed an exhaustive review of the strategic war plan for the third and final time.

They knew the Cuban and Russian guard unit's rotation schedules down to the second and they knew it by heart. They knew the exact height of the concertina fences and the gauge of the steel-reinforced gates. They knew the exact height of the guard towers and the aspect ratios of their varying fields of fire; they knew the number of guard dogs patrolling behind those fences. They knew down to the last cubic foot the interior volume of the three large buildings where they would set their own explosive charges. And they knew exactly how long those fuses needed to be to ensure their timely and healthy departure.

This was, after all, going to be a hit-and-run operation. There would be no hanging around later to mop up and take prisoners. When this one was over, the Stokeland Raiders would just pick up their toys and go home. But right now, as Stoke told his guys, it was nut-cuttin' time.

It was time for Alex Hawke to make one final appraisal of the troops before they went ashore. He left the bridge and headed aft, then down four decks to the stern of the vessel. There, in the aftermost part of the ship, grand de luxe had given way to the austere. Here was the true home of Stokely Jones Jr. and his Raiders. Their no-nonsense assault team accommodations, their mess, their weapons storage, machine maintenance shops, military communications post, and their combat satellite uplink. All were in a state of high readiness.

But Hawke had a personal need to witness and feel that sense of urgency and commitment in the men he was about to send into harm's way.

Here in the spec-ops part of the ship, he found the Stokeland Raiders gathered. They would form two squads for the mission: Redcoat and Bluecoat. Both teams were kitted out in head-to-toe black Kevlar assault gear, looking like some demented alien NFL coach's football fantasy of the most badass damn team in the universe. Which is exactly what the hell these guys were.

Hawke was now down in the ship's well, a large rectangular opening cut into the aft section of the keel inside the very bottom of the hull; he saw black seawater sloshing up onto the surrounding decks. The steel decks were strewn with various items the assault teams had selected but chosen to discard at the last moment.

Extra M16 hot mags, assault knives, gloves, a

couple of pairs of NVGs, even an M110 sniper rifle someone already heavily armed had felt was overkill. Hawke had ordered this undersea-launching platform for the two SDVs (SEAL Delivery Vehicles) built while the boat was still in dry dock back in Key West. It was comparable to the dry deck shelter used aboard U.S. Navy submarines.

The Stokeland Raiders, the sixteen-man platoon divided into two squads of eight, and containing battle-hardened frogmen, demolition experts, and snipers, were already splashing around in the black water inside the ship's enclosed well. They appeared to be simply a bunch of incredibly fit young men without a care in the world, laughing and joking. Beach boys who just happened to be swimming around inside the hull of a megayacht, waiting to climb aboard a pair of highly classified U.S. Navy torpedo-shaped minisubs and go to war instead of playing water polo.

Humor was a great armor to don before battle. It offered a kind of mystic or mythic protection, some of them thought, and those who didn't believe such stuff went along with it simply because, after all, you never know, do you? How many guys die laughing? Prayer takes many forms on the grim eve of battle.

One younger guy hollered to his mirthful brothers, "So this flashy car salesman says to the young black guy, 'You thinking about buying this Cadillac convertible, son?' And the black guy says, 'Hell, no, man. I'm thinking about how much pussy I'd get if I bought this Cadillac.'"

And the echoes of laughter of a bunch of men

who had been there and back more times than they could count filled the steel interior of the ship's well. Every one of them knew that as soon as they deployed inside the two SDVs and were en route to engage the enemy, everything was going to get deadly serious in a hurry. American frogmen were coming . . . watch your ass, boy . . .

Underwater, undetected, and underestimated.

Hawke saw Stoke standing on the deck, looking down at his men, alone with his thoughts.

"You good, Stoke?" Hawke said quietly, standing next to his old friend.

"All good, all the time," was Stoke's standard reply to that one.

Hawke looked down at Brock, already swimming up inside his sub on the port side of the well.

"And Mr. Brock over there in SDV 2? He ready?"

"Good to go. He loves this stuff. Never short on courage, you gotta give him that."

"Right. Listen, because he doesn't, Stoke. Tell him that as soon as he blows that Cuban command bunker, his team hauls ass back down the mountain. I want him at the warehouses to reinforce you and your guys' final attack. I still don't have a good feeling about the human intel on the amount of resistance we're going to see tonight. But, hell. Darkness, element of surprise working for us, superior fighting men, tactics, weapons . . . we're good, right?"

"We got me, remember?"

Hawke laughed briefly, then turned very somber. "You get shot up bad tonight? I want you to re-member what I told you about pain that night in that Hormuz Strait hellhole after I got shot to hell, right?"

"I remember."

"What'd I say?"

"Pain is just weakness leaving your body."

Hawke saw the concern in Stoke's eyes and looked away, embarrassed.

"It's just that the stakes are as high as they can get now, Stoke. High as they've ever been. The world will little note nor long remember what we do here tonight. But—if we screw this up, well . . . you know . . . it's pretty much all over. All of it."

"I do know. And I won't let you down, boss. My guys won't let you down. None of us. Never."

"Give 'em hell, Stoke," Hawke said, giving his friend's shoulder a squeeze.

Might as well try to squeeze concrete.

SIXTY-EIGHT

STOKE DOVE BELOW THE SURFACE AND SWAM UP inside the SDV's plexiglass-canopied cockpit. In the SDV, the pilot was dry from the waist up, wet from the waist down, giving him cockpit-style visibility to drive the boat, monitor the batteries and compressed air supply, and then egress the hell out when it was time to shoot bullets and kick Commie ass.

He pulled himself up into the enclosed pilot station in the port-side watercraft and said hello to his copilot, Gator Luttier. He'd gotten to know Gator pretty well when they'd boarded the Russian spy ship and he'd liked what he'd seen.

Another one of his Raiders, the skinny kid from Kentucky, Fat Jesse Saunders, otherwise known as Fat, climbed up inside to take the helm on the other boat with his copilot, Harry Brock, in the vehicle located to starboard in the well. Gator and Stoke were both smiling.

They loved operating these damn boats. Stoke had the most experience, having first encountered them as a young Navy SEAL in his war, his guys using them for riverine operations in Cambodia and Thailand. Gator had gained experience tearing ass all over the harbor at Tripoli during the dustup in Libya.

Clandestine SDV teams used the submersibles to operate or access ports, harbors, and beachfronts held by hostile forces. Or, like now, areas where military activity would draw unwanted notice and objection. Let's just say Vladimir Putin for starters. The vehicle was flooded during maneuvers, and the swimmers rode exposed to the water, breathing from the onboard compressed air supply or using their own SCUBA gear.

Each of the modified Mark 8 SDVs was lithium-ion battery powered and equipped with propulsion, navigation, communication, and life-support equipment. Each also was capable of transporting one-half of a SEAL platoon composed of sixteen SEALs—two officers, one chief, and thirteen enlisted men, from the mother ship to the mission area. The submersible boat could then be "parked" or loiter in the area, retrieve the troops, and return home to the mother ship.

Blackhawke's interior SDV launch well was crucial to tonight's success in achieving surprise once ashore. The well allowed the vehicles to exit unseen beneath the ship's keel and to remain submerged and out of sight as they began powering away from the megayacht and across the broad harbor toward the mission target, the explosive-laden warehouses on Spy Island.

The two boats, each fully loaded with its complement of eight covert warriors, shoved off. They were both headed in the same direction, ESW to the fortified Cuban navy complex, about a fifteen-minute excursion beneath the sea. After a final video surveillance a quarter of a mile offshore, they would proceed directly to their agreed-upon insertion point.

Fat, working late in the war room the night prior, had determined the single shoreside location where the invaders stood any chance of making landfall without detection. He'd done a thorough search of all the possibilities, located the ideal spot, then created a new map of the harbor that pinpointed their LZ for tonight. They would disembark just off an old and abandoned Soviet area of the port, well beyond the reach of the big searchlights and the big dogs patrolling the perimeter fences.

Fat had pinpointed a dilapidated concrete launch ramp on one of the sat photos, in an area built by the Soviets prior to JFK's Bay of Pigs invasion. This section of the old port was originally designed for launching amphibious vessels to use against the Americans and had not been used since. The ramp and surrounding buildings were in a section of the harbor that was no longer functional and devoid of any visible guard or other personnel.

Back on duty on *Blackhawke's* bridge, Commander Hawke raised the high-powered Zeiss lenses to his eyes. His eyes happened to alight at the top of the ship's flag mast, mounted just forward of the wheelhouse. Damn it. The ship was still flying the Hawke Industries burgee and the yacht ensign, both designed to conceal the ship's true nature while in U.S. ports and in transit to the operation sector.

Irritated with himself for his own sloppy lack of attention to detail, he grabbed the PA mike and depressed the transmit button.

"Ahoy, the foredeck! About time we showed the enemy our true colors, gentlemen."

"Aye-aye, Skipper!" said a young crewman already racing toward the base of the mast.

"Strike the colors," Hawke said, referring to the burgee flying now.

"Strike colors, aye!" was the reply.

The young sailor turned to the flag halyard secured to the mast, eased the lines, and hauled down the offending burgee and ship's ensign. Once they were in his hands, he disengaged them from the halyard and replaced them with a faded and tattered old cotton flag of black and white. Hawke had given the rubber pouch containing it to the sailor for safekeeping while they were still in Key West.

The new colors were now hauled smartly up to the masthead and the flag was soon whipping around in the stiff breeze. Headed yet again into the thick of battle, the yacht *Blackhawke* was flying her true colors once more.

Something stirred inside Hawke at the sight, roiling his pirate blood. He had long admired this artifact from his pirate ancestor's treasure trove of museum-quality artifacts. It had been discovered years ago during the excavation of an area of the port of Kingston, Jamaica, and somehow made its way into the hands of Alex Hawke.

It had been flown by the legendary pirate Captain Edward Teach. Sometimes known by his nom de guerre—Blackbeard.

The skull and crossbones of the mighty Jolly Roger.

SIXTY-NINE

Hawke shifted the Zeiss lenses down to the black coastline of Spy Island and entertained a thought: *When the next war starts, it will start here—here in a forgotten backwater on a forgotten island in the Caribbean Sea.*

He dropped the binocs. Something troublesome on the helm radar screen above caught his eye. An unwelcome blip had strayed from his comfort zone, shifting onto a parallel heading and—

"Hard to port, engines all ahead flank," he said sharply to the helmsman. The man reacted instantly.

"Hard to port, all ahead flank, aye," came Lieutenant Des Fitzgerald's reply. The big boat heeled hard over and carved a tight turn in the rough seas, over onto a new, southerly course. Misdirection was what was called for now, confuse enemy radar as to your true intentions.

"Hard to starboard, Lieutenant. Come to new heading three-two-zero, maintain flank speed . . ."

"Three-two-zero, maintain flank, aye."

Again the boat heeled, this time to starboard.

Hawke looked up at the digital mission clock. He wanted to see if it was concurrent with the Hawke mission clock ticking down in his head: Stoke and the two SDV teams would be nearing the abandoned ramp about now and—his reverie was unpleasantly interrupted by Sparky, the ship's radar/sonar officer.

"Helm, Sonar, new contact bearing three-nine-five . . . range, 36.3 miles . . . uh . . . screw signature indicates she's a Russian Thunder class missile frigate, sir."

"Sonar, Helm," Hawke replied. "What's her bearing?"

"Sorry, sir . . . contact bearing three-one-niner . . . we've been tracking her ever since she steamed out of Havana and made a major course correction . . . she's headed this way . . ."

"Roger. She'll attempt a blockade outside the harbor mouth, attempt to trap us inside . . . what's her armament, Sonar?" Hawke said.

"Thunder class frigate carries four C802 missiles, two 30mm cannons, and two 23mm cannons . . ."

"Christ. What's her speed, Sonar?" Hawke said, immediately heading aft to the sonar station just off the bridge.

"Flank speed classified. She's fast enough though

... Engine turns for thirty-nine knots ... she's got boost gas turbines ..."

"ETA at Isla de Pinos?"

"Roger, if she maintains current speed and course ... 0230, sir."

"Forty-two minutes," Hawke said, looking over at Geneva. "Helm, maintain current heading," Hawke said. "We're going in. We'll find out who blinks first on the way out."

"Maintain current heading, aye," Captain King said. Having relieved Fitzgerald, she was back at the helm. It was not Geneva's first taste of battle and Hawke was glad to note that she seemed preternaturally calm and wholly in command. *A very good sign*, Hawke thought, adding, *Let's just hope it stays that way.*

STOKE WAS FIRST ASHORE.

Cradling his M16, he waded through knee-deep seawater and then up the gradual incline of the wide concrete ramp. Redcoat squad was right behind him. The old 1950s concrete in the harbor was intact, but barely. Great chunks had fallen off into the sea. Russian construction in Cuba was notoriously shoddy. Cheap sand-based concrete was a mainstay of the era, and many of the old Soviet-era apartment complexes surrounding Havana had simply fallen down after the Russians packed up and went home.

Brock and Fat, with the balance of the Bluecoat headbangers right behind them, were slogging the ramp up to solid ground. The weather had ramped up, too, as the eye of the storm approached. Tall palm trees everywhere were bent almost double, their fronds whipping back and forth and clacking loudly in the gusts. The increasingly ferocious wind and driving rain made it difficult for anybody to see anything.

Stoke could barely make out Brock ten feet away, doing a last-minute weapons check along with his guys from Bravo.

Flipping down his IR night-vision goggles, Stoke checked out the guard towers in what he'd taken to calling the "warehouse district," and the fenced perimeter surrounding the naval base camp. Or as much of it as he could see in this crappy weather. He kept on looking, hoping to find a weak spot he'd missed looking at charts and diagrams in the *Blackhawke* war room.

Originally, he'd thought the best way inside was to breach the main gate, storm it, and get it the hell over with. Now, he wasn't so sure. He could plainly see how closely the dense jungle encroached on the base fence line. Yeah, okay. Maybe he could do a feint. A small noisy squad at the front gate . . . meanwhile, the bulk of the Raiders are disappearing into the jungle . . . wire cutters at three locations opening big holes for a lightning assault from the landward side.

Yeah. That was maybe the way to do it.

Surprise, surprise.

QUIET. YOU HAD TO FIGURE THOSE GUYS IN THE towers were busy watching the smoke and fire rising from the two big patrol boats *Blackhawke* had most recently taken out of service. Had to be pissed about that, not to mention seeing one of their fighter planes being blown out of the sky right in front of their eyes. The other three fighters had gone to lunch. So far, anyway, things weren't exactly going their way. But there was a long way to go before it was over.

Stoke, Brock, and two badass machine gunners packing M60s from Redcoat, were all sitting beneath a row of blown-out windows in an abandoned warehouse. From their position, the men looked directly down on the main gate. Redcoat and Bluecoat teams were making their way through the jungle at the rear of the perimeter. Stoke was awaiting the signal letting him know the Raiders had successfully punched a big hole in the wire fencing and were ready to attack.

"Mr. Brock, a word?" Stoke said, imitating one of Hawke's mannerisms just to stick it to Harry. The ex-marine came knee-crawling over, lifting up the face shield used to keep the driving rain out of his eyes.

"What's up?" Brock said, keeping his head down. Searchlights were now playing their beams all over the façade of the old building.

"This is where we part ways, little buddy. You and Gator know what the drill is."

"Bet yo' ass."

"Seriously?"

"Something Gator says. I think it's funny."

Stoke tended to ignore the typical insolence but not this time. He put a big hand on Brock's shoulder, turned him around so they were face-to-face, looked down, and said:

"Harry, listen up, damn it. I'm communicating this to you at the request of the bossman, okay? As soon as you and Gator have taken out that mountain bunker, you get your ass back down here to the waterfront, you understand? The boss is apprehensive about the intel we got from those two Cuban CIA undercover guys. Most especially, the number of armed Russian troops defending the warehouse complex. He's apprehensive? *Hawke?* That means I'm *double* apprehensive. You hear me on the radio looking for your white ass—you get it in gear. *Capiche?*"

Brock nodded his head, sullen, but with respect.

"Something happens, some good reason you guys can't make it, we rendezvous at the ramp at exactly 0400. Don't miss the boat, Harry. You know that 'no man left behind' tradition? Yeah, well. I just might make an exception in the case of your sorry ass."

Brock laughed it off and motioned to Gator. He and Gator got on pretty good now. Neither of them really gave two shits and that gave them a kind of bond. They weren't exactly good old boys but they liked to think of themselves that way. Country, not city. Each of them would be toting a big M60 heavy machine gun and satchels of Semtex. It was a helluva lot of firepower for two guys and Stoke just hoped it was enough.

Harry said something stupid in farewell, but Stoke couldn't hear over the loud hiss of the rain and sporadic gunfire around the town. Brock and his sidekick slipped out into the rain and through the maze of falling-down brick buildings and rusted out trucks and burnt-out Russian jeeps from another war, another time.

Stoke checked his steel Rolex. In four minutes, he was going to open fire on the two towers to either side of the gate and pray for the best while expecting the worst.

HARRY'S OBJECTIVE WAS THIRTY MINUTES AWAY. UP the jungle trail to the command-and-control ops center situated on a hilltop halfway up the mountain. Give him another ten, max, to eliminate any opposition protecting the bunker and missile sites, another fifteen to come down from the hills through the jungle, five to reach the warehouse area if he didn't face any opposition. The *thump-thump* of the big M60s told him Stoke was going in.

Roughly half an hour, forty-five minutes, say.

The weather was shit. Winds had increased, and rain was coming down in sheets now. But it was just as bad for the bad guys as it was for the good guys.

SEVENTY

ISLA DE PINOS

G ATOR! GET YER ASS UP HERE!" BROCK whispered into his lip mike. He took a quick peek
back down the twisting jungle trail they'd just taken
up the mountain. Nada. Where the hell had he got
to?

Somehow, a moment later, Gator was right by his
side, both of them crouched down in the creeping
jungle crud beneath a pair of swaying palm trees
covered with vines. They were about a thousand
yards below the summit of what passed for a mountain on this island. The heavy rains had turned the
dense jungle trail they'd taken up from the port into
a cascading mud bath. Gator had remarked on the
way up that he found it "fun."

Still, where they were situated was a pretty good vantage point to reconnoiter from. The mountain they'd just climbed was offering a bit of shelter from the raging storm coming from out of the south. From his new position, peering through the curtains of rain, Harry could see the whole harbor spread out below.

He saw three of the six big tower searchlights snap on, meaning Stoke's guys had successfully breached the perimeter fence and were on the move inside the warehouse district. Biggest thing out there in the harbor was a big black shape moving slowly through the heavy seas.

It was the dark silhouette of *Blackhawke*, steaming through the harbor mouth. She was ghostlike, with all her lights doused, stem to stern. No running lights, nothing at all showing in the dark.

Harry told Gator to keep his damn eyes open. He stood up and swung his Nikons over to the target and looked around the hilltop for surprises, then zeroed in on his target.

No surprises.

Nothing funky so far. He'd reconned the Cuban command bunker above him down to the nails. He knew how thick the doors were, how thick the walls were. He knew where the windows were and what they were made of and he knew where the outdoor shitter was. The thing was basically a heavily built two-story cement-block building with bulletproof windows only on the seaward side of the structure. The whole rooftop was bristling with antennae, radar dishes whirling around, and all that good stuff, sending and receiving information.

The comms between this building and Moscow were probably humming long about now, Harry surmised. He could hear the Cuban guy inside there now, going, "Hello, Vladimir? Your pal Alex Hawke just showed up in the harbor with a big boat and he's blowing Sukhois out of the sky and sinking all our little boats. What should we do?"

Only one egress door, located on the ground floor at the rear of the building a few feet from the edge of the tropical jungle creepy crawly shit. A lot of lights on inside upstairs. He could see guys moving around in there. Three, maybe four personnel, tops, upstairs anyway.

Nobody out here making rounds on the grounds, at least not so far. Guards probably fast asleep in the dorm on the ground floor. Hell, it was a rainy night. You wouldn't want your dog out on a night like this.

"No guards out here, you believe that, Gator?"

"Yeah," Gator said, "I believe it. Who in their right mind wants to sit outside, soaked to the skin in the middle of a goddamn hurricane? Bored to tears, waiting year in and year out on the off chance they might get to shoot people who never bother to show the fuck up? Who? That's the goddamn question."

"Not the Cuban military, apparently," Harry said.

"Bet yo' ass it ain't."

The good news here and now was this—there was a fairly wide balcony, running around all four sides of the upper story of the building. And it appeared to be empty. Windows on the front, overlooking the harbor, and a wooden door on the side he could see, but no unfriendly activity visible at this point anyway.

Normally, in a situation like this, a CIA field agent like Harry would have gone up a pole and tapped a line. He'd be crouched down here in the weeds, monitoring all the communications going in and out of this building. Finding out who, where, and what the hell is what. Boots-on-the-ground intel. But not now. Tonight, he and Gator were here simply to blow up their shit and take no prisoners.

He looked over at Gator, only his eyes showing through the mudpack, crouched in some cabbage palms. Man looked like a big lanky bug with a great big gun when he had his NVG goggles flipped down. He held that M60 in his arms like it was a newborn baby. Tender. He also had stuck two fat wads of Semtex into the Velcro snap-band around his helmet. Boy was pure badass, that's all, Harry was glad to see.

"You got this rear door, Gator? Ground-floor entrance?"

"Bet yo' ass."

"You, my honky brother, are going to march yourself right up to that back door and rig your charges. I, meanwhile, am going up the side of that wall you're looking at. When I'm all clear up on that balcony? You will hear my signal. You, then, are going to blow that goddamn door sideways, get your ass inside, start shooting that peashooter, and roll right. Keep shooting until they stop shooting at you. Staircase will be to your left. Soon as you've cleared the bottom floor, up the steps you go and step on it. I may need you up there, son. Or you may need me down there. In which case I'll come down the steps. With me, Gator?"

"Bet yo' ass."

"Either way."

"Bet yo' ass."

"You like fried rattlesnake?"

"No."

"Just checking. Ready?"

"Bet yo' ass."

"On my mark . . . five. Five . . . four . . . three . . . two . . . and . . . Mark! *Go, Gator, go!*"

The tough young cracker linebacker came up and out of that green wall of jungle more like a wide receiver on a post route. Harry watched him zig and zag up the hill, staying low, grabbing a little cover whenever he could, every fifty feet or so, working his way up toward the rear of the building. Brock, meanwhile, had his gun up, his sights on the balcony windows . . . nothing much doing up there, not yet, anyway. Playing cards, shooting the shit, looking at titty magazines probably.

Gator disappeared into a clump of palm trees fifty yards from the rear corner of the building. Since he didn't come out, Harry figured he'd heard something he didn't like inside the communications blockhouse. Shit.

Had he and Gator already been made by somebody up there they hadn't seen? One of the Russian Spetsnaz guys actually guarding the joint? Harry came out of his crouch and sprinted up the hill toward the side of the structure nearest to his position on the trail.

The line of sight from the seaside windows above

him was a bit restricted from his angle, and he saw nothing untoward up there as he ran as fast as he could with the heavy machine gun in his hands. Thing either weighed as much as a small refrigerator or he was just getting old.

Gator, sprinting like the athlete he'd been, still hadn't reappeared. Harry, having approached the building on the run and from a different angle, was now crouching beneath the balcony, his whole body pressed up against the unpainted concrete wall, pondering the best way up the side of the damn thing.

He didn't ponder long.

He caught the balcony rail with the first toss of the rubber-coated grapnel hook on the business ending of his nylon climbing line. Didn't make a sound. *Okay, Brock, up you go, easy does it.* He went up the wall hand over hand, his assault knife in his mouth. This, just in case some numb-nuts soldier had decided to spend the night sleeping out in the rain up there on the balcony.

Here's the deal with that. Come over a balcony rail with a jagged dagger in your mouth and you tend to scare people shitless, guard or no guard outside snoozing the night away. He got a hand on the rail and heaved himself up.

Harry took a quick peek over the rail.

The long balcony was empty, at least on this side. Hadn't seen anybody on the sea side either, so he was good to go. He hauled himself up and over and stood for a second, going over it in his head one more time.

There was the louvered wooden door, closed tight, yellow light seeping through between the slats. He could hear noises inside, a chair scraping, somebody laughing . . . and snoring. Loud snoring. Maybe he and Gator would get lucky—maybe they were all shitfaced in there.

He turned back to the rail, leaned over, and gave the signal.

"*Gator's got that Rama Jama, hoo-ah,*" Brock shouted, plenty loud enough for old Gator to hear him down there over all that rain. "*Gator's got that Rama Jama, hoo-ah, hoo-ah!*"

GATOR'S BLAST SHOOK THE BUILDING.

Probably shook up the folks inside it, too. Harry already had his hand on the handle of the louvered door. He yanked it open, almost taking it off the hinges, and dove inside, rolling right. He came up and out of it, bringing the fat bastard of a machine gun up, screaming for everyone to get down or get dead at the top of his lungs.

Harry instantly registered five wide-eyed guys about to piss their pants.

"Get the fuck down on the floor!" he screamed at the Cubans. He liked the look on their faces. He wasn't a man in black right now, he was a maniac in black.

One guy cringed in a skimpy-ass bed with dirty sheets in the far corner by the windows, eating Chinese food; another one over at the windows, hunched over a big telescope, and still three more were moving fast toward him with the pointy end of their weapons pointed directly at Harry Brock himself.

"Okay, don't listen," Harry said calmly.

He pulled the trigger that unleashed the monster.

The heavy thump of an M60 firing 500 to 560 rounds per minute, 7.65mm ball rounds unleashed in close quarters was enough to make anybody nervous. And that was *before* they got cut in half by all that flying lead.

The three hombres who had wanted to shoot him weren't alive anymore, so Harry turned his attention to the other two. Telescope had a nancy little automatic in his hand but didn't seem to know what to do with it. Sleepy over in the corner had both hands under a shitty blanket.

Brock saw movement of the guy's hands under the covers. Something told Harry that not even the coolest of Cuban desperadoes was cool enough to choose this particular moment to jerk off.

"Hands out where I can see them," he shouted at the guy.

Two hands came out, one of them waving a fucking sawed-off shotgun wildly at him and firing both barrels. Harry opened up with Mr. M60 and saw a cartoon of blood, guts, feathers, and Chinese food exploding where once was somebody's son.

He whirled around at the sound of Gator shouting over the fierce gunfire below. He strained desperately to hear him—finally heard Gator yell, "Man coming up the stairs! He's yours!"

HARRY NEVER KNEW WHICH ONE SHOT HIM. TELEscope behind him or Stair Guy as he reached the top step and they looked at each other. But the rounds caught him in the ribs and knocked him backward to the floor. He'd somehow managed to hold on to that bitching machine gun and keep his hand on the trigger.

"Fuck you both!" he yelled, shaking off the shocks as he got up off the floor. Harry just squeezed the damn trigger and spun round and round on his heels, no targets, just laying down a wall of lead in the air between himself and the two dicks who wanted to kill him.

When he woke up, good old Gator was there, leaning down over him, a sweet look of concern on his face, wiping blood out of his eyes.

"Mr. Brock?" Gator said.

"Yeah? Where am I, slick?"

"Don't matter where you're at, sir, you're still alive is all that counts."

Harry coughed up a little blood.

"Oh, shit, that hurts. Fuck!" Harry said, squeezing his eyes shut in pain. "Keep talking to me, Gator. I'm fucked."

"You better unfuck yourself, sir."

"I can't move."

"Well, then, you're just going to have to suck it up, sir. And that's 'cause we got to get out of here before the rest of these boys come looking."

Harry blinked his eyes hard, grimacing as he pressed his fingertips against his ribs, feeling around for bullet holes. He looked around at the room. Looked like a slaughterhouse. The formerly whitewashed walls were awash with bright red blood spatter, and huge chunks of plaster had been blasted out of the ceiling. All the windows overlooking the harbor below had been blown out, only a few jagged panes of glass remaining.

The five previous occupants were scattered in various sizes and shapes all around the room. He saw a big piece of hairy pink stuff with an ear stuck to it up on the ceiling right over Gator's head. Pieces of dead meat didn't bother Harry all that much anymore. That was all that was left of them now. No more telescope, no more furniture, no more Chinese takeout, no more poker, no more nothing . . .

He smiled up at his new sidekick.

"You know, Gator, a top New York decorator might disagree with me on this one, but I think this place looks a shitload better now than it did before we arrived. You with me on that?"

"I gotta patch you up quicklike, sir. See if you can walk."

"Why's that?"

"You're fading in and out on me, sir, not making much sense. Commander Hawke was on your radio just now. He says we gotta move out. He's got another target for us, a 105 Howitzer up there at the top of the mountain. Big damn gun. We gotta take it out."

"He said that? A fucking 105? Shit, boy, we gotta move out."

"Yes, sir, we do."

"Case I die? Let's you and me get something straight, all right? I am not a 'sir.' Never was. My name is Harry. Harry Brock. Got that?"

"I do. But you ain't fucking dying."

"You rig charges all around this goddamn building?"

"Yes, I did."

"And nobody shot you downstairs?"

"Not that I know of."

"Am I going to die? Tell me the truth. I can take it."

"Not today, anyway. Mostly shock. Blood loss. Bullets bounced around off your rib cage. One went through your arm into your ass, and the other is somewhere in your left leg. I shot you up real good with morphine. Bandaged you up."

"Think I can walk?"

"Bet yo' ass."

"Well, I guess we oughta move out, huh, buddy?"

"Why not, Harry?"

"Bet yo' ass."

SEVENTY-ONE

ISLE OF SKYE

SOMETHING MONSTROUS WAS MOVING OFF PORTREE Bay.

And young Colin McPhee could not sleep. Too cold. The howling wind? Perhaps a disturbing dream or two? Perhaps his blankets were too thin for the late summer arrival of an early wave of arctic air.

Colin gave up on sleep, got up, and lit a fire. After a brief period of gazing into the flames looking for hidden meaning, he made himself a mug of strong black coffee and walked outside into the darkness. As he stood on his covered porch, scrutinizing the night world, he was looking for fresh pictures to paint and new music to write.

He was a writer, a novelist by trade, a tyro, and

his innocent mind was still a youthful and hungry organ. He had a novel he was trying to finish, his first. It was a mystery, of sorts, and a damn fine one by his lights. But an unpredicted conundrum in the closing pages of his tale had him stumped.

How did the bloody thing *end*?

Blocked, he sought inspiration everywhere.

A seeker, McPhee had become, not only of wisdom and truth, plot and character, but of sensory inputs to inform and color his written words. All in the fervent hope of finally discovering, in that intransigent final chapter he'd yet to pen, just how his mystery would end.

Luckily, he'd soon realized, there were clues everywhere, if only one took the time to look hard enough. You had to *focus*.

And so McPhee continued his search. Above the land, beneath the stars, a phrase he often repeated to himself. He liked the sound and music of those six words playing inside his head. They seemed to have the power to put a bounce in his step and a smile on his face, even now in the wee small hours before dawn.

He descended five narrow wooden steps from his front door and strode though heavy sea grass, still clumped and wet from an earlier shower, toward the beckoning sea. Everything smelled delicious and alive on the night air. The dewy grass, the salty tang of the wind. In the distance, almost a cliché, he heard the curlew's cry.

His rough wooden cabin stood at the very edge of the land, beneath the stars and high above the sea. He'd built the house himself when the land had thawed, over the course of that spring and summer. One room and one was enough; a hard labor of love, but he had a snug harbor to show for it. He even had lumber left over, logs enough to burn in the stone fireplace as the days grew short and the nights grew long.

Standing now with his legs wide apart at the edge of the craggy promontory, McPhee turned his face into the stiff sea breeze. He inhaled deeply, tasting that trace of iodine on the wind, the scented bite of dried seaweed wafting up from the beaches below.

McPhee was an artist who cherished his senses, primarily because he had so few other blessings to count as his own. But, here, look below! Waves pounded at the frothing shore. He could watch them roll ashore down there, between the toes of his stiff leather boots; they burbled and hissed, sucking at the rocks as they retreated. And fog, the stealthy grey fog, squeezed through the mountains and oozed in runnels down to the sea.

His coffee had grown cold and it was near dawn. He watched in awe as a curved pinkness at the edge of the dark world came to light. Feeling he was on the brink of some illuminating discovery, he came at last to the long flight of wooden steps leading down to the beach. His tiny sandy crescent of the rocky Scottish coast. The wooden steps were wet and shining with moisture and so he trod them cautiously to the bottom.

Just a mile off his rock-strewn beach and the gentle white of the soft sand farther along, wavelets ebbed and flowed, undisturbed, relentless. McPhee raised his eyes to the horizon. Farther out to sea, near the limits of his vision, all was calm. Black and huge, the sea was rolling and swelling heavily beneath pinpricks of starlight splayed across the dome of midnight blue. A perfect sea of tranquility. *Dee-da-da-dee-da-da-dee-dee* . . . words as music.

The music of worlds and the magisterial wonder of creation.

All was undisturbed here save the darting and swooping petrels, terns, and sometimes the distant foghorn. Colin let his eyes drift, his hunger for sight and sound strong, unabated.

McPhee saw the black snout first.

It rose up from the deep and appeared at an odd angle so acute he felt his heart leap within his chest. When, after an eternity, the great beast finally reached its apogee and crashed into the sea, it sent a great wave rolling ashore, an infant tsunami.

The dark now gave way to dawn, and with it came a menacing black vision. Not a whale, no. But it was a leviathan, of sorts, a monster.

Oh, he'd seen them before. The slender stalks. The prying eyes. He recognized that black profile, all right. The enemy. He sensed that packs of these monsters were stalking his waters. They'd been reported off Denmark and Norway, too. But he could scarcely accept the terrible sight of one emerging from the depths so close to home, so close to the wee plot where his tiny cottage stood hard by the sea.

A SUBMARINE. RUSSIAN, MOST LIKELY. THAT IS, IF you believed the papers and pub talk over to Portree Bay. One had been spied in the harbor last month.

The navy came and it was gone. What they wanted, what they were doing here on this night, Colin could not imagine. But he was willing to find out.

This was the very first time he'd seen one of the sinister giants completely surfaced. He ducked back among the large boulders and squeezed between two adjacent rocks that provided good cover. He arranged his body so that he was reasonably comfortable. He had a clear view of the submarine. Although its black skin was lifeless and dull, Colin could hear faint creakings of steel and silvery pings, traveling across the water from somewhere deep inside the great hulking hull.

He zipped up his wind cheater and waited and watched. The first fiery red rays from the eastern rim fired shots across the bow of the death machine. Darkness fled, but not before he saw silhouettes emerging up onto the deck at the foot of the tower. He counted six men, then more, moving forward toward the bow, carrying large rectangular objects.

He heard a splash. Then, another.

Rafts.

The Russians were coming!

He stood frozen, watching the crews of the two rubber rafts pulling at their oars in tandem. Well-trained seamen who rowed with a will. He had a notion to turn and run, but the notion quickly faded when he saw how quickly the submariners were approaching. And how exposed he would be going up the cliff.

Six men in each raft, the first less than a hundred yards away now, and the twelve men were starting to look not so much like fresh-faced young sailors as masked creatures from the deep. Fifty yards now. Twenty.

No, they looked like giant aliens who'd made good their escape from a video game. They were wearing some kind of black body armor that reminded him of Arthurian knights and they all had big, strange-looking weapons, for one thing, and they—

—*better run, Colin!* the tiny author voice in his mind was saying.

Notice they didn't arrive in Portree Bay harbor with flags flying and bands playing, boy. No, they're coming ashore here before dawn because they don't want anyone to see them—and McPhee was nearly struck dumb. He'd simply gone for a walk and—

—it was already too late to run.

He stood inside his shaking boots, rooted to the sandy soil, peering through a narrow slit in the two rocks as the first flat-bottomed inflatable slid up over the smooth round pebbles and onto the sand.

Six men climbed out and stormed ashore through knee-deep water as the other raft beached and discharged its passengers. Five of the first arrivals huddled with the men from the second wave, securing their watercraft and pointing up to the steps climbing the cliff.

The sixth man strode up onto the beach proper to secure his beachhead with a line and a stake.

Colin's legs had gone painfully numb from the awkward, cramped position. He shifted his weight from one leg to the other. And, in so doing, unfortunately dislodged a large stone. A millisecond later, a shout! A brilliant white light burst into life from atop the sub's conning tower. The strong white beam was playing over the large boulders to either side of the wooden steps. The stairway to heaven, Colin liked to say.

McPhee squeezed shut his eyes because he'd read somewhere that the eyes were always a dead give-away, even if one were a mile away, down at the lonesome end of a dark and lonely country road.

But eventually the spotlight came to a stop and he found himself the star of this little seaside drama.

He didn't wait to be told to come out. His leg was in too much pain. He turned sideways and pushed through between the bulging walls of rock to either side until he was free. The blinding light stayed on him and he didn't see the approach of two submariners who grabbed his arms and pinned them behind his back.

A third man, perhaps the leader, addressed him. Who was he, what was he doing here, where did he come from, he said. Made him feel like the usual suspect in this case, even though he was just a lonely man out for a walk, someone encountered by chance, someone completely innocent of any wrongdoing.

"I live up there," McPhee said, pointing to the glowing windows in the cabin at the top of the steps. "I couldn't sleep, so I came down here to get some air. I'll be on my way, if that's all right with you gents."

Naturally enough, it wasn't all right. After a silence, McPhee said: "My name's Colin, and what might yours be?"

"I am Ivan Isakov, captain, Russian Baltic Fleet."

"What can I do for you, Captain?"

"I want you to have a look at something if you don't mind," the Russian said in strongly accented English. He reached inside a waterproof rubber pouch slung from his shoulder. The burly captain had thick black hair combed straight back, pomaded, and heavy black brows framing his dark sunken eyes. Someone who lived beneath the sea, his skin had a deathly white pallor.

"What seems to be the trouble?" Colin asked. An innocent enough question for this ghost.

"We are looking for someone."

He stared beyond the Russian to the far horizon. There, fat cumulus clouds hurried away, pink and purple galleons, setting sail for foreign shores. The sight stirred him deeply, so deep was his grounded place in nature. The true mystery of life, a wise man had once said, is that there is no mystery.

"Who?" was all he could think to say to the ghost.

"None of your bloody business," the captain said, almost barking at him.

He then pulled out a colored and heavily annotated naval military map, an image taken from a satellite no doubt, laminated, and folded in half. Opening it, he pointed to the harbor town of Portree Bay. "We are here, yes?"

"Close enough."

"I want to go *here*," Isakov said, moving his index finger a few inches north. Colin flinched at the sight of the map. The circled location was the old shooting estate where his father still worked. Where Colin and his family had all lived for most of his life. His mother had died and was buried there. Colin had been raised there. Been married there. Would be buried there, beside his wife.

He said: "Nobody home, I'm afraid. It's just an old hunting lodge. The only time anyone is ever there these days is a brief window in the fall. Grouse, you see. Ring-necked pheasant. They come to shoot."

"So do I."

Captain Isakov had a small, nickel-plated automatic. He shoved the muzzle up into the soft flesh beneath Colin's chin. It was painful, but he tried not to flinch. There were times when a man had to show bravery, and this was one of them.

"What do you want to know?" Colin said, beginning to see his denouement at last.

"Do you have a truck?" the captain said. "Or an automobile?"

"Yes. A truck. And an old motorcycle or two in the barn behind the house."

"Good. Give me the keys. All of them."

"I don't have them. They're up there. In a china bowl up on the mantel. Hidden behind a picture of my late wife."

Isakov had no time for sentiment. "Tell me, Colin. What is the best route to this lodge? The fastest route. Show me on the map."

"That would be the road just here. You see? The Old Hollows highway. It follows the coast. Here is the first turning. And the next. Can't miss it."

Colin prayed the Russian would not catch the lie in his eyes. The coast road he was indicating was twice as long as the inland route. But he needed time. He needed to warn his father. To find him and warn him that the Russians were coming.

"Thank you for your assistance, Colin. Most kind. I am looking for a man named Hawke. Do you know him?"

"Yes. Of course. He's my neighbor. He taught me to shoot upland game."

"Is he there now? Hawke? For the shooting?"

"Lord Hawke hasn't been here for years. No one has."

"You're lying. Someone has. A helicopter landed there. Just recently. You didn't see it? Didn't hear it?"

"No."

"Well, no matter. Thank you for your time, Colin," the smiling Russian said, looking deep into the young man's eyes. "And I wish you sweet dreams, my boy."

Colin felt a slight increase of upward pressure from the cold steel muzzle under his chin. And then, in that smallest fraction of a second, just before he finally came to understand the truth, how the great mystery of his life would end, he could swear he heard heaven sigh.

SEVENTY-TWO

Isla de Pinos

HAWKE SAW THE EXPLOSIONS ASHORE BEFORE HE heard them. Saw the spouting geysers of fire and plumes of smoke rising above the warehouse district of the tiny harbor town. The attack on Spy Island had begun in earnest. He left the helm and went out onto the rainswept port bridge wing for a better view, standing in the lee of a bulkhead, which shielded him from the brunt of the raging storm.

He raised the heavy Zeiss binoculars and surveyed the small waterfront village.

The confined harbor was now the scene of sustained heavy machine-gun fire and the bright orange-white flash of rigged explosives being triggered by Stokely's demolitioneers throughout strategic locations within the warehouse district. The explosion of the Cuban's motor pool alone, full as it was of jeeps, troop trucks, fuel, and oil, created a blast that leveled several smaller buildings nearby.

There were already a few skirmishes outside the main entrance to the enemy complex, but the main firefight seemed to be centered in the areas near the main gate.

Hawke could now see heavy fire coming from the six guard towers and a constant barrage of fire emanating from every window on the second story of a burnt-out warehouse. The building was adjacent to the complex's main gate. Had Redcoat already taken up positions inside? He questioned the wisdom of that. The battle plan had called for both Redcoat and Bluecoat squads to storm the main gate and pour into the compound as a unified force.

"What the hell is going on over there?" Hawke wondered aloud. And then he immediately reassured himself. If anyone out there knew what he was doing, it was Stokely Jones Jr. And the men who composed the Stokeland Raiders.

Despite the impending danger of the heavily armed Russian missile frigate now lying in wait for *Blackhawke* outside the harbor, naval resistance inside the breakwaters was negligible. Two or three more undergunned Cuban patrol boats had been sent out to harass him, mostly with their deck-mounted .50-cal. machine guns and carbine fire from crewmen aboard.

Hawke's fire control officer had swiftly ordered the *Blackhawke* commanders and gunners inside the fore and aft turrets to dispatch these and any other hostile craft coming within three hundred yards with 23mm cannon fire. Within minutes of one another, all three enemy boats had been sent to the bottom of the harbor. Hawke had an eye out for more, seeing two rows of them still moored at the docks. So far, at least, none had ventured forth.

"*Blackhawke, Blackhawke*, this is Redcoat One, over."

It was Stoke calling. Hawke grabbed the radio and depressed the transmit button.

"Redcoat One, Redcoat One, *Blackhawke*, what's your situation, Stoke, over."

"Perimeter shows greater strength than earlier intel reports indicated. Bravo Squad now breaching the perimeter on the jungle side. Good thing we didn't wade ashore like they wanted in D.C. Russians got pressure-plate mines everywhere and several rows of underwater obstacles and barriers in the tidal areas. That main gate? Gone. But now I'm looking at two three-ton, fifteen-foot-high interlocking solid steel plates. We're responding to enemy fire while we try to figure a way to take the gates out, over."

"Redcoat One, the ship's fire control officer tells me he now has a missile lock on those gates. You have anyone on the ground out there? Or in the immediate vicinity?"

"Negative, *Blackhawke*, light 'em up and launch when ready, over."

Stokely had barely gotten the words out of his mouth when the whole world outside lit up like day for night. A brilliant flash, a deafening roar, and a hole where the steel gates had once stood. The smart missile Hawke had launched from the ship had just saved Stoke and his Redcoats a whole lot of trouble.

"Target destroyed; Redcoat One is on the move, over."

"Roger that, Redcoat. Status of Bluecoat?"

"Flanking action. Bluecoat is now penetrating far side of the perimeter, entering troops from the jungle."

"Understood, Stoke. I'm bringing the boat closer inshore right now. Moving into position just off-shore of the courthouse location. I'm going in to provide enfilade fire. Raking fire with the machine guns and enable the 23mm cannons to soften up the interior defensive fortifications . . . over. Give me an all clear when we can safely commence fire."

"Yeah, uh, roger that, *Blackhawke* to commence fire on my signal," Stoke said. "Over."

"Affirmative, Stoke, keep your head down. *Blackhawke* out."

Stoke handed his radio over to Fat Jesse and turned to the rest of his guys, now engaged in a fierce firefight with the two nearest machine-gun towers. He had two casualties, the wounded men now being patched up the medical corpsman. One of them was a kid named 12-Gauge who would lead the demo squad.

"Redcoat's on the move and the front door's wide now open, Raiders, let's move out!" Stoke cried out.

STOKE, WITH FAT HARD ON HIS HEELS, WAS FIRST through the blown gates. They sprinted across open ground littered with battle debris, headed for the first of the three warehouses. All were standing side by side on the town square, their backs to the water. The biggest one was the old courthouse building. The two floors of that structure were now being used as a warehouse. That's where, according to that CIA intel, the bulk of the explosives were stored. And, two thousand cases of high-test vodka.

They got good cover from the M60s, his two primary machine gunners laying down thunderous suppression fire both on the ground and up at two more towers that continued to harass his guys' movements below.

After sprinting across a hundred yards of open ground, Stoke and Fat ducked into an open doorway and returned the favor. They poured concentrated fire up into the towers. So far, they'd encountered sentries guarding the warehouses in the town square where the explosives were stored. Two were dispatched with head shots from Fat's lethal sniper rifle fired from the window.

Stoke had used his assault knife to slit the throat of one man from behind before he could sound a warning. Stoke crouched down inside the door with his radio. It was tough to hear over the sound of the pounding fire of the M60 in Fat's hands now.

"Bluecoat, Bluecoat, this is Redcoat One, what's your situation, over."

"Still cutting wire back here. Give us five." Stoke could hear the distinctive sounds of AK-47s in the background.

"You got it, Redcoat One, over," said the wounded ex–Army Ranger known as 12-Gauge, a kid who'd deeply impressed Stoke in all the shipboard briefings. Stoke had finally made the decision to give him leadership of the demo squad when they were splashing around down in the well.

The two squads would soon rejoin forces at the courthouse, the largest of the three designated primary targets.

BLACKHAWKE MOVED SLOWLY, CLOSER INSHORE. FROM the port-side bridge wing, Hawke monitored the developing battle. The ship was returning small-arms fire from locations along the breakwater and out on some of the jetties and piers. Hawke's immediate objective was taking out the guard towers, which were still giving Stoke and his Raiders so much trouble.

He picked up the radio.

"Fire Control, forget this incoming fire from shore. New targets are Towers One, Two, and Three in the area where Redcoat squad now engaging enemy forces in the town square . . . lock on and take them out, over."

"Roger that, sir. Acquiring targets . . . lock one, lock two, lock three . . . and . . . three missiles armed and . . .

"Stoke! Take cover! Incoming!"

And in that instant, Hawke had been staggered, nearly losing his footing and falling to the deck. The boat had just been rocked by an explosion just off her aft beam. Hawke had to grab the bridge wing's handrails just to keep from pitching overboard. He looked back and saw multiple eruptions of incoming fire around the stern—hell, all of a sudden the relatively peaceful harbor was beginning to resemble the Battle of Midway . . . was it possibly fire from the Russian missile frigate approaching through the harbor mouth?

He ducked inside the bridge.

"What the hell is that?" he called out to the radar station. "We taking fire from that big Russian boat out there?"

"Negative, Skipper," the kid said. "Fire from the mountain, sir!"

"I thought we took out that damn bunker up there," Hawke replied, looking at the black smoke still rising up from that location.

"We did. Fire is coming from the jungle area directly above those earlier targets. Gun on the move. Moving along a path just inside the tree line up near the summit. It must be very well camouflaged sir, to avoid detection by spy sats. Or us."

"What the hell is it, firing rounds like that?"

"Those are 105 Howitzer rounds, believe it or not, sir. World War Two vintage. Must be mounted on some kind of tracked vehicle moving around inside the jungle canopy up there."

Hawke grabbed a radio.

"Brock! This is *Blackhawke*, do you copy?"

"*Blackhawke*, Sergeant Luttier, over."

"New objective, Gator, a 105 Howitzer cannon on our butts. He's about to sink the damn boat. Do you guys see this bastard from your position?"

"Just getting ready to move, sir. Brock's hurt. I'm patching him up now. We'll find that bad boy up there, sir."

"You think you two can take him out?"

"Bet yo' ass," Gator said and he was solid gone, over and out.

Hawke stood there with the dead radio in his hand, mystified.

"Did that soldier just say, 'Bet your ass' to me?" Hawke said, looking over at Geneva on duty at the helm.

"That's a big aye-aye, Skipper," she replied, smiling.

Everyone else on the bridge wisely kept their mouths shut.

SEVENTY-THREE

CASTLE DRUM, SCOTLAND

THE GREAT HALL AT CASTLE DRUM WAS FILLED with laughter. It was a chilly but clear mid-morning. Six-year-old Alexei Hawke was sitting cross-legged on a rug before a crackling fire in the open hearth. An arctic air mass had moved down over the islands of the Outer Hebrides the night before. It felt more like early onset winter than fall. A sustained downpour the night before had left the earth sodden and the trees drooping beneath the residual weight of water.

In a leather armchair pulled up near the fireside, Inspector Tristan Walker of Scotland Yard was reading from a book to his young charge. The boy's exuberant black Scottie, Harry, was bounding around the room, charging ahead at full speed from one end of the long room to the other, before turning around and doing it again. Over and over.

Then Harry would abruptly apply his brakes, skidding to a screeching halt right in front of his young owner. The little bowser would then proceed to lick Alexei's face, bringing forth peals of laughter not only from the delighted little boy, but from Walker as well.

Above the stone mantel hung a large portrait of the child's great-grandfather, the Duke of Antrim, sitting astride his fine black steed, Dreadnought. On the ground around the duke were his frolicsome gun dogs, including a few Gordon setters just like the real one now playing with Alexei's puppy. That Gordon, who took its name, Robbie, from the hero Robert the Bruce, was the constant companion of Mr. McPhee, known as Laddie, the caretaker at Castle Drum.

Robbie and Harry were now chasing each other through all the rooms of the ground floor, going round and round the endless oval of the dining room table in a race akin to Michael Schumacher's Ferrari chasing Lewis Hamilton's Mercedes around Nürburgring.

Pelham, who was in the butler's pantry quietly working on his latest needlepoint project, soon came out and shooed the noisy dogs out of his domain. He watched them charge up the wide stone staircase, shook his head, and withdrew into his sanctuary. Pelham had found the quiet life at Castle Drum to be, for the most part, quite salubrious. The recent mad escape from the rooftops of Hawkesmoor had taken a toll on the old fellow; he was glad of the peaceful respite offered by this remote outpost.

Here, in this house, Alexei was at last safe from all those who would do him harm.

At that very moment, the wide front door swung open and in walked Mr. McPhee, as Alexei called the old man everyone always called Laddie. The caretaker strode right through the doorway leading into the Great Hall, curious as to where all this laughter was coming from.

"Hullo?" Laddie called out. "Hullo!"

"Mr. McPhee!" Alexei said, scrambling to his feet and racing over to his new friend. "Is it time? Can we go now? May we go and hunt for the secret of the Lost River, please, sir? You promised!"

McPhee smiled and pulled off his soaking tweed cap, shaking off the dew and scratching the top of his head. He had a full head of thick white hair, bushy snow-white eyebrows, and huge blue eyes that always seemed to be laughing. His cheeks were red with the glow of a long walk of a frosty morning.

"Well, now, laddie boy, I'm not sure as I rightly know the answer to that question. Is it time yet?"

"Look at the clock down the hall, sir! The big hand just went on twelve . . . and the little hand is on ten. It's ten o'clock, sir. Time to go!"

Laddie went down on one knee and hugged the boy closely to his breast. The child was the spitting image of his father, Lord Alex Hawke, at this age. In the child's company, the elderly man felt as if he was reliving his wonderful past with his lordship. Father and son were both full of life, the love of life, really, and all the joy and laughter that each new day brought forth. The boy even had his father's sly sense of humor.

He tousled the youth's unruly black hair and said, "Did Inspector Walker say it was all right? Did you ask the boss his permission yet?"

A dark cloud passed over Alexei's face. "I forgot to ask him, sir."

"No worries, me lad, we'll go ask him now."

McPhee rose and gathered the boy up into his arms. For a man his age, he had enormous strength, probably because he spent so much time felling trees in the forest and splitting logs for the approaching winter.

"Inspector?" McPhee said, entering the great room. "Would you mind terribly if Alexei and I went for a walk in the woods this morning? I've found a secret something I'd like to show him down by the river."

Walker looked up from his book (a tale about King Arthur and his knights) and said, "I don't see why not. As long as Archie tags along. And speak of the devil! Good morning, Archie! Completed your rounds, have you?"

"Aye, and nothing much of note to report, Inspector."

"Good. All that chatter about some mysterious submarine on BBC Glasgow last night had me worried. We'd better be extra mindful until it dies down, Arch."

"Indeed we should, sir."

Sergeant Archie Carstairs had been off on the

ATV for the last two hours. There had been yet another radio report of suspicious submarine activity offshore near the little harbor town of Portree Bay. Rumors of such stuff abounded lately, mostly due to the Swedes' discovery of a submarine in one of their own harbors. Nothing came of it, eventually, but it was one of Archie's jobs to keep a weather eye to sea nevertheless.

"Archie, Laddie here has something he wants Alexei to see down by the river. Have you got time now, before your noon rounds?"

Archie adjusted the sling of the HK MP5 machine gun he carried every moment he was awake. It was the standard weapon of all SO14 Royalty Protection officers and its 4.6mm rounds could penetrate body armor. He had used it to good effect many times in the line of duty and found it satisfactory.

"Indeed I do, sir," Archie Carstairs said.

"Well, then, Laddie, I suppose you boys are off on a wild adventure, then!" Walker said, returning to his book. He'd started reading the old tome as a way to entertain Alexei. But he'd gotten so engrossed in the tale of chivalry, derring-do, and bravery that he couldn't wait to return to those splendid days of yore.

THE HAPPY THREESOME, MEANWHILE, MADE THEIR way toward the river through the cold damp wood. It was slow going, slogging through the wet leaves piling up against the base of old trees like snowdrifts, trees whose tangled roots could send you sprawling if you didn't mind your step. Laddie led the way, with Alexei and Archie tagging along a step or two behind him.

"How old are you, now, Alexei?" the venerable old gamekeeper asked.

"Six!" Alexei said proudly.

"Is that right? Well, isn't that funny? Do you know that when my son Colin, who lives over to Portree Bay, said to me, when he was six years old . . . why, he, he said he was exactly your age!"

Alexei smiled, just to be nice to his new friend, but he wasn't sure that the joke was very funny.

Archie, however, bringing up the rear, laughed loudly.

Out of sight of the boy, Carstairs kept his weapon at the ready beneath his poncho. Something about that worrisome chat on the BBC last night had tugged at him all morning. Made him extravigilant, aware of every sight and sound in the woods.

Finally, they came to a bend in the river where a huge black alder tree stood on the edge of the bank. Its spreading branches and purplish-tinged leaves reached out over the river, hiding the swift flow of currents in the water below.

"Here we are," Laddie said.

"Is this where you fish, Laddie?" Sergeant Carstairs asked, looking at the swirling currents near shore.

"Mebbe I do, mebbe I don't. Fishing holes are secret in the great Scottish outdoors, Sergeant. As me son young Colin is oft to remind, 'In this corner of Scotland, ye have to remember there's a brown trout in every other puddle you stumble upon.'"

Archie sputtered with laughter. "He's serious! He's bloody serious! A trout in every puddle!"

"Is this really the Lost River?" the boy said, looking around for any particular secrets he might spy. "I don't see any secrets, Mr. McPhee."

"That's because you have to *look* for secrets," Laddie said. "We've got to go down this bank here. Careful! Mind your steps, boy; it's muddy and slippery. Don't let him fall in, Sergeant."

"I've got him," Archie said, hoisting the child up in one arm as he made his way down.

"Getting warmer!" Laddie said.

"Where is it, Laddie?" the boy said, peering through the low-hanging branches of the black alder.

"Ah, good question! Hold on. Let's pull this big branch back and—wait—there she is!"

It was a rowboat. And not just any old rowboat either. A brand-new one. She was bright fire-engine red. With two hand-made oars lying on her thwart seat, tied together with a red ribbon bow.

"Oh my!" Alexei said, his eyes wide and his mouth bowing up into a big O. "Oh my goodness . . ."

Laddie said, "I ain't much of a wooden boat-builder, but rowboats I can do to a fare-thee-well. She's a bona fide beaut, isn't she? So who wants to go for a ride? I'll teach the new owner how to row. What do you think, Alexei?"

"Can I, Archie? Can I go row my new boat with Laddie?"

"I suppose you can," Sergeant Carstairs said with a smile. "I don't see why not. Every boy ought to know how to row a boat. Mind that current, though, especially out in the middle of the river."

ARCHIE WATCHED THEM UNTIL THEY GLIDED OUT OF sight around the wide bend. It had begun to rain again, not heavy, but hard enough for him to seek shelter up atop the bank, beneath the spreading branches of the black alder. He sat down with his back up against the trunk of the tree, facing the river so he could monitor the comings and goings of the little red rowboat. He heard the splash of oars and Alexei's laughter nearby, glad Laddie wasn't letting them drift too far downriver.

The sergeant had no idea how long he'd been sitting there when he heard something move above his head. He looked up, expecting to see a squirrel leaping from branch to branch. It wasn't a squirrel at all that he saw, but a heavy black boot. It was dangling down through the dense leaves. He immediately understood that whoever's foot filled that shoe had been hiding right above his head all this time.

Archie moved extremely slowly. He slid his right index finger inside the trigger guard of the MP5. Then he raised the muzzle so the weapon was pointing directly at the bottom of the boot. Then he slowly got to his knees without a sound on the carpet of wet leaves . . . and then to his feet.

The boot was now about five feet above his head.

"I've got a gun," he said, looking up into the tree.

No reply.

"If you don't do exactly as I say, I will blow your right foot off. Believe me, I will do it."

He lifted the muzzle and fired a short burst into the air. The noise was deafening in the silence of the forest.

"No! Don't shoot," a hidden voice said suddenly.

Archie gripped the gun more tightly. He recognized that Slavic accent.

The Russians are coming.

"Throw your gun to the ground. Now. And any other weapons. You've got five seconds before you lose that foot."

A stubby machine gun bounced once off a branch before it fell to the ground right at Archie's feet. A second later, a serrated assault knife. He kicked both away into the leaves and said, "Come down now. Slowly."

There was a rustle of wet leaves above and then a young blond sailor dropped to the ground, his face a mask of fear as he got up off his knees.

"Submarine?" Archie said, already knowing the answer.

He nodded. The boy was barely eighteen, if that. A scared, sleepless Russian kid who'd spent the night being whipped to and fro at the top of a tree in a violent rainstorm.

"Speak English?"

"Little."

"On the ground. Facedown in the leaves. Hands behind your back."

The sailor complied. Archie started to ask another question, but his gaze had strayed to the horizon on the far side of the river. There was no time to question the prisoner: how many, where they were, what kind of arms. No. Right now he had to get the boy back to the relative safety of the house. Time to get Alexei away from the river and get away fast. Who knew how long they had before this fellow's comrades, Russian commandos, would mount an attack on Castle Drum?

Archie placed his boot squarely in the middle of the young man's back, pressed it down to keep him from moving, and called out to Laddie and Alexei. A moment later he saw them hove into view. He smiled at the child and then gave Laddie a warning glance.

The set of Archie's jaw and the dark look in his eyes told Laddie all was not well ashore. He quickly ran the boat up onto the muddy bank and handed Alexei up to the waiting arms of his bodyguard.

"Visitors," Archie whispered to the old man, pointing at the submariner on the ground. "Let's go home!"

"Where'd you find him?" Laddie said; he and Alexei were staring at the stranger with great surprise.

"Found him in that tree," Archie said.

"Who is he?" Alexei said, watching the blondheaded boy get slowly to his feet, brushing the soggy leaves off his peacoat jacket.

"A neighbor," Archie said. "He got sick swimming across the river. Caught a cold. He's coming home with us until he feels better."

"Are you sick?" Alexei said, looking at the shivering fellow. "Is it your tummy?"

"Measles," Laddie said. "Best keep away from him."

"He's contagious?"

"Something like that."

Archie picked up the sailor's gun and assault knife. Then he leaned in close to Laddie's ear and asked him to take the Russian's machine gun. It was loaded, on full auto, he told him. Walk five steps ahead with the prisoner a few steps in front of him, he said. If the Russian made a run for it, shoot him in the legs. They needed the boy alive for interrogation once they were safe. Archie and Alexei would be right behind them.

As they made their way back through the wood, Archie realized that perhaps he knew all he needed to know at the moment. Their young prisoner was just a Boy Scout sent out on a recon. But there were a lot more Russians out there somewhere. They were coming for Alexei. And these men would not even remotely resemble Boy Scouts. They had little time to prepare for this stunning change of events, and he spurred them to pick up the pace.

The men who would come were, in all likelihood, a vicious special forces command sent by the KGB with but one mission. To capture or murder the terrified little boy who now held his hand so tightly.

A happy child who had just, little more than an hour ago, made his way through these very woods with pure joy in his heart, so eager was he to learn the secret of the lost river.

SEVENTY-FOUR

ISLA DE PINOS

BROCK AND GATOR HEARD THE CLANKING TRACKS of the mobile Howitzer chugging steadily onward along the trail just below them. It had just belched smoke as it lobbed two more 105mm cannon shells at *Blackhawke*. The last two rounds had missed, but the gunners were still dialing in the range and these two rounds were much, much closer.

The Russian Army DONAR tracked vehicle was on the move again, no doubt trying to avoid the ship's missile tracking systems.

But, Harry thought, assessing the situation, also trying to gain a better angle on the enemy vessel that had dared to invade the harbor. And that was now pounding the Cuban shore defenses protecting the intelligence installation and huge weapons cache. Once *Blackhawke* was clearly in the sights of the big Howitzer, her fate would be sealed.

"Where the hell's Big Bertha headed, Gator?" Harry said, looking up at him. The kid had climbed a palm tree with his NVG binoculars, trying to get a fix on the big cannon's movements through the jungle cover.

"Headed half a click up the trail. Looks like somebody cut a clearing out of the jungle up there. Artillery emplacement. Definitely one of the Howitzer's preferred firing positions here on the mountain, based on the piles of expended shells up there . . . and . . . we can't let them gain that advantage, sir. Not if we're going to keep them from sinking *Blackhawke*."

"Then what are we waiting for down here, slick?"

"Not me, chief," Gator said, dropping to the ground and grabbing his weapon. "Let's get a move on."

The two men kept low and out of sight, moving in tandem through the jungle, one on either side of the trail. This was good, Harry thought. His leg had stopped hurting so much, thanks to the morphine injection. They hadn't been spotted yet. And they knew exactly where the new target was headed.

"Come to new heading zero-zero-six," Hawke said, his eyes trained on the puffs of artillery smoke rising up near the top of the mountain. The Howitzer crew was already taking evasive action, not waiting around for one of the ship's gun crews to get a lock on the cannon's location. This surprise appearance of heavy artillery was definitely a wild card dealt into the war game at the last minute. Once the gunners up there found the boat's range, all bets were off.

The fighting around the harbor was growing more intense. Cuban shore batteries were now pounding the vessel. Most of the rounds were falling harmlessly into the sea, thanks to the ship's armor plating and the relatively poor training of the Cuban artillery crews by their Russian "advisors."

Also helping the ship were the very effective evasion tactics displayed by Geneva King, manning the battle helm of *Blackhawke*. The shells that hit were inflicting superficial damage, but nothing that could sink the ship. Not so far, anyway.

The Howitzer was another situation entirely. A direct hit in a vulnerable spot by a 105mm shell? "Say sayonara, Suzanne."

Stoke's last situation report had Redcoat moving into the warehouse district proper. Here is where the resistance of Cuban and Russian commandos was heaviest. And where *Blackhawke*'s gun crews had been concentrating their fire to soften up the resistance. Redcoat had rejoined with Bluecoat just in time to present a unified show of force. Both squads had suffered casualties in breaching the main and secondary gates.

Even though the black-uniformed Russian Spetsnaz forces were concentrated in this central location, Stoke said, 12-Gauge and his squad had already managed to rig charges in the two smaller warehouses. They were now working on an approach to the third. The Russians were clearly determined to protect the largest cache of explosives, the cases of Feuerwasser located in the largest of the three warehouses, which butted up to the concrete seawall.

"You've got twenty-eight minutes, Stoke," Hawke said. "Get it done and get the hell out of there. Once that big Howitzer dials us in, I can't guarantee anything anymore."

HARRY AND GATOR RACED AHEAD OF THE SURPRISingly fast-moving tracked vehicle upon which the mighty cannon stood. Their destination was now only a few hundred yards up the winding trail. Gator had a plan, he told Harry, but they had to get up to the clearing first to have any chance of success taking out the monster gun.

"Here, take this!" Gator shouted, tossing Brock a spool of wire he'd pulled out of his satchel while still on the run.

"What the hell is it?" Harry said. He had a bullet in his leg, after all, and he couldn't quite keep up with the star running back from Gainesville ascending a sloppy muddy trail.

"You'll see," Gator said, breaking first into the clearing. He had a spool of his own and was running from palm to palm around the perimeter of the cleared tract, taking a couple of turns around the trunks of each tree with the wire before racing to the next.

"Do the same on the other side," he shouted to Brock, "and meet me in the middle of the clearing with what's left on your spool!"

When they met in the middle, Harry saw that the whole of the clearing was now crisscrossed with the wire web they'd woven in under five minutes. The big gun was coming into view around a wide bend in the trail when Gator pulled a dull black box out of his vest pocket and jammed the two ends of wire into slots in the side.

"Explosive?" Brock said.

Gator smiled as he punched in a sequence on the little black box.

"Sort of. The wires are impregnated with explosives," Gator said. "This is the detonator. Sends out signals. Any metallic solid coming with fifty yards of this box ignites the wires. The wires are coated with stuff called Willy Pete. White phosphorous. Burns at ridiculous temperatures and incinerates anything it comes into contact with—like, say, Big Bertha coming up that trail right now. Better run for the woods, sir; this could get ugly."

They ducked beneath the spiderweb of death and sprinted for the safety of the green wall of jungle at the edge, Brock lagging behind because of his wounds. He stumbled, almost fell, and looked back at the black-uniformed Russian storm troopers coming in advance of the tracked vehicle and—shit—he had about one minute to make it to the trees or he was one gone cat.

"Wrap your arm around my shoulder and hold on," Gator said. "Hurry up, I've got you, sir!"

The man had come back for him. And Brock knew he'd never have made it were it not for Gator's bravery. Bullets were sizzling all around the two men as they neared the green stuff.

Diving into the dense jungle foliage, they just had time to turn around and see the big Howitzer rolling into the explosive spiderweb they'd strung up . . .

The whole world lit up in a blaze of white-hot fire and billowing white smoke—one minute the cannon was clanking forward—the next it had simply burned up along with the wires, turning into white ash and powder before their eyes. The troops who'd accompanied the vehicle were likewise consumed in the chemical fire. And then the 105mm ammo blew sky high. The clearing was a horrific and short-lived nightmare one moment, a smoking emptiness the next.

Brock was staring at the devastation, shaking his head.

"How the hell do I get my hands on some of that funky wire, Gator?" he said.

"You can't, Brah. It's illegal."

Stoke didn't even realize he'd been shot.

He was way, way too busy. He'd gotten his guys this far. The two smaller warehouses to either side of the old courthouse building were gonzo. Now 12-Gauge needed to finish rigging the third. The blackshirts were well entrenched in a small square outside the entrance to the three-story warehouse building. On the top floor were port offices: harbormaster, excise, logistics, and all that crap. On the first and second floors were cases and cases of the most powerful explosive anybody'd ever seen, stacked up to the roof.

Hawke had said this secret stuff of Putin's was

dynamite to the thirtieth power. Hell, President Vlad had knocked Miami off the damn grid with it and sunny South Florida was still reeling in the dark.

Stoke knew old Vladimir was just getting warmed up. Feuerwasser was leaving this port by the boatload on a weekly, sometimes daily basis. Headed for the United States and God knows where else.

"Fat, listen up," Stoke said. He and his wingman had been rigging charges up on the warehouse roof and now they were hunkered down near the oil storage drums on the dock. Not a great place to be hunkered down when the shooting started, Stoke told Fat, but then he had a better idea.

He'd stashed a bottle of Feuerwasser from the second warehouse just before they'd blown the roof off the damn building. You never knew when extremely high-powered explosives might come in handy. Like . . . now.

"Talk to me, bossman," Fat said.

"We need a diversion if we're going to go through those doors alive. This is it."

"What?"

"Our diversion. We use it to blow the used oil dump right next to the warehouse. The fire might even spread inside and trigger the heat charges on the roof. You with me on this? Blow the oil cans and get the hell out. Join the assault mounting in the plaza."

"I guess."

"Got a better idea, Fat?" he said, jamming a fuse through the metal twist cap of the bottle and setting the primer.

"Nope."

"I didn't think so," Stoke said, picking up his radio. "Bluecoat, this is Redcoat One. Fat and I are going to blow the east wall on the count of five. That's your signal to advance into the square and enter through the front. We'll be right with you. First man inside secures a case of the contraband and heads for the boats. Over."

"We roger that, Redcoat One. On five, over."

Stoke said, "Five, four . . . three, two . . . Let's go!" He backhanded the vodka bottle into the midst of the oilcans and the two of them ran like hell for their lives.

SEVENTY-FIVE

WHAT HAPPENED?"

That's what Fat said, running as fast as he could away from the oil dump, trying to keep up with Stoke.

"Nothing happened, that's what happened," Stoke said, looking back over his shoulder at all the oil cans still stacked up beside the warehouse.

"Bad fuse," Fat said as they turned the corner and ran smack-dab into mass confusion. "It happens."

"I guess," Stoke said, shocked at what he saw. "What the hell?"

Redcoat and Bluecoat squads, still waiting for an explosion to signal their advance and the attendant diversion on the rear side of the three-story building, were pinned down by superior numbers. Blackshirts were guarding the wide stone staircase leading up to the second story of the warehouse.

Sniper fire was coming from windows overlooking the little plaza. Nobody pinned by the withering fire could get off a shot.

Stoke immediately raced up the stairs of the empty building. He and Fat had both cover up on the second floor, and the angle on the blackshirts firing from windows in the building across the alley. Fat immediately dropped one with a head shot while Stoke heaved a few grenades through the windows to take out whoever the hell remained undead among the snipers up there.

He and Fat ducked back behind their cover and got on the radio. Bravo wanted to know what the hell had happened to their diversion.

"Bad fuse, Bravo One. No time to worry. We'll just have to gut it out, Raiders. I've got a satchel full of grenades. Fat and I will pull the pins and toss them at the troops down on the steps. We're under nine minutes—we gotta get something going, damn it!"

At that very moment, an old Russian-made jeep, painted jungle camo, came roaring around a corner on two squealing wheels. It got straightened out and barreled into the heart of the square. At the wheel was Harry Brock, driving like a madman on steroids. And, in the rear, manning a smoking .50 cal., was none other than the Gator himself. The gun barrel was red hot and getting hotter as Luttier whirled around unleashing a hail of lead in every direction . . .

It was a sight for sore eyes, and it was all the troops needed to rally.

With a loud "Hoo-ah!" Raiders exploded up out

of their cover and started racing toward the pha-
lanx of stunned blackshirts now being shredded on
the steps under Gator's withering .50-cal. fire and
Stoke's grenades. The man was a blur, swiveling
his smoking barrel through 360 degrees and back
around again.

The roar of cheers from the attacking Raiders
rose in volume and scope, reaching a crescendo that
rose above the square and seemed to hang in space.

"What the hell's all that noise about, Fat?" Stoke
said.

"Let's go!" Saunders responded and lit out down
the stairs.

The two of them ran out into the square just in
time to see another miracle in progress.

"Holy shit, Fat! Will you look at Harry!"

It was Harry. And there was no stopping him
now.

He plowed that jeep right through all the guards
firing at him from the bottom steps. Bodies went
flying as the jeep reached the bottom of the wide
stone staircase leading up to the second floor. That
was where the warehouse full of Firewater was located. Somehow, they had to get inside and check
on the Semtex charges that 12-Gauge had strung all
over the place earlier. They would destroy the rest
of the cache when this was over.

This was the moment when this battle would be
won or lost, and everyone knew it.

But the thing was, Harry's jeep didn't stop at the
foot of the steps. He just downshifted to second
gear, floored the accelerator, and kept on going. He
drove that damn jeep straight up the steps! "Hold

on, Gator!" Stoke heard Harry yell, and he saw that boy holding on to that hot fifty for dear life as the jeep bounced and careened upward until it reached the top. And then blasted forward, splintering the double wooden doors before disappearing inside the cavernous warehouse.

12-Gauge had used Hawke's idea of creating gaping holes in the floors of all three warehouses for the huge vodka runoff. Stoke had been told it seemed to be working. Now he'd see if it was.

Stokely and his Raiders had the Big Mo now.

THE RAIDERS WERE HOPPING AND POPPING ALL OVER the square now, preparing for one last surge that would take them inside the target. Two guys in Bravo were fighting for their lives, being attended to by medical corpsmen away from the skirmish. And the Americans were still taking casualties when the tide of battle shifted permanently. It was the Harry Brock Show once more.

His battered jeep reappeared. Only this time Harry and his wingman, Gator, were going in the opposite direction. They came out flying at full speed, exploding out of that blasted-out building and going airborne before landing with a bang and bouncing and skidding down the rest of the steps. Gator was still hanging on, still shooting when they came out, and Harry was still driving but just barely.

He had it, though. He had Hawke's heavy wooden case of Feuerwasser balanced on his lap. It was interfering with his steering a little bit. But once Harry managed to crash-land the machine back down on solid ground, well, there was just no stopping him.

Brock braked hard, which sent Gator pitching forward, almost over the windshield, but then Harry put the big black wheel hard over, and somehow, maybe God knows how, still managed to keep both Hawke's special reserve Feuerwasser and the kid named Gator from going overboard.

And then Harry and Gator disappeared gone-baby-gone down a twisting narrow side street that led, Stoke knew, directly back to the boat ramp where the two minisubs were waiting to ferry them all home safely to Mother.

It was time to go.

The Raiders melted away into the jungle and toward the docks.

But not before one man slipped through the chaos on the steps and disappeared inside the warehouse to set the timers. The Semtex charges were all in place, set a little earlier by 12-Gauge and his guys. Harry and Gator had made sure they were all set to blow.

It was only fitting that Stoke be the last man out, the one to finally bring down the house.

"*Boom!*" he said to himself as he slipped away.

"All ahead flank speed," Hawke said.

He'd relinquished the conn to the boat's skipper during the recovery of Stoke's Raiders. He wanted to welcome the men back aboard. There were casualties, of course. Four of them had not come back alive. Harry'd been hurt, and Stoke had a bullet in his shoulder. They were bloodied, but unbowed; and they had accomplished their mission. The entire harbor was a smoking ruin. There'd be no more sabotage attacks on America's coastal cities now, not from Isla de Pinos at any rate.

Vladimir Putin knew who the enemy was by now. News of Hawke's naval attack had surely made its way to the Kremlin. He'd know Alex Hawke was coming for him. The two men had old scores to settle. And though fate would play a hand, the Englishman was nursing hopes of final victory. He felt Putin might have overplayed his hand in the global game. And that, maybe, all was not what it seemed in this conflict . . .

The big black warship was finally under way once more; headed for the harbor mouth and open sea beyond. Only one thing stood in her way: a Russian missile frigate armed to the teeth that wanted to sink her.

The Russian skipper had positioned his vessel so that it now lay stationary. It blocked the narrow harbor opening. This clever maneuver put Hawke in a nautical box. Go to port and present a very broad target? Or go starboard and present an equally broad profile? He found himself at a distinct disadvantage before the naval battle had even started.

But Hawke on the bridge was a picture of quiet confidence as they sailed into the thick of it. He was, as many said of him, simply good at war. And moments like the one approaching were what he lived for. His father had drilled a sentence from Kipling into his young head: "If you can keep your head when all around you are losing theirs . . . yours is the earth, my son, and—which is more—you'll be a man, my son!"

"Hard a'starboard, all ahead flank," he said quietly to the helmsman.

"Hard starboard, all ahead flank, aye," came the somewhat nervous reply.

Hawke could read the helmsman's mind, betrayed by his eyes and furrowed brow. Intuition was telling the helmsman that something terrible would happen if they maintained the new heading and— the speaker crackled.

"Helm, Fire Control, enemy vessel now with two missiles locked on, preparing to launch."

Hawke thumbed the radio, only the protrusion of tendons on the back of his hand betraying the tension now everywhere on the bridge.

"Fire Control, Hawke, you on this?"

"Aye-aye, sir. Turrets one and four," the fire control officer said.

The speaker squawked again.

"Missile batteries amidships enemy vessel now preparing to launch . . . suggest AMMS activation to preempt, over, sir."

"AMMS, aye, Fire Control." AMMS was the ship's advanced antimissile missile system. *Blackhawke*'s defensive systems were designed to impact enemy missiles at their slowest point, just when they were leaving the tube. This caused maximum destruction to the enemy.

"Fire Control, five seconds to enemy launch . . . and . . . AMMs away!"

All eyes on the bridge were locked onto the two *Blackhawke* missiles streaking toward the incoming fire.

"Uh, Helm, Fire Control . . . one direct hit . . . and . . . second AMM missed the target . . . enemy missile still incoming!"

Hawke instantly dropped his radio and grabbed the helm, spinning the wheel hard to port. The ship instantly heeled sharply as the boat veered away to a new course. The incoming fire must have missed by a matter of inches. The fierce explosion upon impact with the sea drenched the aft gun crews with a towering tsunami of seawater.

"Helm, come back to course six-zero-six," Hawke said. "Steer her right down that bastard's throat . . ."

"Six-zero-six, aye-aye, sir!"

There was a pervasive attitude of disbelief among those on the bridge that night. Hawke was taking the boat on a collision course . . . did he intend to ram the Russian frigate?

He did not.

Blackhawke surged ahead through the oncoming waves as her twin gas turbines spooled up, delivering power to the four enormous bronze screws churning beneath the stern. Her course seemed intended to take her right into the teeth of the enemy guns. No matter what happened, the Russians on her bridge would have precious little time to avoid this sudden and deliberate incursion into their space . . .

At the last possible moment, Hawke said, "Helm, hard to starboard. Put her damn lee rail down . . .

and . . . Fire Control, launch port-side JDAM . . . Now!"

JDAM, Joint Direct Attack Munition, was the most powerful antiship missile in existence. Two can take out any aircraft carrier afloat. The very idea that such an innocent-looking vessel could even conceivably be armed with such a weapon would be incomprehensible to Hawke's counterpart on the opposing bridge. Still, life was full of surprises, as Hawke intended to remind the Russian captain.

"Fire Control, status?" Hawke said.

"Initiating prelaunch checklist . . . weapon powered up . . . autotrack engaged . . . master arm is hot . . . weapon status go, sir."

"Then go!" Hawke said. "Fire!"

The fish was away.

Hawke's stony blue eyes watched it close the gap between the ships . . . there was a *cra-a-a-ck* . . . men turned away from the blinding sight.

The explosion was nothing short of massive. A blinding, searing flash of white that quickly burned into geysers of yellow, orange, and red climbing skyward out of swirling clouds of blackest smoke.

And when it cleared, a cheer went up on the bridge and from one end of the ship to the other. The missile had literally blown the Russian ship in two, its back broken, blown apart. The two halves, engulfed in flame, were still afloat, canted at odd angles as masses of crewmen could be seen leaping from the rails and desperately trying to outswim the pools of burning oil spreading rapidly on the surface around the doomed vessel.

Hawke said, "Helm, set a course for NAS Key

West, would you please? All ahead flank. I'm going below to grab a catnap. Could somebody wake me when we're about an hour out? Thank you."

And with that he retired from the bridge that had recently seen such intense action. The skipper headed for the owner's stateroom; he was keenly anticipating reconnecting with his favorite goose down pillow.

To the victor go the spoils, after all.

SEVENTY-SIX

CASTLE DRUM

THEY CAME FOR THE BOY AT DAWN.

Archie Carstairs was at his window post in the castle's north tower. It had been a quiet night. From the highest windows, his view was of fjords, fields, and forests stretching away to the sea. Down the hill and to the left, tucked into a copse of black-thorn trees, was a tidy white two-story house with black shutters. It had been home to the McPhee family for generations. When the day was over, it would be a smoking ruin.

Archie got his first sight of the approaching commandos just as the red sun peeked over the eastern horizon. He counted twenty-one. Fanned out across a plowed field, swinging their electric torches to and fro, the twenty commandos began their methodical advance on the castle.

He saw that the leader had called a halt. The big commando went from man to man, pausing a minute or two with each one, checking weapons, issuing last-minute orders for the impending assault on Castle Drum.

Now Archie could make out clearly defined silhouettes. These were spec-ops commandos, that much was certain. They had the swagger, the heavy black combat kit, the serious weaponry that marked the breed. What Archie, the former infantryman, wouldn't give right now for an SBS sniper rifle with a high-powered night-vision scope.

Archie's automatic weapon, his cherished HK MP5, was unbeatable for close combat. But it was never going to be very effective against the enemy when fired from this height. It was a heated subject and one he'd discussed at great length with Walker the night before. All to no avail. He took a deep breath to calm himself. There was nothing to be done now. He needed to use the stillness, the quiet darkness of the hour, to compose himself for the coming battle.

Downstairs, the dogs were sleeping by the smoking embers in the Great Hall, thank God. And every light was extinguished. The Russian prisoner was bound and gagged in one of the countless guest rooms on the second floor. Inspector Walker was posted at one of the library windows on the ground floor. He had the Russian sailor's automatic assault rifle and two 9mm pistols, his own, and one taken from the prisoner down by the river. When the Russian ammo was expended, he had his own HK MP5 as back-up.

If it got to the point where they were using pistols . . . well, best not to go there.

The glass had been removed from the one of the library windows. In addition, Archie and Walker had shoved a heavy wooden table up close to the sill. It would give Walker, the ground-level shooter, a much better field of fire. And an unobstructed view of the final approach up the hill to the entrance of Castle Drum.

Laddie McPhee was the second ground-level shooter. The old fellow was now perched in an open window in the main dining room. He had a brace of Purdey 12-gauge shotguns, loaded, and a .30-06 Springfield rifle with a reasonably good scope. He'd told Archie he could shoot a toothpick out of a man's teeth at fifty paces with that rifle. And Archie had no reason to doubt the man's veracity. His marksmanship would be invaluable. And his boxes of ought-six ammunition.

Pelham was now posted to a window in the nursery on the third floor. Archie had given the old fellow his sidearm and an automatic rifle. As soon as they engaged the enemy, Pelham was to race from room to room, firing from all the third-floor windows. This, to give the enemy the calculated impression that a far larger number of shooters was defending a castle under siege.

Even Alexei would play a part in the defense.

Laddie had spent hours teaching the boy to

shoot, ever since his arrival at Castle Drum. After much heated discussion, Inspector Walker had decided that the boy be allowed to crouch beneath the nursery window with his .22-caliber rifle, loaded. "If something bad happens to Pelham," Walker had told him, "if he cannot shoot any longer, then aim your rifle out the window and shoot at anything that moves. These are bad men, Alexei, they want to hurt us."

Under the circumstances, Archie believed, they had done all they possibly could to prepare for a frontal assault on Castle Drum.

After interrogating the captured sailor all afternoon, the men inside the castle had formed their plan of defense. They'd based it on assumptions formed after hearing the prisoner's story. Two ten-man squads under the command of Captain Ivan Isakov, KGB Special Operations, Baltic Fleet, were approaching. Their mission was to search the house and grounds at Castle Drum. Only one prisoner was to be taken alive. A six-year-old boy named Alexei Hawke.

Isakov's orders were that if he did not have the young heir, dead or alive, in his hands, he need not bother returning to Moscow. To say that Isakov would be highly motivated would be the grossest form of understatement.

Archie caught a glimpse of movement in his binoculars. The enemy had begun to move once more.

He turned away from his lookout and raced out of the small room toward the stairs. It was his first responsibility to warn the others that the enemy had been sighted before resuming his tower post.

He ran out into the hall, then raced down the main staircase to the ground floor first, darting into the Great Hall to alert Walker.

"Twenty-one, total," Archie said, out of breath. "Walking abreast about fifty yards apart. Coming up the hill below the ruins of that old McPhee house. Pretty damn cocky about it, I'd say. We'll give them something to think about, I'll venture, sir. At the very least."

"Indeed. As soon as you've warned Laddie and Pelham, get back up to the tower position. As soon as they're in range, I'll commence firing. Tell the others to follow my lead and commence firing at will. Now, go!"

It took less than twenty minutes for the commandos to crest the hill. They were ranging wider apart, leery of the silence that reigned inside the dark castle. Their recon had never returned. They had to assume he'd been killed or captured. Either way, whoever was waiting up there on the knoll knew they were coming.

Walker knew. He picked a man on the left flank. Braced his weapon against the sill and squeezed the trigger . . . *BAM!* Saw the commando stagger a few steps, regain his balance, and keep coming. Kevlar body armor. His comrades started firing in earnest. Two commandos took off running on a line straight for the windows where Walker's initial shot had come from.

The Russians must have now realized how dreadfully exposed they were on the open ground. Three of them made for the ruins of the old house and ducked inside. The rest took what little cover the open ground afforded them. The barrage of enemy fire in response took effect; huge chunks of stone were blasted out of the castle walls, windows blown inward, doors splintered . . . and on they came.

The men defending Castle Drum gave them everything they had.

Walker fired, reloaded, and fired again, repeating the cycle as fast as humanly possible. He was concentrating his fire on the right flank now, those men closest to the castle.

Laddie, at his post in the dining room, saw one man drop, fired his old rifle again, and saw another man gravely wounded before turning his gun on his own house and the three men inside . . .

Pelham, up in the nursery, saw one of the attackers below crossing his position. He was clearly en route to the Great Hall window where Walker was holding his own. Pelham swiftly brought the 12-gauge to bear as the commando drew near, fired, and saw the man fall to the ground, mortally wounded. That's when the thought first occurred to the old fellow . . . there were just too damn many of them.

And on they came.

He looked down into Alexei's shining face, wondering if this brilliant new day would mark the bitter end of everything he held dear in this world . . . Alexei was tugging at his elbow.

"Can I shoot, too, Pelham? Please?"

He looked down at him with infinite sadness in his old eyes. He now feared the worst.

"No more shooting now, Alexei. Soon, we're

all going up into the tower along with Inspector Walker. He's found a secret hiding place for us up there. We'll be together . . . waiting for the bad men to leave us alone . . . that's my brave boy . . . you can bring your gun, my darling boy."

Pelham's soft blue eyes were brimming with tears, and he brushed them away with the ragged and careworn sleeve of his sweater. He saw the open box of shells and grabbed a handful. He then began firing as fast as he could reload, blinded by tears, but unwilling to cease until he had nothing left to shoot . . .

THE ENEMY WERE SO CLOSE NOW, WALKER THOUGHT, so goddamn *close*. Within a few hundred yards of the barricaded front door. Moments before, the KGB captain had huddled them up near the McPhee house. Walker instinctively knew they were planning a final push, an all-out assault on the entrance now. They had to hold them off . . . somehow.

And now he wasn't at all sure there was much the defenders, staunch as they were, as brave as they had been, could do about it . . . no cavalry was coming up the hill to their rescue. No British paratroopers floating down from above, guns blazing at the merciless attackers now storming the castle walls . . .

But, in the end, Walker was wrong about all that.

Someone had come to the rescue.

It was Archie.

The inspector's heart swelled up, then lifted with pure joy. He saw Lord Hawke's helicopter! It appeared as if out of nowhere, rising straight up from behind the hill, juking this way and that, catching the first rays of the sun on its shiny red flanks.

And now Archie dove again and again on the Russian commandos, strafing them even as he banked hard left, then hard right. He was hanging halfway out of the cockpit, secured only by his harness. He seemed to be firing a heavy machine gun left-handed at the Russians, the enemy scattering in a blind panic now. Somehow the man was shooting with his left hand while he was flying the damn thing with his right hand—it was a bloody, bloody miracle.

The surviving commandos dove this way and that, desperately seeking cover that did not exist. A few made it back inside the old white house, many others did not. Those men died on their feet, raked by lethal fire from above. The desperate survivors trapped inside the house were firing up at the belly of their tormentor, hoping for a miracle that would bring the machine down in flames . . .

But miracles were in very short supply now. And here came Archie and the scarlet chopper once more, skimming low over the ground toward Laddie's ruined house. Then he was hovering above it for a moment, ready to deliver the coup de grâce. He leaned far out and Walker could see him, watched him drop at least half a dozen live hand grenades down Laddie's chimney.

Archie instantly hauled back on the stick and put the beast into a steep vertical climb as a fiery ball of orange flame and black smoke rose straight up out of the house like a cannon blast fired into the early morning sky.

It was over.

PELHAM AND ALEXEI WATCHED IT ALL, CHEERING Archie on from the nursery window. The old fellow was weeping hot tears of joy when he gathered his beloved Alexei up into his arms and hurried down the staircase to find Laddie, Walker, and Pelham, all there, waiting at the entrance.

The three of them, overcome with joy and relief, were standing just outside the splintered oak door, looking up, watching Archie land the helicopter in a rose garden a hundred feet from the castle's front door. He settled the machine, shut the engine down, and climbed out, running out from under the still-spinning rotors toward all his joyous comrades.

They stood as one by the front door, each of them celebrating his victory in his own peculiar way. Laddie and Archie were dancing a Highland fling with Alexei in Archie's arms. Walker and Pelham, well, they just stood there, clapping their hands, applauding, giving the man the hero's welcome he so richly deserved.

Pelham knew the Battle of Castle Drum would never be recorded when historians set down the tales of epic victories on Scottish soil. But for the brave little band of men, and one small boy, who were there that day, who had fought so valiantly against such seemingly insurmountable odds, that fateful day would always have a proud place in their private memories.

These were his thoughts as Pelham left them all celebrating out there in rose garden. And walked through the sunlit rooms to his sanctuary off the kitchens. He pulled up his wooden stool, climbed up on it, and took down a dusty old MI6 high-frequency radio from the cabinet. Hawke had showed him how to work it a long time ago, telling him he was always to use it whenever he had significant news to impart. This would be the first time he had ever used it.

Hawke was off fighting his own battles, he knew that.

But Lord Hawke needed to know one thing. He needed to know that the men to whom he'd entrusted the protection of his worshipped and adored son had not let him down.

Nor would they ever, as long as Pelham Grenville was alive.

SEVENTY-SEVEN

AT SEA

THERE WAS A RAP AT HAWKE'S STATEROOM DOOR. Irritated, because he was tired and because he never took naps but now felt he needed one, he swung his long legs over the side of the bed and crossed the room to the door. Pity the poor person who might be disturbing him for naught.

It was Harry Brock. Brock and his sidekick, the kid the Raiders all called Gator. Catching himself about to say something prickly, while feeling enormously grateful for all the heroics that Harry and Gator had displayed ashore that day, Hawke said, "Why, Harry, I was just thinking about you two gentlemen. I see they patched you up down in sick bay. What's up?"

"Do you mind if we step inside? It's kinda important," Harry said.

"Come in. Have a seat over there and I'll grab my robe."

Hawke sat down on the small leather sofa facing the two warriors. "All right, gents, what's on your mind?"

"Have you met Gator Luttier, sir?" Harry said.

"I've not. Gator, is it? You did a hell of a job up on that mountain last night. You and Mr. Brock."

"Thank you, sir," Gator said, and looked over at Harry to jump in.

"Gator came to see me about an hour ago," Harry said. "He wanted to tell me about something that happened up in that blockhouse we took out. Soon as I heard what Gator had to say, I thought it was something you needed to be aware of. Like, now."

Hawke sat back and lit a cigarette, all hope of any rest dashed. "Go ahead, Gator. Tell me what happened."

"Well, sir, we went in together, see, me and Harry. He took the top floor, me the bottom. Blew the door and found a bunch of guys in there playing poker, Cuban enlisted men and a couple of Russian officers. We weren't expected and we shot 'em up pretty good. Mr. Brock, well, he got hit and knocked unconscious. That was upstairs and, hell, I didn't know a damn thing about it, though. I had one man down, Russian, still breathing. He was hurt plenty bad. Sucking wound in the chest. Knew he wasn't going to make it, but, still, I tried to comfort him a little, like you do, you know. All the rest were dead. He wanted to talk. Crazy talk. About how fucked everything was. How the Russian military didn't want to go to war with America. It was all that damn warmonger Putin. Him and somebody called 'Uncle Joe.' They were the ones would get everybody killed and—"

"*Uncle Joe*? Who the hell is that?" Hawke suddenly leaned forward. "Go on, Gator."

"Well, it was all Uncle Joe this and Putin that. Whoever this Joe cat is, he seems to be running the circus. And then he really got my attention when he said something about a guy called the 'Colonel.' Said that was the one secretly doing all the dirty work for Putin. Said he was the one who shot down that civilian airliner over China. An op he ran from somewhere or other in Siberia. Well, at that point he was pretty delirious, but I felt like I had to keep him talking. And here's the thing about it, sir. What I felt you needed to know about. This guy, the colonel? He's an American."

"What?"

"Yessir. I know because I used to work for him. Did a security job for him at an oilfield in Saudi. He signed my paychecks. His name is Beauregard, Colonel Brett Beauregard from Port Arthur, Texas."

Hawke could not contain his surprise. "Beauregard! You don't mean to say you actually worked for Vulcan, Gator?"

"I did, yessir. Before the colonel got himself in all that hot water and went to ground. He's back, looks like, and working for Putin. He was working here in Cuba until recently, the guy said, coordinating Cuban special operations for Uncle Joe."

"For Uncle Joe. Not Putin, but Uncle Joe. Is that what he said? Were those his precise words?"

"Yessir."

"What else did he say?"

"Not much. He died."

Hawke didn't say a word. Just got to his feet and started pacing back and forth, puffing his cigarette.

Finally he stopped and said, "Harry, I'm going to need your help. I'm finally starting to get an understanding of how this all fits together."

"What do you mean?"

"I mean all of it. Cuba, that goddamn Feuerwasser demonstration, bringing down that airliner and using a bloody Yank to do it! Exploiting American weakness, throwing everybody off their game . . . so he can . . . redraw the map of the world. And convincing himself that nobody will do one damn thing about it."

"I got a feeling that ain't exactly true," Gator said.

"Whatever do you mean?" Hawke replied.

"I mean I got a suspicion *you'll* do something about it, sir."

Hawke laughed. He liked this kid. A lot.

"Gator, I want you and Mr. Brock here, and Mr. Jones, to meet me up in the war room in exactly thirty minutes. I need to get my thoughts together. And, right now, if I can find him, I need to ring up Ambrose Congreve in the U.K.—I hope to God he's back from Siberia—and see if he's found out who the hell this Uncle Joe character is. Our number one mystery man at the moment."

The two got up. Harry paused at the door and said, "Isn't that what they used to call Joe Stalin? Uncle Joe?"

"That's right, Harry. But he's dead. Oh, and do me a favor while you're waiting. Create a digital file for all the stuff you can get on Siberia. Sat maps of the region in question, thermal overprints, you know the drill. Standard stuff."

"We going there next, boss?"

Hawke just smiled and closed the door behind them.

"HULLO? ALEX? IS THAT YOU ON THE LINE?"

"It is indeed, Ambrose. I'm still aboard *Blackhawke*, steaming for Key West. Listen, I'm so glad you're home safe. I've just found out some information regarding recent events in Siberia. During your ill-advised adventure with Halter, did you two run across someone called 'Uncle Joe'?"

"We did indeed. It's a long story, I'm afraid. But I'm very glad you called. I've been worried sick about Professor Halter since I got back here."

"Why is that?" Hawke said.

"I think he may have feigned a heart attack in order to save my life. As I said, it's a long story. But he's either dead of a heart attack in Siberia, or they've got him in some dreadful cell in Lubyanka Prison in Moscow, KGB goons torturing him to death for his splendid treason. I've got to do something to help him soon. Or at least find out the truth. Bring his body home to Cambridge for a proper burial in St. Paul's Cemetery if need be, Alex."

"As it happens, I'm planning another Siberian

excursion at the moment. Like to tag along? With your brains and my charming personality, we're bound to be able to get Halter out of there, one way or the other. Are you in? Diana will kill me, dragging you back there so soon. But there you have it."

"Of course I'm in, damn you! Why didn't you tell me you were going! When and where shall I meet you?"

"St. Petersburg central rail station. My pilot's waiting for me at Key West, Ambrose. I intend to fly nonstop to St. Petersburg on the Gulfstream. Let's agree to meet at the rail station. Checked the rail schedules already. The Red Star, a Trans-Siberian express, pulls out at midnight. Can you be there?"

"Of course. Just the two of us? It could get very spicy when Mr. Putin learns you're poking about in his backyard, even more than you have been."

"Then you'll be happy to hear that I'm planning on bringing a few friends along for the ride. Mr. Jones, for one, likes to travel to exotic locales. As does our perennial favorite, Mr. Brock. And then there are a few other invitees, including a young chap whom I've only just met in Cuba. Fellow named Gator, for some reason or other. Rather one of those one-man-army type of chappies, if you get my drift."

"Good idea, Alex. And, right now, the way things are going in the world, I would say we may well need a couple of one-man armies for Hawke's historic invasion of Russia."

Hawke smiled and said, "'Hawke's invasion of Russia,' did you say? I bloody well like that. Let's reconvene in the ticket agent's office at the St. Petersburg rail station, shall we? Say, at eleven sharp the night of? I'm already ordering your billet online."

"The game is afoot, as the celestial Sherlock Holmes used to say."

"I would say that Holmes, as usual, got it right. Don't forget your cloak and dagger, Constable."

SEVENTY-EIGHT

KEY WEST

STOKE PAID FOR HIS NEWSPAPERS, COFFEE, AND Danish. Then he whirled around, banged out through the swinging screen doors of the Cuban Coffee Queen on Margaret Street in Key West, ran flat out two blocks east, and jumped into his black raspberry GTO convertible. The sound of that monster engine exploding and blatting into life reverberated through the sleepy, shady streets of old Key West on a quiet Sunday morning.

Normally, it took him twenty minutes to get from his favorite morning joe spot in town out to the navy docks. On this particular morning, he did it in twelve. What he had in his hands was something the boss would find extremely interesting.

It was 6:15 A.M. EST when Stokely made it back aboard *Blackhawke*. It was already hot as hell and his carefully pressed Cuban guayabara was sticking to him like a second skin, albeit one of the white persuasion.

He found Hawke in the war room, all alone, carefully studying satellite videos of some new Russian military training facility in Siberia. It was where they were all headed next, and the boss was deep into his brass tacks mode. "God's in his heaven but the Devil's in the details" kind of thing he had going on. Man was definitely in the zone.

"Morning, boss," Stoke said, pushing through the green baize doors.

"Stoke," Hawke muttered, lost in thought, rewinding a scene and staring at it again.

"You gotta see this!" Stoke said.

"See what?"

"This. Just hit the streets."

"What is it, Stoke?" he said, finally lifting his head.

"Have a look, boss, hot off the presses."

Stoke handed him a copy of that morning's *New York Times*. A bold black headline dominated most of the front page above the fold:

US INVADES CUBA, PUTIN SENDS TROOPS AND TANKS INTO ESTONIA, POLAND

Hawke stared at it for a long moment, put his feet up onto the table, stuck a cigarette in the corner of his mouth, and lit it. He exhaled a long, long plume of blue smoke and said: "Well, I'll be damned. Didn't waste any time, did he?"

"That's all you got to say?"

"What else is there to say?"

"Boss! Don't you see what they're saying? They're blaming us for starting World War Three! You and me! Oh, man, we're going to go down in the history books as the nuclear trigger! The two outlaws who started the last World War . . ."

"No, *Putin* is blaming us for starting World War Three."

"You saying there's a difference, boss?"

"Well, technically, no. It is the *New York Times*, after all. *The Daily Worker*. Putin could blame us for inventing wine coolers and they'd run with it."

"This doesn't bother you? Even a little? Seriously?"

"Nope. May I remind you that just last week, Russia tried to blow up Miami? Putin takes out American cities, we then take out his ability to do that. Period. He has zero interest in going nuclear right now. He's just taking it to the next level. Just as he's been planning to do all along. Expand his borders and nobody gives a good hot damn. He knew I'd rise to the bait. Ever notice how he kept putting that bloody explosive of his in my way? First, he demos it on a sunken freighter in France, then we find it on that Russian spy ship leaving Cuba, and then used by proxy terrorists in Miami. I'm surprised he hasn't already had a case of that crap delivered here to the docks as a bon voyage gift."

"Wait, you're saying that Feuerwasser stuff is *phony*?"

"I am. He fooled the hell out of me. Hell, out of all of us. But I just got the results back from independent testing at both the CIA and Department of Defense forensic labs. It's just plain old vodka."

"*Vodka?*"

"Yeah. One hundred percent cheap German rotgut. He's shipped hundreds of thousands of cases throughout the world. Hoping to use them as a bargaining threat against London and Washington when push, at long last, comes to shove. Leave me and my armored divisions alone or I'll blow up Edinburgh . . . or Atlanta. Don't be surprised if you hear him threaten us with exploding vodka in the next twenty-four hours. At the same time, he was going after my son. Attempts to kill him in London, Washington, and, just yesterday, my hunting lodge up in Scotland. Trying to keep me off balance."

"What? Scotland?"

"Yeah. Pelham just called me via radio phone from Castle Drum, our old family lodge up on the Isle of Skye. KGB landed twenty-one commandos off a submarine up there and made a run at Castle Drum and grabbing Alexei. Those Russian thugs are dead now, thanks to Inspector Walker and Sergeant Archie Carstairs. Not to mention Pelham and Laddie McPhee. The bastards did murder Laddie's son Colin, however, and they'll pay for that, too."

"Alexei, he's all right?"

"Absolutely. A bit young to be defending castles right after his sixth birthday, but apparently he was well up to the challenge with his trusty .22 rifle. Runs in the family, I suppose. You didn't bring me another of those aromatic Cuban coffees by any chance, did you? Is that a 'no'?"

"Um . . . I got an extra Danish? So, excuse me, what did they use to level that power plant?"

"Some hybrid method of imploding C-4 that eliminates any trace of itself. Something like that, I think. Ask Harry, he knows."

"Yeah, but what about that freighter you saw in France? What about that—"

Hawke's mind was already back in Siberia.

Stoke just smiled and headed for the door. Man never failed to amaze him. Never.

HAWKE WAS SOUND ASLEEP IN HIS CABIN. HE'D LEFT instructions for his steward to wake him at dawn. His plane was wheels up at six, soaring across the pond for their rendezvous with destiny.

What *was* that noise? Oh. His phone. He rolled over and picked up.

"This better be good," he said.

"It's not. It's Brick, Alex. Wake up. All hell and half of heaven has broken loose up here in the nation's capital."

"Talk."

"The White House went batshit when the morning papers hit the streets. I take it you've seen the *Times*? They're demanding that you get here today if not sooner and explain yourself. They just called me. And Admiral Moore. And probably your boss in London by now. The Big Cheese is looking for you, pal, Sir David wants to know where the hell you are."

"What'd you tell him?"

"That you were tired and taking a sick day."

"True. But, really, what did you say?"

"That I didn't know but I'd try to find out."

"And then what?"

"And then it's up to you. Where are you?"

"Key West. Doing a little fishing. Lots of mackerel around the docks."

"Can you please tell me what you're up to, Alex? I won't breathe a word, I promise. Just in case I have to send somebody out to look for you."

"Well, let's see. How about if you call your Deep Throat at the *Washington Post*. Tell him you've got a great above-the-fold header for next Sunday's paper—'Hawke's Invasion of Russia!'"

THE RED ARROW CHUGGED INTO THE TINY STATION. Tvas was deserted in the predawn hours. It was cold as billy-be-damned here in the Siberian wilderness, a howling blizzard. Gator and the Raiders had enlisted the help of two burly porters to help them get all their gear off the baggage car and onto the icy platform.

Hawke stood, stamping his boots to keep his circulation going and gazing at the growing mound of combat materiel. "One logistics detail, I'm sure you're aware of, Constable. That would be getting to the—"

"Already arranged, dear boy. Chap in the village I put on Scotland Yard's payroll last time out.

Blacksmith named Orlov. Should be here in a tick. Charming fellow, utterly charming."

"What's this Orlov got in mind?"

"Three large sleds. Six strong horses. And mounds of blankets, buckets of caviar, and oceans of vodka for the cross-country run." Hawke wasn't listening.

"I'm looking forward to meeting this Uncle Joe."

"Prepare to be amazed."

"That close to the real thing?"

"Bastard son, or genetically engineered replica. It's positively astounding, Alex."

"What's his relationship with the American? The colonel who blows civilian aircraft out of the sky."

"Stormy, to say the least. When Halter and I first saw him, Uncle Joe was reading Colonel Beauregard the riot act about something and—look!—here's my man Orlov with our sleighs. If we press on, we can be there before first light."

And then Congreve was bounding off through the snow in his bear coat, not quite as streamlined as he'd once been, but calling out for Stokely to get the men moving, for heaven's sake. Hawke smiled, listening to him harangue the team loading the dog sleds with gear. For a man pushing sixty, and a bit on the plumpish side, his energy and zest for life was amazing. Indefatigable, cheery, just the kind of fellow any man might want for a dear friend. And, standing next to you in a gunfight.

Now, for better or worse, these two old friends were waltzing right into the bloody thick of it once more.

SEVENTY-NINE

KGB HQ, Russia

AMBROSE LED THE MEN INTO THE SNOWY WOODS. To the precise spot where he and Halter had hidden such a short time ago.

Their entire team were dressed in the winter combat whites of the Tenth Mountain Division. Congreve had promised snow, and he'd been right on the money. They looked like swiftly moving ghosts, with invisible feet, slipping silently through the trees.

"Here's the spot, just here," Congreve whispered to Hawke. "Clear shot at the main gate just outside the entrance at KGB II headquarters. Something's going on. See the black Audi with the chauffeur asleep at the wheel out front?"

Hawke raised the binoculars and had a look.

"An A8. The kind of car you're likely to see buzzing around the Kremlin," Hawke said.

"Exactly," Congreve said. "I recognized that plate number from the last time I was here. He's back all right. That's Uncle Joe's car and driver, all right."

"Good. I thought we'd end up in Moscow going door-to-door looking for a ghost. Do you know who belongs to the battered old jeep as well?"

"That would be our American cousin, Colonel Beauregard. He lives here on the base. Halter and I both saw his jeep parked out there before we saw him getting dressed down by Uncle Joe and his military tribunal. Halter told me that both the Colonel and old Joe maintain offices in that headquarters building. And private sleeping quarters as well. I think we just got lucky."

"We could use a bit right now. What's at the other end of that road disappearing around the trees over there?"

"That's the original and primary Russian military operation. Four miles away. Nearly ten thousand troops over there. I'd leave that sleeping bear the hell alone."

"What about the guard situation here?"

"Standard ops. Four Spetsnaz fighters outside at the gate, two more off duty inside the guard house. Twelve-hour shifts."

"Okay, let's get this done." Hawke rose and went over to Stokely, who was crouching behind some fallen trees laden with snow, checking his weapons.

"Stoke, sniper time. We're a go in five minutes. Where's Fat?"

Stoke turned around and whispered over his shoulder, "Fat, on me. Now."

"What's up?" Saunders said, crouching down to join them, brushing fresh snow off the barrel of his sniper rifle.

"Two guards. Spetsnaz, nothing but trouble. One on either side of the gate. Take 'em out."

"Spetsnaz? That's all they got? Shit, man." Fat brought up his weapon and sighted in on his designated targets, adjusting for elevation and windage.

"You don't think much of them, Fat?" Hawke said. He always liked to hear what the real deal had to say. The guys who were in elbow deep and knew what they were talking about.

"Tell you the truth, compared to our reduced training lately, those dang boys over there are pure badass. Our current military is so watered down and pussified that it's sickening, sir. I'm former Army Infantry and I'm pretty appalled at the lack of toughness in our current armed forces. I wanted my drill sergeants to kick my butt, 'cause I thought there was more dignity in getting hit in training than getting smoked in combat. But today? That's why I quit. Hard-ass is just not allowed anymore because of the gradual pussification of standards."

Hawke looked at him with new respect. He had the right man with the right gun. Same gun he'd probably carried as an Army Ranger sniper. A 5.56 semiauto sniper rifle.

"Take 'em out now, sir?"

Hawke looked at his watch and said, "Not just yet. More are asleep inside. Gator's going to blow the gate in four minutes . . ."

"Got it, sir."

"The two outside on my signal. The main assault starts in three minutes, Fat," Hawke said. "Take out every guard you see as they come out the door. Then the rest. Wait a beat. Anything else presents itself, you stay here and do your job. Otherwise, double-time it and get with us on the way inside that building. You strong, Fat?"

"Army strong, sir."

"Attaboy. There are your targets, son. On my mark . . . mark . . . four . . . three . . . two . . . FIRE."

There was a barely audible *phfft-phfft* and the targets dropped, instantly dead of head shots.

"Gator? Situation report," Hawke said into his lip mike.

"Gator's in position, sir," Hawke heard in his earbuds. "Charges set. Ready to trigger . . ."

Hawke said: "Mark . . . four . . . three . . . two . . . FIRE."

The night lit up. There was suddenly a hole where the gate used to be . . .

"Let's move!" Hawke cried, breaking out into the open and racing toward Gator's new position inside the perimeter. Stoke and the others were right behind him, charging through the hard-packed snow and racing through the blown gate. Almost immediately, more off-duty guards burst out the door, weapons at the ready.

And, almost instantly, they were dead, smoked by Fat over in the woods.

"Heads up, Fat!" Hawke cried, taking a knee in the snow next to Gator. A group of six more

Spetsnaz came busting out of the HQ, weapons up and charging toward their position . . .

"Fat, fire at will!" he shouted. He and Gator and everyone who had a shot took it. Even Ambrose, who was carrying a Bullpup AR-15 Stoke had given him, was spitting lead with the best of them.

It was over in seconds. The Stokeland Raiders had not only met the enemy, they had shredded them. The team bunched up at the foot of the steps up to HQ; their blood was up now.

"Gator! Go rig those charges around the base of the main door. Fat, grab that cover over there and waste anyone you see."

"Charges set!" Gator said, moving away from the door.

"Gator. On my mark, breach and clear . . . on three. Mark . . . two . . ." The steel doors blew off the hinges and sailed out into the night.

"Go, go, go!" Hawke cried.

Hawke and the Raiders were up the steps and inside in a heartbeat. Hawke, his eyes darting everywhere at once, saw staff, military and clerical alike, throwing themselves to the floor. These men were in a blind panic at the sight of heavily armed military types, in ghostlike white regalia, who had just burst into their lives; all were stunned that this isolated and top secret enclave of the top KGB brass was not as inviolate as they'd been told.

"Chief Inspector, would you please translate something for me?"

"Fire away."

"Everyone stay right where you are," Hawke said,

"facedown on the floor. No one will hurt you if you keep quiet and don't move."

"Done," Congreve said, and told them what to do in Russian.

"Brock, get us a head count, please, and check them all for weapons . . . I said, *don't move!*" Hawke shouted at a man who was rolling over onto his back with his hand going inside his jacket.

"GUN!" Stoke cried. "Boss, he's got a gun!"

Stoke made a move to kick the small automatic out of the man's hand, but he was a second too late. Hawke had pulled his 9mm sidearm from his shoulder holster and put a round between the man's eyes.

Everyone got very still.

"That's much better," Hawke said. "Now, who in this room speaks English? And who is the highest-ranking officer? Please identify yourself."

There was silence.

A moment later, someone on the floor in the far corner spoke up loud and clear and in English with a strong Texas accent.

The big man in khakis said, "Well, since you just shot Major General Yuri Andropov, I guess it's me. Guilty on both counts."

Hawke swung around and stared at him and said, "Beauregard?"

"That's what they call me."

"Stoke, escort that Yank soldier over there to the nearest conference room. Cuff his wrists to a chair and see what you can get out of him. I'll be there in two minutes—need to find out what the hell happened to Gator and Fat. They seem to be MIA and I don't—"

At that very moment, Gator entered the building and a second later he was speaking in Hawke's ear: "You gotta come outside and see this. Fat was helping me finish rigging charges when we saw this guy diving into the backseat of that black Audi out front. Crawled out a bedroom window on the far side of the building and—"

"Let's go," Hawke said, headed for the door.

EIGHTY

THE ESCAPEE, OF COURSE, WAS UNCLE JOE.

Fat had him flat on his back on the ground, hands cuffed above his head, the muzzle of Fat's semiauto two inches from Joe's pale, sweaty forehead. The man's eyes were bulging, sheer terror coming off him in waves. His fingers were tapping on the snow as if he were playing an invisible piano.

Hawke looked down at him and said, "Are you Joe Stalin?"

"*Nyet.*"

"You sure as hell look like him."

"*Da.*"

"Seriously? You're a direct descendant of the man who inspired fear in countless millions? You? Sent millions more to their deaths in the gulags? You have got to be kidding me. Who the hell are you, really?"

"He's nuts, this guy," Fat said. "He comes crawling out of his bedroom window over there, ass-backward and wearing those funky red pajamas . . . I mean, seriously, is this really somebody important?"

"Bring this prisoner inside, Gator. We'll find someplace where we can find out just how important he really is. Come on, Fat."

"Right behind you, Cap'n."

"Gator," Hawke added, "you place those charges around the HQ? Everything rigged?"

"Bet yo' ass, sir. I can turn this place into a Siberian wasteland in about thirty-one seconds."

"That's exactly what I wanted to hear. Fat, you hear all those damn sirens blaring in the distance?"

"Yeah. Three or four klicks away. Those are warning sirens. Coming from the direction of KGB I, I'll bet. Somebody's onto us, skipper. We'd better grill this gentleman, level this combat control center, and get ourselves out of here faster than a bug wink."

GATOR WALKED INTO THE CONFERENCE ROOM WITH Uncle Joe, took one look at the tall man in khakis, already bound to a chair with his back to the wall, and stopped dead in his tracks.

"Colonel?" he said.

"Hell, yeah, it's me. How you doin', Gator? Long time no see. Hell you doing here, sweetie?"

"How about you shut up?" Stoke said to him.

"You're the boss," Beauregard said amiably. "I see you caught the big fish, Gator. My newest pal, Uncle Joe himself. Nice goin'. He tell you he's a people person yet? He will."

"I said, shut up," Stoke said.

Gator cuffed Uncle Joe's wrists behind him and sat him down in a hard chair, right next to the chair where Stoke had stowed the Colonel. Civilian worker, advisor, Hawke had thought, by the looks of him. But apparently not. This was the American who'd built the terror operations command in Isla de Pinos.

"Gator, you say you know this man?" Hawke said, walking up to the Texan.

"Yes, sir, yes I do. That there's Colonel Beauregard himself. I told you about him earlier. Used to work for him at Vulcan. In Saudi."

Hawke looked at the man. "So you are the infamous Colonel, are you? The man who blows women and children out of the sky and blames it on the Chinese."

"Fuck you."

"Your place or mine, you common bastard," Hawke replied.

"Who the hell are you, anyway?"

"Hawke. Commander. British Royal Navy."

"You're Hawke?"

"Last time I checked. Why?"

"Well, hell, Commander, I'm honored to finally meet you, sir. I've been following your exploits for years. Even stole a few moves out of your playbooks."

"I don't kill civilians, Colonel."

"Hell, neither do I. You want to meet the man who does, however? This little shit sitting right next to me. He's the sonofabitch who gave me the orders to bring down that airplane. Told all of us we were taking down a Chinese military transport plane en route to Beijing. Ask him."

"He's lying!" Uncle Joe said, stamping his tiny feet.

"You speak English all of a sudden, Uncle Joe?" Hawke said.

"I spent some time at NYU, that's all. What of it?"

"Did you order the Colonel here to shoot down that civilian airliner over the Chinese borderlands?"

"No. Technically, no. Did not do it," Uncle Joe said.

"Who did? Technically."

"Putin. Wanted to use it as a media diversion to cover his tracks along the borders of certain countries. That crash got a whole lot of airtime on CNN, the Communist News Network. And me? I conveyed the orders to Colonel Beauregard, that's all. So, like they say, please don't shoot the messenger, okay?"

Hawke and Congreve looked at each other in utter disbelief. Uncle Joe had all the earmarks of a visitor from another planet.

"Bullshit," Beauregard said. "Uncle Joe is the one runs the whole damn show. Nothing happens without his signature. Nada. Who do you think is the mastermind behind the massive troop movements last weekend? Into Poland and Estonia? The tank battalions on the roll? You're looking at him. His orders, every last one. General Krakov, head of KGB ops here at Tvas? He even admitted it to me. He told me, 'Putin runs Russia, but Uncle Joe? Uncle Joe runs Putin.'"

Uncle Joe laughed out loud.

"*Me*? Wait, I'm the bad guy? The evil dictator? I'm *gay*, f'crissakes! I love Streisand! I've got a cat!"

"This is such a load of crap he's feeding you, Commander Hawke. His office in the Kremlin? I've been there. Many times. It's twice as big as Putin's! Everybody's scared to death of the little dwarf around there. Just last Christmas he had the three most powerful oligarchs in Russia shot in the head and dumped in the Volga River just before it froze over for the winter. Hell, he even—"

"Putin did that!" Joe said, stamping his tiny feet again. "Putin, Putin, Putin!"

The Colonel continued his tirade. "See? Can't control himself. KGB, Politburo, even Putin himself, they're all terrified of him. You should hear how this character talks to Putin on the phone. It's insane."

"That's ridiculous! I run *Putin*? Me? I don't run anything. Not even my cat."

"What exactly is it that you do, Uncle Joe?" Hawke asked him. He was having a hard time not laughing.

"Me? I'm just a second-rate actor, that's all. Trying to make a buck like anybody else."

"A *what*? Actor?"

"Yeah, yeah, you heard right, actor. Left Moscow to go to NYU Drama School back in the eighties, had a fifth-floor walk-up in Hell's Kitchen. Busboy at P.J. Clarke's. The whole enchilada. Then came back to Moscow to do theater. Ended up starring in a comic opera about Stalin at the Bolshoi Theatre. Called *Me and Uncle Joe*. My biggest gig yet.

My breakthrough role. Nominated for a Tony if they had fuckin' Tonys over here. Putin and his wife were in the audience opening night, front row center. Vlad was laughing his ass off, I'll tell you that. I was great, what can I say? Mr. and Mrs. Putin came backstage to my dressing room and he offered me a job on the spot. That's it, I swear, the whole story. What can I say? The guy was crazy about me."

"Exactly what kind of job did he offer you, Uncle Joe?" Stoke asked.

"Basically? Reprise my starring role in the play. Every day in an office in the Kremlin. 'Just come to work and be Uncle Joe,' he says to me. 'I'll feed you your lines, don't worry,' he says a lot. And just look at me. Perfect casting, right? But, work? God, the hours of footage I watched on that old Commie, the original. Getting his moves down. Looking for nuance. But the look? That I had. Even when I was a baby my aunt Sadie said I looked like Stalin. The kids in my neighborhood screamed and ran when they saw me coming."

"But what the bloody hell did Putin actually want you to *do*, Uncle Joe?" Hawke said, the frustration taking its toll.

"Easy. So, Putin says to me, he says he needs me to divert some inconvenient things away from his office and over to mine. Messy things, you know. Certain unpleasant facts or, you know, iffy events. Like that horrible jetliner thing in China. Messy. And can you blame him? Didn't want to get his lily-white hands dirty on that one, I guess. Never got 'em clean, I'd say, but what do I know? I'm just an actor."

"You sound like a bloody politician," Hawke said.

"Oh, but I am! Now. But I'm also a people person."

"Now, after all the crap he's done, suddenly he's a *people* person? What'd I tell you? He's a people person like I'm a lazy babysitter," Colonel Beauregard sputtered, barely able to control himself.

Hawke just stood there staring at both of them in amazement and bewilderment. Finally, he looked over at the most trustworthy man he knew.

"You believe this guy, Stoke? Uncle Joe?"

"You know what? Crazy-ass as it sounds, I do. I think he's telling the truth here, boss. I really do. How could anyone even begin to make all that stuff up?"

"Ambrose? If anyone can spot a phony alibi, it's you. What do you think?"

"I agree with Stokely. He's telling the truth, Alex. I believe him. Now, I'd like to ask Uncle Joe a question of considerable importance to me, if I may?"

"He's all yours, Constable."

"Recently, a colleague of mine from Cambridge University was here at Tvas on Kremlin business. His name is Stefan Halter. Stef fell ill during a meeting in this very room. You were there. Heart attack, I believe. I'd like to know exactly, and truthfully, what happened to him."

"He was your friend, am I right on that?"

"Perhaps my best friend, yes."

"Listen, I'm sorry to have to tell you this, Mr. Congreve. Very, very sorry. Your friend passed. But it was no heart attack."

"What are you saying? He was murdered? I hope

not because I can assure that if he was, I will not stop until I—"

"Hey—hey, no way! No, sir. Sorry, please. You completely misunderstand what I'm saying here. Fact one, we have a trained medical staff here in the building. Upstairs. Fact two, I had them called as soon as your buddy collapsed there on the floor. We, me included, told the doctors the poor guy had suffered a coronary event of some kind. What kind, I had no fuckin' clue, right? But when they checked him out upstairs, they found out that the heart attack thing . . . was not a factor—"

"Then what happened to him?"

"He had bitten down on a cyanide capsule, see, while the doctors tried to revive him. But here's the thing, and you should know this. Your friend? That guy was the lucky one, I'm telling you. Think about it. That lucky, lucky man, he avoided death at the hands of Putin's KGB interrogators. Whole lot worse than cyanide, and that's the honest truth, so help me, God, if I'm lying."

Ambrose was staring at the floor, straining to rein in his emotions.

After a very long time, he looked up and spoke, barely above a whisper. "He didn't do it for himself. He did it for me."

"Then he's a great hero."

"Yes. He always was."

Congreve, overcome with grief, walked toward the door. He needed to breathe the fresh night air.

"I'm so sorry, Ambrose," Hawke said as he walked by.

"Thank you. I shall miss him very deeply."

The room fell silent for a long moment, out of respect. Everyone felt Congreve's loss, even Uncle Joe.

"So, Uncle Joe, tell us all about Feuerwasser. The Kremlin's miracle explosive," Stoke said.

"It's all bullshit, that garbage. It's no more explosive than a strawberry Frostee. It's fuckin' *vodka*, f'crissakes. Putin asked me to sell the explosive idea around town, so I sold it. I'm a very good salesman. Sell ice to an Eskimo. What else can I tell you? I was making a good buck there in the Kremlin. Gave me a lot of confidence. As an actor I mean, not a real person. Confidence. I got that in spades. And I'm due for a comeback. Next stop for me? Hollywood, baby. Count on it."

Hawke laughed. "My God" was all he could say.

Joe said to him, "You ought to take a run at it yourself. Good-looking hunk of horseflesh like you? Hell. You're the one who oughta be up on the silver screen, not me."

"Highly unlikely, Uncle Joe," Hawke said. "Colonel? What about it, then? You didn't know about any of this? This so-called acting career of Uncle Joe's?"

"Hell, no. Not an inkling. I feel like I'm in the middle of some bizarre reality show whenever I'm around this guy."

"You still think he's lying?" Hawke said.

"Maybe, I dunno. If he is, he's the greatest damn liar since P. T. Barnum met Bernie Madoff. Or greatest actor. But I think he's telling the truth,

Commander. Putin's been putting the pieces in place for this global real estate aggression for a long, long time. Uncle Joe? He was one of those pieces all right. He and Putin were a marriage made in heaven. Both of 'em totally batshit."

"Where is Putin right now, Uncle Joe? If you don't know, just say so. But it'll save us all a lot of trouble if you do."

The Colonel spoke up. "I know exactly where he is, Commander, I've been there. Hell, I'll even take you to him."

"Where?"

"A dacha northwest of Moscow. Top secret KGB hideout. Deep forest. Not on any maps. No marked roads. Ridiculous security. Called *Rus*. But that's where he makes the plans to run this war. And that's where he is right this minute."

"Gator, cut these two gentlemen loose. We've got what we came for here. Let's get the hell out of here and blow this place off the—"

"Commander Hawke, you've got problems," the Colonel said, rubbing his chafed wrists. "I've been counting the frequency of those alarm sirens in the distance. Every twenty seconds now. Coming from the direction of the other camp. KGB I. About four klicks from here. A lot of those troops have already shipped out for Poland and the Estonia invasions. But there are at least ten thousand more under arms and headed this way. They will overrun this base and kill everyone in this room if you don't do something about it. They don't like me and they certainly don't like my men. And frankly, my men hate their goddamn guts. And all of these damn Russians."

"What the hell can we do?" Hawke said, looking to Stokely for help.

"Set us loose on them, that's what," the Colonel said. "I got five thousand of the finest fighting men on the planet right here, living right inside this fence. Every one of them is loyal to me, not Putin. I give the word, and they're weaponed up and marching up that road to meet those Russian bastards halfway here. Man, my guys will roll right over them and won't stop till they get to Moscow. And I'll be right there alongside those boys, too."

Hawke stared at him.

"That sounds a lot like old-fashioned American patriotism, Colonel. Knowing what little I know, I wouldn't think that would be something you were capable of."

"My heart's always been with the farm boys who fought at Lexington and Concord and, finally, Yorktown in 1781, Commander. I stand with the Patriots. Always the Patriots."

"Do it, then," Hawke said. "Call your troops to arms. Have you got enough time to mobilize them?"

"My guys? More than enough."

"You got tanks, armored carriers?"

"Six special-order Chinese T-99 battle tanks, loaded with ammo and ready to roll. The best."

"Good. But you're not marching in front of your boys, Colonel, however much you'd like to be there. You're coming with me. You and I are going to that dacha you told me about. We are going to have a nice little chat with Emperor Putin about changing his plans."

"It'd be an honor to serve alongside you, Commander. Now I'd like to ask you a favor."

"Go ahead."

"My second-in-command is Russian. Good fighter, but I don't trust him worth a shit. So, I'm thinking that I'd like to ask my new friend Gator over there if he'd consider a battlefield commission. I'd like him to step in as commander in charge of all our forces. And lead them into battle against the KGB troopers. Man's got leadership written all over him."

"Gator?" Hawke said. "What do you say?"

Gator had a million-watt smile on his face. "Hell, yeah. *Hell, yeah!* In a heartbeat."

"Stoke? He's your guy . . . yay or nay?"

"Absolutely, boss. Give Gator half a chance, he and his infantry will have those Commie troops for breakfast."

"They're not Communists anymore, Stoke," Brock said.

"Don't be so sure about that, Harry," he replied. "A lot of those dudes would just love to put on those old Soviet uniforms. Including Vladimir Putin."

"Get moving then, Gator," Hawke said. "Show the enemy what you're made of, son."

"Sir, yessir!" Gator said, snapping to attention.

Hawke turned his attention back to the actor.

"Uncle Joe, can you come up with a helicopter at this hour? If you do, I'll give you a seat on it. Out of here."

"For that, you get two helicopters. As many as you need. What else can I do to help?"

"You can spend the entire time we're on that chopper en route to Moscow giving me every single ounce of dirt you've collected on Putin. Everything you've picked up, in all the years you've worked for him. Which buttons to push. Where his weak spots are. How much vodka he drinks. All of that."

"Deal. I love this stuff. You don't happen to know anybody out in Hollywood, do you, Commander Hawke? Agents? I'm just asking."

Congreve stifled a chuckle; Stoke wisely remained stone-faced; Harry Brock laughed out loud and said: "I *love* this guy!"

Hawke, who was about to spend a few hours locked inside a noisy helicopter in deep conversation with Uncle Joe, just looked off into the middle distance. He said, "Okay, that's it, let's go."

EIGHTY-ONE

—

RUS LODGE, OUTSIDE MOSCOW

—

I'LL LEAVE YOU HERE, THEN," HAWKE SAID.

They'd hiked in, the two of them. Hawke and the colonel.

The American looked at him and said: "This is a bad idea, you know."

"Maybe so," Hawke said, peering through the tangled branches of undergrowth in the woods. In the sky, columns of grey smoke were rising from unseen chimneys. He was pretty close now. Close enough. It was cold. It wasn't raining yet, but the woods were heavy and wet. Close. Dark.

"He knows you're coming, Commander. What's to stop him from having you shot on sight? God knows these woods are full of itchy trigger fingers."

"Pride. It would offend his precious pride. And because I told him I was coming. Killing me would solve nothing for him. It would ruin it. He likes the fact that I came. It's hard to explain. He thinks it's funny in a way."

"Funny."

"Yeah. We have a weird relationship. And this is how it has to end. You better head back to Moscow, Colonel. The rest will be worried. Oh, and Colonel?"

"Yessir?"

Hawke handed him a leather envelope stuffed with cash and said, "Keep this somewhere safe. There's quite a bit of money inside."

"You don't have to—"

"It's yours. You're going to need it. And one thing before you go. Make sure Congreve gets on a train bound for England. Yeah? Tonight took a lot out of him. Another thing. I want you to take proper care of Uncle Joe. Despite all evidence to the contrary, he's on the side of the angels. But right now, without our help, he's a dead angel. Smuggle him across the Russian border, out of the country tonight. Fly to Switzerland. Get him to the Zurich airport. Buy that crazy little bastard a first-class ticket to L.A. and give him fifty thousand dollars. On me. And then, tell Stoke—no, that's it, I guess. Take care of yourself, Colonel. That was a fine thing you did back there. Rallying your troops just in time to save our bacon, giving that Luttier kid a break like you did. America doesn't know it yet, but they owe you a great debt. We all do."

"Like you said, not like me. Siding with America. Patriotism, and all that old-fashioned crap. I was a patriot once, Alex. I really was. Before they—destroyed me."

Hawke looked at him, thinking. "I knew about you, of course. Back then. Before it all went to hell for you, I mean. And I want you to know something. You *are* a patriot, Colonel. You proved it tonight."

"Thank you . . . you won't, uh . . ."

"I will never say a word. Who the hell knows? Maybe we'll even share another foxhole sometime. I'd take you in a fight anytime. Take care, Colonel."

"We almost met once, Alex."

"Really? Where?"

"It was in Bermuda."

"There on a fishing trip?" Hawke said.

"Something like that.

"Stay safe," he said, looking quickly away, trying to hide his emotions. But Hawke had seen his face and knew the man had been deeply moved.

"Wait—take this," Hawke said. "I don't need it anymore."

"No—no, don't do that. You gotta at least keep your damn weapon! What if he tries to . . . Christ, what if he—"

"Take it, Colonel. If I do need it, I'm already dead."

HAWKE CAME TO A CLEARING IN THE WOODS. He stepped out into the open, the sting of wet wind on his cheeks. The dacha was large. Vintage Russian architecture. Onion domes. Lights on in a hundred windows. Six tall chimneys, all smoking. In the trees and on rooftops, he knew men watched him through gun sights . . . instinct made him reach for the small automatic in his empty pocket before he remembered that it was gone.

Too late now. Now it was all just waiting to see how it turned out in the end. And so he waited there at the edge of the misty wood, breathing the fresh pine-scented night air. Soon, he lost track of time altogether . . . waiting.

Four men came for him. Plainclothes. One of them, even larger than the others, had a growling Doberman straining fiercely at a short leash. Big men. Hands jammed in their pockets. Long black overcoats. Collars up. Hats pulled low over their eyes. They took their time about it, too. Walking slowly through the pools of light splayed across the lawns. No great hurry.

Making him wait still longer.

"Why are you here?" the man with the slavering Doberman said, shining a blinding white light in his eyes. They gathered round to peer at him. He was the object of sincere curiosity; they chatted about him like he was a new species. Maybe he was, to them.

"What?" Hawke said quietly.

"It seems you don't recognize me, Lord Hawke. It offends me deeply. Are you armed?"

Hawke took a closer look.

"Ah. So sorry. *Der Wolf*, is it not? Fancy meeting you here. I thought you were dead."

"In Cuba we met, yes? Some years ago, now. I remember you left without properly thanking me for my hospitality up in those mountains."

"The Wishing Well. What fond memories."

"Yes. I've moved up in the ranks, Commander

Hawke. I am now President Putin's chief of security. I asked you a question."

"What?"

"Are you armed?"

"No."

"Do I need to check?"

"No."

"Maybe we'll have a look anyway, shall we? He's clean? All right. Come with us."

"Where are we going?"

"To the boathouse. Down by the lake. The president is waiting there. He said you asked to see him alone. He is abiding by your wishes."

"Right."

Liar.

VLADIMIR PUTIN WAS STANDING BY THE FIRE. Shadows flickered across the broad planked floor and climbed walls covered with huge paintings of life in the ancient forest. Flickered across Putin's face. The shaggy black head of a massive bear looked down from above the heavy stone mantel. Gleaming black marbles for eyes. Demonic.

Here we go.

Hawke drew himself up to his full height and strode across the great expanse of worn Turkish carpets and put his hand out.

"Volodya," he said, giving the Russian all the smile he could muster at the moment.

"Alex," Putin said and gripped Hawke's hand. Any trace of warmth the Russian had ever felt toward the English spy had surely gone, fled from his face, his fingers, his cold, cold heart.

They just stood there. Each man looking at the other. After all these years, each had remained intensely curious about the other. It had always been that way. It was what had made it tick between them.

"Have a drink?" Putin said, walking over to the drinks table heavily laden with crystal decanters. "Rum, right? Bermuda?"

"Not tonight, thank you. I'm driving, you see."

Putin smiled. "You haven't changed."

"You have."

"Not really, Alex. Cigarette?"

"Yes. Thanks. This may sound odd, but it's good to see you," Hawke said, flicking his lighter and inhaling deeply. The Russian tobacco brought him immeasurable comfort.

Putin smiled and said: "I know what you mean. Odd. But it's good to see you, too, Alex."

"Sorry it's come to this, Volodya. It didn't have to."

"Yes, it did. It was always coming to this, Alex. We both knew it from the beginning. Even in that damnable cell of mine at Energetika Prison. Remember that? The night we met?"

"Of course I do. You saved my bloody life."

"So I did. You look well."

"I see you have a dog, Volodya. Handsome chap. What's his name?"

"Blofeld. Russian wolfhound."

"Ah, Blofeld, of course. Ian Fleming, wasn't it? Ernst Stavro Blofeld. In *Thunderball*, as I recall."

"An evil Russian genius with aspirations of global domination, remember?" Putin said, with a wry smile. "Blofeld, Putin, what's the difference?"

Hawke laughed. "How could I forget? I loved that book."

"Let's sit down, shall we, Lord Hawke?"

Hawke looked back at him and smiled.

"Don't worry," he said, "my title still irritates me."

Putin laughed. "Good. I'm glad to see it. Some things never change."

THERE WERE TWO LARGE LEATHER ARMCHAIRS FACING the fire and they took them. A half-full tumbler full of vodka stood on the table beside the Russian president. He took a sip and stared up at his bear. Putin seemed so benign, almost wistful, that Hawke began to worry about his state of mind.

A man at home on a rainy night. His faithful dog sleeping at his feet. Not a care in the world. Except perhaps the end of that world at daybreak.

Hawke was first to break the silence.

"Look. It goes without saying that I appreciate your agreeing to see me here tonight. Especially under these circumstances. And, despite how this evening may or may not end, I strongly believe this was the right thing for us to do."

"I agree. How do you wish it to end, Alex?"

"Sensibly. We both walk it a step back. Anything less would not be the act of any rational human being. We've got everything to gain. Just as we've got everything to lose. We both need to clearly understand which is which. And act accordingly. That's really all I have to say."

"Who do you speak for?"

"Myself."

"Good. You are a warrior. Perhaps one of the very finest who ever lived. And therefore I have every hope you will understand me when I tell you I cannot retreat from the status quo. Mighty Caesar has crossed the Rubicon, Alex. *Alea iacta est*—the die is cast. No turning back."

Putin eyed Hawke, took another sip of vodka, and waited for Hawke's response.

"No. I cannot accept that."

"Apparently you believe you have a choice."

"At least hear me out, Volodya. For both our sakes."

Putin said nothing. He reached down and scratched his dog's head, whispering sweet nothings to him in Russian.

The meeting seemed to be over before it had even begun.

EIGHTY-TWO

"Funny thing," Putin finally said.

"What's that?"

"I've been reading Plutarch's *Caesar*. While I waited for you this evening. That book on the table beside you. There it is. Hand it to me, won't you?"

"Here you go."

"I came across a passage . . . Let me find it. Ah, here we are." He began to read aloud. "And Caesar stood on the banks of the Rubicon and said, 'Here, will I abandon peace and desecrated law. Fortune, I follow only you. Farewell to treaties. From now on, only war shall be our judge.'"

"War is our judge?"

"Hmm."

"Whatever you believe, Volodya, you cannot possibly believe that 'war shall be our judge.' That doesn't even make any sense!"

Putin took another sip of vodka, smiled at him, and said, "And now you disparage my beloved Caesar? Tell me. Upon what meat doth this our mighty Hawke feed that he is grown so great?"

"Volodya, listen to me. Caesar was talking about breaking Roman law by crossing a river into Italy. That was a small civil war in 49 BC, for God's sake. Not risking modern global warfare with billions of lives hanging in the balance."

"War is war. In both Caesar's finest hour and in mine."

Hawke, veering toward despair at all this, said nothing for a moment or two. Desperate for time to marshal his whirling thoughts, he said, "They will destroy you, you know."

"Who will destroy me?"

"The Americans."

"The Americans have grown weak."

"No. Her leaders are weak. Her generals and her people are strong. As are those in my own country. They are closely allied against you, America and Britain. The Allies will not let this stand. The attacks on American and British soil. The brutal invasion of Estonia. And even now, your troops and tanks are rolling across the Polish border. Two NATO countries whose freedom our alliance is sworn to protect."

"Farewell to treaties, Alex. That time has passed."

"You believe I come to bury Caesar. But I came here to try to help you. To make you see reason. I'm offering you a bloody lifeline, damn you! To try and *save* you."

"Say what you have to say. I am weary of this conversation."

"The generals are waiting for a sign from you."

"What do they expect?"

"The cessation of hostilities against my country and the U.S. The immediate and permanent withdrawal of all Russian air, naval, and infantry forces inside the two besieged nations and on the borders of the others."

"Never."

"They will go nuclear then. The American and British generals. There will be no stopping them and no turning back."

"Over a mere political dispute? Laughable. Land that was stolen from the motherland by centuries of illegal treaties? War over that? Never. It will be the same as before, Alex. Deliberation, sanctions. Negotiations, delays, and more demands. Disappearing lines in the sand. Ultimatums and mythic deadlines, just as the foolishness with the Iranians. More fucking sanctions. But, war? No, Alex. They are too afraid to do that."

"You really believe we are afraid?"

"I do."

"Feuerwasser? Is that it? That magic potion of yours, the one that will end all your problems. You think to threaten the world with it. You don't drop bombs, you have them delivered by the caseload. By now, you've shipped hundreds of thousands of cases of it to cities around the world. You claim you can blow the whole world up at the press of your mighty button. As you demonstrated so convincingly with that freighter in France, you are become death, the destroyer of worlds."

"One does what one can, Alex."

"Warehouses in places like Isla de Pinos, Los Angeles, New York, or London, packed to the bloody rafters with that stuff, suddenly become Ground Zero, is that it? A plague of simultaneous Hiroshimas? Is that your dream? A worldwide apocalypse with one flick of your finger. Is that it?"

"Don't go down this road, Alex! I warn you, do not—I repeat, do *not* go there!"

"I must go there, Volodya! It's the only road we've got left. And you, you're headed straight to hell in a hotrod, going over the cliff. Because you somehow still believe you now hold the world hostage. But the generals arrayed against you no longer fear you, Volodya. Not them, not the politicians, and certainly not me. Not anymore."

"You should."

"Perhaps, but I don't. Because it's all a bloody lie! An outright fraud. That elaborate demonstration you staged for me in the sub, that underwater light show. Revealing your new secret weapon so convincingly with a vial going down a smokestack. But it wasn't true, was it, Volodya? No! It was all an elaborate hoax you spent years perfecting. That sunken tanker you blew up had been prerigged by divers. Traditional plastic explosives, I'm quite sure. But I was your friend and I trusted you. That was my own stupid mistake. I won't make it again."

"Try convincing them of that. Your mighty American generals. They saw what happened in Miami with their own eyes. And Texas. And that little coastal town in England. Vaporized. And was there even the slightest trace of a traditional explosive found? No. If there had been, why in God's name have they not gone public? Pointing the accusing finger at the guilty? Presumably, me!"

"My friend Kelly at CIA told them not to. At my request."

"Why would he ever do that?"

"Because I was looking for irrefutable proof of your duplicity. Now I have it."

"You have nothing of the kind."

"Trust me."

Putin considered. Just long enough.

"You're lying." Putin said finally. He seemed exhausted and out of bullets.

Hawke saw his ray of hope. He needed to let what he'd just told him bake inside Putin's brain. Needed to give him time to reflect before taking another step.

Hawke said, "Unless you've got serious objections, I've changed my mind about that drink." And this, unsurprisingly, brought a smile to the Russian president's face. "Gosling's?" he said.

"Perhaps a vodka?"

"When in Russia . . ." Putin grunted, getting somewhat shakily to his feet.

Hawke smiled and sank back in his chair. Slowly but surely, he felt he might be gaining the upper hand. He'd needed this small chunk of time to consolidate what he believed to be his strategic gains thus far. Then he would strike.

Putin went to the drinks table. Ice and the tinkle of crystal. He returned moments later and handed

Hawke his glass, sloshing a bit over the rim, and saying: "Careful, you don't know what's in that."

Hawke smiled up at him.

Always the consummate poker player, the president collapsed back into his chair and picked up his drink. Raised his glass and said, "*Prost!*"

"Thanks. This is an awfully fine vodka. Might I ask what it is?"

Putin could not hide a sly smile.

"You wouldn't believe me if I told you, Alex."

"Not Feuerwasser?"

"Hmm."

"Seriously? Oh, come on, Volodya."

Putin just smiled and sipped his drink, staring with those bloody black poker eyes across the rim of his glass at the Englishman.

And then it came to Hawke. Something Uncle Joe had told him en route to Moscow. Perhaps Putin had been sitting in that same bloody chair all afternoon. Drinking vodka, listening to Beethoven, and feeling sorry for himself. Mulling over the stirring words of his mighty Caesar, using alcohol and the ancient glory of military history to stiffen his spine . . .

Hawke held his fire.

The two men sat drinking quietly in the deep silence that pervaded the drafty wooden building. There was only the soft lapping of the waves washing ashore beyond the windows, the snoring of Putin's wolfhound, and the distant ticking of a great clock in a distant hall . . . Hawke's troubled mind slowed and drifted . . . back to the dark Siberian wood. It was near dawn and . . .

EIGHTY-THREE

Hawke was sitting on a fallen log, he and Ambrose studying the enemy compound gate. He was thinking then about how this would all end. Where the hell did it all go from here? War? Peace? Death? He tried to think it through. It was like driving through a dark wood with the headlamps off. He felt the clouds of self-doubt and despair rolling in, sought desperately to stave them off. Had he, finally, simply taken on too much? Overestimated himself, deluded himself about his lifelong ability to overcome even the most insurmountable of challenges, the most impenetrable of—

And then, without warning, dawn broke. It was all perfectly clear! He would contact Putin tonight. Hawke suddenly knew that somehow Putin might actually agree to see him. And therein lay the only way forward. The beckoning open door swung wide. His opponent had built his fortress of fear atop a weak foundation. Neither a castle nor a fortress, but a house of cards. Yet, thank God, the Russian president still believed the stronghold of his lie still held fast!

And in that cherished belief lay the seeds of his downfall.

And then came yet another illuminating ray of light: Putin knew now that Hawke had, only days ago, gone to extraordinary lengths to destroy his Cuban warehouse full of Feuerwasser. And therein, perhaps, lay Hawke's salvation. And perhaps the world's as well.

Putin still clung to the belief that neither Hawke nor anyone else knew his secret . . .

HAWKE SNAPPED OUT OF HIS REVERIE.

He sensed, no, he *knew*, that now was the moment to go in for the kill. In the last few minutes, he had come to a realization: in any negotiation, when your opponent's only defense rests upon a foundation of his own lies and deceit, then your opponent will, more often than not, be first to fold. It was Hawke's only chance and he knew it.

Strike now, Alex, he heard his mind say. *Strike now!*

And so he struck.

"Please listen to me carefully, Volodya. I am going to tell you precisely how it stands now between us. There are no more bargaining chips on the table. No more shadow armies in Siberia waiting to pounce on your defenseless neighbors. No secret weapons of mass destruction. No Feuerwasser. Nothing. There is just you. And just me. And the words we now say to each other. That's it. That's all we have. For better or for worse."

Putin stared at his enemy for a long moment, assessing the truth of his statement. He said, "Go on."

"Take this."

"What is it?"

Hawke handed it to him.

"It's a vial of that stuff. Feuerwasser. You gave it to me that day in the library aboard *Tsar*. I slipped it into my pocket and forgot about it. Found it again a few days ago. Notice the metal seal remains unbroken. It's still armed."

"Yes, I see that."

"Ignite it. Vaporize both of us the way you vaporized that sunken freighter."

"What?"

"You heard me. I'm ready to die if you are. Twist the bloody top, man. Or smash it on the floor. Use your mobile to pull the trigger. Boom. We're history . . ."

"You are a fucking madman, you know," Putin said. He turned and hurled the vial, smashing it to crystalline bits against the stone fireplace.

They both stared at the puddle of clear liquid and the broken glass in silence.

Hawke said, "I may indeed be mad, but you most certainly are a liar. Don't you see? You're walking around naked, Volodya. Emperor Putin has no clothes. And the whole world can see him for a poseur and a charlatan. A destroyer of worlds."

THEY SPOKE FOR ANOTHER HOUR. PUTIN WOULD thrust and parry, looking for the slightest of holes in Hawke's position. On, and on, and still on. At the very end, both men were exhausted. They simply could not find a way to end it.

In the tall eastern windows of the lodge, the light beyond took on a pinkish cast.

Hawke had finally had enough. He got to his feet and started pacing back and forth before the fireplace, just to get his blood flowing again. He finally spoke.

"Look here, damn it. You don't seem to understand that the Americans have already gone to Defcon 3, Volodya! A state of war already exists! America and Britain are on a war footing. Just waiting for an excuse to get rid of you once and for all. Don't give them that excuse, Volodya. Don't be remembered as the one who bet it all and lost."

"Fuck you. You hear me? *Fuck you.*"

Putin was plainly drunk now. Hawke knew he had to hurry. The last vestiges of sobriety were evaporating, and with them, any hope of peace with Russia. His mind turned to something else Uncle Joe had told him aboard the chopper . . . Putin's fierce pride in his legacy.

"For God's sake! Look at yourself! You're up to your knees in shit. And now Western economic sanctions have brought you to your knees. The ruble is underwater. Plummeting oil prices have emptied your coffers. You're broke. And now you would go to *war*? You don't want to be remembered by future Russian schoolchildren as history's fool, do you? I

know you. And you don't want that. You're far too
bloody narcissistic for that. Am I wrong? That was
a question, damn it. I said, *Does the great Vladimir
Putin want to be remembered for all time as history's
fool?* Or not? Now is the time to decide, God damn
you!"

Putin paused a moment. Then, he rose, quite
wobbly now, to his feet. He threw back his head,
drained the last of his vodka, and hurled the crystal vodka tumbler against the stone. More shattered
bits of glass scattered on the hearthstone, glittering
in the firelight.

Everything was broken now. It was all broken.
And the end was very near.

"How long have I got?" Putin said, his voice
shaking.

"Forty-eight hours. They want you to sign this
document to that effect in my presence."

Hawke handed the Russian president the document he'd had printed at KGB Headquarters. The
one the American secretary of state had frantically
e-mailed him before he left hours earlier.

Putin took it and went to the drinks table and
poured himself another. He read the terms without speaking and with trembling hands. He turned
and regarded his old friend, now his adversary, with
those hooded brooding eyes. When he returned to
the fireside, he spoke, the words parsed out slowly,
barely audible.

"I have made the decision to stand down. I will
sign your fucking papers. I will tell my commanders
in the field to withdraw from Estonia and Poland.

To retreat back within existing Russian borders. Also, I shall similarly instruct the navy. The air force. And then I shall call my wife to . . . what was I saying?"

Hawke was elated, but what came next was an eerie reminder of Nixon's bizarre farewell speech in the Oval Office.

"I would never mind being defeated by you, Alex. Never. There is no shame in what happens on the battlefield. There is only honor and blood and bravery among warring knights. But this, tonight, was no field of battle. No. You have come into the sanctity of my home and you have humiliated me. Abused the favored status I have always granted you as someone fervently respected and admired. And that abuse, my old friend, is something I can never, nor will I ever, forgive."

"Volodya, what would you have had me do? Would you rather I had just turned away and watched you fall into a wretched pit of—"

"Silence!"

His enemy's face was white, and he was bathed in sweat. His breathing was a desperate rattle, as if he had just run a race.

"*Silence!* I cannot stomach the sight of your face nor the sound of your words. You had better leave now. Take your fucking papers and go! I can no longer hold myself responsible for your safety, Alex. Now, please go while you still can."

Hawke saw Putin reach inside his woolen jacket with his free hand, the other still clutching the signed documents. Out came the small silver Walther PPK he always carried for protection. Hawke's heart stopped when he saw the man eyeing the roaring fire turn to face him.

His intent was clear. He had changed his mind. He was about to hurl the signed treaty into the fire. A red spark of anger filled Hawke's blue sailor's eyes as he took a step toward the madman, who was now batting the scorched treaty at the licking flames.

"Get out, I said!" Putin cried as Hawke moved closer toward him.

"I'm sorry, Volodya. This is not what I wanted. To insult you, to offend you, was never my intent. I wanted only for the two of us to find the truth together. Seek a peaceful resolution that protects this imperfect old world as we know it for a little while longer. I hope you can come to believe that."

"And I hope *you* believe this," Putin said.

He raised the weapon and pointed it at Hawke's head. If he wanted Hawke to flinch, he was sorely disappointed. Hawke took one and then two steps more toward the president, a cold fury in his eyes. And then, as Hawke reached out to snatch the treaty clutched in Putin's left hand, the drunken leader fired his weapon at point-blank range.

He missed.

Hawke took another step closer. His right hand shot out like a piston. In desperation, he wrenched the precious document away from the drunken Russian. Now, somehow, he had to get out of here alive with the cease-fire treaty in his possession.

"Damn you!" Putin said, raising the pistol again.

"Don't do it, Volodya."

Two more shots rang out, striking the ancient plaster just inches above the Englishman's head. Hawke stared at Putin, knowing full well that the end of this story was very near now.

It would be so easy for Putin to simply kill him . . .

One way or the other, Hawke would stand his ground; he would do what he had always done. He would stand fast.

The gun wavered wildly as Putin gave full vent to his righteous anger, firing shots into the ceiling high above. He was shouting now, "I don't believe in your old world, Hawke! I believe in a new world to come. And someday I shall have it . . ."

"All things are possible, Volodya."

"Yes, they are. Over your dead body."

"That is clearly your choice, Volodya. I took you at your word. You're the only one with a gun, remember."

Putin laughed, but it was mirthless and hollow.

He took dead aim once more.

Hawke stood fast and unflinching, looking into the cold dark eyes above the barrel. He saw trickery and he saw death. He could feel the spot on his forehead where the bullet would strike; the spot, a small circle of fear, was there even now. It felt cold and icy and final.

"You really are a murderous bastard, aren't you?" Hawke said, keeping his voice steady.

Putin smiled. "Anything else to say?" Hawke was watching his trigger finger and saw the pressure whiten the knuckles . . .

"Just one thing," Hawke said evenly. "You'd better make the first shot good, Volodya. I will get my hands on you before you can fire that bloody thing a second time . . ."

Fired.

Hawke, a blur, dove forward. He had both hands around his assailant's neck, crushing fingers digging brutally into the larynx before Putin even knew he'd missed. He tightened his fingers cruelly around the Russian's throat.

"Drop it. Now."

The gun clattered on the stone hearth, and Hawke shoved him away, disgusted more than anything else. Putin backed up against the wall, rubbing his bruised throat, his eyes glaring and red. His voice was raw when he finally spoke in a harsh whispery croak.

"Oh, what a noble image of yourself you've always had! The valiant Arthurian knight on his black charger. But you hear this, Hawke. The second you walk out that door, you will no longer enjoy my benevolent protection. Nor will your beloved son. Nor even the Russian whore who bore you your bastard child. So I suggest you run for the woods once you step outside. Run as fast as you can. Do I make myself perfectly clear? Now, get out of my sight!"

"Good-bye, Volodya," Hawke said, walking away. But he paused at the doorway then turned around to face his enemy. Holding up the treaty, the Englishman said, "You've summoned a small semblance of honor here tonight. And done a courageous thing. The right thing. And, despite what you say you believe, I can only pray that one day you'll realize what I say is true. That, on this one night in history, both of us have done the very best that either of us may ever be capable of doing."

Putin had no reply. Not that night, anyway.

His final answer, tragically, would come to haunt Alex Hawke. But it would come later.

Much later.

Hawke turned his collar up against the cold and walked on into the night, under starry Russian skies.

The woods ahead were dark and deep.

"On we go," he whispered to himself.

On we go.

ACKNOWLEDGMENTS

I WOULD LIKE TO OFFER HEARTFELT THANKS TO MY literary agent, Peter McGuigan, as well as Emily Brown at Foundry Literary + Media, and to my dear wife, Lucinda Watson, for putting up with me during the completion of this manuscript.